The Girls That Break

Killer Signatures 1

Christine Winston

The Girls That Break © Killer Signatures Book 1 by Christine Winston, previously The Breaking Wheel by Christine Winston.

Editing

Developmental Nicole @ Emerald Edits

Tiffany Taylor

Copy Editing Jill @Bright Owl Edits.

Proofreading @Orla Doyle

Read-Through editor Deirdre Winston

Book Cover Design @Alison Celis

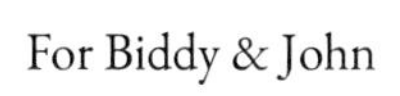
For Biddy & John

Contents

PROLOGUE

Rose

THAT SONG plays on a continuous loop, a tormenting tempo as he spins me around the room. I'm aware of every sensation: the dress lightly brushing the back of my legs, the searing blisters, the broken bones grinding together and the frigid grip of fever. My stomach whirls too. The nausea, pain, and disorientation aren't enough to distract me from this nightmare. He turns me again and my mind whirls with memories of my mom. I feel her presence, a gentle whisper in the back of my mind urging me to be strong. I draw from the precious memories of her warm embrace and sense her with me, guiding me through this hell. He choregraphed this dance for failure, but I'm taking what little spirit I have left and cashing out. I slump in his arms, my weight becoming his burden and on one final, heart-wrenching twirl, my toes graze the unforgiving wooden floor. "Stand up," he demands.

Clutching my waist, he struggles to keep me upright, and it brings me nothing but pleasure. All the fear I've harbored over the past few weeks oozes out, slipping through the cracks of my fragmented bones.

His furious voice is already a million miles away from where I'm headed. *The devil can't follow me to heaven!*

"Fix yourself," he hisses. "Open your eyes, Rose." My eyelids ignore him. My soul has moved from the windows and is ready to leave this house for good.

"Oh no, you don't!" is the last thing I hear before lapsing into unconsciousness.

CHAPTER 1

DETECTIVE JOHN WALTERS

We've found Rose.

Tucked between the rusty railway tracks of the Old Appleton swing bridge. The body of Rose Bernstein lies with her head at my feet. Her once vibrant blue eyes now stare lifelessly at corroded beams overhead while the Fox River roils beneath. Glancing back at the Lawe Street entrance, I scan our desolate location. Despite being well-traveled during the day, the overpass is hidden from the main road at several points. Beyond the crime scene tape that is stretched tautly from one beam to another, the graveled path disappears around a bend.

With my notepad and pen in hand, I circle her body. I can't help but think of the countless victims before Rose who relied on me to find answers, to deliver justice. Gazing down at her reinforces my commitment to that cause. I begin to carefully document my finding. Despite some light bruising, her face appears to be the only body part unbroken. The sickening reality of my failure cuts through me like a knife. While chances of finding Rose alive had been dwindling daily, hope persisted. Everyone who knew her described an energetic and sweet young woman; I wanted to bring her home.

Not like this.

Now, red lipstick stains full lips and is smudged across her cheeks, the color fading to pink as it meets the black mascara streaks that outline the tracks of tears. Her blond hair, save for a few loose strands has been meticulously tucked behind her ears. The blue, full-skirted dress she's wearing is in complete contrast to what her father Arnie Bernstein said she wore on the day of her disappearance. Three gold buttons and a loose thread adorn the bodice. I write "missing button" in my notepad. With a deep breath my focus turns to her injuries. I start with her legs: bruised and twisted unnaturally, they have a peculiar pattern above and below her knees.

What the hell caused that?

My pen stills, suspended in thought as my eyes travel to the soles of her bare feet. They have multiple cuts and bruises, obvious blisters across the balls and back of the heels. Black high heels lie idly next to her. I squat down closer to her body. Note the same distinct pattern of bruising on her arms, that are swollen to twice their size.

My head moves back and forth, unable to fully comprehend the extent of her injuries. Her arms, her fingers, her legs, her neck, every inch shows considerable signs of trauma. Standing up, I growl out an angry breath, my eyes sting with fury and I close them on another deep inhale.

I try to visualize, internalize her terror as he inflicted his dark and violent desires onto her. My fists tightens around my notepad and pen, my own thirst for blood drying my throat as I swallow back my rage. Whoever did this went beyond the scope of brutal into pure savagery.

Arnie Bernstein's face flashes to the forefront of my mind. A tall man with kind eyes and an already broken heart, his world is about to get a whole lot darker. Witnessing the aftermath of murder is part of the darkness that haunts my career as a homicide detective. It never gets easier, and, on those days, I doubt I'll ever bring a child into this cruel world. I hang my head low, indulging in the disappointment this development brings before stowing those personal feelings away.

A flurry of action draws my attention to the end of the walkway. The forensics team has arrived, along with a news van. I flip my notepad closed. Looking down at Rose, I offer up a new promise. "I'll find who did this to you," I whisper, knowing that whoever he is, his face was the last she saw before dying. I will be just as obsessed with finding him as he was the morning he went hunting for Rose. Knowing his capability, *how can I not be?*

"Can you get a tent up before the choppers get here?" I ask Maria, who is head of the crime scene unit. She is covered, head to toe, in a white bunny suit and carrying her kit as she steps onto the bridge. I don't miss the eye roll through her goggles.

"Sorry, I don't want them blasting this image on the TV," I sigh.

She pats my shoulder as I pass.

"We've got her from here, John. You go find the bastard who did this." She smiles sympathetically. I take some comfort in knowing that Rose is in caring hands now. I look back one last time as Maria crosses the bridge and burn the image of Rose into my mind. This is how I will remember her, for now.

I leave the scene in my car. My first stop will be telling Arnie that we found his little girl.

CHAPTER 2

SCOTT

Tonight's true crime segment was scheduled to cover the disappearance of Rose Bernstein. However, in the early hours, Savannah Phillips, one half of our true-crime duo, called to inform me that police have discovered a female body. Formal identification has yet to be made, so I've arranged a pre-show meeting for Savannah and her co-host Faye to prepare fresh content for the schedule.

As always, Faye's early. Her cherry-red beret grabs my attention as she wanders into the studio. From behind the glass of the control room, I watch her stand inside the door. I shouldn't stare, but as they so often do, my eyes gravitate to hers. The baby blues look lost as they scan the empty studio.

Faye is beautiful. No man could be indifferent to her sex appeal, but as her boss, I need to be. Though, it's her inner beauty that invades my thoughts more often than I care to admit, too often to consider myself a professional when she's around. Being her producer means we're around each other a lot. For the most part, I can handle it, but oh boy, it's moments like these, when she's vulnerable or lost in thought, that slay me. Her journey to where she is now has been fraught with heartbreak and loss but through it all she kept smiling. There is a quiet strength that she carries with her, one that I've drawn from through my own pain.

Still unaware of my presence, she turns back out of the studio, no doubt heading to the communal office space. My stomach muscles tighten, my emotions too entwined with her to simply resume my paperwork. I'm right behind her when she reaches her desk.

"Nice hat!" I say.

Turning, she takes off her winter coat, throwing it on the back of her chair.

"A gift from Luke."

"He's got taste, for a big brother."

"I wasn't sure about it." She blushes, pulling the soft wool hat from her head before combing her fingers through her messy blond hair.

"I like it. Looks good on you." My eyes are fixed on hers. "Are you OK?"

Surprised by the question, confusion creases her brow.

"Yeah, of course. Why'd you ask?"

"I saw you come in ... you looked upset?"

Swiping a hand in the air, "I'm being silly. Really, it's nothing."

"Is it about the body they found this morning?"

Since the beginning, the striking resemblance between Faye and Rose has been impossible to overlook. They could pass for sisters, a fact that never fails to give me goosebumps.

"I'm being ridiculous: all morning I've had this ache in my chest, and ..." her eyes swim with emotion. "We've been covering her disappearance, I can't help feeling that ... I've lost a friend. It's silly, I know." She's shaking her head, dismissing the emotions again.

"I don't think it's silly. I hoped our coverage of the case would somehow help; we'd be robots not to feel disappointed."

She nods. "Yeah, you're right. It's just very raw. I wonder how Savannah is feeling."

"Where is she actually?" I check my watch. "It's not like her to be late."

"I'm wondering if she ever sleeps. You know she phoned me at six a.m. when the news broke?"

"Yeah. Me too."

"Maybe it's a Texan thing?" She grins.

"What?"

"Eh, maybe they sleep with one eye open!"

"Nah. Believe it or not, I googled that before and it's not humanly possible. So, it's a Savannah thing," I joke, happy to see her shoulders shake with laughter.

"Scott! You did not! Seriously though, maybe she keeps a police scanner under her bed?"

"I don't want to imagine the things under her bed!" My words elicit another rumble of laughter from her chest and my day—no, my week is made. As if right on cue, the door bursts open.

Savannah's backing into the office, the curve of her hip pushing open the door. The two coffees she's carrying spill onto the sleeve of her white blouse. "Oh, for fuck's sake!" she grumbles, before the paper tray tumbles from her hands.

"SHIT!" She throws her head back. "Can this shitty day get any worse?" she huffs, the heavy sigh blowing the strands of her auburn hair from her eyes. Faye and I jump to help her. The same sadness that held Faye's eyes moments before fill Savannah's. I get busy cleaning up the mess while they embrace one another in consolation.

FAYE

"Good evening, Green Bay! Welcome to True Crime Tuesday here on the late show, with myself, Faye Anderson, and my wonderful co-host, Savannah Phillips."

"Yeah, thanks, Faye." Savannah leans into the mic. "Y'all, I'm sure you've heard the sad news that a body has been found in Appleton. I think we all know it is most likely Rose Bernstein."

"Shocking news. I really, really hoped for a different outcome." My voice catches, the news still playing havoc with my peace of mind.

"We all did, we're three weeks into covering this case. It's the worst possible outcome."

"I can't stop thinking about her poor father." My thoughts drift to Arnie Bernstein, my heart aching for him. The helpless reality weighs down on my chest. We did all we could, which feels like absolutely nothing at all.

"It's unimaginable, what he must be going through: the loss of his only child. I'm just hoping the detective on the case can catch this guy fast."

Savannah's voice is steady as she takes the lead.

"Hopefully Detective Walters can work his magic here, too." Savannah's tone carries some hope.

"Ladies, we're getting texts in asking who the hell Detective Walters is." Scott's soothing voice floats through our headphones. Savannah's eyes round in shock.

"Oh, come on, y'all! Surely you know who he is: he was lead detective on the Lucy Clax case, two years ago."

My forehead wrinkles in recognition of the name, my mind trying to connect the dots.

"Lucy Clax ..." I repeat the name, as the piece fits into place. "Wasn't she the little girl kidnapped out at Fox River Mall?"

"Yeah, her mother was putting groceries in the trunk of the car and Karl Lipton went and snatched her, right from the back seat! Thankfully, police located her within forty-eight hours, and alive!"

The details of that case flood my memory "That's right! Impressive police work ..."

"How could you forget?"

"Now, now my serial-killer-obsessed co-host, not everyone knows true crime like you."

"Whoa, whoa, whoa! Let's not get all carried away. 'Obsessed' is a very strong word. 'Intrigued' is a word I might feel more comfortable being associated with." She cocks a dark, perfectly manicured brow at me. My eyes dart to the true-crime paperback sitting next to her coffee and tease her further.

"That would be misleading to our listeners. You, my friend, are obsessed."

"Ad break coming up, ladies." Scott interrupts our banter.

Reaching for my water bottle, I rest the rim on my bottom lip, while my eyes drink in Scott through the acoustic glass. His head's down, concentrating on the monitor in front of him. His floppy brown hair, as laid back as he is, curls around his ears. When his gray eyes lift and catch me staring, the deep grooves of his dimples burrow into his cheeks as an easy smile unfurls on his handsome face.

Scott was already working here when I joined the station as an intern five years ago. His guidance and unwavering support have been a cornerstone of my career. Savannah was way ahead of me too; she was already hosting her own early morning show. Her sultry drawl roused our listeners out of their beds and into their day. Now it's those sensual tones that help ease them into a good night's sleep. Our friendship has been a lifeline to me in the bustling world of media and true crime, without it I'm not sure I could talk about the horrors we cover day in day out.

"And we're back in five, four..." Scott's voice pulls me from my musings. Sitting up straight, I get back to work.

The rest of the show goes off without a hitch. Wisconsin is engrossed by this case, and while most of our conversation is conjecture, talking about it has been a welcomed topic.

"Brilliant show, guys ..." Scott says, walking into our small studio. "Now, let's get the hell out of here."

"One second!" I say, reaching for my coat and hat. They both wait for me, Scott reaching for my laptop case as I bend to collect my purse.

"What have you got in here? Bricks?" he asks, throwing it over his shoulder.

"I printed off info on Detective Walters's cases. I thought he could be a guest speaker on the show. We could also try to get some info on Rose's murder."

"Have you got the printer in here too?" he jokes, earning him chuckle from Savannah and me. I reach out to take it from him, but he steps back. "I got it," he insists, already leaving the studio and me with no choice but to accept his kindness.

Savannah looks back over her shoulder as she follows, wiggling her eyebrows at the stupid grin on my face.

"I like your idea about the detective," she says, as we walk toward the exit.

Scott agrees. "I'll phone the Outagamie Sheriff's department tomorrow to put the feelers out."

"You did an amazing job tonight, Savannah." I nudge her with my shoulder.

She swipes her hand in the air. "Hush now, we're a team." Her tone, raspy from fatigue and talking, leaves no room for argument. Scott's eyes scan over her head to find me. The appreciation in his gaze causing my cheeks to burn.

"The A-team." He winks before his attention wanders back to Savannah.

"I gotta admit, Savannah, you were right about the true crime segment. I'm impressed. The podcast will really help solidify those loyal listeners."

"That'll teach you to doubt this duo." She waggles her thumb between us both.

Wrapping his arm around her neck, he musses her hair. "Never again!" he laughs.

"Scott!" Wriggling free, Savannah shoves at his broad chest, her eyes alight with humor. My fingers tingle with the urge to join in.

I admire Savannah's talent to charm him, everyone for that matter. Scott's easy-going nature shines around her. I quash any envy, knowing their relationship resembles that of siblings rather than secret lovers, and I'm genuinely happy for her. I have my brother Luke here in Wisconsin, while Savannah's family are in Texas. Scott and I are like her extended Green Bay family. Stepping into the frosty November air, we disturb its stillness as we walk across the empty parking lot.

"OK. Night, y'all!"

"Night," Scott and I say in unison as Savannah climbs into her car.

We watch her back out of her parking spot, waving as she drives off, before we take a leisurely stroll to my truck. Parked next to Scott's shiny black sedan, she looks forlorn. But I love every inch of my Dodge D-100: the chipping, turquoise paint, rusted edges, dents and dings included.

"Will you be OK driving home?" he asks.

"Yeah, I'll be fine, I've got old Sally here." I hip bump my truck.

"Is that thing even roadworthy?"

Craning my neck, I stare up at him with wide eyes and amusement in my tone "Hey! Leave my baby alone."

Laughing now, he leans against the truck next to me. "Where did you get this old thing anyway?"

"It was my mom's." One of the few relics I still have from her. He inches closer, guilt marring his face. I don't talk much about my mom and dad passing away.

"Shit, I'm sorry."

"Don't be silly, I've never told you before and besides, you were just teasing."

"In that case, this here ..." his hand pats one side of the truck. "Is the finest hunk of junk I've ever seen."

"It sure is." My mouth drops open, a deep yawn holding it wide until my tired sigh escapes. "—Ooh! Sorry." I shake away the shiver it brings. His soft laugh warms my weary limbs and tugs the corner of my mouth up again. His gaze roams from my smile to my eyes.

"By the way, have you and Savannah RSVP'd for Karen's wedding yet?" he asks. Karen is the marketing manager at Green Bay Radio. She's getting married next month, and they invited most of the station staff.

"Yeah, we did a few weeks ago."

"Oh, you did?" He leans back. Seconds tick, the silence stretches, and the cogs of his mind turn as if trying to figure something out. There has always been an unspoken connection between Scott and me. One that threatens the boundaries of our working relationship, a boundary we flirt the edges of too often. Electricity crackles in the air and I wonder what he is thinking before he reveals it to me.

"Well, do I know the lucky guy?"

"Yeah, you do actually!" I tease.

"Who?" his eyes widen.

"Savannah!" I laugh, my stomach whirling when relief flashes across his face. "What about you?"

Clearing his throat, he sidles next to me. "You know Don from the tech department? He asked me if I would bring his new girlfriend's sister."

"Like a blind date?"

He shrugs. "it's more of a favor than a date. She's nervous about meeting us all for the first time so he wanted her to have someone she knew there."

I nod along, smiling politely, pretending to be surprised. I don't tell him that Savannah found this out weeks ago. Although, I am relieved to know it's not an actual date.

"And you agreed?" I push on.

"Yeah ... reluctantly, I might add."

"But who knows? She could be the love of your life!"

"Well, my plan is to spend the night with the A-team!" he leans in closer, nudging me with his elbow.

"Not when Savannah finds out we're second best." I can't stop myself from teasing him.

"You wouldn't do that to me!"

"Nah. If it doesn't work out, you know you can party with us."

"It's not a date!" he insists, his eyes searching mine.

Scott's eyes can both comfort and unsettle me. My head and heart are in a constant tug of war when he's around. My stomach is the collateral damage, clenching and unclenching under his attention. Stepping back, I climb into my truck and roll down the window.

"Hey, you don't have to explain yourself to me!"

His hand curls around the doorframe "Have you ever considered that I might want to?"

"Want to what?"

"Explain myself." He knocks on the roof. "Safe driving, Faye." He smiles, stepping away to give me space to drive. The warmth of his grey eyes continues to tug on my heart before I manage to say.

"Goodnight, Scott!"

CHAPTER 3

FAYE

Forty minutes from the laid-back city of Green Bay, the road narrows, welcoming the country lanes. No streetlights guide my pickup truck as it snakes around their inky black bends. Flanked on either side by an expanding forest, this stretch of road can be treacherous when icy.

Dropping gears, I slow down and turn onto the narrow drive toward my cabin. Moonlight filters through the bare branches of the maple trees that border the gravel road. Tall and linear, they stand like foot guards, leading to my castle.

Hauling my tired limbs out into the chilly night air, I steal a moment to soak in my surroundings. When my grandmother passed away and left this property to me and Luke, we chose to keep it. A decision rooted in our shared childhood memories of watching our mother struggle after our father's death. He was a fit young farmer; his sudden death floored us all. Mom did her best to keep the farm afloat, but ill health and heartbreak plunged her into debt until we lost our cherished home. At times, the long drive can become tiresome, but no one can take away our home and that makes every mile worth it. Heading to the moonlit, stone-faced cabin, I glance toward the woods. Stars hang overhead, as far as the eye can see. The calm waters of the lake behind our cabin reflect the night sky's beauty along its surface. I love nothing more than swimming in that lake during the summer and hiking the surrounding woods all year round. I drag myself up the two steps and across the small wrap porch to the front door, listening to the welcoming creak of its hinges. Luke has been promising to oil them for months. Not bothering to turn on the lights, I drop my bag and coat by the door and head upstairs to bed. Crossing the threshold into my bedroom, I realize that I left the door unlocked. But sleep beckons and my bed is too close to deny myself another second of comfort.

The cabin is isolated, my mind reasons.

The entrance is hidden.

I fall asleep happy that unless you know the rural town of Abrams, you wouldn't even know we were here.

A crash wakes me with a jolt. Snapping upright in bed, my eyes struggle to adjust in the darkness. The whines of the screech owls outside my window are the only sound I hear until the deep grumbling of a man's voice filters up the stairs.

Pulling back my duvet, I step onto the cool wooden floorboards and tiptoe toward the stairs. My heart pounds in my ears until there is another muttered groan.

"Aw, shit ..."

Relief washes over me and I rush down the stairs, grinning when I see Luke, bent over, with his head in the refrigerator.

"Don't you buy any food?" he asks, his big head still inside the fridge.

"Food! You just scared the shit out me and you're worried about your belly ..." I admonish, already walking to the cupboard to take out some bread. "And don't you know how to switch on the lights?" I ask.

Grabbing a bottle of beer and closing the fridge door, Luke turns his bearded face lazily toward me. An amused smile hitches up one of his cheeks. "I was trying *not* to wake my annoying little sister."

"Ha! What was that bang, twinkle toes?"

"That damn table needs to go," he grumbles. I look back into the hallway and notice that the side table, which is usually flush against the wall, is askew, and one of the ornaments toppled over.

I laugh. "How do you always manage to bump into it?"

"It's hazardous." He lifts the bottle of beer and takes a long swig. "But I'm sorry I woke you."

"It's OK. I'm glad you did. I miss you when you're gone ..." I smile up at him. "Now sit down while make you a sandwich."

He complies and wanders to the other side of the kitchen island.

"We just flattened a patch in Oregon. I have a few weeks' leave before we fly to Washington," he informs me, leaning over the kitchen island to take the cheese sandwich I've just finished cutting in two. Luke is a lumberjack. He travels from camp to camp around the country, working away from home for weeks at a time. He was recently promoted to a chainsaw-wielding feller. His love of the wilderness and need for adventure combined to make this the perfect job, in his opinion. Despite his reassurances that he is properly trained and wears safety equipment, I still worry.

"So how have things been here?" he asks.

"Good. I've been busy with work. We've been putting in a lot of overtime on the podcast, hence the lack of food."

"Yeah, I've been listening. I worry about you working so late, especially when a girl who looks a lot like you has just been murdered."

"Another beer?" I ask, reaching into the fridge for my own. His concerns tug on mine, but I ignore them and change the subject.

"You do know you're a walking stereotype right now, don't you?" He looks down at his worn jeans and red flannel shirt and shrugs, smiling.

"The ladies love it."

"Shut up!"

"You better believe it; I'm fighting them off with a stick. They're crazy for the guns." Stuffing the last of his food in his mouth, and lifting one of his burly arms, he flexes, the bicep bulging. I roll my eyes dramatically.

"God, you're so vain!"

"And you're great at leaving doors unlocked," he growls.

"I forgot ..." My cheeks burn under his scrutiny. "It was silly," I admit.

"I'm surprised you took such a risk."

"You're right, I know, it was stupid. But after the scare you gave me, I doubt it will happen again."

"I hope so, because covering a murder investigation on the show doesn't seem to have done the trick. Why are you talking about this anyway?"

"It was Savannah's idea, but I'm enjoying it. And the listeners love it."

He grunts. "When am I meeting this Savannah? I'm not sure she's a good influence."

"Not a *good influence*?" I scoff. "What are you talking about?"

He shrugs unapologetically. "She comes across as very opinionated on the show, and now she's roping you into all of this true crime stuff."

"So, she should be quiet and suggestible? Is that what you think of me?"

"No, don't twist it!"

"Don't be so judgmental of my friends."

Pasting a smile on his face, his hands lift in defense. "OK, shit I'm sorry. It's hard to be so far away sometimes."

"I know you worry, but Savannah is my friend! And since you're home early, you should know she's staying over this weekend. So, you better be nice!" the hoarseness returns to my sleep-deprived voice.

"I will," he promises, standing as he drops his beer bottle in the recycling bin. "I hate when you give me that look ..." His eyes pool with warmth as he moves around to my side of the island. "I'll play nice this weekend. But now—" He pulls me into a bear hug, his meaty fingers pinching my waist before he spins me around and bounds off. "You can lock up!"

"Ow—You asshole!" I call after, the sounds of his heavy feet already pounding up the stairs. "And take a shower: you smell!"

Detective John Walters

It's been a long, grueling few days. Breaking the news to Arnie Bernstein was devastating, his grief-stricken face still weighs heavily on me as I climb the steps towards the ME's office. My chest burns with the need to catch my breath. A grim reminder that I'll never be as fit as I was before my injury. With each upward stride, the steps blurs beneath my feet as I consider every decision made in this case so far.

Could I have done more to bring Rose home alive?

The pursuit of evil often comes at a personal cost, one I've paid many times over. The war between good and evil is never-ending, and I know, no matter how many killers I catch, the only real victory is preventing these monsters from doing harm. This case hits harder and I can't help but wonder if my work has made a difference at all. A life spent forsaking all else and still innocent victims like Rose suffer at the hands of the depraved.

Reaching the top, I release those doubts on a deep exhale and stare up at the tall gray government building. It bears down one me as does my commitment to justice. I'm here again because there is another battle to fight and another promise to keep.

On the second floor, I find the office of Dr. Ronald Lacey, medical examiner, and the first port of call in any murder investigation. A man in his midforties, he is one of the finest MEs I've worked with, remarkably thorough and knowledgeable. He will help me to bridge the gap between Rose's life and her death. Understanding the enemy, and how he treated her, will impact how I move forward from here. Having a well-planned and thorough investigation strategy is important. Ronald's reports help me to prepare for battle.

As always when I visit, he's waiting with his door open, reading over his notes behind his desk. I knock lightly and he lifts his head from the page.

"John." He stands. "Good to see you again." I return his firm handshake before dropping into the seat across from him.

"I was reading over my notes from the autopsy just now. I must tell you, John, this one ..." He pauses. "Well, let's just say, I won't be forgetting it any time soon."

"Yeah, I thought it might be challenging."

"Well, brace yourself, because her injuries are extensive. I've never seen anything like it."

"That doesn't sound good."

He refers to the files in front of him. "Cause of death is homicide; he broke every bone in her body."

"When you say every bone, you can't mean *all*—"

"*All* her bones. Every bone, John! He broke them all ..."

"Fuck ..."

"Yeah. She suffered a broken neck: he crushed all seven vertebrae. Both collarbones were fractured and dislocated. Both arms had multiple breaks—above and below the elbows. *All* her fingers were broken ..." He looks up and we both silently shake our heads in disbelief.

"Her ribcage was crushed, causing secondary injuries to her lungs and heart, which were pierced by the jagged ribs. Her lumbar was shattered; hips, dislocated; pelvis, multiple fractures. Both femurs. Both shins, ankles, and feet all broken in multiple places. All toes broken. And to top it all off, she had severe sepsis."

"What the fuck? was she run over?"

"No." He shakes his head.

"How can you be so sure?"

"Because of this." Lifting the files laid out before him, he turns them to face me, dropping the autopsy photos of Rose's legs and arms on top.

"What am I looking at?" My eyes scan the deathly pale skin. Each leg and arm is marred by the same pattern of bruising I'd noted at the crime scene. I lift my eyes to his. "A baseball bat?"

"No." Leaning forward, he takes back his files.

"As you can see, the bruising on both shins and thighs are all consistent with one another. All four inches wide and parallel with each other. He broke the femur on both legs. It's the longest and strongest bone in the body, and very hard to break. Whatever he used was extremely heavy because, quite frankly, ripping the hip from its socket and breaking not one, but *both* femurs, would require tremendous force!"

This guy's a monster!

My stomach turns. Swallowing back the bile currently crawling up my esophagus, I force myself to ask.

"Was she sexually assaulted?"

"The short answer is no. Her internal injuries were too extensive to determine for sure, but I couldn't find evidence to say that she had been."

There is some relief knowing, that despite everything else he took from her, she may have been spared that cruelty.

"How could he dislocate her hips?" Images of a man with superhuman strength are flashing in my mind.

"Either her legs were spread so far apart that the ball joint dislocated, or some other unimaginable contortion. I don't know. I can't say for sure. That will be for you to figure out, but it is unlikely a man could do it alone. Some instrument or ... device would be needed." He sighs.

A strange mix of emotions burns in my chest, imagining the terror she must have gone through. But no, I couldn't have imagined this level of excruciating pain and horror and I've seen the worst in humans.

"So, we're talking torture then?"

"Maybe. The evidence does suggest it. However, the cause of death was blunt force trauma to the chest area, causing internal injuries, resulting in heart failure. I can tell you this, her fingers were broken first, then her arms, a day or two apart. Both legs— an hour or two before death. All other injuries were done postmortem."

"Wait." I inch forward in my chair. "Are you saying that he continued to break her bones *after* she died?"

"Yes."

"How do you know the order of injuries?"

"When a bone breaks, tissue tears at the site of the fracture. Blood will begin to clot there and spongy tissue forms at the center of the bone, beginning the healing process. Her fingers were broken first, so they were further along into that healing process." He rubs his eyes.

"Wow." I stand, report in hand. "Thanks, Ronald. This is ... a lot to take in." Following my lead, he moves around his desk, walking me to his door. The same routine as always, but this time, the air between us is thick with astonishment and disbelief.

"John, I racked my brains on the murder weapon. I'm sorry I can't come up with a real suggestion, but I do remember a case, a few years back, over in Brown County. Remains found out by Wequiock Falls. I recall the victim had some broken bones. It could be irrelevant, but you might look into it." He shrugs noncommittedly.

"I will. That is interesting," I nod. He lightly pats my shoulder.

"Thanks again." I offer one last, tight smile and leave. My mind is full now with the last three weeks of Rose's horrifying existence. I'm charged. The implications of this report are off the scale. I have work to do to catch a madman!

CHAPTER 4

JEFFREY

The radio is tuned in to a talk show discussing Rose's case. With my eyes firmly on the road ahead, I listen. Rose, Rose, Rose. Her name, her face, seem to be everywhere. I should be rattled, concerned about all the attention Rose is receiving and yet I'm glued to every news report. I'm hooked on the case, reveling in the outrage. There's even a podcast on the subject: the first episode will be available tomorrow, and I'm counting down the hours.

The first time, I was less composed. I kept expecting the police to knock on my door, for everyone to see right through me, like they knew what I'd done. Then weeks passed. Then months, then years, and nobody talked about it. It was as if no one cared. And then I met Rose.

The need to fill that void was intensifying daily. The first time my eyes met hers, I knew she was special. Watching her subdued the hunger, until the longing to dance and touch her became overpowering. My control was slipping and taking her became the only solution. That morning, I waited with my car stopped on Julius

Road. She pulled up behind me, trusting me enough to roll down her window. She leaped from her car when I lied about having hit a stray dog. Utter confusion twisted her features when she ran to the front of my car and found the road empty. I was already covering her mouth and dragging her to my trunk before she realized what was happening. The chloroform rag I used helped to subdue her. It took less than sixty seconds, and I was in my car and moving out of the area. In the end, Rose was a disappointment to me.

Turning off the country road, I navigate my car down the uneven drive toward my house. The wheels bumping through the potholes as I pass the barn on my left before parking. The headlights cut out with the engine, darkness and silence shrouding me. There are no streetlights, no nearby homes. Nothing but a cold stillness that weighs against the pent-up energy coursing through my veins. I rarely come here midweek. The journey is too far for daily commuting, but the recent media circus has stoked my excitement too much to wait for the weekend. I need to let off steam, to release my enthusiasm. The only way I know how is here, in dance.

The house is cold, but it always sizzles to life when I enter. Each step brings a piece of the past back into the dull room. When I dance, the floors gleam again, the fire crackles, the table lamp provides a warm glow as my feet glide around the room. Practice was mandatory under Mother's strict watch. Stay focused. Stay dramatic. Stay in control. Our own *Paso Doble* playing out night after night after night. One stamp of her foot demanded that I follow her lead.

I was a rebellious child and fought her every step of the way. Mother and son in a dance to the death, each misstep like a red rag to a bull. For a long time, Mother was stronger, but I became more daring. There was a cold cruelty to her; a crucial tension between us that I couldn't understand then. Now, I burn to feel it again. This room is my arena, a safe space to reclaim my power. Here I recharge, regain my strength, return to the ring.

Dress for the dance and the danger, there are simply no other options. Bending, I wipe a smudge from my otherwise shiny shoes. It's blood. Rose's blood. My jaw ticks with irritation. It's another reminder of how she failed me. Quickly washing my hands, I pull my black suspenders over the white leotard and fasten them to the waist of my black, straight legged slacks.

A cool breeze whistles through the wooden slats of the house as I move to the turntable. Dropping the needle between the grooves of the old vinyl record, it spins and wobbles, releasing a rustle of static before the room fills with the sound of famous lyrics.

The Everly Brothers' "All I have to Do is Dream" begins to play.

Mother's favorite song.

The steps are second nature to me now. My empty arms feel heavy: the weight of failure is a huge burden to carry. I should have had more patience with Rose. I should have helped her to understand how important the dance is to me.

She should have tried harder. My jaw clenches.

She should have been more grateful. My teeth grind together.

She should have wanted this as much as me. My feet move with fervor.

As the foxtrot comes to an end, the urge to samba takes hold. I don't usually cut the practice of a dance short, but the foxtrot did little to dampen my high spirits. Shifting my weight between my left and right foot, my hips sway freely, my arms fluid but controlled as I dance vigorously around the room. Every muscle in my body works: back straight, head up, my legs are powerful enough to withstand the demands of such formidable movement.

"Show no weakness Jeffrey: no loose arms." Mother's words echo through my mind as I command the room. Sweat drips from my forehead as I stamp back heavily on my left foot, holding it in place to push up onto my right toes. With one hand on my hip, the other raises above my head in salute. The rush of endorphins floods my body in this pose. My shirt is soaked through with sweat and my breath heaving as a wide smile spreads across my face. Releasing the hold, I suck in a deep breath, before returning to the foxtrot. This is exactly what I needed tonight.

FAYE

It's Saturday. "Where is Rose?" and "The Old Swing Bridge" went live yesterday. The first two episodes of our podcast covering the Rose Bernstein case have already had huge listenership figures: not just in Wisconsin, but across the world. At lunch hour, a fan added us to the *Talking Truth and Crime in Green Bay* discussion page on social media. A group of amateur sleuths have deemed our podcast "very informative" regarding Rose's case. With the podcast's success comes a huge responsibility. From now on, we owe it to everyone to continue our investigation with respect and dignity for Rose's family and community.

Sitting at my desk, my eyes are pinned to the laptop in front of me. Rose's photo fills the screen, and it is as if I'm looking in the mirror. I should be working, instead I study her face, knowing how easily it could have been me he chose to kill. How easily it could be any woman. A wave of fear adds to my already jangled nerves. I want to believe I'm smart enough, strong enough to avoid this kind of grim ending but looking at a face so like mine, I feel afraid. Rose had no control. She was just like me. It's an unsettling thought.

"How ya doin' over there?" Savannah calls to me from across the office. We're all putting in some extra hours today, giving up our Saturday to be here working on the next episode of the podcast.

"I'm doin' nuttin." Mimicking Savannah's accent adds some sparkle to my dreary tone.

"You've been staring at that photo for ten minutes now. Wanna spit out what you're chewing over?"

She pulls her hair back into a ponytail, working an elastic from around her wrist to hold it in place. Her now unframed face reveals every worry line of her concerned expression.

"Can I ask you something?"

"Shoot!" She nods firmly.

"You know more than me when it comes to murderers. You said something to me a while back about how killers have a type. Would I be his, I mean Rose's killer's—" I stumble over the word— "type?"

Her head bobs up and down, her eyes refusing to leave mine as she considers her answer.

"Yes, you would be. You look just like Rose. But that doesn't mean he's a serial killer or that you are in danger."

"I know you're right. It's just ..." a ragged breath passes my lips.

"What ya feelin'?"

"This whole thing sends the hairs on the back of my neck standing. Since day one, something has felt off. I don't know if it's because we're covering the case, or if it's because I look like Rose, but it's driving me crazy that I can't figure out if my gut is warning me of some unknown danger or if I'm overreacting!"

"Well, there's nothing 'over' about reacting this way. I think your feelings are valid, considering we have no idea who did this, and these killers tend to follow media coverage of their crime. He could very well be listening to us on the radio."

A cold chill gallops down my spine.

My body sags into my chair, as I unburden myself of the question that has tormented me for days. "What if he looks up the website and sees my photo?"

"It's a scary notion ..."

"What's scary?" Scott's voice startles us both causing us to leap in our seats.

"You! Creeping up on us like that!" Savannah scolds him.

Strolling to her desk, he drops a brown paper bag. "I come bearing food."

His smile is still in place when he turns toward me. The sudden squeeze of my stomach muscles has nothing to do with fear and everything to do with the long, lean body heading in my direction. Scott works out at the gym next to the radio station and all of his effort is greatly appreciated.

"You didn't have to get us food!" I smile as he reaches into another paper bag and tosses a waxed-paper package in my direction.

"It's a bagel." He shrugs, falling into the free seat next to me. I watch him unwrap his own food, his bicep curling as he brings it to his mouth. His presence is a welcome relief from staring at the screen. Looking at Scott instead is certainly helping me to forget my gloom.

"How are you two coming along here?" he asks.

"We're making headway. Maybe we could record the next episode today and head out to Finley's for a beer after?" Savannah's suggestion will put us ahead of schedule.

"I'm in!" I say, happy to go for drinks.

Scott checks his watch before sinking his teeth into his bagel, nodding as he chews and considers Savannah's suggestion.

"Do we have enough talking points?" he finally asks, before taking another bite. Savannah flip-flops her hand in a so-so motion as she too chews over her food. We all sit with full mouths, nodding at each other before all three of us smile.

"If you give us another hour, I think we'll be ready. What do you think, Savannah?"

"Yeah. If we quit burning daylight, we'll be sipping on suds in no time!"

"It's settled then. Let's finish up eating and get back to it. What do you need from me before I head back to the control room?"

"Nothing." I shrug.

"Great! I have some calls to make," Scott says. "I've been trying to get Detective Walters to call me back all week. I'll try him again."

"Good thinking," Savannah calls out, her eyes firmly fixed back on her laptop.

"Thanks for lunch." I smile, throwing Scott a small wave as he leaves. "First drinks on me at Finley's."

"Yee-haw!" Savannah crows, not bothering to glance our way.

I laugh. "And on that note, let's get to work."

FAYE

Finley's is alive with anticipation for the night ahead. Staff from surrounding businesses fill the popular watering hole to the rafters. The dark wooden floors and neon signs on the walls are complemented by the smell of stale beer and sweat. We were lucky to make it through the doors, but hit the jackpot when Scott secured a small table in the corner.

Music blares from the speakers overhead. Leaning closer, Savannah shares that she once left her mic on and spent ten seconds, live on-air, talking about the previous caller's sexy voice.

"Scott, your turn! Tell us your biggest on-air catastrophe?"

He thinks for a moment. "OK, I have one. When I was studying in Madison, I was juggling work at the college radio station, writing scripts for the news reports. I was also interning on the weekends at a local television studio. My plate was full. So, this one time, I wrote a report for the opening of a new diner on the college campus. It was called 'Rusty's Rolls'..."

He pauses for dramatic effect. Savannah and I lean forward in our seats.

"I wrote 'Students flock to eat Rusty's holes'."

Savannah squeals.

"Oh my god! That reminds me of a report I read about a new nightclub called 'Fuzzy Holes.' Imagine, calling your bar 'Fuzzy Holes'!"

My stomach aches from laughing.

"Oh stop! 'Fuzzy wuzzy was a woman ...'" I manage through fits of laughter, remembering a line from my favorite movie.

We all cackle like a pack of hyenas. Drying her eyes, Savannah turns to me. "OK, Faye, you're up! Biggest on-air catastrophe. Spill, or we're doing shots!"

"OK, OK! But I'm still traumatized to this day."

Scott's eyes widen with intrigue. "Hold on. Let me get comfortable." He leans back into his chair.

"One time, I referred to Tom Cruise's dick!"

Savannah chokes on her beer. "Shut up! You didn't!" she splutters louder than ever.

"Whoa, whoa, whoa ... Please clarify, Ms. Anderson. You called him a dick?"

"No, I was referring to his nether region." My eyes drop to Scott's crotch, my cheeks heating as I note the thick bulge. He shifts in his seat. My gaze lifts to find stormy gray eyes and a mischievous dimple popping.

I clear my throat. "It was in college. The new 'Mission Impossible' was out in the theater, and I was reviewing it with my co-host. Man, Tom Cruise can run. I was so impressed and blabbering on about it. She said, 'But he's the size of a thumb!' to which I replied, 'I'd take his thumb any day of the week.' It just came out!"

Savannah's head falls back, her eyes watering. "I'd like a bit of thumb Cruise myself."

"Thumbs up to that!" Scott chimes in, both of them teasing me further.

"Stop, stop! It just thumb-led out of my mouth!"

"I reckon that man has a 'schlong'!" Savannah winks, more serious now.

"'Shlong'? Are you drunk? Do you mean he's 'long'?"

"Noooo. It's 'ssshhhhhlong'!" Her Texan drawl oozes over the word. "It's actually German, for snake. I think 'snake' captures the essence of penises around the world."

"Yeah, there is a certain *je ne sais quoi* to it." We're giggling like schoolgirls.

Scott turns pink beside us. "Oh, you speak German now, do you?"

"No, Scotty, I speak the language of penis. In Spanish it's *pene*, in Sweden they say *snopp*. In Finland it's *kulli* ... must I go on?"

Savannah never fails to surprise me with her quirky, yet completely useless facts. A multilingual knowledge of penises should be no different, and yet I'm impressed.

"How the hell do you know this shit?"

"Now, that's a story that requires tequila, time, and a two-way conversation! For now, it's my round." She jumps up, disappearing into the crowd within seconds. Feeling tipsy from the alcohol and laughter I turn to Scott, his fresh scent even more intoxicating than the beer in my hand.

"This is so much fun!"

His eyes sparkle. "You're cute when you're drunk."

"*Only* when I'm drunk?" I boldly ask.

"No, but I can *only* admit it when *I'm* drunk!"

Butterflies fill my stomach, enough to bring me to dizzying new heights.

"Oh ..."

"Shit, that was inappropriate. I shouldn't have commented on your appearance like that."

I reach for his elbow. "No, It's OK! Outside the studio we're friends, right?"

"I guess." His eyes fall to my fingers, still gripping his wool sweater. "But even then, I'm still your boss."

"So, hypothetically: if I told *you* that you're cute, would I be issued a warning?"

"I'd have no choice."

"Verbal, or written?"

"You're on dangerous ground right now, Ms. Anderson."

I glance at the floor, searching playfully. "From where I'm sitting, I think I'm pretty safe." I wink.

"Did you just wink?"

I bite the edge of my lips. "I had something in my eye."

"Is it gone?" His Adam's apple bobs.

I lean closer, feeling more brazen than ever. "No ... can you take a look?"

His finger gently tugs on my bottom eyelid. I breathe him in again, giving new life to the butterflies that flutter furiously. Our breaths mingle, our noses graze and the noisy bar fades to the sound of my throbbing heart.

"Look up," he whispers into my hair, "I can't see anything."

"Hmmm."

"Definitely, a verbal warning." His gruff voice sends a shiver down my spine.

Pulling back, our eyes catch again. "Can't you look the other way, this time?" I say.

"I'm not sure I can look *anywhere* else at this point."

"I got shots!!" Savannah's interruption sends us leaping back into our chairs. "It's hotter than a honeymoon suite at this table!" She's grinning wide. "I'm going to grab the beers," she announces already whipping back toward the bar before we can respond.

"Will you be OK to drive home?" Scott nods to the shots.

"I was planning on thumbing a lift."

Easy smiles spread across our faces. "Actually, Luke's picking me up soon." Retrieving my phone from my bag, I notice three missed calls. Oops. I scan the bar and spot him coming through the door. "Oh. There he is!"

All the alcohol rushes to my head as I jump to put on my winter coat. Reaching to steady me, Scott's hand lands on my hip. the heat of his touch burns beneath the denim of my jeans. We share another knowing smile.

LUKE

Coming home is always an adjustment: from working long days with early starts and passing out as soon as my head hits the pillow, to sleepless nights and idle afternoons. The only activity that helps ease me back into the slow pace of Wisconsin is fishing. Dragging my weary ass from my truck, I go in search for Faye. Walking through a busy bar wearing navy fishing bibs and rubber boots was not part of tonight's plan. Eyes size me up as I squeeze between the well-dressed clientele of Finley's. At six foot three and smelling like the East River, there was no hope of being inconspicuous. Spotting Faye in the back corner, I'm making my way in her direction when the sound of breaking glass and an aggressive male voice stops my wet boots.

"Watch where you're going, lady," he growls, towering over a woman half his size.

Anger fuels the heat creeping up my neck as I turn in their direction.

"You knocked the beer from my hand, asshole!"

"You walked into me, cowgirl," he spits.

"It's always the dirty dog that howls the loudest."

I'd recognize that raspy voice anywhere. That Texan accent is unmistakably hers. With hair the color of autumn and sapphire eyes fierce enough to slice the guy in two, all the oxygen is momentarily sucked from my lungs. I hadn't expected Savannah to be so beautiful.

"Fuck off, lady ..." The guy's furious eyes quickly fade to fear when he sees me standing behind her.

I exhale gruffly. "You owe the lady a drink, dickhead."

Savannah turns, her shoulder bumping my chest to find me towering over her. She cocks her head to one side; her eyes travel slowly and deliberately up my body.

Fuck, she's sexy.

"Luke, I presume?" she drawls lazily.

"Nice to meet you, Savannah. Need some help?"

She glances over her shoulder, to find that the fucker who spilled her drinks has left. "Apparently not." A sardonic smile hitches up one side of her face. "I take it you didn't catch any fish today?"

"Why do you say that?"

"Surely you scared them all away." She arches her eyebrows. "I could handle him, you know."

"I didn't know, but I'm *catching* on." My pun manages to elicit a chuckle and an eyeroll.

"Hmm. I suppose I should go easy on you. After all, you are Faye's big brother ..." She offers her hand. "Nice to meet you." My rough skin caressing her smooth palm is like two opposing charges meeting, sending a surge of desire throughout my entire being.

"Nice to meet you too." I take a step back and out of the danger zone. "Let me buy you a drink," I offer.

"Thanks, but I got it."

"I'd like to, being it's the first time we're meeting." I'm reaching for my wallet when her Texan drawl turns cold.

"I said no. I can buy my own drinks."

I feel a stitch of unease in my chest. "Fine. I was just trying to be nice."

"Yeah, well, don't. I can handle myself and I can buy my own drinks." She whirls away, leaving me to stare at the back of her head. My first impression of Savannah came from listening to her on the radio. Seeing her in the flesh confirms those perceptions.

She's a ballbuster!

I'm ready to leave when Faye's sweet and slurred voice comes up behind me.

"You guys met!"

We both turn, forced smiles in place.

"Sure did." Savannah says.

"Great! Come say hi to Scott before we go." She beams at me before turning back to Savannah. "Do you need some help with the drinks?"

"Oh no, she's got it all under control." My voice drips with sarcasm, but Savannah's controlled expression is unflinching as she answers Faye.

"Thanks for asking, but Luke's right. You go on ahead and introduce him to Scott. I'll see you tomorrow." Her feisty eyes narrow on me as Faye leans in for a goodbye hug. I forgot Faye invited Savannah for dinner tomorrow. Now, the idea of it has my stomach swooping with anticipation. The entire drive home is filled with thoughts of Savannah Phillips. Women usually appreciate it when I offer to buy them a drink, but not her. She set fire to that idea and left me speechless.

CHAPTER 5

SAVANNAH

Fuuuuuuuuck, I'm cold!

I've just spent the last thirty minutes trying to jack up my Ford Bronco, at the side of a muddy road. Soaking wet, I jump back into the warmth for a few moments' reprieve. There's no sign of the weather letting up. The wind, whistling louder than a fifty-pound bag of lips, has my vehicle wobbling from side to side. Craning my neck to look through my steamy windshield, all I can see is the tops of the birch trees and thunderclouds bringing some real rain. The empty road is barely visible beyond the safety of my car.

I'm in the middle of nowhere ...

Rainwater drips from my nose onto my lips as another shiver rakes my body. My irritation at slipping three times, ruining my new leather pants and swallowing dirt, are now overshadowed by concern of the vulnerable position I'm in.

I turn over the engine and crank up the heat. With my boots plumb full of water, I'm madder than a wet hen. I was hoping to wait it out, let the rain ease and try again until Faye called. She insisted that Luke come to help me while she finishes cooking. He's on his way, and for the second time in twenty-four hours, he's coming to my aid. I don't like it.

Don't like him.

My gut squeezes in protest. Desire, stronger than I've ever felt before, sends a surge of heat coursing through my veins. It unnerves me. I don't cotton to the idea of a helpless female needing a man.

I'm no damsel in distress!

Bracing myself for the cold, I set out to prove just that, by collecting my discarded tools from the side of the road and returning them to the trunk before he arrives. My hair whips around my face. The icy rain joins forces with the wind as I battle the elements. Moving quickly along the solid asphalt, I pause before stepping into the grassy sludge at the shoulder. Armed with my tire iron and jack, I hold onto the car with my free hand and use it to guide me back to the trunk. After depositing the tools and pulling out my overnight bag, I gratefully drop back into the driver's seat. Sucking in a lungful of air through chattering teeth, I prepare myself for one last battle with Mother Nature and the spare tire. I get back out as headlights come around a bend. A black pickup emerges from the bleak surroundings and slows next to me, the driver's window sliding down.

His bearded face frowns in disapproval, his tone too curt for my liking when he asks, "What are you doing?"

"Putting the spare back in the trunk." I yell over the howling wind. As I turn, my foot slides forward, bringing me down onto one knee, my hands sinking into a slurry of grass and cold muck. Within seconds, Luke's hands come under my arms, lifting me from the dirt and back onto solid ground.

"Wait here," he orders. There's no room for discussion as he moves around me to reach for the spare tire. I twist, reaching as he does.

"I got it!" I yell.

"You got nothing. Look around you, woman!" His growl deepens the groove between his brows. "You're covered from head to toe in mud and a bad attitude."

Suddenly self-conscious, my muddy fingers swipe through my hair. "What the hell did you want me to do? I got a flat!"

"You should have called as soon as it happened! Instead, you're out here, Ms. Independent, risking your neck! You should know better!" his face drops closer. Anger shoots from his eyes forcing me to look away. My eyes land square in the centre of his heaving chest, noticing for the first time that he isn't wearing a jacket.

"Don't lecture me, especially if you're dumb enough to come out in this weather without a jacket!" I scold him.

Rolling back on his heels, he shakes his head. "You're a real piece of work, you know that?"

He hurried to help you.

He's right. Even I was starting to worry before he arrived.

"Go get in my truck. I'll grab your things."

"I—"

He doesn't wait to hear my reply, lifting the spare tire into the trunk and slamming it shut in seconds. I do as I'm told, too cold to consider how dirty I am as I sink into the passenger seat of his truck. My elbows pull tight against my body as I try to stem the constant quaking. The door behind me whips open and my bags land on the backseat, the book I'm currently reading sliding onto the floor.

"Fuck, it's cold out there!" he curses through quivering lips. His long-sleeved black t-shirt is soaked and sticking to every muscle of his body. I scan his thick, masculine chest, drawing down to his lean waist and tight abs before dropping my eyes to his belt buckle, lower again I drink in his strong legs. Sturdy like a tree, Luke makes Samson look sensitive as he jumps into the driver's seat.

"I told Faye not to bother you."

His eyes narrow. "I didn't say it bothered me, did I?"

"I ain't tryna sound ungrateful."

"You didn't mean to *be* ungrateful, or you didn't mean to sound it?"

"Both!" I snap back.

"Are you sure you're not trying to rub me the wrong way, Texas?" He grins.

"I don't want to rub you, any which way!" I finally manage through gritted teeth.

"I think you'd love to get the chance actually."

"I think you've overestimated your effect on me."

"I think there is more to your immediate 'dislike' of me than you want to admit."

"I think, you think too much," I huff, "I would've been just fine; you should've stayed home."

He laughs at that. "Looked to me like you were far from just fine."

"I grew up on a farm: fixin's my middle name! I've changed plenty of flat tires, more than you could shake a stick at. The weather just knocked me back a little."

The air between us turns icy. With a shake of his head, he turns to drive back in the direction he came from.

"Oh, and I suppose you could fight off a would-be attacker too?" he growls, keeping his eyes fixed on the road ahead.

"If I had to, yes." The words seem silly even to my ears. "I would at least try."

"This coming from the woman I lifted off the ground with one arm. You'd better come up with better self-defense, if you plan on putting yourself in harm's way on a regular basis," he snorts.

"I slipped! I didn't need your paws picking me up—" I swing around—"And I certainly didn't plan on getting a flat tire! What if a maniac *did* happen by and murder me? I suppose you'd say it was my fault!" My throat burns.

"Of course not, I'd blame the sick fuck who did it." He pauses, his lips hitching upward. "Although, you are a royal pain in the ass. I imagine, if you'd been talking to him for a while, he might ..." he bites the inside of his cheek.

"That's not funny!"

"No, it's not. Look: you think I'm pissed because I was dragged out into the rain? No. I'm pissed because ..." I notice his knuckles are white as he grips the steering wheel.

"Because ...?"

"I'm sure you can stand on your own two feet just fine. But I don't know, seeing you struggling in the dark like that, it ..."

"What?"

"It disturbed me, OK?" His frown is fixed on the road ahead. I refuse to admit that he disturbs me too. *I met him twenty-four hours ago!* He's already gotten under my skin and is busy shifting parts of me that took years to set in place. I don't like it.

I don't like him.

"Well, I can't take all the responsibility. I'm pretty sure you were disturbed long before you met me!"

"I wouldn't go that far, darlin'.'" He mimics my accent.

"Don't you *darlin'* me. But do I apologize for the inconvenience, nonetheless." I concede to his point. Somewhere beneath his antagonism, he makes a valid one.

"Well, don't fall over yourself on my account, Miss Savannah. It takes more than a hard-headed female to hurt my feelings." His smug face turns toward me as we drive down the lane to their cabin.

"No need to look so pleased. You're no Sunday picnic, yourself!"

"I only ever give as good as I get," he says playfully.

"You don't give as good as you think!"

"Oh, you've no idea of just how good I can give it—" his gravelly tone's a warning that he might just show me. "Maybe you should lay it all on me sometime, see who comes out on top."

"I always come out on top," I harrumph as he puts the car into park. He turns in his seat, his eyes meeting mine with unbridled glee.

"I'm counting on it." He winks, before climbing down from the truck and opening the back door to grab my bags.

Reaching around into the backseat, I pick up my book from the floor, turning it for his attention. "Sweetie, you'd better hope that if you ever find yourself beneath me, I'm not holding a knife." I wink back, taking myself and my copy of *Women Who Kill* into the cabin, leaving Luke with an open mouth and my bags to carry.

Noise from Luke's football game floats down the hallway and into the cozy kitchen. Sitting across the island with nothing but two glasses of wine between us, Faye and I gossip.

Ending up in Green Bay was never part of my life's plan. In the end, my passion for true crime led me here. I'd been online, reading about a Chicago woman missing in Wisconsin, when the website for Green Bay Radio popped up. Among the ads was an internship application. I applied, and three weeks later, they offered me the job. The timing was perfect, and despite differing vastly from my hometown of Edom, Texas, Green Bay felt like the right choice. Meeting Faye and Scott has been the greatest surprise of it all. Hittin' the road at a young age brought many challenges and I sure learned the hard way, the lonesome way, that true friendship is a rare gem. Thankfully, I got savvy about spottin' it when it's right under my nose. That's why Faye's concerns about her likeness to Rose Bernstein has poked at my own. She's topping off our glass of wine when I ask.

"How you doin' after our chat, yesterday?"

Her shoulder lifts. "Better."

"Good, but I'm here if you need to talk, OK?"

She sighs, some of yesterday's sadness returning to her eyes. "Thanks, Savannah. I got caught up imagining all the worst-case scenarios."

"Our night out with Scott seems to have put a pep in your step!" I smirk over the rim before sipping on the crisp white wine.

"It sure did."

"Faye Anderson! You are as loose as ashes in the wind!"

She splutters out a laugh, "Hardly! We just flirted." She flushes red.

"Spill the beans now. What happened with Scott?"

"Oh God. I embarrassed myself."

"Good, it's about damn time! You two are so slow you could gain weight walking!"

They've been dancing around their attraction to one another for two years and it's painful to watch. Faye was dating a douchebag when she first joined the station, but I'm surprised Scott didn't seize the opportunity when they broke up.

"Out with it. I want all the details."

Leaning back on my high stool, I listen as Faye regales me with her antics from last night.

"I can't believe you faked an eyelash in your eye!"

We're both howling with laughter as Luke walks in. He eyes us suspiciously. A devious glint lingers in my direction before he looks to Faye.

"Your friend threatened to stab me earlier." He flashes a smug smile at me before ducking into the fridge.

"That's OK." She leans closer. "I've considered killing him myself, but I couldn't deal with stabbing him. Too much blood." She shivers at the thought.

"I agree, but whenever I imagine myself in a 'fight to the death' scenario, I'm always armed with a knife," I shrug.

"You're so weird! Who thinks about that stuff?" Luke moves to the opposite side of the island.

"Um, me? Did you know that how we choose to kill someone aligns with how we approach life?"

He turns to his sister. "Faye? I've just told you she threatened me—"

She lifts her hand to silence him. "Hush for a second. I want to know about this." Both Andersons train their eyes on me now. "So, if I choose to shoot Luke, what does that say about how I approach life?"

"Great, now I'm getting shot and stabbed in one night!" Luke throws up his arms.

"OK, but first, Luke: your turn. How would you kill somebody?"

"I'd use some form of torture," he deadpans, his eyes darkening. He means it too.

Faye turns, thumping one of his burly biceps. "That's cruel!"

"Great. Now Faye, would you shoot your victim from the front or behind?" I clarify.

"This is all very graphic, Savannah. Are you sure you're not getting a little kick out of this?" Luke inches closer, more intrigued than he wants to let on.

"A coward shoots from behind, but I don't think I could look someone in the eyes," Faye finally answers.

"OK perfect. So, from a completely psychological point of view, how you would choose to murder someone is in line with how you present yourself in everyday life. I, for example, would probably reach for a knife. That means that I get the job done, no matter how messy, and I'm direct—hands on, willing to get up close and personal." My eyes slide to Luke's. I'd never actually want to take another human life, not even his, but he doesn't need to know that.

"What about mine?" Faye looks excited.

"You'll accomplish the mission, even if you don't want to—"

"Just like thumb Cruise!" she interrupts. Her reference to last night's joke sends me into a peel of laughter.

"I don't even want to know," Luke says.

"OK, sorry, where was I? Oh yeah. You'll get the job done, but you are prone to tiptoeing around people instead of just pulling the trigger and telling them what you want."

"That's so me. I'm working on being more direct." She blushes. "What about Luke?"

"It won't surprise you to learn that Luke's answer is the most disturbing." I smile. "Luke takes his time, because he likes to draw out the pleasure for himself and the agony for his victim ..."

"Drawing out pleasure has always been welcomed, in my experience ..." He interrupts. Heat creeps into my cheeks. Choosing to ignore the innuendo, I continue.

"He's strategic. Everything is planned, nothing is left to chance. He delays instead of just getting the job done."

"If I'm going to do it, I'm going to take my time. *Every* time."

Suddenly parched, I sip from my wine glass and take a moment to regain some control.

"However, his work is completed to the highest standards, even if he is—" I smile, crookedly— "a little slow."

"Bullshit! I'm as direct as you'll get!"

"That is *so* you!" Faye points at him before turning back to me. "He doesn't buy a new shirt without thinking it over for six months."

"Now, why doesn't that surprise me?"

My eyes meet his across the island, my pulse racing at the unmasked desire that stares back. He stands up tall to leave. "Faye, keep this killer away from me. She's dangerous."

I call after him. "Hey, wait! I've one more ... unless you're afraid we'll see inside your twisted mind."

"Try me!"

"When I say a word, y'all have to say the very first word that comes to your mind. Got it?"

"It's not rocket science, but to be sure, you'll say a word, we just answer it, with whatever word comes to mind?" Luke asks, confirming that he is in fact a control freak, afraid to get a game wrong.

"Yessir, that's right. Y'all ready?"

"Go for it," they say in unison.

"The word is ..." I pause. "Coffee."

The words "bean" and "cream" leave their mouths. A burst of laughter leaves me as they both stare at me, waiting for me to explain.

"Come on, don't leave us in suspense," Faye begs.

"Coffee is a stimulant, so it's linked to our feelings around sex and what stimulates us during sex. Luke likes the bean, and Faye, you like the cream." I howl again.

"I'm out of here." Luke claps his hands to his ears, horrified to be talking about sex around his sister. An excited thrill floods my core. Payback for his earlier innuendos is beautiful. *Direct, my ass!*

"I see you, Luke!" I wave two fingers between my eyes and his, still laughing as he runs from the kitchen.

"I do love the cream," Faye confesses, once Luke is out of earshot.

"And a good thumb!" I say.

We both erupt into another fit of laughter.

CHAPTER 6

DETECTIVE JOHN WALTERS

The shrill of my desk phone drags my attention away from my computer screen. Rubbing my strained eyes before glancing around the room, my vision adjusts as I reach for the handset.

"Walters."

"Hey, this is Detective James, over in Brown County. You called about a case I worked a few years back?"

"I did. Did you have a chance to look it over?" I called the sheriff's office after leaving the medical examiner's to talk to the detective in charge of the unsolved case mentioned by Dr. Lacey.

"Well," he says, "not much information here, to be honest. What was it you needed to know?"

I roll my eyes in frustration. I've got no leads, a tension headache building behind my eyes and this guy took three days to tell me he *has nothing to tell me!*

"I'm working on the Rose Bernstein case. I wanted to know if there are any similarities with your case. So, if you could outline what you have, that would help."

"OK ..." He sighs, rustling his papers over the line.

"Yeah, here we go—" He coughs—"One sec." he chokes, then there's the sound of him slurping back a drink before the thud of a mug being set down.

"Sorry about that. Yes. Partial skeletal remains were found in early November 2019, in a shallow grave, by the walking trails at Wequiock Falls, near Champion, in the town of Scott. The lab identified the remains as female. No cause of death was determined. The body has yet to be identified. DNA didn't match anyone in the system."

Both victims were found in November.

"Did you have any leads on who she was?"

"My guess? Homeless woman took a walk into the forest area there and succumbed to the elements."

Fuck me, this guy's a detective?!

"Do you have the medical examiner's report on file?"

More ruffling.

"Yeah. Dr. Daniel Stanley, the forensic pathologist for the crime lab wrote it ..."

I interrupt. "Could you email me over the full file? I'll go over it myself. I don't want to take up any more of your time."

"Yeah, sure. Give me your details," he agrees.

Ten minutes later, the case file lands in my inbox. Clicking through some of the overview crime scene photos, nothing stands out at first glance. Until a photo, labeled *OV 19, Bridge*.

She was found near a bridge, just like Rose.

Loosening my collar, I remind myself not to jump to conclusions. A wooden bridge comes into view. Again, like Rose, this victim's remains were discovered on a nature trail. The area is a popular beauty spot.

It could be a coincidence ...

Moving on, I click into the closeup photo file. The photographer focused on the remains. Unfortunately, the bones look to have been disturbed, more than likely scattered by wildlife throughout the area. It's unclear from the photos if any of the bones are broken. In truth, I wouldn't be able to decipher a femur from an ulna. So, I move on to the mid-range file, my eyes scanning instantly over the clothing found at the scene. Reaching for my phone, I call Detective James again. He answers on the first ring.

"Brown County Sheriff's office."

"Yeah. Walters here, from Outagamie again. I'm looking at one of your crime scene photos here," I begin.

"Oh, right ..."

"You say you reckoned this was a homeless person, out for a walk?" I remind him of his outrageous theory.

"That's right."

"I'm not sure about you, Detective, but I've never seen a homeless person wearing stiletto heels and a fancy dress taking a walk through a forest." I hiss through gritted teeth.

"Listen, I followed up on all the missing persons in the area. I got no hits. There was nothing to say this was a homicide. I have a backlog of cases here. If you come up with something tangible that I can follow up on, let me know."

"I will," I growl before dropping the receiver. "Incompetent fucking asshole!" My curse echoes around my empty office. Needing to move, I whip on my jacket and stalk through the station, my jaw ticking as I grind down on the fury that Detective James's shoddy work has unleashed.

"Jones!" I call out to a deputy. His head lifts from his desk as I storm toward the exit. "Call ahead to the Brown County State Lab and let Dr. Stanley know I'm on my way." Without waiting for a response, I head straight to my car, clipping the Jane Doe's anthropologist's report to the outside of Rose's autopsy. Exiting the parking lot, I turn toward Brown County. I have two reasons to believe that these cases are connected. I need a third.

Fifteen minutes into my journey, Deputy Jones called. Dr. Stanley is not at the state crime lab. Instead, I can find him on campus, at the University of Wisconsin, Green Bay.

Signposted, the forensic sciences department is located at the back of the campus in a one-story red brick building. Walking through the double doors, a warm blast of heat welcomes me in from the cold. Noting the empty seat behind the reception desk, I walk over to a nearby janitor. He's at the top of a tall stepladder, struggling to place a star on top of a large Christmas tree. The foyer is a wide, open space. Students huddle in groups of four or five on sofas, no doubt too busy studying for their end-of-term exams to offer help. Dropping my case file on a small table next to him, I steady the wobbly stepladder.

"Thank you," he says, looking down. Youthful eyes light up his weathered face. Setting the star in place, he climbs down.

"You're welcome," I smile back. "That time of year again." I cock my head toward the tree. I don't dislike Christmas, but I've no time for all the madness. All the partying brings added stress for the police.

"My favorite. I love it!" he looks proudly at his work.

"It's a good-looking tree. I hope they appreciate your hard work." My eyes shift to the students.

"That bunch," he points to the students, chuckling softly. "They're good kids, but I could dance around here naked in a Santa hat and their eyes wouldn't leave the books!"

I laugh along. "Please don't! I'd hate to arrest you."

"Aha, a copper! You have the look about you."

"Is that so? I'm afraid to ask."

"It's that sharp look in your eye. Plus, you carry yourself with an air of authority. Nothing wrong with that," he replies, patting my shoulder.

"Well, thank you. But I could do with some directions."

"Sure, fire away!"

"Could you point me toward Dr. Stanley's office?"

"Sure." He turns and points to the unattended reception desk. "Go right down the hall. He's the last office on the left. I think he's in a lecture, but his assistant is working in the lab. He'll let you in."

"Thank you, and merry Christmas." It's still only late November, but the old man's eyes light up just the same.

The double doors that lead down a long hallway to Dr. Stanley's office have the words *Department of Forensic Anthropology* written above them. A deep male voice booms from a lecture hall as I pass. Following the janitor's advice, I head toward the lab, rapping on the door before entering.

Pale blue eyes assess me from over the top of a laptop before a tall man stands, his eyes looking to the empty hallway behind me.

"Can I help you?"

"Yes. Are you Dr. Stanley's assistant?"

"Yes, I'm Dr. Carson." His head tilts. "And you are?"

"Detective John Walters, with the Outagamie County Police Department. I was told that Dr. Stanley would be free soon, and to speak with you about seeing him."

"Of course. Can *I* help you with anything? I've worked in the field with him on several cases," he informs me.

"No, thank you. I've some questions regarding a report he wrote up a few years ago." Disappointment mars his features, but I don't elaborate further. People talk and the press is already having a field day with Rose's case. The last thing we need is them getting wind of a possible second victim.

"Ah. Here he is now."

Dr. Stanley barrels into the lab behind me. All five foot three inches of him, bringing a burst of energy to the room. His tawny-brown eyes alight on me as he reaches for his white coat, turning to face me, as he buttons it over his shirt, hiding a round belly. He smiles through his full black beard.

"Who have we got here?" His voice rumbles loudly.

"A detective from the Outagamie Police Department," Dr. Carson answers before I can introduce myself.

I take his chubby hand in a firm handshake. "John Walters."

"Oh yes, your deputy called. I don't have much time before my next lecture, and we are behind on our research." He glances to a clock on the wall.

"I appreciate you're a busy man. Do you have somewhere we can speak privately?"

"My office." He walks to the door, letting out a loud breath. "Carson, please call me if you need me."

His office is tiny. Bookshelves line the walls, leaving him with just enough room for a desk and two chairs. He has three framed *Forensic Science* magazine covers on one shelf. I move closer, reading the article titles.

"'Forensic Scientist of the Year'! I'm impressed."

He shakes his head, uninterested in the attention. "We received that award based on the research that Carson and I are conducting in the field of facial reconstruction. The award belongs to him too, but I am the poster boy of this fine institution." He frames his face with both hands, grimacing.

"I take it you don't do the job for the money or the glory?" I laugh.

"Oh no, the money's great." His deep laughter rattles the frames on the shelf. "So, what can I do for you, Detective? I really am short on time." He sits behind his desk, directing me to the chair opposite. Pulling the manilla file from under my arm, I rest it on my knee.

"I was hoping you could shed some light on a case you were involved in, back in November 2019. Out by Wequiock Falls?"

"Yes, I remember that ..." He steeples his fingers underneath his chin. "Female skeletal remains, scattered by wildlife. As I recall, not all the remains were recovered."

"That's the one. You listed the cause of death as 'undetermined.'"

"Yes, Detective. While we discovered her remains in a shallow grave, I couldn't determine without a shadow of doubt whether her death had been a homicide or an accident."

"Did you notice any unusual breaks on the bones recovered?"

His brown eyes widen with interest. "Yes ... yes, I did."

"Have you heard of Rose Bernstein?" I introduce the reason for my visit.

"The young lady found dead two weeks ago?"

"Yes. Our medical examiner determined she suffered some unusual injuries to her person. In particular, the femur was snapped in both legs—" At this statement he stands, moving to a large filing cabinet and begins to sift through his files. "I wondered—"

"One moment, Detective." He raises his hand. "Both femurs, you say?" At my nod, he removes a file and places it on his desk. He props a pair of silver spectacles on the end of his nose before flipping through pages in his file. He stops at a photo and looks at me over his glasses. "Do you, by any chance, have an x-ray of your victim's femur?"

I hand the copy to him. He's holding his photo next to mine when his assistant enters.

"Apologies. Professor—"

"Carson, come in: look at these. See here, look at the similarities in the fractures," he muses. Looking over the rims of his spectacles, he hands Carson the photo and x-ray. He turns back to me.

"Was this a closed fracture, Detective?"

"Yes. Her arms and shins, too."

"You thought these cases were related when you came to me. Why?"

I look at his assistant, reluctant to reveal too much. Noting my hesitation, he hastens to assure me.

"Dr. Carson works alongside me in the field. We consult on all cases."

I nod before continuing. "We found clothes on our victim, which didn't belong to her - an old-fashioned dress and black heels, just like your Jane Doe. Additionally, the killer left the bodies in similar locations." I stop there, needing more time to concretely connect both cases.

"Hmm." He ponders, his eyes alight with intrigue. "What's your assessment?" he asks Carson.

"These fractures are too alike. The probability of two different weapons causing these injuries is minimal. Look at how the fracture travels in the same direction on both."

"I agree." Dr. Stanley stands. "We did question how a fall could break our Jane Doe's femur." He sighs, his tone laced in regret.

"Your input helps, Doctor. I felt this crime was too sophisticated to have been his first. I'll follow up with the Brown County Sheriff's office and investigate your Jane Doe." Sensing my time is up, I stand to leave. "One last question. Can you shed any light on what type of weapon he might have used? The medical examiner suggested something heavy."

"I'm sorry, Detective. Offhand, I don't know." Dr. Stanley shakes his head.

"There was that ..." Dr. Carson begins, before dismissing his idea.

"No, please. Any suggestions are welcome," I encourage him. Perhaps I was mistaken to exclude Dr. Carson from the entire interview.

He turns to Professor Stanley.

"Do you remember your lecture on medieval burial sites?"

"Yes ..."

"You talked about a device called the Catherine wheel ..." his pale complexion flushes red.

"I suppose that could apply." Stanley moves to a bookshelf, taking down a navy hardcover tome handing it to me.

It's titled *Medieval Capital Punishment*.

"I don't follow."

"Take it with you."

Following at his heels, I listen as we exit his office. "There was a form of torture and execution used until the mid-nineteenth century called the Catherine wheel, or more accurately, the breaking wheel. Imagine a large wagon wheel, like the ones found on a horse cart. The executioner used the wheel, with its heavy iron rim, to slam onto the limbs of the criminal, breaking their bones while they were tied to another wheel. Gruesome stuff. Maybe far-fetched here, but it would do the job." His nose wrinkles in disgust. "I must go, Detective. Call me if you need anything else. I'll hold off on contacting the coroner's office with regards to changing the death certificate to homicide until you update me further. I suspect Detective James won't be too happy about the extra work." His eyes roll. Seems Detective James has a reputation.

"Well, thank you for your time, Dr. Stanley. And thank you, Dr. Carson," I turn to his assistant, hefting the heavy book in my hand "I'll look into this and be sure to get it back to you."

We part company outside the lecture hall, and I find my way to my car. Turning on the heat, I review the new information. *I have another victim*. This development is progress, but this killer's potential for killing again is high, which means I need to find him, and soon. Leaning my head back, I close my eyes, mulling over what I know of him. He holds his victims captive, dresses them, breaks their bones over a prolonged period, tortures them until they succumb to their injuries and then leaves the body at beauty spots around the greater Green Bay area. This is a level of depravity I haven't come across before. It may only be getting started.

Grabbing my phone, I look up the FBI's Milwaukee office. Pressing dial, I fasten my seat belt and head back to the station.

FAYE

Cringing from the backseat of Scott's car, I wait for him and Savannah to pause before speaking up.

"You both realize this is crazy. We can't just walk into the police department and demand to speak with the detective." I can't believe that I let myself get dragged into this harebrained scheme.

Scott's eyes meet mine in the rear-view mirror before shifting back to the road ahead. "We're only going to see if we can get two minutes of his time. He's not returning my calls: it's worth a shot."

Savannah, who came up with this genius idea, nods in agreement. "Faye, he's a cop. It's his job to deal with the public! Trust me, he won't show you his handcuffs." She winks.

Scott clears his throat. Savannah, in the passenger seat, has a clear view of his face.

"That is ... unless you're into that sort of thing?"

I shove her shoulder. "No, I'm not!"

"Assault! Assault!" she calls out dramatically, "I could have you arrested for that."

Scott remains quiet, which doesn't go unnoticed by Savannah. "What about you, Scott?" she asks.

"What about me?"

"Handcuffs in the bedroom: yes, or no?"

Scott's our boss, but Savannah never seems to care about those boundaries.

"Yes." He nods, his eyes meeting mine in the mirror again. Images of being handcuffed to Scott's bed have no place in my mind, and yet, they're here now, I doubt they'll ever leave.

Savannah is unfazed. "Interesting, Scotty. Now, would you wear said cuffs, or would you hold the key?"

His eyes are back on the road. "That you'll never know. Certain things are only discussed between a man and his lover."

"I agree." I swallow. I don't miss the small smile that spreads across his face as we turn into the Outagamie Sheriff's department parking lot.

Climbing out of Scott's car together, Savannah takes the lead as we walk into the station.

"How was your weekend?" Scott asks as we follow behind.

"Great. I had fun on Friday ... did you?" I glance up at him from under my lashes. Our conversation has been replaying in my mind all weekend. Each time, my stomach whirled with excitement.

Savannah disappears into the police station. Scott reaches for the door handle but stills.

"I did. I'd like to do it again some time." He hesitates, looking over his shoulder into the station.

"Me too."

"Good." He grins widely. "We'd better go in." He holds the door for me.

Hearing us, Savannah swings round from the reception desk, her auburn hair breaking free from the haphazard bun on top of her head. "Apparently, 'he's not here.'" She eyeballs the officer behind the desk as we join her.

"I've told you already: he's out on call and won't be back today. If you leave your name and number, I'll have him call you. If you want to report a crime, Deputy Jones here can take your statement." He thumbs toward another officer, who has come over to help.

"Are you the ladies from that radio show?" he asks.

Savannah's eyes light up. "Why, yes! We wanted to speak with Detective Walters. Do Y'all listen to the show?" she drawls, angling her body in his direction.

"I'm a huge fan, but Detective Walters, not so much." He grins.

Ignoring her attempts at southern charm, the officer simply nods, turning his attention to Scott.

"You must be Scott?" he reaches out a hand to shake. "I'm Deputy Jones. We spoke over the phone."

"That's right. We hoped to get five minutes with the detective."

"He *is* out. But even if he was here, I doubt he'd see you guys ..." He's in the middle of turning us away when the front door swings open again. All eyes shift to the man who enters. He removes his winter coat, revealing a fitted black shirt and slacks. My eyes move from his dark brown hair with its silver threads, past his chiseled jaw and broad shoulders, down long muscular legs and back up to the gun on his hip.

Holy hell!

"Detective Walters! I'm Savannah Philips ..."

He shifts the book he's carrying to his left and takes her offered hand.

"Good to know." his dark eyes glance from her to Scott continuing his quick assessment before his eyes land on me last. He pauses, his stern expression flickering. "Let me guess: reporters?" he scoffs, already walking away from us.

"We're from Green Bay Radio—" Savannah tries to salvage the situation.

"No." He continues down the hall.

"Wait—!"

"No." He doesn't even look back.

Savannah's charm has never met with such blatant indifference.

"Asshole ..." she mutters. "You two could have said something!"

She turns to face the officers behind the desk. "If he changes his mind, could you give him this card? It's the direct line." She hands her business card to Deputy Jones.

"Do *you* have a direct line? Maybe we could grab a drink sometime."

"Darlin',' if you were five years older, maybe. But the only thing I want from *you* right now, is to convince that insufferable man to sit down with us for thirty minutes." She bats her eyes.

He winks back at her. "Can't blame a guy for trying."

"I can. Get your ass back to work." His colleague is unimpressed by their exchange. "And you three: you heard the man. That was a clear *no*." He nods toward the exit. Politely, if not literally, telling us to *fuck off*.

Outside, Scott nudges my shoulder. Savannah's steaming ahead to the car.

"She is so annoyed!" I bite my lip, trying my best to not grin at her expense.

"What's it she always says?" His brows crease in mock concentration. "Oh yeah: 'she's got her tail up'!" Dipping our chins, we both snicker into the collars of our jackets.

"Faye, you take the front seat: I need room to explode." She's fuming as we reach the car, already pulling open the door to the backseat.

"Don't let him get to you. We knew it was a long shot."

Scott turns on the engine. "Exactly. you did your best."

"That man could strut sitting down. Can you believe how rude he was?"

Oh boy. she's as mad as hell.

I nod sympathetically. "He wasn't friendly."

"Friendly! He was as friendly as a bramble patch. I have a notion to go back in there and give him a piece of my mind. Although ..." Her tone shifts dramatically as a mischievous smile crosses her face. "I think I might enjoy getting tangled up in those brambles."

"He *is* handsome," I eagerly agree.

"A regular old silver fox. Whoo-ee, I nearly forgot my own name." She reaches over, nudging me playfully. "He had a good look at you. You might come around to the idea of handcuffs, after all!"

"Enough about handcuffs, already." Scott clears his throat irritably. "We have work to do."

Savannah and I look at each other, both of us surprised by his sharp tone.

"Don't get your shorts in a bunch, Scotty. You know we think you're a handsome devil, too." She keeps her own tone playful, before smoothly bringing the conversation back to work. "We'll need to source someone else to interview for the podcast."

"I agree. We can't air the episode on John Walters—"

"*Dick* Walters, you mean!" Savannah cuts over me.

"Exactly! We can't release the episode without more information on him."

"What *do* we have so far, Faye?" Scott asks.

"He was born in Milwaukee. Moved to Madison ten years ago, headed up the missing persons and homicide division there. Moved to Green Bay four years ago." I list the facts as I remember them.

"Why would he leave Madison? Appleton is a third its size! Plus, he was head of the homicide division. Was it by choice? Was he demoted?" Savannah looks suspicious.

"He might have wanted to take things easier."

"He's a man, Faye," she scoffs.

"What's that got to do with anything?" Scott turns incredulous eyes on her.

"Ego, Scott. A man, in his prime, would not leave a homicide division in a bustling city like Madison, for a smaller office with less prestige, in a place where the crime rate spikes once a year for illegal hunting." She rolls her eyes.

"You're wrong: he solved that missing girl's case two years ago, and now he's working the biggest homicide case Wisconsin's seen in years," he argues.

"True, but that was purely because of proximity and timing."

"Give me a break. How?"

"Look. He's obviously a good cop, but I'm just pointing out that those cases are rare for the Outagamie Sheriff's office. He's unlikely to see anything like them again in his jurisdiction, so why leave a homicide division at the peak of your career?" she shrugs her shoulders.

I chime in. "He still works on big cases, so it doesn't matter where he lives or works."

"I'm saying, why give up being head of the homicide division? Maybe our silver fox has something to hide." She's like a dog with a bone, won't let it go. And if it's buried, she'll start digging.

CHAPTER 7

FAYE

We're live on-air, discussing homelessness in Wisconsin, when a fresh wave of nausea hits. Stronger than the last, it forces me to clamp my mouth shut and miss my cue. Savannah picks up the slack, while I sit quietly, breathing heavily through my nose, fighting the urge to be sick.

"Everything OK, Faye?" Scott's concerned voice floats through my headphones. Finding his eyes on me through the partition window. I'm shaking my head in response when my mouth fills with watery acid. Jumping up, I pull off my headphones before rushing from the studio. Covering my mouth with both hands, I make it to the washroom just in time to reach the bowl. Lurching forward, I violently empty the contents of my stomach.

"Faye, can I come in?" Scott's voice echoes from somewhere outside the cubicle.

"I'm OK," I call back, feeling anything but.

"I'll get you some water," he says, the door creaking shut.

Dragging myself to the sink, I splash some cold water on my face, rinsing out my mouth. I felt fine all morning. The queasiness began after lunch.

"Faye?" Scott's head peeks around the door again, his eyes widening at the sight of me. *Jeez, that bad?* I glance into the mirror at my pale face and watery eyes. *OK, so I've had better days.*

"You need to go home."

"No, I'm OK," I protest, unprepared to abandon Savannah.

"If it's a bug, I can't have you infecting the whole of Wisconsin." He smirks.

"You know they can't get it over the airwaves, right?"

"Seriously, you look awful. You'll need to sit out the rest of tonight." Tilting his head, he stares intently at me, openly assessing my condition. Puffing my cheeks out, I try stem off another wave of nausea.

"Did you eat something funky?"

"No ..." I pause, remembering Luke brought home some take out last night. "Other than some take out." Memories of yesterday's supper turn my gut again.

"Hey, you OK?" Savannah comes jogging down the hallway as we walk toward the cafeteria.

"Yeah, just something I ate." I shrug. "Wait—how are you out here? What about the show?"

"Don't worry about that, hon, the six-minute version of 'Bohemian Rhapsody' is currently playing. I wanted to check on you. You look like you've been chewed up, spit out and stepped on."

She turns to Scott. "She can't drive home in this state. I need to get back on-air: you make sure Luke comes to get her," she directs him, before turning back to me. As if reading my mind, she reassures me. "Don't you worry about the show: we only have an hour to go. You need to get home and rest up. I'll call you later." She wraps her arms around me, then rushes back down the corridor. She's a whirlwind, much like the new one wreaking havoc to my insides.

"Oh, shit ..." I groan. Tossing Scott my bottled water, I run back into the bathroom. Round two runs my energy levels right down. All I can do is stay still as my body fights my roiling stomach.

Scott calls in that he phoned Luke, who is also vomiting. That does it. *I'm never eating take out again!*

"Your place is too far, so I'll just take you to mine, get you into bed." Scott's arm is around my shoulders, guiding me toward the exit and to his car. Somewhere, amid the nausea and fear of throwing up on his shoes, I notice he has my stuff in his hand. I nod, too sick to argue. The bouts between each spew are shortening. The ride to his apartment is a blur.

"Bathroom's on the right," he calls after me as I rush over the threshold. Sometime soon, I'll remember my unladylike dash to his toilet bowl and feel my soul shrinking with extreme mortification. Tonight, I hug the bowl, thankful I made it in time. He's waiting for me when I come out.

"My bedroom is this way. There're fresh towels out. Water and Tylenol on the bedside table." The concern in his voice is adorable, and despite feeling like hell, I smile a little. I follow him into his room and fall straight into his enormous bed.

"I'll need to go back to help Savannah and Don wrap up. I'll be back soon. Your phone is next to the water, so call if you need anything."

"Thanks Scott. I'm sorry about this."

"Don't be silly. Get some rest: it will pass in a few hours." His hushed tone follows him out of the room, switching off the lights as he goes. I'm out cold within minutes.

Scott's scent brings a smile to my face as my eyes flicker open. The room is dark. A heavy awareness settles into the stillness, bringing me upright in his bed. My tummy hollows out, tightening as last night's events replay in my mind. My hand lifts to the damp skin on my neck, waiting for that uneasy feeling in my throat. Relieved when the nausea doesn't return, I reach for my phone to check the time. It's after four a.m. I'm in Scott's bed, alone. Inhaling deeply, I greedily soak up the scent of him again. My fantasies of a night in Scott's bed did not include puking in front of him. Satisfied the vomiting has eased, I push back the blanket and tiptoe toward the bathroom.

"You're up."

"Shit!" My hand leaps to my chest and I jump, startled to see Scott getting up from the couch.

He chuckles gently. "I didn't mean to startle you."

"No, I'm sorry. I woke you. I needed to use the bathroom." I whisper.

"I was awake. You go on, I'll make some peppermint tea," he offers.

"No, don't do that, I've been enough trouble!"

He's already moving to the kitchen. "Nah, I want some too."

His sleepy gaze roams over my face from across the dimly lit room. He's wearing a black t-shirt and red pajama pants, and with his mussed hair curling around his ears, Scott's sex appeal punches me square in the chest. Resisting him is becoming impossible.

"OK," I croak before removing myself to the bathroom. I take the opportunity to steal some toothpaste and to splash some cold water on my face.

As promised, he's carrying two steaming mugs to the sofa when I return, placing them at either end of the coffee table.

"Sit out here with me for a bit." He pulls back his blanket. I drop into one corner of the sofa, curling my knees to my chest and facing him while he gets comfortable on the other end. I wrap my hands around my hot cup, the fragrant steam filling my senses as I take a sip. The peppermint soothes the raw edge of my throat.

"I'm sorry again for being such a pain in the ass."

"Quit apologizing. Besides, it's my back that will suffer, not my ass." He groans playfully.

"There's some Tylenol left over."

"How are you feeling?"

"Much better—a little weak, but no more nausea."

"Good. Savannah was worried about you."

Guilt heats my cheeks. "How did the rest of the show go?"

"Without a hitch. She managed fine. It has me thinking that we might not need *two* hosts on the payroll." Amusement flashes in his eyes at my horror before he winks.

I can't resist. "Do you have something in your eye?"

"Do you want to check?" His eyes darken.

"Maybe next time." I hide my smile behind another sip of tea. "Is that your family?" I ask, pointing to a framed photo sitting on his coffee table.

"Yes." He reaches forward to pick up the wooden frame, handing it to me. "That's the whole gang."

My eyes land on a younger-looking Scott. "How old is this photo?"

He shrugs. "A few years. It's one of my favorite photos of us all together. Mom, Dad, Pete and Rob." He points out his two brothers.

"Good-looking family. And I like your chubby cheeks."

"Yeah, I was a bit chubby. Mom liked to feed me. You can see she baked a lot. It wasn't a good look."

"I bet all the girls were chasing you! Who could resist those cute dimples?"

He gazes fondly at the photo. "I suspect they were after my mom's cookies." He laughs to himself.

"What?"

"I'm just remembering her when my first girlfriend broke my heart. Mom made me dance around the kitchen, music blaring, with wooden spoons for mics. We sang at the top of our lungs every day after until I felt better. She was my hero."

"She sounds amazing."

"She was." He places the photo back on the table.

"Do you see them often?"

"Yeah, most weekends since Mom died. Dad likes to fish, so we get out during the summer. They love ice fishing, but I'm not a fan, so I'll see them less over the next few months."

"Luke loves fly-fishing. He's good," I smile proudly.

"You're close to him. It's nice that you have each other."

"Yeah ..." I sigh. "I don't know how I would have coped without him when our grandmother passed."

"You strike me as a strong woman."

"Don't be so sure. My grandmother's death hit like a sledgehammer. I'd already lost my mom, dad, and grandfather. I knew what grief was, but still tried to control it."

"How *did* you cope?" he asks.

"I cried. A lot!" I sigh again. I risk asking about his mom. "How about you?"

"I went onto autopilot. I couldn't eat or sleep for a long time. Started going to the gym, got a little obsessed with that for some time. It was like, if I stopped moving, I'd fall apart. I found it hard to cry, but when the floodgates opened, man did I feel it! Even now, when I visit my dad, I walk in, expecting to see her reading in her favorite armchair, and it hits me all over again. She's gone."

I nod, knowing how true and how real those moments are.

"For me, grief is like barbed wire being wrapped around your heart and having it pulled through, taking chunks of who you are with it. Your heart has to find a way to heal so it can beat without those pieces. Life's never the same."

His large hand spreads across his chest. "Wow. What a very apt description. So true."

Scott's mom passed just a few weeks before we started working on the show together. I've wanted to ask more about her, but it's always felt like prying. Now, it's the most natural thing to chat about our similar experiences with loss.

"Can I ask how she passed?"

"Cancer. She fought it tooth and nail—" His voice breaks. "She loved to sing and dance, and even on her worst days, she'd turn up the radio and, if she was too sick to dance, she listened, she sang, she closed her eyes and allowed herself to just feel the music."

My eyes well. "I love how much you love her."

"She taught me how to love. Showed me how it feels to give it and receive it."

"Was it her love for music that inspired you to work in radio?"

"Yeah. Saturday mornings, Mom would crank up the radio and dance around while we cleaned the house. Chores were made easy, having the radio on. I remember the buzz when a great tune came on. The volume went higher, and we sang at the top of our lungs. So many good memories. I like to think we're creating them for our listeners today."

I smile. "I couldn't agree more. Our topics can be heavy, even uncomfortable, but if we're helping one person feel less lonely during our shift, we're doing our job."

"Can I tell you something?" he asks.

"Sure,"

"When I first met you, it took me a few minutes to reconcile the person across the table from me with the person I'd been listening to on the radio."

"Why?"

"On-air, you seemed to be this chatty, bubbly person. In the flesh, you seemed shy. It intrigued me. Where do you find the confidence to perform so well in the studio?"

"When my parents died, I was young. Dad died of a heart attack when I was seven, and five years later Mum died of pneumonia. She was so young and healthy, but she got a chest infection that kept getting worse ..." I sigh deeply before continuing.

"When we moved into the cabin with our grandparents, I spent so much time alone. Luke was off with friends. My grandparents had their own heartbreak to deal with and two teenagers to raise. There wasn't enough time to focus on me, so I would lock myself into my room. I became most comfortable in that little box, and the tv and radio kept me company. I would pretend to be a TV reporter." I laugh, thinking how silly I was.

"So, the studio is your new 'little box'?"

"Exactly. So many people rely on us. We keep them company on the lonely nights and knowing that switches me into *Faye Anderson, reporting for Green Bay Radio* mode," I laugh, doing my best reporter voice.

His gray eyes smile. "I'm lucky to experience both sides of you."

"You think there are only two sides?" I smirk.

"Oh, no! You're dangerous, too!"

"I've never been called dangerous before. It makes me want to live up to it ..." His deep intake of breath fills me with excitement. "Would you like to see that side?"

He exhales roughly. "You're already killing me, Faye!" he growls.

"I didn't think I had it in me!"

"Well, you should stop, because I'm not sure I can survive much more of it." He pokes my feet with his under the blanket. We stay like this, chatting until the birds chirp, before falling asleep together on the sofa.

CHAPTER 8

DETECTIVE JOHN WALTERS

I've spent my morning walking the crime scene again. The Appleton swing bridge has three access points, but only one road would give the killer enough cover to park his car and dispose of Rose's body without fear of being seen. Along that same road is a gas station with CCTV cameras. We submitted the request for the footage. With some luck, having this visual evidence will give us a lead on the killer's vehicle.

Once I'm satisfied that I've overturned every stone at the scene, I head back to the station to find Deputy Jones waiting for me at the entrance. *This is new.* Jones has been hanging around my office for weeks, taking whatever tasks I throw his way. He's two years into a criminal psychology degree and I admit, he's got a nose for it. But this level of eagerness is a bit much.

"There's an FBI agent in your office!" he calls, hurrying toward me.

I'm surprised that my call to the FBI Behavioral Analyses Unit yielded such a quick response. They warned they deal primarily with "time sensitive" cases. At most, I hoped they would draw up a profile and email it to me. I hadn't expected them to send an agent here.

I hand my coffee cup to Jones. "What did he say?" I ask, shrugging out of my jacket. He's grinning at me now, unable to mask his delight.

"Just that *she* was here to see you and that *she* would wait in your office. Very assertive."

That explains it.

"Has she been here long?" I sigh.

"Only thirty minutes ..."

I ignore him, looking at my watch. It's just nine a.m.

"What do you want me to look into today?" he asks before I can walk away.

"Follow up on the gas station footage."

"It arrived first thing. I've been going over it."

"Anything on it?"

"I ran the plates of everyone who bought gas that night, but nothing stands out so far. The images of the main road are pretty blurred, but it catches headlights and taillights passing all through the night ..."

"Go over it again. Find me something I can work with," I growl. *Another dead end!*

"You got it."

"Oh. Did the Madison forensics lab pick up the evidence fr—"

"Collected and transferred yesterday evening," he interrupts me, a smug smile spreading across his face.

Dr. Lacey phoned me yesterday to let me know he was ready to release Rose's body back to her father. All physical evidence collected from the body was sealed and ready for collection. I contacted the Madison forensics lab right away to prioritize the evidence transfer.

"Should I bring our guest a coffee?" his eyes drop to the coffee he's still holding for me.

"*My* guest," I remind him. "No, I doubt she'll be staying long. Now stop smiling and give me my coffee."

He's good, but he's cocky and that can be a dangerous mix. He'll need to shadow a homicide detective, eventually. Maybe I'll help him hone his skills. One day. If I can find the patience.

AGENT DELLA PEREZ

His office is tidy, spartan. The desk, free from clutter, faces the door. His back is to the wall when he's working. *Our Detective Walters may not like surprises.* I smile to myself, my eyes sliding to the venetian blind pulled halfway up and hanging crookedly. *So, not compulsively tidy.* The obsessive compulsive in *me* is already moving to the window to straighten it out. There are no family photos, nothing to suggest he is married or has children. *Single?* I wonder, my eyes moving to the wall adjacent the door. A large map of Appleton, crime scene photos, newspaper articles, post-it notes with dates, times, theories are all laid out in chronological order and pinned to a corkboard. A photo of Rose Bernstein hangs there too. From his desk chair, her image is in his direct line of vision. *He cares about the victims.* I take it all in, impressed.

My eyes slide to a dying weeping fig resting on the windowsill. The neglected plant, parched and drooping sadly toward the dish beneath, begs for water. The only personal touch in here and it has been left to wilt. *Does he, perhaps, struggle with providing TLC to the living things in his care?* I'm considering whether pouring some water onto the soil would be stepping out of bounds when a throat clears behind me. My preconceived image, of a paunchy middle-aged man shatters when I turn from the discolored foliage.

Detective Walters enters the office. Standing over six feet tall, his confident stride makes quick work of the space between the door and his desk. I stand a little straighter, taking him in. Brown hair, styled loosely and graying at the temples, tapers toward his clean-shaven jawline. He doesn't speak, his granite expression giving nothing away as our eyes meet. Impossibly brown and fanned by thick black lashes, his eyes darken suspiciously over my face, assessing me. His dark brows rise, challenging me to speak first.

Uncharacteristically swayed by his presence, my brain short circuits. Walters is arguably the most attractive cop I've worked with. The gentle thud of files dropping onto his desk snaps me back to reality.

"Detective Walters, I presume?" the corners of my lips lift.

Sitting on the edge of the desk, he nods toward the plant. "It was dead when I got here," he deadpans.

Astute too!

"You didn't think to investigate?" I allow my smile to spread. "I'm Special Agent Odelia Perez, Della for short."

"What can I do for you, Agent?"

"I'm with the BAU. I'm here to assist with your investigation."

He stands, the displaced air of his advance carrying his fresh scent toward me.

He extends his hand. "John Walters. I wasn't expecting you." His voice is abrupt. Breaking eye contact, he rounds his desk. "Please."

He gestures to the empty chair across from him. A coil of confusion tightens in my stomach, the knot absorbs his cool welcome, winding tighter. *He* reached out to us. His prickly attitude is uncalled for. Straightening my shoulders, I take the offered chair and sit facing him.

"I read over the case notes *you* sent and got on the road this morning. Why would you not expect a response?"

"I did. I expected a profile to be emailed."

"I guess you got lucky! We typically work remotely, but I requested to come out into the field on this one."

"Why?"

"He broke their bones. I've never seen it before."

"And that means what, exactly?"

"It means I am here to figure out why."

I refrain from sharing my theory on why he breaks their bones. It's my job to understand the nature of this killer's obsession. It would be unprofessional for me to speculate further, without having done my due diligence.

His eyes drill into me. "This is my case. I'm lead investigator: understood?"

My tone is flat, my shoulders stiffening. "Oh, I understand just fine."

His eyebrows draw tight, molten brown eyes weighing his options before he speaks again. "What do you need?"

"Access to everything you have on the case so far."

His tone thaws. "What about a coffee first?"

For now, he is suspending hostilities between us, and the tension melts from my shoulders.

"Sure." I accept his peace offering "Then maybe we can go over a few things. I'd like to interview the witnesses again, visit the crime scenes."

He nods. I've passed some unknown test, enough to get my foot in the door. But I've yet to convince Detective Walters that my intrusion on his case will be worthwhile.

DETECTIVE JOHN WALTERS

Having an inquisitive streak comes with the territory when working in law enforcement. However, the bottle-green eyes, bright and alert that assess me from across my desk, glisten with habitual curiosity. She was analyzing me from the moment I walked through the door. Filing away her assessments under a mass of unruly, chestnut brown hair.

She's attractive, which explains why Jones was grinning like a schoolboy when I first arrived. Her eyes are striking against the warmth of her golden skin. Her hair falls in waves around her shoulders. The singsong of her dusky tone hints at her Latin decent. She's beautiful. But good looks aside, a phone call to let me know she was coming would have been nice. We've spent the morning going over every aspect of the case. I'm impressed on a professional level. She has left no stone unturned, asking everything I might ask myself. She looks up from the paperwork that Detective James sent over.

"Are there *any* leads at all on this Jane Doe?" Her eyes roll in disapproval. Detective James seems to have that effect on everyone.

"I'm looking into missing women out of state, starting with Minnesota, Iowa and Illinois. One stood out to me as similar to Rose's disappearance. Her car was found abandoned; all her belongings left undisturbed. It could be nothing, but the timeline fits."

"Sounds promising. We will need to visit our Jane Doe's crime scene, interview any witnesses listed in the case file, although we don't have much to work with."

"What are your thoughts, so far?" My fingers lightly tap the desk, stilling when her observant eyes fall to them.

"On the killer, or your investigation?" she asks.

Her words poke at my chest. My physical reaction silences me, my mind already running through every aspect of my investigation, self-doubt pounding in my ears before I regain control over both.

"Are you here to psychoanalyze me or the killer?" I finally say, irked further by the flash of humor in her eyes before she dives in.

"He's organized. Smart too: we're not dealing with a loose cannon. He's always in control of his victims. The clothes and the posing of the bodies are closely connected, with regards to his psychological needs. Even after death he wants to control them, possess them, manipulate their bodies so they are found exactly how he wants them to be found. The breaking of the bones," she pauses, cocking her head "I haven't reconciled that element of his behavior in my mind, just yet. I know he will kill again, Detective; you were right to call us."

"Serial?"

"Right now, you have two victims, a third will certainly put him into serial killer status. Let's hope we can prevent that from happening."

"OK, let's head to the Jane Doe crime scene." I suggest.

"It is better that we start with the most recent murder, as it's fresh in the mind of our witnesses." She stands, lifting a large briefcase that rested against her chair. It's teeming with papers, and I wonder what importance they hold to this investigation.

"Would you like help carrying that?" I offer.

"Top secret." She taps it, smiling openly now. Her red lips part to reveal a row of white teeth. She waits for me to take the lead out of the office. I walk ahead, happy to free myself of her company and the uncomfortable feelings it generates within

JEFFREY

How dare they. How dare that bitch accuse me of being a coward? Reaching for my phone, I hover over the radio station's toll-free number and pause. *Take a deep breath*. The fire in my stomach burns for me to act, react even. I've been following the podcast for over two weeks now, and so far, it has amused me how little they know. Then tonight, live on air, Savannah called me a *sniveling coward,* and the urge to set her straight was palpable. But I can't call them from my own phone: I'm angry, but I'm not stupid. The need to clear my mind has me pulling on a tracksuit and sneakers. It's late enough that the streets of Green Bay will be empty. Without another thought, I plug in earbuds and listen to the rest of the show as I jog.

"I think we're dealing with a clever killer," a caller argues, and a smile spreads across my face as my feet pound the dark streets.

"Calling him that does nothing more than massage the ego of a deranged psychopath ..." Savannah's twangy southern accent cuts across the listener. My molars grind together. She's managed to get under my skin, like a fucking parasite.

"There are different types of killers, Savannah, let him finish," Faye's sweet voice interrupts, trying to bring order to the conversation. Faye is my favorite.

"I know that. I just don't agree we should be feeding into the theory that this guy is somehow clever. It's only been two weeks: we have no idea what the police know, so to assume he is clever, is, in my opinion, idiocy." She huffs.

"That's all true, but we don't know how clever he is. He may get away with murder. Accepting that he might be clever doesn't glorify what he did," Faye continues in a soothing tone that I could listen to for hours. I jog past a payphone, a rare find these days in Green Bay. The temptation is too strong to ignore. I'll just say one thing before hanging up. Looking around, I confirm the street is empty and dial the station's number.

A male voice answers on the other end. "Green Bay Radio, you are through to the late show with Faye and Savannah."

"I have information on the case. I'll only tell Faye." I try to disguise my voice as best I can.

"Can I get a name ...?"

"No. Can I speak to her or not?" Paranoia begins to creep in. This was a bad idea.

"Hold on ..." There is some silence before her voice crackles through the phone line. "You're through to True Crime Tuesdays. This is Faye, can I get your name?" she sounds even sweeter over the phone.

"No need. Am I on the air?" I ask.

"Not yet. We have a two-minute delay. What did you want to add?" Her warm tone is like a drug.

"I don't like how Savannah speaks about me. She should know better than to poke a bear." My voice is deeper than normal, bringing with it a sinister tone—which I like.

"She wouldn't want to offend you. What's your name?" she asks again.

"Who I am doesn't matter! What I did, what I *can* do isn't just clever, it's an art, a skill—"

"Bullshit! Hey, Scott, pull the plug on this prank call." Savannah cuts in again and I lose all reason. My hand squeezes the metal phone cord until it hurts.

"You listen here, you fucking bitch, I will snap that pretty neck like a twig!" Before I know what I'm doing, I pull the cord in my hand, snapping the handset free of the phone box and cutting off the call.

Fuck. I can't believe I lost control like that. Wiping the buttons of the payphone with the sleeve of my sweatshirt, I stick the receiver into my pocket and resume jogging toward the Fox River bridge. As I throw the receiver into the river, I scold myself for having been so stupid. Savannah was right, this time. I'm not as clever as I think.

FAYE

We often get prank calls on the show, but this one has startled us both. Something in his voice sent shivers down my spine. His threats toward Savannah felt real.

"I'll call the police tomorrow, invite them to listen to the call and see if they want to investigate further," Scott informs us, as we walk to our cars.

"If anything, it might buy us five minutes with the dick-tective," Savannah smiles slyly before climbing into her car.

"Just call me as soon as you've locked your doors, so I know you're safe," I beg her. Scott and I wait for her to pull out of the parking lot before walking the short distance to my car. It's been nearly a week since we woke together on his couch, our eyes meeting in a moment of sleepy intimacy before we sheepishly untangled our limbs. Scott made pancakes before taking me to my truck. Since then, we've changed. I feel comfortable when our eyes meet through the glass. I'm settling into the idea that Scott feels something more than friendship too, and trying to figure out what comes next.

"Do you think it was him?" I ask. I already know Savannah isn't convinced, but something in my gut tells me the call was legit.

"I don't know. The police will look into it and get back to us. Are you OK to drive home?"

"Yeah. I hope they can trace the call." My hand rests briefly on his forearm.

"It's likely nothing. I don't want you worrying. Are you sure you're good to drive?"

"You're not trying to play doctor again, are you?" My lips press together, holding my smile at bay.

"God no, that was awful! I'm not much of a doctor."

"Nah, you did great! "

"You slept through me walking the floors!"

"Aw, that's sweet. Why, did you think I was dead?" I laugh.

"No way. You snore—loudly!"

My laughter erupts around us in the car park. I should be embarrassed, but I can't help but be amused.

"Oh no, was it bad?" I manage.

"You kept me awake with it, and then spent the rest of the night yapping," he teases, his fingers playfully pinching my side.

Without thinking, I lift my finger to my nose, pushing back the tip. "Just call me Miss Piggy." I'm rewarded by the deep rumble of his laughter. Wiping his eyes, he turns to me.

"Faye, that is the cutest thing you've ever done."

"A laugh a day keeps the doctor away!"

"Not this doctor."

"Good to know," I nod. The air is thick with tension as we stand, both rocking back and forth on our toes. I don't really want to leave, but not knowing what else to do, I turn to get into my truck.

"Goodnight, Scott."

His hand grabs mine, turning me around.

"Text me when you're home." He gives my fingers a gentle squeeze.

CHAPTER 9

DETECTIVE JOHN WALTERS

A thin layer of undisturbed snow coats the ground when we arrive at Wequiock Falls. Light sifts through the bare trees, reflecting off my windshield and the road ahead.

"We'll have to be quick; the forecast is calling for more snow later," I warn Perez, backing my car into a parking space next to the trail head. Yesterday, we interviewed witnesses and visited the site where Rose's body was found. This morning, Agent Perez requested I bring her to the location where we found our Jane Doe.

Peering around, she scans the wide-open spaces of Wequiock Falls. "I can already see the similarities between the locations," she announces, ignoring my comment about the weather.

"Yes, it's difficult to ignore them. Both victims left beside a body of water, with a bridge close by, along nature trails, and both locations are just off a highway."

Unbuckling, we both step out of the car, my boots sinking into the powdery white snow. I point toward the main road that runs parallel, beyond the walls of the park. "He most likely drove along that road, pulled over, and found an entry point after hours."

"Is this lot open twenty-four seven?"

"No. The gates close every evening at seven p.m. ..." the buzzing of my phone interrupts our conversation. I hold it up in apology, answering Deputy Jones.

"Walters."

"John, are you sitting down?"

"No, I'm out at Wequiock Falls with Agent Perez." Hearing his eagerness, I allow him time to steady himself before asking. "What's happened?"

"That crew from the radio station called, first thing this morning. They had a strange call from a listener, the man threatened one of the hosts—"

"Jones, surely you can handle a prank call," I sigh.

"That's the thing. They think it might be our guy, the killer." His voice skips over the line.

"We can't assume every nut who phones a radio station is our killer. Get a copy of the tape, and I'll have a listen when I get back."

"In my course, they say killers can reach out—" I fight the urge to hang up. I appreciate his enthusiasm, but I'm freezing my balls off while he rambles.

"I'll listen to the tape and decide if we need to look into it further," I interrupt him again.

"The producer said you'd need to come by ... *I* could go listen?" He stumbles over his words, doing a poor job of hiding his insecurity, but a great job at making me feel like the bad guy. *What is happening to me?*

"Jones ..." I know I'll regret my next few words. "Meet me and Agent Perez at the radio station in two hours."

"Yes! will do, boss. You won't regret it. I'll bring coffees: does Agent Perez prefer—" This time I do hang up.

Agent Perez purses her lips. I'm pretty sure she heard every word of our conversation, so I don't bother relaying it all back to her. "Come on." I nod toward the trail head, pausing to scan the signpost to figure out which path we should take.

"He looks up to you." Her mouth curves with tenderness for Jones.

My eyes roll toward the gray clouds in exasperation. "He's a pain in my ass. But he's keen to learn. He's halfway through his criminology course, thinks he knows it all ... It makes most sense to go left, follow the path closest to the main road, but let me double-check."

Leaning over, her body gently presses against my arm to examine the signpost. "You like him ..." Her devious green eyes flick toward me. "And you're right: we head that way." She glances casually away, pointing left.

She's enjoying herself, I determine with a nonchalant shoulder shrug before striding off up the path.

"He's a good kid. Overly enthusiastic, but a hard worker. That's all," I finally say.

"Oh, you like him a lot more than I originally thought!"

Her hand comes to my arm, nudging me gently ahead with the kind of contact old friends share. The kind that skirts too close to edge of my boundaries. I glance sideways, meeting her gaze as we stride side by side. The path runs parallel to the main road before curving around a wide bend, the wooden footbridge coming into view.

"I'm starting to like him less, the more we talk about it. Let me see those crime scene photos again." As she passes the folder over, my eyes narrow on her shaking hands.

"I'm still getting used to your Midwestern weather. I sometimes forget how cold this state can be," she explains, rubbing her hands together before stuffing them into the pockets of her winter coat.

"I left my gloves in the car. I've got a spare pair in the trunk. I'll get them for you when we get back."

"Thank you."

"How long have you been in Milwaukee?" I ask, flicking through the stack of photos.

"Two years. Before that I was in California. I think we're close to the trail." She leans over again to peer at the photos, blocking the little light left in the sky. The weather might turn sooner than I thought.

"We should move fast. According to the crime scene report, her body was discovered about two hundred yards in this direction. She was found off the trail fifty yards into the woods." I move ahead of Perez. "Through here ..." I climb up a small incline, turning back to help her. Reaching out, she folds her soft hand into mine. She stares at me for a second, a slow smile playing on her lips. The tips of her cool fingers grip tighter as she pulls herself up next to me.

"Thanks." She arches one brow before stepping around me, her hand sliding from mine, cold air seeping back into the space she just filled.

"OK." Clearing my throat, I turn. "This is where the clothing was found."

I point to a small patch of open ground, not far from a fallen tree. Perez walks around the spot, creating a circle of footprints in the snow as she goes. Leaving her to assess the scene, I struggle further into the brush, toward the main road. The whizz of passing traffic tells me I'm close to the highway, and before long I arrive at the wall that separates the park from the road. Looking at the stone wall, I decide it would be too high for a person to scale with a dead body. I follow the wall as it curves, coming upon a set of old, wrought iron gates. The rusty gates are held together by a chain and padlock, not quite as worn as the gates themselves. *Replaced in the last few years?* I wonder. Stepping back, I take photographs of the gates, and the hardware. I set the timer on my watch to clock my walk back to the location where the body was found.

I find Perez lying on the ground, staring up at the sky.

"Don't tell me you're sleeping on the job," I joke.

"This is definitely not a method I've used before."

Biting back my smile, I refrain from offering her my hand again and wait for her to get up.

"I was trying to imagine what he wanted his victims to see, to hear, to feel ..."

"He killed her. Don't you think he just wanted to dump the body?"

"Come on, John—"

Oh, so we're on a first name basis now.

"Well, Della." Her name on my tongue feels strangely intimate. "I agree it's a lot of effort to go to, to dispose of a body. But couldn't it be as simple as, he frequents the area and wanted to be able to visit her?"

"Yes, but it's more than that. He is posing his victims in a way that pleases him."

"What's your point?" I ask.

"This is art to him. He is meticulous in how he portrays himself and his victims. It's part of his signature and this guy has a few."

"Is that unusual?"

"We might see one or two signatures normally. But this killer dresses his victims, he poses their bodies, he continues to break their bones after they are dead, he chooses locations that are scenic. That's four signatures so far, and if our guy made the call to the radio station, that's a fifth."

"How does knowing this help us catch him?"

"Let's get to the radio station and listen to those tapes. We can go through the profile in full, tomorrow."

I nod in agreement "There's a set of iron gates, about seven minutes' walk from here. The padlock and chain seem recently replaced." I thumb in the direction behind me. "He might have cut the lock and carried her from there."

"Which means he scouted out this location in advance. He brought the tools to cut through the lock," she surmises.

"I trekked through that brush; he must be strong." I found it tough *without* the weight of a dead body on my shoulder.

"He'd have to be, to carry one hundred pounds of dead weight that distance," she agrees. "He wanted Jane Doe to be found, but she wasn't found in the way he hoped. Rose was found along a trail that is frequented more often by the general public. Which means he is developing his skills, learning from his mistakes." She spins in a slow circle, her eyes blinking rapidly, as if capturing the scene, storing the images in her mind to recall later.

I wipe away the cold caress of a snowflake from my nose. "Let's go meet with the radio crew, see if it's our guy." Jones's earlier excitement is catching, and I move eagerly back to the footpath. Perez follows, the snowfall already filling our footprints, erasing the evidence of us being here.

The studio is tiny. The six of us; the two hosts, their producer, Perez, Jones and I, all squeeze into the cramped space. Perez's eyes round on Faye's face before snapping to mine. The similarities between Rose and Faye is uncanny, there can be no mistaking the shift in Perez's thoughts.

"Thanks for coming, Detective." Scott Allen, the producer, reaches across the small desk to shake my hand. Jones, who was already here when we arrived, is sitting on a small stool in the corner. He leaps up to hand out the coffees he'd promised.

"Thanks Jones," Perez smiles, her eyes softening at him.

"No probs! I was just telling these guys you're from the FBI ..." He blushes under her grateful glow. My hard stare shuts him up as he hands over my much-needed caffeine. Realizing he's overstepped, he breaks eye contact, retreating sheepishly to the corner. This is police work 101. He knows better than to reveal details of any ongoing investigation to the public. Worse, he told the media! It won't be long before the whole world knows that the FBI are involved in this case.

"Don't worry, Detective, we won't share any information that could damage your investigation." Faye's kind voice is little reassurance against the curious stare of her co-host Savannah.

"This is *not* an interview. Anything we discuss here is off-limits." I scan all three faces. Faye and Scott nod yes, but Savannah is shaking her head. *I knew it!*

"Nothing further is getting said until you agree!" I glare at her.

"OK, fine." She throws her hand up, obviously frustrated.

"We listened to your first episode in the car on the way over here," Perez informs them and my temper simmers. I don't like this one bit: between Jones and Perez, we're leaking information all over the place.

"OK, play the tape," I interrupt before they can get organizing a slumber party together. I take one of the two empty seats at the small desk.

"Put on the headphones, I'll play it from the production room." Scott leaves, reappearing through the small window in the next room. Perez and I place the headphones on our ears.

"*Who I am doesn't matter. What I did, what I can do isn't just clever, it's an art, a skill ...*"

I look to Perez. The words she used, less than an hour ago to describe these killings, are like a cold breeze to the nape of my neck, the hairs on my body standing up as his aggression toward Savannah increases.

"*You listen here, you fucking bitch, I will snap that pretty neck like a twig!*"

The line goes dead. Perez and I take off the headphones. It is not public knowledge that our killer has a kink for breaking bones. It could be a coincidence, but I doubt it.

"You said that this didn't go over the airwaves?" I confirm.

"No, we have a two-minute delay. It helps us weed out the prank calls," Savannah confirms.

Scott re-enters the studio. I address him.

"And you said, when he first called, he asked to speak with Faye?"

He nods, his eyes narrowing. "Yes."

I mull this over, ignoring the growing tension in the small space. Faye could be Rose Bernstein's twin sister. If he is taking an interest in her, that makes her a potential target. Unsure of how to proceed, I refrain from saying much more, for now.

Savannah leans forward. "Don't keep us in suspense: is it him?"

"Who, outside of this room, knows about this call?" My voice is slow and steady, my tone serious as I examine each face carefully. All three look to each other. Scott answers first.

"Don: he works the switchboard. He's due in later tonight, for the show."

"Have any of you told family, friends?" Perez keeps her voice friendly. Savannah shakes her head, followed by Scott and Faye in unison, answering no. I look to Scott; he seems to be the man in charge.

"We'll need a copy of the tape. Do you have the call logs from last night?"

"I'll need to get permission to release that information ... the station may require a warrant," he informs us, an uncomfortable look on his face.

"I'm sure they would be more than willing to cooperate if, say, you did a sit-down interview for our podcast," Savannah chimes in. *Savvy,* I'll give her that.

"John, can I talk with you for a minute?" Perez touches my arm, her head nodding to the door. I bite my tongue on the flat out *no* that I was about to deliver to Savannah.

Once outside, Perez eyes me seriously. "Hear me out," she begins, and I'm already regretting agreeing to this side chat.

"I think you should do the interview. Not for the podcast: they have a live show. Sit down with them. This killer wants his ego massaged. He's clearly following the case closely; he might call in again. If you can get him on-air, we can get him to talk more. Try trace the call."

"You can't be serious!" I put my hands on my hips, huffing in disbelief.

"This is the best lead we have so far. He listens to these women."

"No. We have other leads! We don't even know for sure that it's him!" I interrupt her train of thought.

"John, if it is him, then he's already zeroed in on this show and threatened Savannah."

"He asked for Faye. Considering her likeness to Rose, doesn't that concern you?" I growl.

"Of course, but he reached out to the show. We need to use his behavior against him. He threatened Savannah because she was disparaging. She called him a coward, his control slipped."

"If we do it, how do we ensure their safety?"

"We are going to manipulate him, flatter him this time. If he's already fixated on Faye, then we need to gain control of this situation," she implores.

I shake away the doubts, mulling over possibilities. "OK. We set ground rules and we make sure to always stay in control of the situation." I'm not happy about this, but I agree. We need to draw the killer out of the shadows again, and it looks like Savannah and Faye might be the key to it.

We walk back into the studio. Perez takes the lead.

"All right. We will agree to an interview with Detective Walters. It needs to be live, on-air, and one of our police officers will man the incoming calls. We will have a set list of questions you can ask—"

"No going off script." I eye Savannah, who's grinning like a kid at the county fair.

"Deal!" she hoots. "We can open up discussing this Friday's vigil for Rose and introduce them from there." She turns to Scott, already outlining the show.

There is a candlelight vigil this weekend for Rose. Perez and I are already setting up police surveillance at every intersection, including plain-clothes officers among the crowd. Perez has convinced me that the killer will likely show up and taking note of every license plate that passes or enters the area or parks, could be useful later on in the investigation.

"Sure, whatever we can do to help—" Faye begins to agree before Scott cuts her off, his arm snaking around the back of her chair.

"Now wait. Is this going to put the girls in any danger?"

"All we know so far is that he threatened Savannah. He asked to speak with Faye, and we can't ignore how much you resemble Rose." Perez offers Faye a sympathetic smile. "All of that means nothing until we know a little more about what we're dealing with."

"We have no definite proof that this is our guy. I'd prefer if you didn't attend the vigil." I address Faye directly.

"We promised Arnie Bernstein we would read a prayer," Savannah argues.

"Yes, and like you said, there is no *definite* proof it's the killer. Let's not overreact." Faye's voice gives little away, but the wringing of her hands tells me she's worried. I stand up and Jones follows suit.

"We'll get back to you with the list of questions in the next few hours. We'll need the tape and telephone records within the hour." I eye Scott, who nods in agreement. Perez stands now and shakes their hands goodbye. I simply nod in their direction before turning to leave.

In the hallway, Jones speaks up. "Do you think it's him?"

"It is a possibility. If we can get him on the air again, we might be able to pull more information from him. Get him to say something only the killer would know." Perez fills him in.

"This is great. Can I help out?" Jones practically skips alongside us, Perez smiling at him like a proud mother.

"Jones, we're going to need all hands on deck over the next twenty-four hours," she announces.

"Are we now?" I growl. This case feels like wet glass slipping through my fingers.

She ignores my obvious irritation. "I'll deliver my profile when we get back to the station. Everyone should know what to be looking out for at the vigil."

AGENT DELLA PEREZ

Walters hurried off as soon as we got back from the radio station. The man intrigues me, I can't deny it. He was very obviously annoyed that I forced his hand with the interview. In truth, I needed the hour to gather my notes and hone my profile, before delivering it to the team.

I arrive in the conference room to find him alone. His back is to me, I take the opportunity to silently observe him. His hands are on his hips as he steps back from the investigation wall he has created in my absence. Crime scene photos, maps, and bullet points of the investigation so far are written out in black marker on the whiteboard. I take in his powerful shoulders and tousled hair, appreciating how hard he has worked to have this ready. He turns slightly allowing his side profile to come into view, highlighting his strong jaw. The warmth of his brown eyes lands on me but there is nothing inviting in his tone. He is still annoyed. *Good.*

"Are you going to stand there psychoanalyzing me all day?"

"I was just thinking to myself that maybe you'd like to express what it is that you're annoyed about?"

Narrowing his eyes now, he turns the rest of his body to face me. "I'm not annoyed," he shrugs.

Terrible liar. That's good too.

"Have I hurt you then?"

"You're joking, right?" he snorts.

"You're clearly upset about our interaction at the radio station. I'm simply giving you the opportunity to express that to me, clear the air and move on with the investigation."

"Look, I appreciate you coming all this way to help but I am not the one under the magnifying glass. I'm too busy for this nonsense. I'm not annoyed, so can we get to work?"

He's right. It is the curse of my profession, I suppose. Human behavior is not something I can unknow. Like noticing how John's body closes down, how when he returns to his investigation wall, his back to me, his hands are back in place on his hips. He is not avoiding further conversation; he is flat out denying it. I move to the conference table, set out my files and get ready to deliver my profile. In less than an hour, this room will be crammed with officers. Many will be eager to use all tools available to them to catch this killer, but some will be doubtful of criminal profiling, some even more so of a female profiler.

Jones pokes his head in the door, a large grin booming on his face when he sees me. I like him. He reminds me of my younger brother. A playful flirt, but a determined person none the less.

"John, call on line one. Do you need anything, Agent Perez?" he asks.

"No, thank you, Jones." I smile.

"Thank you, Jones," John barks, dismissing him. Clearly used to Detective Walters's moods, he rolls his eyes before leaving. I turn my attention back to my files, trying not to listen in to John's conversation.

"This is Walters—"

A pause, as he listens.

"Wow, that was quick. What you got?"

His tone shifts to one of intrigue and my ears prick up.

"How soon can you get the reports to me?" He nods, ruffling through some files as he listens. Hanging up, he hands me a photo before launching straight into what he's found out.

"That was the Madison forensics lab. They ran the DNA swabs I sent of our Jane Doe against the DNA in the system for missing persons; we have an identification and the name of our second victim: Katherine Clifford."

My eyes drop to the photo. "Wow, she certainly looks like Rose. What do we know about her disappearance? How did he cross paths with her if she was living in Chicago?"

"I have her missing person's report here ..." He's sifting through his files again before landing on a manila folder. "OK, here we go. She finished her shift as a retail assistant at nine p.m., but never made it home. Like Rose, nothing was disturbed in her car." He skims the document further, his eyes widening on a particular passage.

"She was in Green Bay three weeks before her abduction!"

"Wow. How old was she?"

"Twenty-seven at the time of her abduction." He takes back the photo and pins it to the board. Wiping out the words 'Jane Doe,' he now writes the name 'Katherine Clifford.'

"I'll need to speak with the detective who investigated her disappearance, get as much information as I can. Will you be OK to finish up here?" he asks, flicking his wrist and checking the time.

"Yes! We have an hour. I'll alter my profile to include this information. You go, this is promising. Well done."

"OK. I'll be in my office; call if you need me. But I'll be back in time for the meeting."

He's buzzed. "Well done, John," I say again. He shrugs, confused by the praise.

"It's what they hired me for."

Note to self: Detective John Walters doesn't like to be complimented!

Smiling, I shake my head before returning to my profile.

Detective Walters introduces me to the room.

"Thank you, John." I scan the faces of the deputies seated around the conference table and everyone standing at the back. With Walters and the investigation wall to my right, I begin.

"We as law enforcers must be as obsessed with catching this killer as he is with killing. My job here is to offer you some insight into the type of killer we are dealing with. I formed this profile based on what we know of his behavior to date. This involves looking at his victims and everything he does before, during and after."

I turn to the whiteboard and point to the two photos of his victims.

"Understand that this killer didn't just wake up one day and decide to murder Katherine Clifford and Rose Bernstein. He fantasized about murdering long before our victims crossed his path. He would have played every scenario out in his head, over and over, until it consumed him. Until the fantasy did little to satisfy his murderous desire. These women were carefully selected. These were not random acts of violence. We are dealing with a very organized killer." My words are slow and firm, driving home this point.

"It's likely he tracked his victims before the abductions. Both women were in the Green Bay area in the weeks leading up to their disappearances. This indicates that our killer either lives or works in Green Bay. The information that Katherine Clifford was kidnapped from Chicago supports the notion that he pursued his victims and brought her to Wisconsin. Rose was living in Appleton. He could not have abducted these women, in such isolated areas, leaving zero evidence at the scene, without having watched them first. This was all well thought out and planned in advance."

I look around the room. Everyone nods along. I'm relieved to see they're engaging with the information that I'm relaying to them. It can be a lot to absorb at once. I push on.

"He is a predatorial stalker. He stalks his victims over a short period of time, without making contact until the attack. Rose lived a fairly regular, or predictable, lifestyle. As did Katherine. He would have quickly figured out their routines, determining how best to isolate and ultimately take control of them."

"He chooses young, Caucasian women with blond hair and blue eyes. Both were single, living with their parents and led quiet lifestyles. He hunts for someone who fits a specific physical description and who he can easily overpower. What we know of both victims so far is that they were quiet, nonconfrontational women. This is no accident. He seeks to manipulate, dominate, and control his victims."

A female deputy's hand shoots up, her body leaning toward me. I smile at her interest. "Yes?"

"Why keep Rose alive for so long?"

"Great question. Once he gains control of his victim, she becomes part of his fantasy. Both victims were dressed up, wearing makeup. In Rose's case, food contents in her stomach suggest that she ate a steak dinner, just hours before he killed her. Imagine the juxtaposition in which she found herself. She was in the company of a man who dressed her up, fed her steak dinners, then tortured her. That control, that psychological and physical torture, fed his depravity. Rose was playing a role, most likely of a mother figure in his life."

"Why his mother and not a girlfriend for example?" she asks.

I pause, reaching for my water bottle. My eyes meet John's, and I find them strangely reassuring. He offers me a slight encouraging nod.

"Like I said, it is most likely his mother or a maternal figure and that is because most often killers like our unsub have strained or complex relationships with their mothers. They're usually from a broken home or have suffered some maternal abandonment or abuse as a child. As a result, he chooses victims that resemble his mother physically. Although, I do suspect that his interactions with his victims are more in line with a courtship. That is indicative of his need for love, which might have been lacking throughout his formative years. He expects them to dress a certain way, behave a certain way, and return his affection. When they refuse or cannot live up to the fantasy in his mind, he punishes them. Those punishments become more violent until he finally unravels and murders them.

"These acts are all part of his 'signature.' The signature satisfies his psychological need and isn't necessary for the execution of the crime. It's his calling card, and if dealing with a serial killer, you will see the signature repeated across all his crime scenes," I explain.

"Let's take each signature individually. We've already touched on why he dresses them up so let's move on. He held them captive, so he likely lives alone. Your killer will be a single man. This kind of fantasy requires privacy. He may live in an isolated area or have access to one. How he disposed of the bodies ties into my theory above. These locations are romanticized in his mind. He lays them down in beauty spots, their eyes open and looking up at the stars. There is a reason, unique to him for choosing these locations. He may live close by. He may have visited them as a child with his mother. But let's not forget the most unique and unusual element of his crimes. That is the breaking of his victims' bones."

"Can I ask another question?" The same female deputy's hand shoots up again.

"Absolutely!"

"Was there any sign of sexual assault?"

Another great question.

"Rose wasn't sexually assaulted. But there was a sexual element to these crimes. Why? He broke her bones both while she was alive and after she succumbed to her injuries. He felt the need to continue to mutilate her body. Consider the killer who chooses a knife as his weapon. The knife is a phallic symbol. The act of plunging the knife into the body of his victim is the sexual release. A crime that is sexual in nature might not always have a sexual assault. Our killer breaks their bones. His sexual release, I believe ..." I pause to take a breath.

"Is the *sound* of their bones snapping and crunching. This fetish is known as *Auralism.* It is rare but it exists, and I believe may play a factor in his crimes."

A pin could drop as I continue.

"It arouses him, feeds those emotional and sexual needs. This fetish will have tell-tale signs and bleed into his everyday life. He could be a rheumatologist, a physical therapist or even an orthopedic surgeon. His obsession with bones will reveal itself to you. Does he crack his knuckles while talking to you, or roll out his neck? These sounds help him calm down under pressure. They are unique to him, but when you know what you're looking for, you will spot it quickly." I fold my hands together.

"Can you tell us what he looks like?" another deputy calls out.

I chuckle. "Not exactly, I wish I could! But we can decipher some physical descriptions, based on years of research and his chosen victims. Rose and Katherine are white females and it is well documented that serial killers rarely kill outside of their own ethnicity. So, we can assume he is a white man. He lured his victims from their car, so he is unassuming and charming, possibly attractive. If they trusted him enough to feel safe, could he be cunning, clever and sociable? It is very likely he is all of these things. His social skills will afford him the ability to hold down a steady job, most likely a nine-to-five which allows him time to carry out his stalking and eventually his fantasies. He knows the highways well and may travel along them for work. He carried Katherine Clifford's body through dense brush, which means he is strong. Most likely well-built and in his mid- to late-thirties. How he kills his victims might help you to eliminate potential suspects. He tortures them over a period of time. He will have a basement, or a second location that he takes them to. He assumes the role of dominant, so is likely to have had a very dominating or controlling mother. His hatred for his mother is exacted onto his victims. He keeps them on edge, enjoys their fear. These crimes give him a satisfaction he cannot achieve in any other area of his life. That is why he will not stop. He chooses to do this. It makes him feel powerful."

I take a deep breath. "OK. Any questions?"

"Do we eliminate smaller and older men?" John asks.

"Not automatically. This profile is a tool to help you when investigating. You should never rule out a suspect based on this profile alone. However, use your powers of discernment when questioning a suspect. A man in his seventies is unlikely to have carried Katherine's body."

"Anything else?" I ask the room.

"At the vigil, what do we look out for?" John asks again.

"An event like the upcoming vigil will be too tempting. It's likely he'll make an appearance. We'll be leaving a personal item of Rose's at the memorial site to lure the killer there. Hoping that the prospect of a trophy from his victim will be too much to ignore. Many of you will be in attendance: take note of cars that come in and out of the area. He may park, he may simply drive by and leave. He could be brave and be on foot. Ask yourself, who is lingering in the shadows? Who is walking the vigil alone? Who is more interested in what law enforcement personnel are doing than the ceremony itself? It will be up to each of you to keep your eyes and ears peeled." My eyes meet theirs around the room, happy to find them all taking the information in.

I spend twenty minutes fielding questions, before handing the floor over to John. He stands to address the room. I've noticed that John speaks only when he has something important to say, so when he does, people listen. You could hear a pin drop right now. His colleagues respect him.

"First, I'd like to thank Agent Perez for taking the time to come help us with this case. I want to remind all of you that these streets are our responsibility. Rose and Katherine died on our watch. I don't care where you're stationed: whether you're on patrol or running down leads, doing foot patrol or manning the front desk; when you're on duty, I expect you all to take this profile seriously. Keep Rose and Katherine in the back of your mind. Question everything and everyone that seems unusual or out of place." They all nod enthusiastically.

"OK, let's get to work."

CHAPTER 10

JEFFREY

He's clever.

The deep voice of Detective Walters booms through the speakers of my car as I maneuver the country roads back to Green Bay. After my call to the show, which I suspect was the catalyst for this interview, I spent the night at the cabin in dance. Savannah, as usual, is taking the lead on questioning the good detective. They're calling it a 'bonus true-crime segment' to mark tomorrow's vigil for Rose.

It's a trap!

"Detective Walters, are you any closer to catching the man responsible?" she asks.

"I can't answer that question without compromising the investigation. However, I will say that whoever killed Rose is an interesting person. I'd love the opportunity to sit and speak to this person. If they wanted to call tonight, I'd be willing to hear their side of the story."

Ha! Does he think I'm stupid?

"Why is it you find him so interesting?" Faye's sweet voice replaces his. Her input is always gentle, always empathetic.

"There have been few times over the course of my career that a suspect has impressed me. This killer knows what he's doing. I'm intrigued, and like I said, would welcome any conversation with him."

My chest bursts with pride.

Faye asks, "How would he get in contact with you?"

"He could call your show tonight or call the Outagamie Sheriff's office. I'll be attending the candlelight vigil for Rose tomorrow in Appleton, if he wanted to talk in person."

My fingers twitch on the steering wheel, gripping it tight, squeezing away the urge to fall for it.

"We'll be attending the vigil for Rose too—" My ears perk, my heart suddenly pumping a little harder as I listen to Faye. "We were asked by Rose's dad to lay her favorite teddy bear next to the place where her body was discovered."

Savannah made a great first impression when I started listening to their show, but Faye has won me over as a true fan. She's always the voice of reason. The opportunity to meet her, put a face to her singsong voice far more enticing than the bait Detective Walters is dangling.

It's settled, no more risks. I'll attend the vigil instead.

AGENT DELLA PEREZ

Snow has been falling steadily all afternoon, dusting the streets with white and filling the footsteps of everyone that has arrived for Rose's vigil. Police cruisers line the packed sidewalks, their lights silently flashing and illuminating the mourners in waves of blue and red as they wait to walk the short distance from the Appleton library to the old swing bridge. My fingers shake as I check my earpiece. My sleeve holds the microphone, the wire running to my collar. Securing the clip and coil tube over the back of my ear, I zip my heavy winter coat back up to my chin and pull on my leather gloves. I fill my lungs with cold air, my eyes scan the sea of faces, trying to concentrate despite the biting temperatures. Further along the street my eyes land on the broad shoulders of a lone male before recognizing it's Walters. We separated to cover more ground. As if sensing my eyes on him, his rough voice chatters in my ear.

"Perez, this is Walters. What's your current location?"

"I'm crossing onto Birch Street now."

"OK, stay alert."

His comment should grate on me, but I'm too cold to react. Instead, my focus returns to the faces in the crowd. My eyes shoot to every doorway, building and alleyway, until I spot a man lingering alone at the entrance of a side street. Keeping my eyes firmly on him, I move in his direction. He's dressed all in black, shifting from one foot to the other. *He's agitated,* I note to myself, before spotting Rose's missing person poster in his hand. He's staring at it, a sinister smile spreading across his face before he slinks into the shadows behind him.

Not agitated. *He's excited!*

I dip my chin and speak into the mic on my sleeve.

"Walters, this is Perez. I'm on foot, following a potential suspect into the alleyway between Old Navy and CVS—"

"I'm turning back now. I'm thirty seconds away, wait for back up—"

"That's a negative, I'll lose him. Stay with Faye and Savannah, I'll check this out." I cut him off, already turning down the dark lane, following the only set of footprints disturbing the blanket of fresh snow. Halfway down the alley, the tracks veer off between two dumpsters. Snow crunches beneath my feet, an icy breeze swooping up my spine. I hear heavy breathing echoing from behind the dumpster. Instinctively, I draw my gun and flashlight from my hip, holding both outstretched as I round on him.

"FBI!" I scream, clicking on the bright light and beaming it into his startled face. His hands go up in the air. His trousers fall to the ground.

My gut churns with disgust as I grasp the crude reality. This guy is masturbating at the vigil for a murdered girl. I hear heavy footsteps and John, breathless with anger and exertion, enters the alleyway.

"Perez!" He reaches me in seconds and takes in the scene before him.

"What the fuck?"

"I was just ..." the suspect speaks.

"Don't move," I growl, keeping my gun trained on him, while Walters speaks into his radio.

"Jones, get a squad car and some backup to the alleyway on Fifth."

The suspect dips, lowering his hands. "HANDS IN THE AIR," I repeat.

"M-my pants are down."

"Don't move an inch," Walters barks. He slaps him in cuffs before roughly pulling up the man's pants. The ball of revulsion tightens in my stomach as I holster my weapon, noticing for the first time the wedding band on his finger. With his round tummy, thinning hair and greasy appearance, I doubt he's our killer. The physical description doesn't match up: he can scarcely carry himself, let alone a dead body. However, this kind of lewd behavior can't be overlooked. At minimum he's facing charges of indecent exposure. We'll need to alibi him and run a full background check to confirm it, but if I'm right, he's not our guy.

The squad car arrives from the opposite end of the alley. Faye's due to take the podium any minute, so we hand him over to deal with later, and return to the vigil. Walters storms ahead. His eyes, colder than the damn Wisconsin weather, narrow on mine over his shoulder.

"Don't do that again."

"Excuse me?" I match him in tone and speed as we hurry toward the podium.

"Cut the bullshit. You're here on my territory. I know these streets like the back of my hand. There's at least five entranceways along that alley where a killer could hide. I was thirty seconds behind you."

"He could have escaped. And now we have him in custody: we did our job," I huff, my chest tightening between the cold, the pace, and the anger Detective Walters is managing to stir within me. Dropping behind him, I indulge his need for control, allowing him to continue leading the way. Distracted and frustrated, my shoulder bangs into a group of mourners as we're reaching the podium. Turning to apologize, a flash of pale blue snares my attention before another pedestrian blocks my line of sight. A chill gallops along my spine, halting my forward motion. My head whips back around, searching for those eyes again. Nothing.

"Do you have something?" Walters comes up behind me.

"No, I just—I bumped into someone, but he's gone. I'm sure it's nothing."

"We can circle back," he offers.

"No, let's get to the podium. I'll look from there."

JEFFREY

"Thank you all for joining us this evening." Her voice soars through the microphone, its wistful lure enough to silence the mob. I too, am left speechless, but it's her winsome face that enthralls me. Over the heads of a thousand people, she's a beacon of beauty. Her face glows under the floodlights as she recites a prayer. The words blur as I reconcile that this is Faye, and not the soul of Rose. Haunted and thrilled at once, I swallow back my surprise. My legs, almost of their own accord, pull me deeper into the horde. Closer to her. Faye commands attention, but too many eyes are diverted to the crowd, alerting me to a heavy police presence. I adjust my scarf around my face, thankful for the snowfall and the anonymity it provides me. I stop next to two women and huddle close to light my candle. I turn just as Detective Walters, followed by an attractive female cop, cuts between us. Her shoulder bumps into mine as she goes. Glancing back, she apologizes. Her sharp eyes narrow just as I drop my gaze to engage the ladies.

"Do you have a light?"

By the time I look back up, a thousand flames burn around me for Rose, igniting the passion of a thousand flames within, for Faye. It's ironic: she has been seeking me out. Her fascination with this case, *with me*, has been playing out over the airwaves like a siren's call, night after night. Compelling me, luring me here, and demanding that I find her.

I'm surrounded by solemn expressions and a heavy sadness pervades the air, but it does nothing to stop the smile from spreading behind my scarf. Skirting the edges of the congested streets, I follow as Faye and Savannah lead the way to the bridge. Arnie Bernstein weeps next to Detective Walters, who offers a simple hand on his shoulder. A gesture of strength and quiet reassurance. He is too close to Faye today, and nowhere near me any other day of the week. There will be plenty of opportunities to be by her side. For now, Detective Walters narrows his steely glare on the crowd, hopping from face to face. Stepping back, I move into the shadows, just as his gaze lands on the now-empty space I occupied. Intrigued, I watch his eyes flick back and forth, his brows furrowing as he searches the gloom. When his mouth moves to the collar of his shirt, I find Faye's face once more.

"Soon." The promise passes my lips in a whisper before I leave along the edge of the Fox River.

FAYE

Pulling off the highway toward home, I flick on my high beams to navigate the dark country roads. Traffic at this hour is non-existent, but I like the eerie tranquillity of my drive and my truck is regularly serviced to prevent any car trouble while driving alone. The very idea of car trouble makes me think of Rose Bernstein again. Her vigil earlier this evening has left a hollow feeling in my chest. Her father stood next to us, his hopes pinned to Detective Walters's plan to coax her killer out of the shadows. Nothing stood out to me as unusual, but according to Agent Perez, that doesn't mean the night was a failure. Rubbing my tired eyes, I glance at the clock. It's two thirty a.m. It's been a long, emotional day and I still have another twenty minutes of driving time. I turn up the radio and crack open the window, allowing a gust of cold air into the truck. Karen's wedding is tomorrow. With so much to prepare, it will be an early start in the morning.

The sudden appearance of headlights in my rearview mirror grabs my attention. The blaring high beams jolts my senses, kicking the air from my lungs and my reflexes into gear. I urgently tap the brakes to alert the driver to his tailgating and to back off. My jangled nerves settle when he pulls back but the relief is short lived when he accelerates again, resuming his aggressive pursuit. Dazzled by the lights, I slow to encourage him to pass, but he remains on my tail. My anxious fingers maintain a death grip on the steering wheel as my eyes dart back and forth between the road and my rearview mirror. The radio show caller's threat combined with this driver's menacing antics amplifies the nervous energy thumping against my ribs.

When I signal for my turn, he pulls back again. Relieved, I take the last bend toward home, soothing my frayed nerves when the end of our lane comes into view.

My brain is scrambling to make sense of what just happened when I spot the car again in my mirror. This time it rolls to a slow stop at the end of the drive. Inside, the silhouette of a man sits, his head turned in my direction, his features obscured in the darkness.

Danger!

Panic grips my chest, shaking me into action. Parking, I lock the doors of my truck and dial Luke's number. Pulling my eyes from the strange car to Luke's bedroom window, I offer a silent plea for him to answer, just as a warm glow lights up his room.

"Are you OK?"

"Luke! I think a car followed me home. He's stopped at the end of the laneway."

A rustling sound comes over the line. "Lock your doors. I'm on the way."

Seconds later, Luke is out the front door with a flashlight in one hand and an axe in the other. Fear for my own safety is replaced with the thought that now Luke could be at risk. I jump out of the truck as the car speeds off. Luke runs past me.

"Get inside. Lock the door, and don't open it," he calls over his shoulder. My head whirls. Panic, relief, and fear for Luke all pin me to the spot. Luke's flashlight blinds me.

"FAYE. NOW."

The light turns off. Back in darkness, I watch his large silhouette disappear into the night.

I hurry up the steps and into the cabin. Locking the door behind me, I pace back and forth, trembling. I punch 911 into my cell but pause over hitting the call button.

What if I'm imagining it all?

I wait. Seconds turn into minutes. Minutes feel like hours, before I hear footsteps on the porch. My heart stopped until Luke's gruff voice came through the door.

"Faye? open up."

I pull open the door and he rushes in.

"Lock it behind me," he orders, his breathing heavy. His grim expression does nothing to ease my concerns as he picks up his cell phone.

"Who are you calling?"

"Hi. Yes, this is Luke Anderson. I'm out here on Oak Orchard Road, off Route 41. Could you send someone out? My sister was followed home from work." His words to the dispatcher answer my question.

"What happened?" I follow him into the kitchen. The thud of his axe hitting the kitchen table startles me as he paces around the island.

"Luke."

"I'm thinking," he barks back. His eyes soften when he finally looks at me. "Sorry." he sighs. "The car was stopped further down the road. I crept almost right up to him, but the fucker spotted me and sped off." His fists curl at his side.

I rack my brain for a reasonable explanation. "Maybe he was lost?" I offer, weakly.

"Who was that cop you had on the show the other night?"

"Detective Walters, but—"

"Have you got his number?".

"No, Scott might, but—" His finger silences me as he makes another call.

"Scott? It's Luke Anderson—" I hear hurried talking from the other end. "No, someone followed her home. Could you send me that detective's number? ..."

Frustrated, I exit the kitchen in time to see the flashing lights of the local sheriff's car pulling into our lane. We spend the next thirty minutes recounting the events of the last hour to the sheriff. Luke identified the car as a dark Chevrolet with a Wisconsin license plate. He saw the numbers 3 and 9. I only knew it was a dark sedan. When the sheriff leaves, Luke grabs me into a bear hug. I rest my head on his shoulder and feel safe again. We decide there is nothing more to do except get some sleep and check in with Detective Walters in the morning. Climbing the stairs to bed, I notice I have three missed calls from Scott and quickly fire off a text.

Hey, sorry for the late text. I missed your calls earlier, the sheriff was here. All is OK, I'm fine. Talk tomorrow.

My phone buzzes with an incoming call straight away.

"Hey," I answer.

"Jesus, I've been worried sick. You OK? What happened?"

"It's a long story ..." I fill him in on the night's events, apologizing that Luke woke him to get the detective's phone number.

"I don't care about that. Are *you* OK?" the soft timbre of his voice soothes away my concerns.

"Yeah, the sheriff just left. There's not much they can do, but they'll write up the report and keep an eye out for the car."

"I gave Luke Detective Walters's number. I should have made sure you were safe ..."

"Don't—"

"No, I should have insisted you and Savannah be pulled out of the vigil service tonight—"

"Let's not all get too carried away. I'm fine."

"Well, Detective Walters needs to know what happened. Will you be OK for tomorrow?"

He has me smiling now. "Yeah. You worried I might miss the wedding?"

"Obviously! Gotta have my priorities straight."

The sound of his laughter fills me with warmth. Only Scott could turn such a horrible night around.

He clears his throat. "Leah's sister is still going, but it's just a friendly thing."

"You mentioned. You've got a lot of women in the friend zone, Allen!"

A soft chuckle comes over the line.

"Faye?" His voice is a whisper and my stomach tightens in anticipation of his next few words. "I'm hoping there'll soon be one less."

FAYE

Karen booked a beautiful lakeside retreat for the ceremony and reception. The hotel itself is designed to look like a log cabin, its intimate atmosphere provided by the forest surrounding it.

We arrived over an hour ago and checked into our rooms to get ready. Savannah drove. Always one for mysteries, she kept an eye on the rearview mirror for the entire trip here.

Seeing both her and Luke so rattled about last night has done little to ease my own nerves. I'm so distracted that I burn my forehead with the curling iron. Tears prick the corners of my eyes as I assess the red welt starting to form. Frustrated, I throw the iron on the dressing table and let go for a cry. Large, self-pitying tears fall down my face, ruining my makeup, but also freeing me of the knot in my stomach. The past few days have taken their toll.

After the worst of the waterworks are done, I look up. My sobs turn to laughter when I catch sight of myself in the mirror. Sniffling back my tears, I wipe my eyes, clean off the wrecked makeup and start over.

Everything is OK, you're safe! I repeat these words over in my mind as I get dressed.

Running my hands over the soft material of my black dress, I admire it one last time in the mirror. The Bardot neckline leaves my shoulders bare before cutting into a deep V. It shows a little more cleavage than I'm comfortable with. Savannah coaxed me into buying it, insisting it was "sexy as fuck." Sexy is the last thing I feel right now, but I can't deny the dress hugs my figure beautifully.

"Everything is OK," I whisper to myself in the mirror, before making my way to meet Savannah.

Savannah's back is to me as she leans against the bar with one hip cocked. Her floor-length, navy dress flows over her curves like water. Her auburn hair falls in waves down her back. I already think she's the most striking woman in the room as I sidle up next to her.

"Holy cow. You look stunning." My eyes widen in awe of her beauty.

"Sugar, I could be wearing a flour sack and you'd think I was the best-dressed person in the room." She shakes off my compliment with a smile. "But look at you! Scott will have to pick himself up off the floor when he sees you in that dress." She wiggles her eyebrows, before reaching back to pick up two glasses of wine. She hands one to me.

"I think we've earned these." She lifts her glass to clink with mine.

As we wait with the other guests, I'm constantly searching the room for Scott. He hasn't arrived yet when we're directed to the converted barn for the ceremony. The flagstone pathway has been cleared of snow. Savannah and I link elbows, laughing as we navigate it in our heels. The path is flanked on either side by a dense pine forest. The soft smell reminds me of Luke and home. Inhaling deeply, we lean on each other, admiring the fairy lights hung to guide us toward the barn door. Two wide doors are outlined in fairy lights, with a smaller door off to the right welcoming us in from the freezing cold air.

"Wow."

The massive, rustic pine structures that rise from the floor to the ceiling, each draped in sheer white voile fabric, carefully wrapped around the beams before unfurling and meeting again overhead. At the room's center, a magnificent chandelier is suspended.

"Wow ..." Savannah echoes. "I love the vintage decor." She points out some old wooden crates. White roses spill out of jugs resting on top of each crate, surrounded by tealights in old jam jars. We take our seats along the aisle, then turn just in time to see Scott, Don and their dates arrive. Leah and her sister are extremely attractive. Both with silky black hair, high cheekbones and full red lips against their pale complexions. Heads turn as they all walk in together.

We both look at Scott, who smiles our way, offering a small wave before taking his seat. My hand lifts, gingerly waving back, as my eyes swallow him whole. The ultra-slim, tapered fit of his black suit with a crisp white shirt and black tie, molds perfectly to his toned body.

The urge to unbutton his shirt sends a tingling sensation through my fingers.

"Earth to Faye: you're staring," Savannah hisses next to me. My eyes snap back to her, before shifting to the wedding program in my hand.

"Oh my God. I was fanning myself while looking at him!" I burn with mortification.

"Uh-huh. But to be fair, he does look hot as Hades."

"He does, doesn't he?" I sigh.

The wedding ceremony is lovely. The barn is quickly transformed into a magnificent reception area. Savannah visits the ladies' room while I find our seats. The Green Bay Radio crew are all seated at the same table. I'm sitting alone when Scott's deep voice whispers in my ear, his warm breath caressing my neck. I turn to look up at him inches from me, his eyes smiling with mischief.

"Are you having fun?"

"I am now. You?"

"I will be, once I ..." reaching over, he proceeds to rearrange the place cards, "... do this." He winks, conveniently seating himself next to me.

"Scott!" I laugh, loving this playful side of him. "I'm telling Karen," I tease. I'm about to ask after his date when his hand comes to my face. His thumb gently skims over my forehead. The light touch has the welt burning all over again.

"What happened here?"

"Curling iron." My eyes roll.

"You should be more careful, they're hot!"

"I like hot stuff!"

"Me too ..." his eyes fall to my lips "although it hurts when they burn."

"Do you burn?" I'm openly flirting with him again, but if I've learned anything over the last few days, it's life's too short. I'm crazy about Scott. I want him to know.

"You think I'm hot?"

"Yeah ..." my breath hitches.

There's heat in his eyes now. "I don't burn. But ..." he stares right at me. "I might set you on fire." The gentle caress of his thumb is no match for the intensity of his gaze. My heart pounds wildly.

"I think I'm about to combust."

His laughter is soft, his body leaning out of my space. "Can I ask you something?"

"Sure," a nervous laugh passes my lips.

Sweetness replaces the flirtation in his tone. "Why are you so beautiful?"

I forget how to breathe. I forget how to speak.

"Am I interrupting something?" Jumping back, we both turn to Savannah. Her eyes flit between us.

"No," I blurt.

"Yes," Scott says.

"Good." Savannah smirks. I'm pretty sure it's Scott's response that has her looking pleased.

It's after supper, and the speeches are finished. The DJ's popular choices have a lot of people out dancing. Scott is still next to me but he was gentleman enough to move his date's place card to his other side. When Savannah goes to the bar, I turn to him, resting my cheek in my hand, my elbow on the table.

"Where's Jordyn?"

"On the dance floor with Leah." He nods that way, and I see her swinging her hips to Abba's "Mamma Mia" and laughing with her sister.

"She's pretty. And seems really friendly."

"She is, but ..." He smirks playfully, gently touching the charms hanging from my bracelet.

"But ...?" I laugh.

"But she's not the prettiest girl in the room tonight."

"Dare I ask who is?" My stomach twists in excitement.

"It's obvious, isn't it?" His eyes twinkle with mischief. "The bride!" He chuckles at himself. Pretending to be offended, I lean away, swatting his hand from my bracelet.

"Leave my charms alone," I laugh. Then I'm stunned when he captures my hand in his.

"Sleepwalking," by Skinny Living begins to play, the soft piano chords filling the room as the lead singer's voice croons deeply, making the air heavy with romance.

"You have such dainty wrists." He lightly grazes the inside of my wrist, stopping to feel my pulse pound at his touch. My head spins.

"You have such strong hands." My voice shakes with pleasure.

"You have the cutest freckles." His eyes refuse to release mine, his fingers trailing up my bare arm.

"You've got a great ass." I swallow.

He laughs. "Ditto!"

His hand reaches my throat. "You've got the prettiest neck." His eyes drop to my exposed collarbone. My chest is rising and falling to match my erratic heartbeat. My eyes fall to his lips.

"Let's dance." He's already standing. His hand returns to mine as he gently tugs me from my seat, making our way to the dance floor. Savannah winks in my direction as we pass. Still holding my hand, he lifts it between our chests, his free arm wrapping around my waist and holding me close to his warm body as we sway gently to the music. our feet moving in sync. This shift happened so suddenly. There's something real between Scott and I, and I'm tired of pretending otherwise. I relax into the moment, and just enjoy. We remain embraced until the song ends. He's not afraid to wiggle his hips and shimmy his shoulders with me. Scott has a goofy side, and it comes to life on the dance floor. We spend much of the evening together.

I'm taking a break later when Savanah drops into a chair beside me.

"Where's Scott?" she asks, massaging one tired foot.

"He left to walk Jordyn back to her room. Don and Leah left over an hour ago."

"Oh, here he is back now." Savannah nods toward the door. Turning, I see him strolling back toward us. His jacket is off, his shirt molding to his lean muscles as he carries it over his shoulder. Despite the casual pace, his long strides eat up the distance between us in no time.

"Are you ladies ready to leave, or shall we have another drink?" He looks around the barn.

"I'm beat," Savannah answers and I nod in agreement. Scott retrieves our coats before we all return to the vestibule. We walk Savannah to her room first, waiting as she enters, only moving on when her door is securely closed.

"You don't have to walk me to my door."

"Are you kidding? I've been waiting all night to walk you to your room."

Scott leans against the wall waiting for the elevator with me. His suit is rumpled, his messy hair tempting me to run my fingers through it. My stomach clenches when he catches me staring.

"You shouldn't be looking at me with those eyes." His ragged tone is arousing.

"You shouldn't have told me that I'm beautiful."

"I should have told you long ago, how beautiful you are." The elevator doors slide open. The sexual tension around us fills the small space.

"Why didn't you?"

He presses the button for the third floor, turning back to me. "I'm your boss. I didn't want to cross a line."

I swallow. "And now?"

"Now," he begins, stepping forward, closing the distance between us. He yanks me against his hard body. His free hand tangles in my hair, his lips find mine. His warm tongue slowly coaxes my lips apart, with almost painful precision.

"Scott!" I moan, my head falling back as his lips race down my neck. Trembling with need, my patience falls to the wayside as I pull his lips back to mine. Dazed, I fist his shirt, rubbing my aching body against his. His skillful mouth sets the rhythm of our intimate kiss.

"Which room is yours?" His voice is hoarse as he walks me backward out of the elevator and toward my room.

"302," I reply, hungrily pulling his lips back to mine. At the door, my hand trembles as I struggle with the key card. I'm too tangled up in his scent, his touch, the feel of his arousal against my ass, to think straight.

Stepping forward into the room, I leave the door open and turn back to face him. My bold invitation hangs in the air between us. Still standing in the doorway, he grips the frame with both hands, a pained expression on his face.

"You're killing me." His eyes leave mine, looking to the double bed behind me.

"You can come inside, you know. I promise not to bite." I pat the bed.

The hunger in his eyes has me feeling more powerful than I ever have before. Closing the door, he walks to me and in an instant his lips are on mine again. His large body leans over me as I fall back on the bed, pulling him down.

"Faye." He moans, his full weight landing on me, pinning me beneath him, his arousal searing into my flesh. Rearing up, I grind against him, deepening our kiss.

"Faye!" I'm forced to respond when he rolls away. Breathless, he lies next to me, gripping his hair with both hands. "I don't want to rush things," he manages.

"I think we've waited long enough."

"Jesus, Faye, this is torture, but we've both been drinking and after everything you've been through over the last twenty-four hours ... I don't want this to be something you regret." He turns to face me, his eyes full of sincerity.

"I'm fine!" I try to reassure him, until I realize that he's right. My stomach turns and my eyes fill. "I'm sorry," I sniffle, as he pulls me into his arms.

"You're safe," he whispers. "We *will* find out who it was. You don't need to be afraid." He leans back, wiping away my tears.

"I'm sorry. I don't know what came over me," I croak.

"Please don't apologize. The last thing I wanted to do was upset you." Dropping his head, his lips find mine, softly rousing me out of my fears. "Can I stay with you tonight? I don't want to leave you while you're upset."

Distracted by his tender ministrations, I simply nod. He holds me like this until my breathing evens and my eyes feel heavy.

"Scott?" I whisper.

"Yeah?"

"Can I ask you something?"

"Anything." He kisses me in the darkness.

"Why are *you* so beautiful?" I smile, feeling happier than I have in the longest time.

CHAPTER 11

LUKE

The incoming text alert rouses me from my slumber. Turning in my bed, I reach toward my bedside table. Last night's events, still fresh in my mind, have had me on edge all day. Lifting the phone, I see Savannah's name on my screen and swiftly sit up to read the message.

> The wedding was a success, nothing strange to report. I've been thinking that you really need to get some home security in place. You're away so often, it's not safe for Faye to be in that house alone right now.

I'm comforted by the notion that Faye has somebody looking out for her when I'm not around. She's right too. Maybe nothing else will come of last night's scare, but it's a wake-up call to all of us.

I agree, I was thinking along the same lines myself. Did you have fun at the wedding?

A photo of Faye and Savannah fills the screen. Faye looks as beautiful as ever. Savannah looks like a siren. I can't help but zoom in on her curves. Her bright eyes in the photo are alight with humor, as they both make faces in the mirror. *Fuck,* I groan, I really shouldn't be creeping on my little sister's best friend.

You both look great. Thank you for looking out for her.

Her thumbs-up reply ends our conversation. Throwing my phone back on the nightstand, I'm relieved to know I'll get a few worry-free hours of sleep.

JEFFREY

The center of the large wagon wheel rests on top of a steel pole. The pole, extendable and reinforced, holds the wheel, allowing me to spin it easily. Four feet from the floor, it turns now, the smooth iron rim sliding through the palm of my cupped hand, the uneven grain of the wood caressing my fingers. The silent whirl has me captivated. The spokes blur and I look down on what appears to be a spinning tabletop. I grip it tightly to stop the rotation. The urge to see what they see is too much to resist and I climb on board. Lying across the wooden structure, I wriggle in discomfort against the hub digging into my spine. The wheel turns. I stare up at the tin roof of the barn. It screeches in protest of the wind sneaking beneath its ridges, threatening to lift it clean off. I turn my head to one side, my gaze gliding around the barn. I take in the bales that line one wall. The barn's blood-red paint is flaked and chipped, bits falling in the moldy straw. I pass the lightbulb that hangs over my workbench, illuminating falling dust, before the old farm machinery that fills this barn comes into view. I love this space, from the gigantic cobwebs to the smell of mildew that lingers.

I'm starting to feel nauseous from the motion. I drop one leg between the spokes of the wheel, my foot stopping the rotation. Pride washes over me. Designed to resemble the methods of past executioners, I built it with punishment in mind. My wheel surpasses all previous limits, allowing me to experience so much more pleasure.

I remember Rose's mangled limbs between the spokes. The splitting and cracking sounds of her breaking bones echo in my mind and reverberate around my body. She was easy to break, weak in every way. I crushed her from above with another wheel first, and she died before I could use the rope. It didn't stop me. I tied one end of the rope around her ankle and the other to one of the barn's steel beams. Once secured, I pushed the wheel hard to the right. Her knee popped before her hip was ripped from its socket. The method exceeded my expectations on the first try. I had to repeat it on all of her limbs.

Turning out the lights, I leave the barn and head for my station wagon. Memories of Rose were enough until I saw Faye. I was foolish to follow her home after the vigil. I got carried away, revealing my presence along those dark country roads. My mind, no matter how preoccupied with Faye over the last thirty hours, always comes back to *him*. I need to know who he is. My knuckles turn white with my hard grip on the steering wheel, as I recall the axe in his hand. *Is he her lover?*

I glanced up into the rearview mirror, spotting him creeping through the night, just as he reached my car. The moon illuminated the gleaming axe he held, and I sped away.

Once the adrenaline receded, rage took over. My steering wheel bore the brunt of my violent response. I wasn't expecting someone to sneak out and follow me on foot. He's clever, looks strong, and is an unexpected complication. But he's no match for me.

To avoid any suspicion today, I found a rest area and parked there before setting out into the woods. I trekked over a mile, coming to the treeline that runs along the edge of the small clearing that holds her cabin. Alone, it sits on a vast stretch of land, the lake behind it bordering the entire property. I admit, despite the inconvenience, this is the kind of home I would choose too. Another confirmation of our connection.

Ducking low behind the brush, I find the best vantage point. I'm not close enough to see what's going on inside the cabin, but I can see her truck parked out front. She's home. Next to her truck is a second vehicle, a black truck. New compared to Faye's vintage model, the Chevy Silverado must be his.

I regret scaring her. I know it will make getting close to her more difficult. Faye has me taking risks. I feel daring and bold. The stakes are higher, the tension alluring. I can't walk away. Keeping low, I focus on the cabin, looking for any signs of life. The sun has risen, but I'm shielded by the dark forest around me. The cold morning air has me longing for the comfort of my heated car. Rose's life was simple. Her routine monotonous. But Mother always said that hard work brought the biggest rewards. It was all leading here: to Faye, my greatest challenge.

I walk the edge of the tree line, taking in as much information about the property as possible. The first sign of life comes from a light turning on in the kitchen. For a few brief seconds, *he* comes into view, moving briskly about before disappearing again.

In spite of feeling stiff with cold, I move stealthily back to the front of the cabin, just in time to see him come out onto the porch. Tall and broad with big burly arms, this man is clearly strong. A lesser man would be intimidated, but he's no match for me. His eyes scan the treeline and I stare back, daring him to find me. For a split second, I think he does. I admire his ability to sense danger.

The sound of tires crunching on gravel pulls my attention to the black BMW coming down the drive. Detective Walters and his female colleague step out of the car. A slow smile creeps up my face. I knew the detective was laying a trap. In many ways, he did me a favor. Without his interference, I might never have attended the vigil. I watch them climb the porch steps and shake hands with the man before they all go inside. Keeping low, I crawl behind the brush, sinking lower when the three reappear, framed by the kitchen window. They stand talking. All I can do is watch their silent exchange, rolling out my neck to try to ease my stiff shoulders. None of these people have any place in *our* lives. Answers about who he is will have to wait. I won't be gaining access to the cabin while the police are hanging around. I fade back into the forest, moving with speed back to my station wagon. There was no sign of Faye. Hopefully tomorrow will be more promising.

SCOTT

I didn't think it was possible, but somehow Faye is even more stunning in the morning. Rolling over next to me, her eyes flutter open and my heart stills.

"Good morning." Her words, sleepy and soft as though wrapped in velvet, bring an overwhelming need to be close to her.

"Hey." I smile. "How are you feeling this morning?"

"Safe."

Her response strikes a protective chord within me. Reaching for her, I pull her into my arms, her chest pressing against mine as I wrap her in my strength.

"I like that," I admit. My heart lurches madly when she looks up into my eyes.

"I like this." Her heart thuds against mine, beat for beat, and our eyes reveal more than either of us is ready to put into words.

"I know it's a little late to ask, but are you OK with all this? Me being your boss doesn't bother you?"

"I'm more than OK with it. Besides, I'll be the boss in the bedroom!" She giggles.

"You drive a hard bargain, but OK." I'm grinning from ear to ear. "Can I take you on a date tomorrow?"

"Yes, but right now, you're on the clock ..." A seductive glint flashes in her eyes. "And I'd like you to kiss me."

"Yes boss!" I smile back, my lips meeting hers.

LUKE

"You're early." I scowl at the two detectives climbing the steps to my porch.

"We anticipated getting lost."

I turn to the pretty detective who spoke.

"Agent Della Perez." Her green eyes hold mine as she stretches out her hand, introducing herself. Her soft Spanish accent is doing wonders at easing my irritation.

"*Mucho gusto.*" I smile, taking her hand.

"Ah, you speak my native tongue?" Her eyes widen, her handshake remaining firm.

"Just the basics. I spent two months in Chiapas, a few years back."

Detective Walters steps forward. His bored expression tells me he doesn't care much for small talk.

"I'm Detective Walters. We spoke on the phone yesterday."

"Luke Anderson." I nod and we shake hands.

"Well, come in. Faye isn't back yet, but she is on her way." I explain as we walk through to the kitchen.

"Coffee?" I offer, already pulling cups from the cabinet.

"Please," Perez answers, and Detective Walters follows suit. I look over my shoulder to find them both standing around the kitchen island. Walters's eyes are moving around the room.

"Maybe you could go over the events of Friday night, while we wait." Walters takes his coffee.

Happy to do so, I lean back against the countertop, taking a sip of my coffee before beginning. We spend the next while going over everything. Faye and Savannah walk in just as I'm about to make a fresh pot.

"Just in time." Seeing Faye's smiling face lifts my mood. Savannah trails behind her with her own happy expression.

"How was the drive?" I ask.

"Great," Faye replies. Moving her attention to the cops, her eyes light up. "Detective Walters, Agent Perez!" She smiles at them both.

"Hello ladies." Perez welcomes them, Walters following with a curt nod. I listen as they discuss, once again, the events of Friday night. They're thorough, I'll give them that much. They haven't missed a beat and double back a few times to confirm certain points.

"What I don't understand is how my sister got mixed up in your investigation?" I step forward, voicing the question that has been plaguing me since Friday night.

Walters looks uncomfortable, but meets my eyes, his expression unwavering. "Unfortunately, the show's coverage of Rose's murder drew unwanted attention. An individual called the show who is now a person of interest in the investigation."

"Oh, so we brought this on ourselves? If that's not victim blaming, I don't know what is!" Savannah huffs back.

"This is the problem with the media: they all want to 'be in' with police investigations to get the scoop, when they just interfere! We have protocols to prevent the public becoming mixed up in an investigation. *You* pushed for information and found yourselves on the receiving end of unwanted attention." Walters thumbs to himself and Agent Perez. "*We* are here to help." He keeps his tone cool.

"Hold up here! Why didn't you tell me someone threatened you!" I'm furious with Faye.

"I—" she begins.

"*I* was threatened, not Faye. And don't you go blaming us either," Savannah cuts in again.

"OK, simmer down," Walters's drones out. I round on him, close to boiling.

"*Who*, exactly, pushed for information?" I ask, although I have a guess.

Silence . My eyes find Savannah, who blushes under my gaze. I turn to Faye.

"I knew it was a bad idea for you to be doing that true crime stuff!"

"In case you missed it, your sister is a grown woman!" Savannah's second interruption fuels my irritation toward her.

"Does that ease your conscience? You're the one pushing all this true crime shit and now look what's happening," I snap.

"Oh yeah, jump on the bandwagon, blame the victims!" She spits.

"Bullshit, Savannah. You started this fire and now it's getting out of control!"

"Let's all settle down—" Agent Perez begins, but Savannah and I both turn on her.

"No!" we spit in unison, before facing each other again. With only Faye between us, we go at it.

"We were doing our job!" she growls.

"I'm doing mine. She's my sister. Family. You might not care much about that, but we do!"

"Luke!" It's Faye's turn to be mad. "Don't blame Savannah. This is nobody's fault!"

Looking around the kitchen island, she addresses everyone. "Detective Walters, Agent Perez. You both should be off solving

Rose's murder. If anything, else strange happens, we will contact you immediately."

"And as for you." She pokes my chest. "You have no right to speak to Savannah like that, ever! When she is in *our* home, she will be treated like family. *Flesh and blood*, do you hear me?"

Faye rarely gets this mad at me, but when she does, I'm usually at fault.

"I'm sorry, Savannah," I mumble.

"It's fine." She drops her chin, her voice breaking over her words.

"We should go." Agent Perez's soft voice interrupts. "Faye?" She waits for Faye to turn toward her. "I hope that I'm wrong, and I don't mean to frighten you. If the incident from Friday night is connected to Rose's case, and I believe that it could be, then you need to be aware of your surroundings at all times."

"If you need us, call my cell. Anytime of the day or night," Walters cuts in. Perez continues.

"If it is the same man, he will likely be a white man in his mid- to late thirties. He will be charming; to all appearances just a normal man. His aim will be to get you alone, so if you come across anyone who tries to lure or take you from the location you're in, call for help. He will be strong too. I'm telling you this, so you know what to look out for." She signals to Walters that it's time to go. We follow them as far as the porch, then watch as they get into the car.

"Wait—" Faye calls after them. "What do I do if he succeeds?" The fear in her voice stops my heart.

He won't succeed! I offer the silent promise.

"As much as you can, do whatever he wants. Try to avoid upsetting him or making him angry. Get through it as best you can, and don't lose hope." Perez walks back to Faye, resting her delicate hand over her shaking fingers. "*If* he succeeds, remember, so will we. We will find you."

Faye nods, but the ominous conversation has unsettled us all. As they drive off, we go back inside. When the front door clicks, both girls ignore me. I don't miss the emotion in Savannah's voice or eyes when she reaches for her bag.

"I need to get home. You good?"

"Yeah, go. I'm going to run a hot bath and chill out for the day. Are you OK?" She pulls Savannah into a hug. Faye's disappointed eyes meet mine over her shoulder, further needling at the guilt I'm feeling for upsetting her.

"I'm good. Just a little tired," she promises before heading for the door. I hold my hand up to Faye when she moves to walk her outside.

"Savannah, I—"

She whirls on me when we step out onto the porch.

"I know you're worried about her, OK? But I am too." A single tear falls down her cheek. With the power of a thousand waves, it crushes my earlier anger. Wiping it away, she moves to her car.

I take a long shaky breath. "I know."

CHAPTER 12

FAYE

We decided to meet at the station's parking lot. Light snow patters against my face as I round the front of my truck, meeting Scott at the front of his sedan.

Facing each other, we remain silent until the nervous energy between us makes us laugh.

"So, should we go in your car?" I ask.

"Actually, let's walk." He offers me his elbow.

"Well, I did wear comfortable shoes, like you suggested," I pick up one foot, wiggling my winter boot before grabbing hold of his wing.

"Very sexy." He laughs. "OK, let's go." His long legs already striding out of the lot.

"Oh, we're taking this to the outside world, are we?" I tease. I was a little worried that he planned on circling the building.

"I considered taking you to the staff lounge but decided against it," he deadpans.

"Glad to hear it. As much as I love stale coffee and stained tables, I was hoping to broaden our horizons."

"I think you'll like this walk." His eyes, full of confidence, sparkle under the Christmas lights lining the streets.

"The lights are so pretty," I sigh as we cross the intersection toward Lambeau Field. Home to the Green Bay Packers, the stadium is the largest in Wisconsin, and famous for the "cheese head" supporters.

"The Packers have opened their gates to the public. I thought we could check it out." Scott takes us on to the grounds of the stadium.

"Oh, OK, but you should be warned, I'm not a big football fan. Don't be offended if I don't offer much in the way of conversation on the topic." I can't hide my reluctance. My fantasies of romance and Christmas lights burst as we near the entrance.

"Well, I'm a huge Packers fan, but for the next few weeks, they've turned their parking lot into a skating rink and Christmas market." We round a corner and see a pathway of brightly lit Christmas arches. The warm yellow lights and decorated pine trees restore my faith in our date.

"Oh, wow! It's so pretty!" Giddy now, I wrap both arms around his elbow, squeezing tightly as we walk through the arches. I'm looking everywhere at once, committing it to memory.

"You're happy?"

"I love it! Can we skate?"

"How well can you penguin?" His lips spread again in amusement.

"Is doing 'the penguin' a thing?"

"No, but they don't slip on the ice because they waddle. I'm wondering how well you waddle."

"I could try." Dropping his arm, I angle my feet outwards on both sides and with my arms at my side, I waddle. Three steps in, filled with humor and embarrassment, I burst out laughing. Scott joins in, his own laughter bolstering mine until both of our eyes blur.

"Let's get a hot drink to warm you up first. The tip of your nose is red ..." Dipping his head, he rubs his nose gently against mine before his lips, soft and pink, press against mine. "That's an Eskimo kiss," he whispers. "I couldn't resist, you look so cute."

My heart oozes affection for him.

"I could say the same thing about you." I nibble at the corner of my bottom lip, hesitant for just a moment, before I rise up on my toes to return the chaste kiss. He grins. Then, grabbing my hand, he pulls me toward the first market stand.

"I'll take a hat with a pompom, and a scarf." He hands over twenty dollars and pops the green and yellow striped hat on my head. His lithe fingers fiddle with the pompom before wrapping the scarf loosely around my neck.

"Oh yes, this is doing it for me." He chuckles. "Come on, let's get that hot chocolate." And he's moving again.

We walk the market, sipping hot chocolates and sampling from different food stalls before entering a big, heated tent selling Christmas ornaments. I leave Scott's side, heading to the first stall, where a lady is painting ornaments at her booth.

"Wow, these are wonderful!" I scan her table, awed by the glitter and gold decorations in all shapes and sizes before moving to a tree of ornaments. "Scott, look at these," I call just as he sidles up next to me. Lifting an ornament into my hand, I'm enthralled by the intricate design.

"Is that Lambeau Field?" I look over my shoulder to find the artist joining us at the tree.

"Yes, I made that one especially for this event: no two ornaments are the same!" Her warm smile, revealing slightly crooked teeth, lifts her chubby cheeks and deepens the creases at the corner of her eyes. I admire her style. Long, wiry gray hair in a messy bun on top of her head is wrapped in a pink silk scarf that floats down her neck, resting over her shoulder. There's kindness in her smile and youth in her eyes.

"It's like a snow globe ..." I look through the clear bauble to the delicate scene inside. Two skaters embrace on a tiny ice rink with a miniature model of Lambeau Field behind them. The base of the globe is covered in snow, with tiny Christmas trees filling the rest of the small space. The artist managing to freeze this moment in time perfectly. I break away from the scene and look back at the lady.

"It's so lightweight!"

"It's blown plastic and the pieces inside are polystyrene," she informs me as I hang it back on the tree.

"Can you hold onto it for us?" Scott asks, "we're just about to go skating; can we pick it up after?" His smile brings out his dimple again.

"Of course! You kids go on ahead." She reaches for the bauble, taking it from the tree and placing it behind her stall. No woman is immune to a dimpled man.

"Thank you!" I beam, as Scott gathers me under his arm again, walking us to the ice rink.

We skate together for over an hour, both of us wet and gasping as we pick ourselves up from yet another fall. On the ice, Scott has two left feet. His weight pulls me down every time his skates go out from under him. However, there are worse things in life than landing on Scott's body, so I relish every fall. We make our way to the edge of the rink, using the barrier to propel ourselves toward the exit. My feet are sore, and I need to rest a little.

"That was so much fun!"

"It's been years since I've skated, I'm a little rusty," he explains.

"I noticed!" I laugh, nudging him playfully when he lands next to me on the bench.

Bending, we untie our skates and switch back into our own boots. "I might have a few bruises tomorrow but I'm glad you enjoyed it. Are you hungry? I'll take that as a yes," Scott says when my stomach rumbles my reply.

We return the skates before walking back to the stall to collect our bauble. This has already been the best date I've ever been on, and the night is still young.

"Don't even try it, Anderson, it's an early Christmas gift." Scott gently pushes my purse aside when we arrive at the stall. He reaches into his back pocket for his wallet, lifting his coat as he does and revealing his cute ass. I bite my lip to stop myself from smiling.

"Are you staring at my butt?" he laughs, shaking his head in mock disappointment.

"Well, if you're going to flaunt it all over the place."

"Oh, I'm flaunting, am I? I'll have to rein myself in next time." We continue to tease until our designer friend finishes up with another customer.

"You two again! Back for more baubles?" she asks eagerly.

"Thank you, but we just want to get the one you set aside for us," I remind her.

"I gave it to your friend." Seeing our confusion, she clarifies. "Tall guy, blue eyes?" She looks back and forth between us expectantly.

"We came alone. Maybe it was another client?" Scott prompts her gently.

"No, he came over just a minute or so after you left. Said he wanted to surprise you both with it ..." Realizing that we have no idea who bought the bauble, her mouth drops open in dismay. "Oh my! Oh, I am so sorry. He must have wanted the same piece and lied to me."

I'm disappointed but I feel for her. She looks upset.

"Please, don't worry about it! You're very talented and obviously in demand."

"I have another, similar piece at my workshop. I'll bring it with me tomorrow evening."

"Unfortunately, we work nights, so we won't make it back, do you have a card, or a website?" Scott asks.

"Yes, yes ..." She fumbles in her apron pocket, pulling out a white business card. *Kitty Harmon Designs* is written in a pink script font across the front. "I'm sorry, again. My email is on the back. Make sure to let me know who you are, and I'll mail you any design at no extra charge."

"We'll find something just as magical on your site, I'm sure," I promise her. I fully intend to find a bauble similar to the one she sold.

Breathless and wet, we tumble into Scott's apartment. Facing each other inside the doorway our eyes meet. The zing of electricity is palpable. In a heartbeat, Scott's fingers curl around the nape of my neck and in one smooth movement, he draws my lips to his. My hands slide under his wet coat, pushing it away. Stumbling forward we fumble over each other, our lips still locked.

"Come here." Scott's voice is low and seductive. His hands drop to the curve of my ass, lifting me from the floor and into his arms. I wrap my legs around his waist as he walks us to his bedroom.

"Let's leave the curtains open," I whisper when he reaches for the light switch. The moonlight casts a romantic glow in his bedroom. It's enough to see the hunger in his eyes. I can't believe we've resisted this moment as long as we have.

"Yes, boss!" The deep timbre of his voice sends me plunging forward, grinding against him as my mouth, hot and fast demands more.

"Holy fuck ..." Pulling away, he drops me next to his bed, his hands already helping me undress. I smile at his urgency, falling back on the bed as he pulls at my damp jeans. We both laugh when they refuse to come away at my ankles. With one strong tug, he frees my legs and slides between them, capturing my mouth again.

"Scott!" His name passes my lips on a breathless plea. I burn for more, there can never be enough. His body, fitting perfectly to mine, rolls, his hips grinding against my core, the temperature rising with each thrust. I grapple for his jeans, desperate to feel his flesh. Aroused further when his teeth nibble on my chin, the scrape of his five o'clock shadow against my neck releases another moan.

"Faye ..." His stare could melt all the snow in Wisconsin. When he rids himself of his clothes, my eyes round with pleasure and surprise.

"Oh," I purr, greedily devouring him with my eyes. In this moment, there is nothing soft about Scott. He is hard lines of steel and sex. "Jesus, you're perfect!"

His mouth crushes mine, capturing the tail end of my whimper. My fingernails are moving through his hair, a maddening urge to feel him pressed against me again ricochets around my body. My hands find his ass, and I pull him flush against me.

Consumed by his taste, his scent, the feel of his hot, damp skin against my own sends a new tremor through me, building faster than ever before. I quiver beneath him as he positions himself, then sinks into me. Warm and wanting, I take him. My legs wrap around him as he thrusts forward, my back arching with pleasure. His arms snake around me, his hot tongue circling my nipples.

"Oh God ..." I cry out, my nails digging into his shoulders. The pressure is building, layer by layer. I feel him everywhere; in the quickening of my pulse, the heat flooding to my core as his tongue trails across my breasts.

"Scott ...! I'm going to ..." My insides vibrate.

"Look at me." He slows down, the moonlight reflecting in the deep hue of his eyes. The tenderness they hold is almost unbearable, connecting us on a level I've never experienced before. His confident control continues as he gathers me in his arms, one hand at the small of my back, the other losing itself in my hair. He thrusts deeper, faster than before. Our bodies move in sync. Heat centers inside me, pooling around him, my body gripping him tightly. Desperate, we are a flurry of teeth, tongues and pounding flesh, as our bodies pulsate and release together.

Trembling, he collapses against my chest, his damp hair tickling my neck. Every muscle in my body is limp from pleasure.

"Wow." His warm breath fans over my slick skin, causing me to shudder.

"That was …" Dazed, my mind struggles to form complete sentences.

"Yeah, it was." His weight shifts, his eyes still dark with desire as he rolls over, taking me with him. Straddling him now, I lean back. My hips turn and grind slowly against him. Cupping my cheek, Scott sits up to kiss me.

"You are amazing," he whispers.

We take our time and with slow and steady movements we climb to another intense climax.

CHAPTER 13

JEFFREY

The floor creaks under my feet as I make my way down the hallway to the living room. The distinct smell of wood lingers in the air. The tips of my gloved fingers graze the yellow pine as I go. The narrow hallway widens into a large open living area. The gabled roof is lined with rugged-hewn beams, adding to its charm. Chopped logs sit next to a granite fireplace, the remains of last night's blaze still lying in the grate. The faint smell of firewood clings to the fresh air that blew through the open back door. Two oversized leather sofas face each other next to the fireplace. My eyes are drawn to the coffee table centered on the cream rug between the sofas. Stepping further into the room, I pick up a used mug. Pink lipstick marks the rim, the last few drops of last night's hot chocolate dried at the bottom of her cup. Sinking onto the sofa, I imagine her here, just a few hours ago. Her feet tucked under the gray throw next to me, her face flushed from the heat of the fire. Her eyes admiring the large Christmas tree in the corner while she sips her drink.

Approaching headlights coming down the drive cut my musings short, bringing me back to the present. In a few minutes, she will turn on the tree lights and light the fire, sip another hot drink and breathe life into this room again. Voices from outside draw me to the window. I watch her step out of her old truck, boots sinking into the fresh blanket of snow. Unable to drag myself away, I watch a man come around the other side of the truck, his greedy eyes and hands on her.

"Wow, you live here?" I hear him say, before his hungry mouth finds her lips.

The sweet sound of her laughter needles me. A combination of urgency and rage flow through me. I hear a small snapping noise and look at the cup in my hand. I've broken the handle off. This man is another distraction, although it's clear now that the axe-wielding man who chased me must be family. *A brother, maybe?* That he lives here is certain. His routine has been easier to track than Faye's. Frustration burns again. Faye's life is a lot more complicated than I expected. Her work, her brother, her friend, her interview with Detective Walters, and now this new lover. I watched them on their excursion to the market. Seeing her leaving in his car last night was the final straw. There is too much interference. *He can't have her!* Time is running out for their affair.

As they step toward the cabin, I move back into the dark hallway. Pain shoots through my hip as I run into the corner of an ill-placed table. The sound of turning keys pushes me back through the kitchen. I drop the broken mug on the counter and am out the back door.

"Luke must have forgotten to set the alarm," she says as the lights come on. Ducking under the window, I hear them move around in the kitchen. Laughter fills the room as I quietly reinsert the battery pack into the alarm panel. Their security system is diabolical. Rushing back through the forest, I'm thankful for the heavy snow. My footprints will be covered in minutes.

FAYE

Scott comes up behind me, his hot lips on my neck, as I pick up my favorite mug, broken in two pieces on my kitchen island.

"I could kill Luke," I grumble, as Scott turns me in his arms.

It's so unlike Luke to leave the place in such a mess. The floors are wet. He broke our cardinal house rule: no traipsing through the cabin in boots.

"I take it he broke your mug?" he grins.

"Not just that, the floors are slippery and the table in the hallway is out of place. He's a big child sometimes," I moan.

"Are you a clean freak, Anderson?" His smile deepens, dimples popping as his gray eyes run over my face.

"No!" I protest. "He's just a big oaf. This is my favorite mug!" I pout.

"I'll buy you a new one." His lips find mine, their gentle caress replacing my disappointment with desire before his stubbled jaw dips to my neck. The tingling sensation tickles dreadfully.

"Scott!" My joyful yelp only spurs him on as he continues to torture me.

"Do you want to see my room?" I gasp out through my laughter. My question works and he pulls back.

"Is Luke due home soon?" his serious expression has me laughing again.

"I told him I was cooking supper for us, so he's gone to visit a friend. Could be gone all night ..." I lean into him, my teeth gently nibbling his bottom lip. My hand slowly travels south in time to feel him grow hard beneath the rough material of his jeans.

"Lead the way," he grunts in pleasure, his fingers combing through my hair, his tongue hot and hungry as he devours me.

LUKE

I got the call first thing this morning. I'm needed on site in Oregon within the next week. I'll be gone for at least a month. My gut turns, thinking about Faye alone for a whole month. I've never doubted her safety before, but now I can't shake the feeling that someone is watching her. Us. The cabin. Moving out onto the porch to get a better signal, I pull the phone from my ear and check the time. I've been on hold for sixteen minutes now.

Needing to move, I walk around the side of the cabin, my eyes scanning the ground as I go. Still holding the line, my attention moves to the alarm panel under the kitchen window. My eyes widen as a footprint, directly beneath the sill, comes into view. My heartrate increasing with each step, I duck down to examine it more closely. There's a boot print in the snow. It's the only one around—the projecting windowsill must have prevented last night's snowfall from filling it in. I jump up, my eyes searching the treeline beyond the clearing.

"Stone Security. How can I help you today?" A bored male voice finally picks up my call.

"I'm here. I need to speak with someone about moving up my installation date." I hurry, calling out my details, still looking into the woods.

"Mr. Anderson, yes. I see your order here. Unfortunately, our specialist security engineers are booked through until next Tuesday. However, we do have a team of electricians, who could begin the rewiring on the property. Would that be of any help?" The line crackles, my coverage waning. My eyes are still laser-focused on the trees as I move toward them.

"Book me in for tomorrow. What time can I expect them?" I sigh, frustrated by the lack of signal and fear of the call dropping before the appointment is made.

"Between eight a.m. and noon tomorrow. They will need access to the front and back doors of the house, including any loft or basement spaces within the property. The security engineer will see to the implementation of advanced sensors and cameras and set you up for cell phone updates, allowing you to monitor the property on your cell from anywhere in the world." His sales pitch is delivered in a chirpy voice. I should be grateful that they're speeding up the process for me, but every fiber of my being is screaming for me to pack Faye up and take her with me.

"Great, thank you." I hang up the call and continue beyond the tree line.

FAYE

"No, of course not. We were inside the entire time."

Luke is on the phone. We are in the middle of our show. An ad break was playing when he called. Savannah lifts her head, her eyes narrowing in concentration as she listens to my end of the conversation.

"I don't like this, Faye. Somebody has definitely been on the property. There are footprints along the treeline. I'm waiting for Detective Walters to get here now."

My hands shake, my blood runs cold.

"Could it have been hunters?" My frazzled mind is desperate to come up with another explanation.

"Unlikely. Did you notice anything strange last night? Hear anything outside?"

"No, other than the mess you left," I huff.

"What mess?"

"You broke my favorite mug, for one, and knocked the hall table out of place again. Not to mention the wet footprints all through the house. I had to mop up—" My mouth dries as the words pass my lips. Instinctively, I stand up out of my chair, my heart jackhammering in my chest.

"Oh God ..." My hand comes to my mouth, realization dawning. I was so wrapped up in Scott visiting, I didn't even consider that someone else might have been in the cabin.

"Faye," Luke begins.

"Don't say it," I cut in, not wanting to hear him confirm my fears. My eyes dart to Savannah who has risen from her chair, to Scott who's staring at me from the control room.

"What's going on?" Savannah demands.

"Faye, I didn't make that mess," Luke's voice is low, and dead serious.

"Luke, I'm afraid." Swallowing back the lump in my throat, I try to regain some composure. Savannah's at my side, with Scott coming into the recording studio. Adele's "Love in the Dark" filters through the discarded headphones. We have only minutes before we're back on air.

"Let me talk to him," Savannah gently urges me. I pass her my cell as Scott takes my hand.

"Luke, it's Savannah. What's going on?"

I turn to Scott, filling him in.

"Jesus. We need to phone the police." He's already reaching into his back pocket for his cell.

"OK. We gotta go. We're back on-air in a sec." Savannah hands the phone back to me.

"Luke, I'll call you when the show is done," I assure him before hanging up. The end of Adele's song has me reaching for my headphones. Savannah's already back in her seat.

"Scott: Call Detective Walters. Keep trying until you get through," she calls to him, before getting back on-air. "Welcome back to the late show with Faye and Savannah! That was "Love in the Dark," by the soulful Adele."

I'm grateful for her ability to remain calm.

Scott nods in her direction, his eyes sending me a *don't worry* glance before he quietly exits the studio. The rest of the show passes by in a haze of Christmas chatter, songs and light-hearted conversations. I do a terrible job of sounding upbeat. I'm so grateful to have such a professional co-host.

"I'm so sorry, Savannah. I've left you carrying the show. Again." I'm sniffling after we finally say goodnight to our listeners. Relief washes over me that the show is over. I can properly focus on the new developments.

"Detective Walters and Luke are both here," Scott pokes his head in the door, the others coming in behind him.

The detective addresses me directly. "I've just left your property. Luke showed me the footprint. He says you found some items out of place when you arrived home yesterday?" Fatigue is evident in his tone. He takes a notepad and pen out of his pocket. "Tell me everything you can remember."

I relate everything to him, including that Scott was with me. Our relationship is so new, I'm terrified it will be too much for Scott to deal with.

"Is there anywhere you can stay, while Luke is away?"

"No need, I'm going to cancel the job."

"Faye will be staying with me," Savannah steps forward and wraps her arm protectively around my shoulder. "How about some police protection?"

My head spins as everyone in the room starts talking at once. Scott's telling Savannah that if I stay anywhere, it will be with him. Luke's telling them both not to bother arguing, since he's staying put in Wisconsin. Savannah's growling at them both, protesting that she is more than capable of managing the task. Detective Walters simply rubs his tired eyes in frustration.

"Can you all just stop?" I massage my aching temples. "Luke, you need this job, you're going. Savannah, I appreciate the offer, but you've only got one bed and I don't want to put you at risk too." She opens her mouth to argue with me, but I push on, my eyes falling to Scott.

"If it's OK, could I stay with you for a few days?"

"You can stay as long as you like."

"And, Detective," I say, with a sigh. "Anything you can do to help ensure my safety would be appreciated."

Smiling, he offers a small nod. "We will do everything in our power to prevent you from coming to any harm," he promises.

"Are you saying then, Detective, that this is the same guy? We need to know what we're up against." Savannah presses him again, and I can see his patience beginning to wear thin.

"I'm saying," he says through gritted teeth, flashing her a warning look, "we are working around the clock to catch Rose's killer. I can't ignore a possible connection to the case. Which is why—" his eyes find mine again, softening—"I would suggest you take extra precautions while traveling in your car. I will organize some extra patrols around the radio station. You have my direct line. I will be available to you any time of the day. So, call."

"I will."

Detective Walters leaves and with him goes my confidence. There is an undeniable strength about him, a determination in his eyes that reassures me. He is closing in on Rose's killer, and potentially my stalker, too. I'm comforted by the fact that he is on the case. I look around the studio of worried faces before me and smile. All three blink in surprise.

"I've never felt so loved," I tell them.

"Let's get you home," Luke says, wrapping his arm around my shoulder.

CHAPTER 14

DETECTIVE JOHN WALTERS

Two weeks have passed since the vigil, and six days since Agent Perez was called out of state on another assignment. The investigation has been making headway. I traveled to Chicago to interview Katherine Clifford's friends and family. We're working on a timeline of her activities while she was here in Wisconsin. We're doing our best to cross-reference that information with Rose's routine, but so far, we haven't found a link. The answer will be there, we just need to keep digging. Thankfully, nothing else strange has happened with regard to Faye Anderson, but my concerns for her haven't abated.

"John, Brown County is pulling the twenty-four-hour surveillance on Faye Anderson." It's rare that I get a summons from the chief sheriff. I should have known there was something wrong.

"Now hold on a minute—" I lean forward in my chair, glaring across the desk into the hard stare of the chief.

"Look, I was on the line with Brown County. They're short-staffed and can't spare any men."

Faye's protection is within their jurisdiction, so it's out of my hands.

"We have a potential third victim here, and you want to remove her police protection?"

"No, John, but I can't dictate how they run their station! They've already stretched themselves thin to help out here. They'll have a car patrolling the radio station, and I have a task force working around the clock to catch this guy. The media are hounding me, and I have the mayor's office breathing down my neck." She sighs, relaxing back into her black leather chair.

"It's all necessary."

"That may be, John, but look around. We're all overworked, trying to cover all bases. I can't justify keeping a man on her at all times. How can I expect Brown County to? When does it end?"

"When he's long gone," I growl.

"The decision is final. They'll sign off on another week of patrolling the radio station," she warns.

"This guy is dangerous!"

"John, we have hundreds of dangerous criminals walking the streets right now. Every single one of them has the potential to cause harm to one of our citizens. We see muggings, carjackings, and armed robberies, every day of the week. I can't abandon those responsibilities. It's your job to find Rose and Katherine's killer. It's my job to lead this unit in serving this community and to look out for the well-being of everyone who works here."

I like the chief. I've always found her to be fair and reasonable in her decision-making. She rarely interferes in my investigations. I listen to her point of view, and I see the regret in her eyes. These murders have weighed heavily on this department.

I sigh. "When will they be removed from twenty-four-hour protection?"

She glances at her watch. "The current shift is due to finish at eight p.m. There's no more after that."

"Just like that." I shake my head, standing to leave." I hope you're right about this, Chief."

She calls after me. "Oh, and John? You look like shit: go home and get some sleep."

I don't turn back. Instead, I head straight to my office. I call Faye's cell, but it goes to voicemail. She must be in the studio. I leave a message informing her that the police protection has been lifted.

JEFFREY

The police have been everywhere: at the radio station, the cabin, and patrolling her lover's apartment. I couldn't get close to her. Until today. All morning, I've watched her and Savannah Christmas shopping. Arms linked, heads falling back in laughter as they move throughout the mall. Nothing, not the Christmas music filtering through speakers, or the holiday cheer all around, not even seeing her now can replace the frustration of *their* interference. The need for connection draws me closer to where she queues for coffee, close enough to inhale her feminine scent. It compels me to reach out until my lightly fingers lightly graze the ends of her silky hair.

I need more.

Walking straight to the carpark, I sit, waiting, watching as they exit the mall and climb into her truck. I expect them to turn towards Green Bay radio station but instead the truck heads towards the motorway. My pulse picks up its pace first, then my car as I push down hard on the gas.

She's going home!

A plan forms in my mind. Overtaking the truck is the first step, getting there before them is the second. The increased speed feels good, a heady mixture of danger and excitement. Faye is never alone. There is always some irritating complication trespassing on our lives.

It's now or never.

I glance at the clock, time is not on my side. Their show airs in just a few hours, which means they won't be staying long. I double down on my speed and find a layby not far from the cabin. I have everything I need in the trunk. Once I neutralize Savannah, Faye will be free. They're all working to keep us apart. The thrill of knowing they've failed spikes my adrenaline as I rush through the clearing, reaching the back porch just as her truck pulls up the drive.

FAYE

The drive has Savannah snoozing beside me. Pulling into the drive, I nudge her.

"Wakey, wakey."

Her eyes peel open "Shit. Sorry," she murmurs.

"I'll just run in and get a few things,"

"No way are you leaving me out here on my own."

She jumps out of the truck with me, we link arms and scamper through the snow toward the cabin. We have two hours before our show starts. We're running behind.

As I'm turning the key, my cell phone rings. I look at the caller ID to see Luke's name flashing on the screen. He's been checking in every few hours since leaving for Oregon.

"It's Luke," I tell Savannah, pushing open the door and letting her head in first. The *beep, beep, beep* of our new alarm system has me running to the keypad as I answer the call.

"Hey, great timing! What's the alarm code again?"

"Why are you at the cabin? Your police detail has been pulled!" His angry tone is loud enough through the receiver for the whole of Wisconsin to hear. Savannah rolls her eyes.

"I'm grabbing some clothes."

"No need. I've decided I'm coming home. My flight is booked for tomorrow."

"I'll make us coffee for the drive back," Savannah whispers, heading to the kitchen.

"You don't have to come home. Luke, what's the code?" I ask again.

"Zero, nine, eight, two, three," he reads out. "Hey, who's at the back door?" he asks, as I punch in the code. A shuffling sound comes from the kitchen, distracting me as I press enter.

"Hmm? Savannah must have ..." I look over my shoulder into the darkness, suddenly aware that she hasn't switched on any lights.

"Savannah?" I call into the silent cabin, my feet glued to the floor.

"What the fuck is going on?!" Luke's gruff voice only manages to scare me even further.

"Savannah!" I call out again, this time taking one small step in the direction of the kitchen. "This isn't funny."

Savannah wouldn't play tricks like this.

Maybe she can't hear me?

"Savannah?"

Dead silence. My heart pounds in my ears until Luke's firm and insistent voice begs me to listen.

"Faye: listen to me. You need to get out of there."

"Luke," I whimper in a hushed tone.

"FAYE. Get out of the house!" he snaps. "Pete, call this number ..." His directions to someone with him are a blur as I step closer to the kitchen. My eyes are fixed on the open door, the darkness sucking me closer.

"SAVANNAH!!" my voice trembles ",She's not answering me, Luke."

"Faye, I'm calling for help on another line. Listen to me. You need to leave. Please. Leave!" his voice breaks and tears stream down my face now.

"I can't leave her, Luke."

"Faye! Don't—"

"I love you..."

"Faye, NO!"

I take the phone from my ear, but I don't hang up as I reach for the light switch. I'm too afraid to face whatever's waiting in the dark. Fear for my own safety is immediately forgotten when I see Savannah lying on the floor. I rush to her.

"Oh my God. Luke, she's hurt!" I'm lifting the phone to my ear when it's violently swiped from my hand. Suddenly I'm fighting, flailing against strong arms that have wrapped around me.

He's so strong.

A strong metallic taste burns my mouth and nose, making my eyes blur. Overcome by a sense of powerlessness, my limbs grow heavy. Choking on the heavy fumes, I lose consciousness.

LUKE

I hear heavy breathing over the line.

"Faye!!" I'm frantic. I could hear her struggle. Hear the silence as her muffled screams grew fainter. Tears sting my eyes. I've failed her.

"Who is this?" I plead. More heavy breathing, before the line goes dead.

"Detective, tell me you have a car close by," I lift my buddy Pete's phone to my ear. Detective Walters picked up his call, just as Faye entered the kitchen.

"Please tell me she left the cabin," he barks.

"He has them."

"Them?"

"Savannah was there too," I inform him. Pete and I running for his truck.

"Luke, can you log in to the home security footage?" he asks.

"I'm trying!" I bark, pulling up the camera feed. I watch in horror as a man, dressed head to toe in black, carries my sister's unresisting body to her truck.

"He's putting her in the truck. Where are the cops?" Pete drives, kicking up dirt as we speed out of the site. I need to get to the airport.

"Listen to me. What is he doing? Tell me everything as it happens, Luke. I'm in my car, I'm heading there now. I need you to tell me which direction he takes at the end of the drive," he orders.

"He's leaving, without Savannah. Why?" My brain struggles to piece together what is happening before my very eyes.

"Which way is he turning?" Detective Walters repeats.

"Right."

Holding onto the dashboard as we bounce over potholes, I freeze. I'm watching my sister's kidnapping in real-time. I listened, unable to help either of them as Faye fought for her life, and now he's leaving Savannah behind. The possible reason for that is too terrible to even contemplate.

"Why did he leave Savannah?" I ask again.

"She was never part of the plan. We have an ambulance on the way, they're five minutes out, Luke." His reassurance does nothing to ease my fears.

"Is she ... dead?"

He pauses and that second of silence is the only answer I need. "We don't know that," he reasons, trying to pull it back.

"I'm on my way home. You had better find him before I do." I hang up Pete's phone, letting it fall into the middle console. In three clicks, I download the footage from the security cameras and forward them to Detective Walters. He needs all the help I can give him.

DETECTIVE JOHN WALTERS

In her profile, Agent Perez called him a predator. Watching him on-screen, dressed from head to toe in black and moving with the speed of a panther into the cabin, there is no other way to describe him. The ladies came in the front door only seconds after he entered through the back door. The sensors picked him up, but Faye inputting the alarm code erased the alert to the security company. He got lucky, but he's made his biggest mistakes yet. I phoned Perez as soon as I hung up with Luke. She's on her way back to Wisconsin.

The narrow entrance of the driveway is sealed off. An officer lifts the crime scene tape for me to drive under. Flashing blue and red lights illuminate the cabin and the surrounding forest. The bright colors intrude on this seemingly idyllic setting.

Two officers stand guarding the main entrance. "Detective Walters, Outagamie County SD." I flash my badge, then take a moment to don latex gloves and plastic foot coverings.

They step aside to let me through. I look around, observing the scene. Two purses are on the floor, just inside the door. I assume they belong to Savannah and Faye. My eyes shift to the alarm panel. The white cover is still open, the blue LED blinking at me.

I scan the living area before moving toward the kitchen. The back door is open. Just inside, a dark pool of blood stains the wooden floor. The paramedics stabilized Savannah at the scene before moving her to hospital. Other than the strewn medical remnants and Faye's phone across the floor, there is nothing to suggest there was much of a struggle. This was child's play to him. I head back outside.

"I'll need everyone to step off the porch. This is an active crime scene," I call out. Jones arrives just then.

"We found the truck."

I had a feeling we would find it abandoned close by.

"OK, let's go." I'm already moving back to my car. There's nothing more I can learn from this scene. Forensics will be here soon.

"I want Savannah Phillips under police protection at the hospital," I direct Jones, who makes the call.

Starting the engine, I turn to him again. "When you're done with that call, phone Luke Anderson and advise him to meet us at St. Mark's hospital when he arrives back in Wisconsin."

The killer has changed his MO. Breaking into his victim's home is new. Faye wasn't even supposed to be here, and Savannah was never part of his plan. This was spur of the moment: he's escalating. It's only been four weeks since Rose's body was found. He's beginning to unravel, and I need to catch him before he kills again.

We find Faye's truck parked at a rest stop two miles from the cabin. Directing Jones to stay behind me, we circle it.

Looking through the windows, I confirm it's empty.

"Tire tracks." Jones points to an area of disturbed snow at the edge of the rest stop. "They're smaller than the tires on the pickup. He drove her here and transferred her to his car." He hunkers down to get a closer look. The road is plowed so we won't get any more tracks than this.

"He went this direction." I point toward Pensaukee. Beyond that, there are only miles upon miles of forest.

We both turn to the arriving squad car. We help the officer seal off a perimeter around Faye's truck, waiting until the crime scene photographer arrives before heading back to Green Bay. Forensics will finish up here, then the truck will be impounded. We're halfway to the station when a text comes in from Agent Perez. I pass my phone to Jones so he can read it to me while I continue.

Just landed. Meet you at the station.

I dictate my reply.

Meeting Luke Anderson at the hospital. Will pick you up outside the station in thirty minutes.

CHAPTER 15

FAYE

My throat burns. My head throbs as I try to lift it from the pillow. My vision is blurred, and I strain to take in my surroundings as that metallic taste sends a flood of panic throughout my body. I twist and turn on a bed, fighting for freedom. My bound wrists and ankles begin to burn. My heart is pounding and there is a ringing in my ears. The memory hits me hard. Savannah. She was on the floor, bleeding. I ran to her. I remember his strength, how easily he picked me up, how easily I was overcome. Shaking my head to dispel the memory brings a new flashback. I woke up, briefly, dizzy and nauseated, inside a strange car. I remember reaching for the door handle, then a stranger's surprised cursing and the car coming to a sudden stop. He reached into the back seat, taking my head in both hands. I struggled weakly against the rag that covered my mouth again, before waking here. Tears sting my eyes as I try to focus. Sunlight streams through the window of the bedroom, the rays landing on a vanity at the end of the bed I lie on. A damp smell lingers in the air. Dust motes dance in the light and coat every surface. I don't remember arriving here. My hands tug on the binds tied to the wooden bedposts above me.

Tears sting my eyes again. The pressure in my chest is too heavy to bear. I can't contain the loud sob that rips free, filling this silent room with my terror.

The sound of floorboards creaking beyond the door bring a new wave of fear. I press my lips together, stifling my sobs to whimpers, my nose flaring with each shuddering breath as my head falls back on the pillow. Trembling, I listen to his footsteps. The hinges of the door groan as he enters. I turn my head away, my entire body tense as I try to control the shakes that rake through me.

"It's all right, Faye. You're safe here." Tears manage to seep between my tightly closed eyelids, pooling at the base of my neck and soaking my pillow.

His voice is smooth. "Open your eyes, Faye," he whispers, his fingers softly stroking the top of my clenched fist.

I shake my head. "No! I haven't seen you. You can let me go." The words wobble free from my tight lips.

"Open your eyes, Faye."

"Please release me," I plead. The mattress dips with his weight. I feel his breath on my neck as he leans closer. I twist away from him, my shoulders straining against the pull of the ties above my head.

"Open. Your. Eyes." he growls in my ear.

"Please! Just let me go!"

His fingers slide up my arm, his large hand cupping my fist.

"Let's try something else ..." His even tone has an eerie calmness to it. "We'll start with relaxing your hand. Open your hand, Faye."

Warning bells ring in my mind. Agent Perez's advice filters through the fear: *do whatever he wants. Try to avoid upsetting him or making him angry*. I'm on my own here. Surviving this until help arrives feels like an impossible task, but I have to try. My fingers uncurl, slowly. I keep my body twisted away from him as he holds my hand still with one hand. The fingers of his free hand run along the inside of my thumb, slowly, then sweep up my index finger.

"Did you know that each finger is made up three bones called the phalanges?"

"No." I exhale sharply. I hadn't even realized I was holding my breath. His fingers continue their torturous journey, tracing each finger, pausing when he reaches my little finger.

"Even this little pinkie." He applies more pressure, until suddenly a sharp pain shoots through my hand. The definite snapping of bone is a violent disruption to the stillness, followed by a low guttural sound vibrating from him. His moan has my eyes flying open before my own scream of pain tears through the room. Instinctively, I arch my back and dig my heels in, trying to rise from the bed, escape my only thought, before my bound arms pull me back down with a thud against the hard mattress.

"Now you see me." His face hovers above me, a wide grin dripping in pleasure. He breathes heavily, a lock of dark hair falling into ice-blue eyes. A cold shudder runs down my body at the sight of him. The devil lingers above me. A burning ache runs from my pinkie to my wrist. I glance at my hand and see my finger twisted strangely. I can't move it.

"What do you want from me?" I sob. The image of Savannah on my kitchen floor reminds me that I need to be strong and find a way out of this mess.

"I want you to stop crying, Faye. You're safe." The back of his hand, the same hand that just snapped my finger like a toothpick, comes to my forehead. Pushing the wet hair from my face, he runs his hand gently down my cheek. Our eyes lock and there's a look of adoration in his eyes, scarier than his anger. *This guy is a psycho!*

"I'm going to prepare supper and then I'll be back, to help you get ready for practice." The mattress bounces back as he stands up. "I'm so happy you're here." His freaky smile sends another chill down my spine.

I hear the clicking of a door lock. Relief floods me as the creaking of floorboards fades down the hallway. My frazzled mind tries to contend with everything I know so far. One thing is abundantly clear. *I need to get the hell out of here!*

LUKE

Fear is too small a word to describe what I'm feeling. Trepidation, terror, complete hopelessness, and raging guilt all swell within me. By the time I reach the hospital in Wisconsin, I'm ready to explode.

The nurse's station refuses to give me any information on Savannah. My body rattles before I release some steam on a gruff demand to see her. I don't have time for this "family only" bullshit. She was with Faye, she's hurt, and she has no family here in Wisconsin. Right now, I tell the nurse, I'm the only family she's got. I don't see Walters and Perez until they're right next to me.

"Luke," Perez's sympathetic tone pulls my attention to her green eyes.

"They won't tell me anything about Savannah!"

"Savannah is OK. And we're going to find Faye."

"Dead or alive?" I pin Walters with a cold glare.

"Luke, you can't lose hope. Faye needs you to be strong." Perez reaches out as she steps forward, resting her small hand on my forearm. I jerk away. I need to keep moving: I need to speak with Savannah, I need to know what happened, and then I need to find the motherfucker who took her.

"Shouldn't you two be out there looking for her?!" I turn my back to them as my eyes start stinging.

"You're right." Walters speaks up. He sounds less sympathetic, but at least he admits they're wasting time. "We should be out there. But right now, we need to go over every single detail with you, and then we need to speak with Savannah."

My simmering rage boils over. "None of this would have happened if you hadn't pulled her police protection!"

He narrows his eyes at me. "Get your finger out of my face." He steps closer.

"Both of you, stop this now! We have a job to do here!" Perez snaps, but neither of us looks away. "Luke, step back now. And John, keep it together."

It's the first time I've seen the man show any emotion. I should be grateful that he's as riled up as me, but I'm not.

"She's all I have left: my only family." My vision blurs, and I need to clear my throat. Walters steps back.

"I'm going to find your sister," he promises. "Savannah's resting. She should make a full recovery. While she is resting, can we go through everything? Then we'll leave you to visit with her."

We go over everything that has happened. They both nod along, interrupting from time to time, probing me for finer details. I try to recall the phone conversation verbatim.

"I need to know ..."my stomach turns at the very thought of what he could be doing to my little sister, but I need to know. "If this is the same guy who killed Rose ... what did ... I mean how did he—?"

"We can't reveal that." Walters's curt response is softened by Perez's kindness.

"Luke. Focus on being there for Faye when we bring her home." She forces a thin smile, then stands briskly, Walters following suit. "Let's check on Savannah."

He leads the way. "We'll need to be in the room with you, at first."

Savannah's sitting up in bed when we enter the room. Perez and Walters walk straight to her. Gripping the door frame, I'm forced to hold myself upright at the sight of her. Her blue eyes find me and everyone else fades into the periphery, as I take her in. There's deep black and blue bruising on the right side of her face. Her auburn hair, seeming darker against the pallor of her skin, is tangled up in the cotton bandage wrapped around her head. My vision blurs. Savannah, the feisty, outspoken siren, looks broken. An overwhelming surge of emotion paralyzes me.

"I'm sorry, Luke," she croaks, dropping her face into her hands. The pain in her voice pulls me to her. I take her in my arms, crushing her to my chest.

"This is *not* your fault." My resolve breaks, and my own tears flow. Seeing Savannah so frail, devoid of her usual grit and vitality makes me want to fall to my knees and beg for forgiveness. She went to the cabin because I insisted that Faye couldn't be alone. I never considered the risks she was taking in all of this. Worse yet, I told Faye to leave her behind.

"Savannah ..." I pull back, ready to tell her, prepared to beg for absolution, until our eyes meet. She's so vulnerable. Those deep blue pools urge me to just be here.

"What are we going to do, Luke? We need to find her."

"We will, I promise." Kissing the top of her head, I try to reassure her, as Walters and Perez did with me. I mean every word. I'm hoping they do too. Walters and Perez are about to step forward when a commotion outside the door has them reaching for their guns. Walters throws me a warning glare.

"Stay here," he barks. Both he and Perez rush out of the room.

"I need to see her!" We hear a man's desperate plea, mingled with shouts for him to get down on the ground.

"Oh my God, it's Scott." Savannah grips my shirt again. "Luke, you have to help him." I'm going to do just that when Walters calls out a loud *stand down*. I reach the door in time to see Walters help Scott off the hospital floor.

"Luke, please. Say it's not true," he pleads, as though there's no one else here. I shake my head. I can't tell him what we all want to hear. I watch as he crumples forward. His elbows on his knees, his face falls into his hands.

"Let's go in here," Perez rubs his back, urging him into Savannah's hospital room. He's a mess. We all are.

SCOTT

I promised her, time and time again that she was safe. Each time, a niggling doubt at the back of my mind whispered *liar*. I didn't want to believe it, and now I can't breathe with the fear of losing her permanently.

"Why didn't you call me?" I lift my face from my hands and narrow my eyes at Luke. Nobody called me. I only found out when two officers showed up to question my whereabouts.

"I ..." He looks to the floor. "I wasn't thinking straight, but I wish I had called you first." He shoots Detective Walters an accusing glare.

"Yes, you should have! I would have driven there. I could have—"

"You could have gotten yourself killed!" Walters interjects.

"Better me than Faye!" I bark at him. At them all.

"Scott." Luke's voice is more controlled than I expected. "Better *him*, than any of us. And I'm going to find her," he promises through gritted teeth.

"Now, listen up, both of you—" Detective Walters begins, but Agent Perez lays a hand on his arm.

"Everyone in this room has one objective, and that is to *bring Faye home*, safe and sound. To do that, we all need to stay calm." Her voice is soft and clear and does absolutely nothing to reassure me. Fear and anger knot inside me and become a new wave of panic that churns in my stomach.

"Oh God, I can't lose her." Feeling breathless, I drop my head in my hands, my fingers digging into my hair.

"I'm not going to let that happen," Luke growls angrily.

AGENT DELLA PEREZ

My eyes burn for sleep. The cold air against my face is a welcome relief when we leave the hospital. It's four a.m. The clock started ten hours ago when he took her. Every second is vital: sleep can wait. John is on a call next to me as we walk to his car.

"Roger that." He hangs up, his eyes focused ahead. There's a shift in energy. If it wasn't already cold outside, I'd think John was responsible for the chill. I'm curious but decide not to ask.

We move quickly through the snow, and in no time are seated in his car and buckled up. He remains silent. We both do. Turning over the engine, the fan heaters blast against the windshield. The frost clears before he finally speaks.

"When were you going to tell me?" His tone is flat.

"Tell you what?" My body still shakes from the cold.

"That was my chief. As of tomorrow, you and the FBI are lead investigators on this case."

Damn it! I forgot. I intended to speak with him about it, but in truth, I've been too busy to think of anything other than finding Faye.

"Oh." I sigh. "I haven't had a moment, but yes, the FBI will be heavily involved as of tomorrow." There is no guilt in my tone, but I feel it, nonetheless. John has worked this case hard from day one. It's never an easy pill to swallow when a case is taken out of your hands.

He nods. His hand moves to the gear stick, his foot pushing down on the gas. We leave the hospital. The silence between us stretches the entire ride to the police station. The only sound is from the steady beat of John's fingers tapping the steering wheel. He's upset.

"A heads up would have been appreciated." He speaks again but doesn't look at me, choosing to keep his eyes straight ahead as we walk into the police station.

"I apologize. I'm sure you understand we've had other, more pressing matters to deal with since my return," I stop walking, forcing him to turn and face me. He nods, pouting again.

"You need to remove your ego from this, John. It's not about taking your case away from you, it's about finding Faye and the FBI can help. Surely you agree that we need help?"

"I do. I'm sure *you'll* do a great job, Agent Perez." His hands are stuffed into the pockets of his winter coat. The steely glare in his eyes waiting for me to take the bait. I won't do it. I don't do passive-aggressive.

"We." I waggle my pointer finger between us. "*We* will do a great job. This is still your case, John. I suggest you build a bridge and get over it! My lapse of communication was unintended."

"Great. Let's get to work, Agent." He turns and resumes his climb up the steps and into the police station.

DETECTIVE JOHN WALTERS

The FBI are not the enemy. My main objective is catching this guy.

I leave Perez and walk straight to the chief's office. Faye Anderson's abduction has made this a federal crime: this killer kidnapped three victims, one across state lines. He's escalating at a high rate of speed. I drop wearily into a chair across from her.

"They arrive tomorrow. Agent Perez will oversee the team and you will work alongside her," she explains to me.

"I can't say I'm jumping for joy, but it is what it is."

"Can't say I'm too happy myself, but we need the help. With the use of the ViCap database and our crime lab, we'll be able to analyze information and evidence quickly and effectively. Time is not on our hands."

"I'll get the job done either way." I sigh.

"I don't doubt it! You're one of the best detectives I've got. But you need to work on ..." she smiles, her eyes rolling as she tries to find the right words. "Being part of a team."

"Hmm. If that's all?" I stand, anxious to get back to the case.

"For now. Will you tell Agent Perez that I'd like to speak with her? I need to finalize a few things ahead of her team's arrival."

Her head has already dropped, her eyes scanning the paperwork in front of her. I bristle with anger and I don't like the feeling. I've poured myself into this case, just like every case before it. I consider it work, a job worth doing and doing well. *I'm just tired.*

AGENT DELLA PEREZ

"The chief wants to see you when you're free."

"*Por el amor de Dios!*" I jump, heart pounding. Swiveling in my chair, I see a disheveled Walters in the doorway. He looks slightly amused.

"Are you OK?" he asks.

"I feel as rough as you look, John. I think we should get some sleep."

"No, I'm good. I need to go over everything."

"You need some sleep." My words are more deliberate now.

"How would you know what I need?" His tone is flat.

"Because, John, that's my job! I'm a profiler. And what I see in front of me is a fatigued man with an ego the size of Texas who just won't let go." There's no hiding the frustration in my voice. "We'll break for four hours and meet back here at nine a.m." I huff.

"Is that an order?" He moves in from the doorway, hands falling to his hips.

"YES!"

An awkward silence extends around us, then his heated stare loses its fire when he speaks.

"I think it's time for you to start building ..."

"Building what?"

"A bridge!"

His smile, full and unexpected, spreads across his handsome face. He is a man of few words and fewer smiles. My breath hitches at the rare sight. It disarms me, freeing me from a place of pure frustration and exhaustion. Our giddy laughter echoes down the hallway.

"I'll see you in a few hours." He heads toward his office.

CHAPTER 16

DETECTIVE JOHN WALTERS

We're back at the hospital. There's a press conference due to take place soon, informing the media and the general public of Faye's abduction. We've already questioned her employer and close family. It won't be long before the media gets hold of her name, especially since she works in radio: she's one of them. They will take it personally, which means that we will have to field a lot of attention and questions from the press. While their intentions can be good, just one bad write-up could lead her kidnapper to snap.

Luke is gone when we arrive.

"He borrowed my car. He was restless, needed to be doing something," Savannah explains. My eyes slide to Perez. Luke is a loose cannon. Pushing on, I interview them both again, starting with Savannah and then Scott.

"We believe he was waiting for them at the cabin. Scott, can you tell us if you've noticed anyone following her, before last night?" I ask.

"No, never. Wait." His head pops up, his gray eyes finding mine. "Last week."

"Yes?"

"We went on a date. We were at the Christmas market, and Faye was looking at this tree ornament. The lady said she would hold onto it for us while we went skating, but when we got back, some guy had bought it. We thought it was so strange; he told the lady he was our friend, but we were there alone. Oh God, I feel sick. He was right there! I should have seen him following us." His face pales.

"The lady at the stand saw him?" I ignore his distress, hoping to refocus his mind.

"Yes, she said he came straight up after we left."

"Where's the Christmas market?" I press.

"Over at Lambeau Field. I was going to go back and buy her a different ornament, for Christmas." Deep sadness fills his eyes.

"That's a good idea. Why don't we head there now? You can take us to meet this artist and you can pick up your ornament." Perez gently suggests.

I must admit, Perez is good with people. She has a knack for putting them at ease, even during these highly stressful situations. I watched her do it moments ago when she took the lead on questioning Savannah. As it happens, Savannah heard the kidnapper just before he struck her. She turned and caught a quick glimpse of pale eyes and a black ski mask.

We ride with Scott to Lambeau Field. He scans the twenty or so stalls before shaking his head. She isn't here. Perez and I speak with a few of the other vendors, only to be told that the artists rotate each week.

We find an employee who calls the stadium's event manager. She directs us to the city council. The Packers have simply opened their doors for the event to take place. They have no hand in the management of it.

"Oh!" Scott remembers. "The artist gave Faye her card. She put it in her purse."

"Great." I'm relieved, we have Faye's handbag in evidence.

FAYE

Dust and grime coat the surface of the old wooden dressing table, clouding the three oval-shaped mirrors. The items on top, while shabby, have been used more recently. I pluck one of the perfume bottles from its position atop a black jewelry box. The delicate glass vial, with its intricate design compels me to remove the stopper and lift it to my nose. The soft musk smell reminds me of my grandmother, but my present circumstances taint the comforting memories. I drop the antique bottle. Before I can think, I lunge to catch it, and the heavy glass hits my injured finger before crashing onto the dresser. I groan in pain. The ache is unbearable and fresh tears gather behind my closed eyelids. Cradling my hand, I rock back and forth, willing the pain to subside.

"What happened?" the door swings open, his furrowed brows framing furious eyes as he glares across the room at me. He untied me only moments ago. Told me to wait here for his return.

"I ... wanted to smell nice," I lie, my eyes falling to the perfume bottle in explanation.

He softens in an instant. "Please be more careful," he says, kneeling next to me. The three-legged stool I sit on wobbles with the shaking of my body. "You've already hurt yourself once. We don't want any more accidents, do we?" He turns, righting the perfume bottle and putting it back in its original position.

"Now." He stands, coming behind me, the weight of his hands on my shoulders pushing me further into the stool. "We need to get you ready." The tips of his fingers graze my neck, pulling my hair away from my face and over my shoulders. I sit in terrified silence as he produces a comb from the pocket of his slacks. I bow my head, allowing him to comb my hair. He's humming a familiar song, but I'm unable to place it as he continues to groom me like a child.

"I'd like you to look pretty for me, Faye." He leans against me, placing the comb on the dresser before stepping away. I don't dare lift my head to watch him, but I listen intently. The floorboards creak, the hinges of the wardrobe squealing, as he opens the doors, sounding as if they too are frightened of him.

"There's makeup inside the black jewelry box. I expect you to be at your best when you come down for supper." Metal hangers scrape against wood before one is plucked free of the wardrobe "You'll look pretty in pink," he continues. Keeping my head down, I risk a sideways glance, watching as he lays out a pink dress on the bed.

His movements are swift and sure as he flows about the room. "Your heels are by the bed too. Wear the red lipstick." He snaps his eyes in my direction, making sure I hear as he delivers the rules of his game. I dare not look away while he plays the romantic suitor. His soft tone, meant to woo me, is betrayed by his sinister demands. I'm repulsed. Remembering again Agent Perez's advice, I force my mouth into a tight smile.

"OK."

Slowly, his tongue wets his lips. He rolls them, like a man tasting his lover's kiss, his eyes burning with pleasure.

"Good. I'll be outside." His husky tone confirms my suspicions. He's turned on. All of this is foreplay for him, which means there is a lot more to come. The door clicks shut behind him, the turn of the key bringing me some relief. Right now, that rickety old door and lock are all that stand between me and that monster. I don't have much time. I move straight to the window. My fingers grip the wooden frame, tugging it upward with no success. It's bolted shut, refusing to budge even a little. Splinters come away in my fingers when I remove my hand. The floorboards creak from beyond the doorway. A quick glance over my shoulder tells me he hasn't come back. Yet. My heart jackhammers in my chest, each beat bringing me closer to his return.

Leaning my face into one corner of the windowpane, I strain to see everything around this two-story house. From the second floor, the night sky throws shadow on most of the property, but I can make out some landmarks. An old tractor sits under a yard light, next to a red barn. The long grass growing around flat tires indicate that the tractor hasn't been used for many years. I focus on the barn. The structure will be easier for police to find, if I ever get out of here to identify it. A rusty, corrugated metal roof sits atop the red-painted, wooden panels. Surrounded by woods, the eerie stillness brings a new sense of dread. *There's nobody around for miles!* Moving to the opposite side of the window, I crane my neck, hoping to see more of the property, but it's clear: I'm in the middle of nowhere, completely at his mercy.

"Faye, are you almost ready?" He's calling from beyond the door. Reality dawns. I'll need to meet him if I'm to find a way out of this house.

Careful not to snag my throbbing finger, I strip away my jeans and sweater. I slide the musty old dress over my head. Covered in tiny pink and white flowers, the pattern, the heavy fabric and style belong to a time long gone. It's meant to be fitted around the waist and should fan out into a full skirt. On my slim frame, the sleeveless dress droops unattractively. Ignoring the concern building in my stomach, I quickly move back to the dressing table. With trembling hands, I open the black box, finding it stuffed full, not of jewelry, but of cosmetics. I smear some red lipstick on and apply some foundation and blush before moving on to my eyes. Despite the bad lighting and grimy mirrors, I'm relieved that I don't do a bad job and that makes my stomach turn. The realization that I *want* to look good, causes me to dry heave.

The black satin heels, with their scuffed soles, have clearly been worn before. I can't think about that. I slip my feet inside them as he enters.

Silence. His black hair is slicked back off his face, his piercing blue eyes slowly evaluate me. Standing with his hands behind the back of his black tailored suit, his lips are pursed. He twirls a finger in the air, motioning for me to turn full circle. I do as I'm told. My eyes travel from the neck of his white shirt to the shiny shoes on his feet. He looks like he just stepped off a ballroom floor.

He finally breaks the silence. "You look beautiful. Supper is ready." He steps forward, and with one hand still behind his back, he offers his other hand, palms up. I jerk backward. The last time his hand touched mine, I ended up with a broken finger.

"Faye, you are a tonic!" he sneers before erupting into cold laughter. "I'll only hurt you if you misbehave. Now, take my hand." His eyes narrow until I step forward, my feet wobbling in the shoes.

"The shoes are too big," I whisper as we move to the door.

"You'll manage."

He ignores my struggle to walk, pulling me along a narrow hallway before coming to the top of an open wooden staircase. I grab hold of the banister with my free hand as we descend, minding my step. We're halfway down when I notice the large oil painting hanging opposite the foot of the stairs. Dark blues and navies create a magnificent depiction of a starry night sky, above two lovers lying next to a river. Illuminated by the moon that hangs over them, they're locked in a romantic embrace. I try to soak in the image: the wooden bridge, the forest that surrounds them. It's breath-taking and a far cry from the peril I face right now.

He pulls to the left. I glance back over my shoulder. There's a living room with dusty furniture pushed against the walls, leaving a vacant floor space at the center of the room. We enter the kitchen before I spot any escape routes. This room is in major disrepair. The cabinet doors barely hang on their hinges, drooping toward the worn wooden floors. Sitting me down at the small dining table, he reaches for some matches to light tall candles between our place settings. *We are having a romantic meal.* Bile creeps up my esophagus, stinging the back of my throat. I try to swallow against it.

Instead, I focus on the pale blue crockery that sits, chipped and cracked, in front of me. It rests on a lace tablecloth next to a water glass with painted cherries dotted all over it. I twist the wooden-handled knife at my place slowly in my hand, preferring to count the cherries on my glass than look toward the man preparing supper next to me. I don't hear his approach, but the hairs on the back of my neck scream for me to pay attention. When I look up, his eyes are on the knife in my hand.

"I hope you're not thinking about doing anything crazy?"

I want to laugh. *Me, crazy? Yeah, I'm the crazy one in this scenario!* Instead, I adamantly shake my head no, dropping the knife and keeping my lips sealed as he fills my plate with food and my glass with water.

I wait for him to sit across for me, I wait for his direction. Lifting his own cutlery, he nods for me to begin. The smells of warm chicken and vegetables seize my senses, causing my stomach to churn in distaste. Despite my hunger, I am not interested in being here. I don't want to participate in this sick charade.

"Is there something wrong with the food?" he asks. I lift my eyes to meet his.

"No, it smells delicious." My throat tightens. "I'm very thirsty," I say, reaching for my glass of water. The cool liquid offers a welcome relief against the struggle of swallowing back my disgust.

"I wanted everything to be perfect. You should eat up; you will need energy for practice." He dips his head, his knife and fork tearing the white meat.

"Practice?" I dare to murmur. His eyes snap to mine.

Irritated, he drops his cutlery. "We will discuss that later."

"I..." I can't keep my voice from shaking or the tears from falling free. Navigating his brittle temperament is exhausting. I want to be with Scott. *Scott* ... his dimpled smile and kind eyes flood my memory. No longer able to keep my resolve, I allow myself to whimper openly.

Not even the screech of his chair against the wooden floor, or the sound of dishes landing heavily in the kitchen sink can pull me back to his game. I want to go home. To Scott, to Luke, to Savannah.

His roar is violent. "STOP THIS NOW. YOU'RE RUINING EVERYTHING," he screams, stepping closer. My hands come up to my head, curling into the wall. I try to protect myself from any oncoming assault.

I wait, huddled on the dining chair for the attack. When it doesn't come, I slowly drop my hands. Turning to locate him, I'm surprised to see him sitting back in his chair, across the table. His jaw ticks, his anger shifting toward himself.

"I apologize for screaming. I don't like to get so worked up." He straightens his lapels, brushing a stray lock of hair back into place.

"I want to go home," I sniffle.

"You are home. I know things are off to a rough start, but once you get to know me, everything will fall into place."

"I don't even know your name," I regret saying it the moment he responds.

"Jeffrey." Flesh and blood with a first name. He's more real to me now, more dangerous than when I considered him a monster. When he was simply a monster, he was a figment of my imagination. Something to be slain, something to wake up from. Now he is Jeffrey, my real-life kidnapper. The man who is likely to kill me. The man I must escape to survive.

I decide to bite the bullet. I need to know what happened to Savannah. "Is Savannah OK?" I swallow hard, not sure I'm prepared for the answer.

"You know, she said some pretty nasty things about me, Faye. You always stuck up for me." His shoulders shrug, so dismissive of Savannah, like she was dirt on his shoe. "She was hurt, but that blow wasn't enough to kill her. She's fine, I'm sure. She might think twice before bad-mouthing people again."

My heart leaps for joy, the beat *thump, thump, thumping* in my ears, until I think of something. My heart stumbles, the blood freezing in my veins as I piece together exactly who he is.

"*You* killed Rose." I whisper it aloud, a statement rather than a question, but he answers anyway.

"That was an accident. Rose wanted to leave me. She hurt herself."

I focus on the door behind him. I noticed it earlier, keenly aware of the metal locks above and below the handle. He looks to the door and then back to me. A sly smile creeps up his face.

"Go ahead." He waves his hand toward the door. A cruel trick. His eyes say: *Leave me, and you'll end up like Rose.*

I slowly rise from the table, and my own eyes answer. *Stay here, and I'll end up like her anyway.* I step one foot out of the shoe, dropping it to the floor, before kicking off the second heel. He continues to watch me, leaning back into his chair as I reach for the knife. Holding it out in front of me, my hand shakes as I move around the table. He doesn't move, not an inch. Once around the table, I walk backward to the door, keeping my eyes on him at all times, until I feel the door at my back. I keep the knife pointed at him, as I turn to one side and slide the metal bars out of their locks. The knob turns easily in my hand, the door opening from the frame. And still, he makes no movements. I step forward, pulling the door open without looking away from him once. He laughs when I let it swing behind me and when his head falls back in glee, I take that moment to run. Turning away from him, I run straight into a cement block wall, then fall backward onto my ass. The doorway is completely sealed off from the outside world. He stands over me.

"There's nowhere to go, Faye." He laughs. Scooting back on my hands, I turn before pulling myself up, taking off for the living room. I reach the windows and whip open the curtains, only to find more cement blocks. I run through another door into a hallway, finding the front door. More cement blocks. All the while, Jeffrey's laughter rings through the house.

Pounding against the cold bricks, I scream. "Please! Won't you just let me go home?"

"Faye, this is your home." His voice nears me. I rush back into the living area, facing him once again. The doorway to the basement comes into sight. *That must be the exit*. I move to it, this time running into his hard chest as he grabs hold of me.

His long fingers bite into my biceps, shaking me roughly. "Faye, darling, please calm down. Can't you see how good we have it? I knew the moment I laid eyes on you, nothing else and nobody else could ever compare to you. To us. Didn't you feel the same?" his voice booms around me, his fingers digging deeper into the flesh of my arms. His words, his tone, a complete contrast to the physical pain he's causing me.

"Ouch!" I wince.

"Am I hurting you, darling?" He relaxes the pressure of his grip.

"I don't want to be here: to be with you!" I cry, unable to control myself.

"Do you *want* to be punished?" He sneers, dragging me to the middle of the room.

"No, please. I'm sorry, I'll be good!" I beg.

"You *will* be good." The cool edge of his tone sends a shiver down my spine as he finally releases my arms. I don't move, standing still as he circles me once before moving to the record player.

Music fills the room as he returns. "It's time for practice." His hot breath is on my neck as his hand slides across my waist. "Take my hand," he demands.

The lyrics of his chosen song fill the air and I hesitate. One beat too long. Storming away, he stops the music.

"I misunderstood!" I lie. I jump when he storms back to face me.

"Your hand," he hisses. I know what he means to do. I can't.

"Faye, give me your hand!"

My shaking fingers curl into a fist, clenching and unclenching. His hand snakes out at speed to grab hold of my wrist.

"Open." His voice trembles with rage. I force my fingers to uncurl in his hand.

The sound, like a walnut in a nutcracker, cracks in my ears before my body registers that he's broken my ring finger. Excruciating pain shoots from my knuckle up my entire arm. My mouth opens to release some of the agony in a scream.

"Shussssssssh, Faye," his breathless voice is heavy with pleasure.

Agent Perez warned me to do whatever he wanted, and to avoid making him angry, but watching his eyes fill with gratification, I know, one way or another, he'll discover a reason to be angry. He'll find a reason to hurt me. Cradling my broken finger, I slump forward with my head hanging low and sob. The pain is too much.

"It's time for dance practice," he announces smoothly. Walking over to replay his song. This time, I don't hesitate in taking his hand.

LUKE

The call from Detective Walters wakes me up. I sit up straight on the hard hospital chair, stretching my back, legs and neck. I see Savannah, still asleep in bed beside me, and Scott in the chair opposite. We both stayed with her all night. Neither of us knows where else we should be, or how else we could help.

"Luke, it's Detective Walters."

"Do you have any news?"

Scott stirs at the sound of my voice.

"Not yet. Forensics have signed off on the cabin, if you need to go there. You can get me on this number all day. I'll be out following up on leads," he informs me.

"I'll be following up on my own leads." I'm not prepared to sit by and do nothing. I drove around aimlessly yesterday. Today will be different. I need a plan.

"Luke." He sighs, his voice losing its air of superiority. "You need to trust me to do my job. When families get involved, things never work out well."

Scott's sitting up, his eyes trained on me as I speak. "Faye is all the family I have, so understand this: I was involved long before you, and I'll be involved long after I bring her home. I'll be in touch, Detective." I hang up.

"What's the plan?" Scott asks, standing up from his seat, preparing to leave.

"I'll need to get back out to the cabin. You'll have to stay here ..." I'm standing too, meeting his eyes across the bed, hoping he understands.

"No! I won't be babysitter while Faye needs me," he hisses quietly. My eyes drop to Savannah, relieved to see she's still sleeping.

"What about Savannah?" I remind him.

"She has twenty-four-hour police protection." He gestures to the door to prove his point.

"Look how well that worked out for Faye," I snap.

"I love Savannah, but right now she is safe, while my girlfriend is out there, scared and alone. Take me with you or don't. Either way, I'll be looking for her."

I roll my eyes to the ceiling. This is the last thing I need.

"We can't leave Savannah alone!" I reconcile myself to the fact that if he's not with me, he'll be running around on his own, trying to find Faye.

"I won't be alone," Savannah's husky tone has us both jerking our heads in her direction. I move to her side, helping her sit up. "Scott, do you have your car?"

"Yes, I parked here last night."

"Luke, you said you flew here, so I take it you need a car?" she smiles knowingly.

"Your point?" I growl.

"Scott can drive you. Faye needs him as much as she needs you. I have police protection. Now y'all go find our girl." Her eyes well up.

"We'll be back tonight,"

"Could you do me a favor?"

"Anything," Scott says.

"The keys to my apartment are in the pocket of my jacket." She points to the clothes she wore during the attack, now folded on a table behind me. "Could you bring some fresh clothes with you? I plan on getting out of here tomorrow."

"No problem," Scott answers. Reaching down to kiss her on the forehead, he heads to the door as I get the leather jacket. My back is to her when I spot her blood-stained cream blouse.

"I'll meet you outside," I tell him, my eyes glued to the bloodied blouse. I turn it over in my hands. My heart begins to pound in my chest, my breathing shallow as I turn to face Savannah. I need to look her in the eyes and tell her how much of a coward I am.

"What is it?" she pales. I lift my eyes to her, my words catching in my throat when I try to speak. "Luke, you're scaring me."

Moving back to the bed, I sit down beside her.

"When I was on the phone with Faye. I ... told her to ... leave you." The words break free, and I drop my head in shame. Faye had more courage in that moment than I do in my whole body. She walked into the kitchen to try to save her friend.

"I don't know what you mea—" she stops as it dawns. "Oh."

Reaching for her hand, I grab hold. "Savannah, I'm so sorry. I was afraid for Faye." My eyes water.

"Luke," she croaks, "if it was the other way around, I would have done the same thing."

"That's different."

"No. I'm *so* mad at her for coming into the kitchen. She should have run. Luke, your sister has a mind and a heart of her own. She's stronger than you realize. We'll find her." Her small hand turns in my mine, offering me a reassuring squeeze. We lock eyes, her bruises reminding me that I need to avenge her too.

"I'm going to kill him, for what he did to you and Faye. " Consequences be damned, no one gets away with hurting the people I care about.

"Only if you get to him before me, sugar," she retorts and I'm relieved to have some of the sassy Savannah filtering back to me. I chuckle, and before I think about it, I lean forward and kiss her cheek, my lips brushing lightly against her bruised eyelids before standing off the bed.

"I'll be back tonight."

She touches her cheek, eyes round as she nods. The cop at the door gets a hard stare and a few choice words of warning to keep her safe before I meet Scott outside.

"Where to?" he asks.

"I need to go home." I sigh, dreading returning there.

Halfway to the cabin, I turn to him.

"Slow down! Neither of us are any good to Faye dead." I pat his shoulder when he eases off the throttle.

The blood on the floor stops me in my tracks. Shaking, I try to take it all in. The cold air is filled with a deathly silence. Blood-soaked bandages litter the floor and fingerprint dust covers most surfaces. Violence doesn't belong here, but somehow it slithered its way into our home. My throat burns as I close the kitchen door, shutting out the mess, and my fears.

I scour the house for anything unusual but come up empty. After showering and a change of clothes, I stuff extra clothing, my phone and my wallet into a bag. I meet Scott back in the downstairs hallway within minutes.

"There's nothing here that can help us."

"Where to now?" He asks, as he waits for me to buckle up.

Joe's Guns and Ammo is located on the edge of town. I've driven by it so often, never once considering that I would ever cross its threshold. We walk past the racks of hunting gear and equipment, straight to the sales counter. The clerk has a strong Wisconsin accent and several missing teeth.

"How's it goin' wid yous guys, now?"

"I want to buy a gun," I whip out my ID and slap it on the long glass cabinet that houses an array of guns. Bushy gray eyebrows frown disapprovingly at me.

"Ya know, I'm obligated to get you to fill out a background check, by law." He turns, pulling a metal clipboard from the shelf behind him. I take it from him, quickly filling out the form and handing it back over.

"I'll take a handgun and a long shot rifle. And just give me a box of ammo for both." I'm already handing over my credit card when he starts laughing.

"Now look here, sonny. I gotta submit the form to the DOJ. It can take 'em upward o' five days to get back to me, ya know?"

"I don't have five days."

"Well, Jeez. Hold your horses, boy, n' let me finish. I was sayin', it *could* take up to five days, but often they come back in twenty-four hours. I'm sure you can hold off on murdering until then." He looks squarely into my eyes.

"I hope not," I growl impatiently.

"Now you just wait a minute! I never sold a gun that wasn't used for huntin' or protectin'. And I'm not gonna start now, ya know? So yous just turn on around, real quick, and go find yourselves another gun dealer." He picks up the clipboard, turning his back on me.

"Thirty-seven hours ago, my sister was kidnapped, out there on Oak Orchard Road. I'm sure you've heard about it on the news. I'm sure you've also heard about that other girl, who was found dead a few weeks before that." His back is still stiffened righteously, but he turns back around. "Look at my name on that form: Luke Anderson. My sister is Faye Anderson. I'd appreciate if you would run that background check and give me a call, sir."

"It's terrible, what's happened to them girls. I'll call you when I get the approval." He offers me a solemn nod. I thank him before getting back on the road.

CHAPTER 17

DETECTIVE JOHN WALTERS

The business card for Kitty Harmon Designs was inside Faye's purse. The address listed is only a ten-minute drive from the station, so Perez and I go.

Perez breaks the silence, her eyes on the road ahead. "This snow is coming down pretty hard."

"It might ease off. We don't usually see heavy snowfall until January," I say, hopeful. "OK. We know he lives off-grid once he abducts his victims. The County Highway Department usually does a good job of plowing and laying down salt."

"Yeah, I'm learning. Since moving to Milwaukee, I've become well acquainted with snow boots and snow tires." Her laughter is soft, genuine and marks the first time she's relaxed around me since I found out the FBI are arriving.

"What time do your colleagues arrive?"

"This evening." Her smile falters a little.

"Good." I smile back.

We drive over the Walnut Street Bridge, passing the Green Bay Correctional Facility before driving through a suburban neighborhood. Locating the house, I park along the curb before we exit the car together. Climbing onto the wraparound porch, I knock firmly. I wait a moment, then rap on the door again. Through the small pane of glass, I spot an old man hobbling down the hallway. He pulls open the heavy solid wood door, leaving the storm door between us closed. “What can I do for you?” he asks.

“Hi, sir. My name is Detective Walters, and this is Agent Perez. We are from the Outagamie Sheriff’s department. We’re looking to have a word with a Kitty Harmon. Is she here?” I smile.

“Kitty ...” he calls behind him, before shuffling back down the hall.

“Daddy, what are you doing out of your chair?” a frantic female emerges from the basement, meeting her father in the hallway.

“They were bangin’ down the door and you had that darned music playin’. What do you expect me to do?” he groans. Perez giggles beside me. The old man must be a handful for his daughter. Moments later, Kitty Harmon comes to the door. We introduce ourselves and show her our badges. She kindly invites us into her kitchen, offering tea.

“It’s chamomile.” She pours steaming liquid from a ceramic teapot into matching teacups, while Perez and I sit at a small table. I’m not a big fan of tea but it’s cold outside, so I accept.

“Now, what can I help you officers with?” She smiles warmly.

“We wanted to talk to you about an incident you might remember, from your time at Lambeau Field last week,” Perez begins.

“Oh, I’m intrigued. Although I must admit, I don’t remember anything too exciting happening.” Her round cheeks are flushed when she finally sits down. I take out the business card and slide it across the table.

"Do you remember giving this card to a pretty, young, blonde woman? She was with her date. They had been admiring one of your ornaments?"

"Oh, of course! They're a very handsome young couple. That was the strangest thing: I was holding the ornament while they went skating. This young man came over, pretending to be their friend. I guess he liked the ornament too." She flushes proudly.

I keep my tone gentle, careful not to startle her. "Ms. Harmon, that young lady was abducted from her home, two nights ago. We believe the man who purchased the ornament may have been stalking her."

"Oh my, oh Lord! That poor girl. She was so polite and friendly ..." Her eyes fill with pity.

"Do you think you could describe him to us?" Perez cuts in.

"Oh yes! I could draw him too: I'm an artist. I'm quite good actually."

"That would be very helpful. Can you give me any details now that can help us?" Perez smiles warmly.

"He was very tall. About the same height as you," she says, glancing toward me. I'm six foot three.

"His eyes were a striking shade of blue and he had jet-black hair and eyebrows. Very handsome, I'd say movie-star good looks. He was charming and friendly—are you sure he's involved? I just can't imagine—" She stops herself, thoughtful for a moment. "I guess that's what everyone said about Bundy."

"He may be innocent, but we have to follow up on every lead. How old do you think he might have been?" I ask.

"Oh, late thirties." She responds without hesitation, looking to Perez. "He had some fine lines, but not crow's feet like you. You must smile a lot."

Perez laughs. "I'm not quite 'late thirties' yet, but I know what you mean."

"Oh, that was rude. Excuse me." She flushes a deeper shade of red.

"Not at all, you're being very helpful!" Perez reassures her, the fine lines I'd never noticed before adding character to her face as she smiles at this lady. Perez and I both take notes, questioning her about any small detail that might help us track him down.

"Do you remember how he paid?"

She looks up and to the right as she tries to recall.

"I can't remember off-hand, but I sold quite a lot of ornaments that evening. There were more credit card sales than cash. I could give you all the receipts, if that helps.

"Yes, please." My heart races. He might have slipped up!

JEFFREY

She looks so angelic. Her long blond hair is fanned out across her pillow, her eyelashes resting against her cheeks, fluttering lightly as she breathes. Moving closer, I allow myself one touch. Her delicate ankles are swollen from the tight restraints, but her behavior last night left me with little choice. I can't risk her trying to escape. In time, she will join me in *our* bed. Faye is perfect. Everything and everyone else led me to this moment. I am hers and she is mine. Cupping her ankle, I slide my hand up her calf, allowing it to travel further, under her dress, over her knee, before it stills on her thigh. *No.* I pull my hand back. *Not like this.*

Stepping away from the bed, I turn out the light. By the light of the hallway, I observe her one last time before closing the door behind me. Unfortunately, I must leave her for work. Usually, I would have planned: I'd have taken some time off, so we could get to know each other better. But everything with Faye has been a whirlwind. After last night's escapade, I expected her to fight me when I gave her the pills. Instead, she swallowed them, welcoming the sleep.

It made me realize she is still resisting our new life together, but tonight I will put up the Christmas tree. It will set the tone, help her become more compliant.

She'll need to bathe too. Thoughts of Faye lying in my tub, bubbles to her neck, her gaze settling on me as I help her bathe, starts a flurry of excitement in the pit of my stomach. I'll be gone from the farm for almost ten hours. That time apart suddenly feels monumental. Every mile that passes on these icy roads is a mile too far from Faye.

The Christmas break begins on Friday, so I need to catch up on my workload before we stop for the holidays. Besides my home, work is the only other place I feel at ease. This time of year is always quiet. I'm not surprised to see the sidewalk hidden under inches of undisturbed snow as I trudge toward the entrance.

"Jeffrey?" Tom the janitor calls out to me as I walk through the double doors. "What in the dickens are you doing here today?" He walks toward me, pushing his mop and bucket to the entrance.

"Sorry Tom," I smile ruefully, looking down at the melting snow I've tracked in from outside, which is now pooling on the floor at my feet. "I have some work to complete, before finishing up on Friday."

Waving away my apology, he squeezes out the mop and gets to work wiping up my mess. "Well don't let me stop you. If I don't see you before Friday, you have a merry Christmas, OK?"

"I think it will be my best one yet," I chirp, genuinely thrilled at the prospect of spending the holidays with Faye.

I head toward my lab, tapping the sign, *Department of Forensic Anthropology*, as I walk through the double doors that lead to my office.

This is where I first encountered Detective Walters. He suspected a link between Katherine and Rose and for a few seconds, I felt knocked off balance, unsettled, afraid even. However, I quickly gathered myself to accept the unexpected challenge and even found myself handing him the murder weapon on a plate. He shook the hand of their killer and walked out carrying a gigantic piece of the puzzle. I watched him, an air of authority in every stride, go back to his car. He lobbed the book onto the back seat.

"Good morning, Dr. Carson." Dr. Stanley waves from his office as I pass through to the lab. I wave in his direction, deciding to pass on the niceties for now. I have work to do and the perfect woman waiting for me at home. Remembering the gift I bought for her spurs me on even further. I can't wait to see her face.

FAYE

The sleeping pills should have given me a few hours of respite from the reality of this place. I needed to escape the physical pain of my broken fingers and the bonds that dig into my flesh. To escape the emotional rollercoaster that has me nauseated one moment and spiked full of adrenaline the next.

Instead, I woke up groggy and more confused than ever before. It took me at least half an hour for the woozy feeling to pass, and another for the fog in my mind to clear.

Lying still, I strain to pick up any sound in this abandoned house. *How did he come to find this place?* Its furnishings and decorations, even the clothes that still hang in the wardrobe, are pieces of the past. I've been dragged back to a different time as he forces me to dance in the shoes of someone who came before me. There have been no creaking floorboards, no clattering of pots. And that song hasn't played once today. We danced to the Everly Brothers on repeat. I fell asleep with the lyrics swimming around my head. I had always liked that tune, but the lyrics take on a whole new meaning when a psychopath plays it for you, over and over and over!

I rotate my wrists and wince against the rope burn. My fingers throb: the pain is becoming unbearable. I try to refocus my mind, away from the pain and toward a plan. I need to stay alive until they find me. Until then, I need to manage this monster. First, I'll have to gain his trust enough that he stops tying me up every time he leaves. *I'll have to pretend to enjoy his company*. My entire body shivers at the very thought, jerking the ropes again.

I know the basement is the only way out. I didn't know that yesterday. If I keep my wits about me, I'll learn more this evening.

Then the unmistakable sound of a car accelerating up the drive draws my attention to the window. Headlights illuminate the room before the engine cuts out. *He's outside!* Seconds turn into minutes of silence. *He must be in the barn*. The house remains still until a clatter of doors disturbs the hush. I listen for his movements as he enters the house. Nothing, until a floorboard lightly creaks. *He's back!* Each mental note elevates me from this pinned position on the bed, giving me something to analyze, something to focus on. Maybe knowing his routine will offer an opportunity. I train my ears, searching for his light footfall as he moves toward the door. The dull thudding of my heart is louder than his approach. The turning doorknob mimics my twisting gut. The heaviness in my chest feels like impending doom.

The light from the hallway streams in first, blurring his face and casting him in shadow.

"Hello, darling." His sickening pet name breaks the silence, sucking all of the lightness from the air. My aching fingers prompt me to speak.

"Hello." I smile weakly. "Could you—" The words lodge in my throat, struggling to break free of the lump forming. "My fingers hurt. I hoped you might release my hand for just a minute," I finally manage.

"I'm going to run a bath. The warm water will help to soothe them," his pale blue eyes wander over me.

"Thank you," I croak, hoping to gain some trust. I'm delighted with the idea of being free of this bed. He leaves the bedroom door open. As my eyes adjust to the light, my ears tune into the squeak of old metal fixtures, the rush of water and his humming. Steam rolls down the hallway, carrying with it the scent of lavender. A squeal of the taps turning off. He returns and frees my ankles. He places his knee on the mattress, rolling me toward him as he frees first my left hand, then my right.

"Your mascara is running."

His displeased tutting has me squirming back, bringing my knees to my chest. Grooves have formed in the flesh around my ankles and wrists. As much as my broken fingers will allow, I massage the dark contusions, ankles first, before gently encouraging blood flow back into my swollen fingers.

"I'll help you bathe."

His pale blue eyes darken, challenging me to defy his authority. Agent Perez was right about him without having ever met him.

As much as you can, do whatever he wants. Try to avoid upsetting him or making him angry. The soft Spanish lilt also promised: *if he succeeds, remember, so will we. We will find you*. The memory gives me enough strength to nod.

I drop my feet over the edge of the bed. There are certain moments in every woman's life. We imagine what we might do in a situation as dire as the one I now face. I always thought I would fight, that I would rather die than have a man invade my space, my body. Here, I find myself fighting all my instincts, just to stay alive. I feel like the weakest woman alive.

"Turn around," he orders. When I comply, he swipes my hair from my back and around my shuddering shoulders.

He whispers into my ear. "I would never force you. I'll wait until you're ready."

He slowly unzips the dress, fingers grazing along my spine, revealing my bare skin to him. I can hear his heavy breathing, his hums of pleasure, as his hands slide up my shoulders, easing the dress from my body.

"Shushhhhh. I told you, I won't rush this," he squeezes my arms. The dress falls at my feet, and I step out of it. He directs me down the hall to the bathroom. My arms cross over my chest, warding off the cold air and his perusal of my body. A cast iron bath sits in the middle of the bathroom. The deep tub, with long taps, is another piece of the past frozen in time.

My eyes search the room, scanning the broken tiles for a weapon. For anything I could hit him with.

"I'll turn while you remove your undergarments." He swallows, lust dripping from each word. My shoulders slump as I obey, gingerly stepping into the scalding water.

"It's too hot," I wince.

"It's perfect!" he snaps, his head jerking sideways to show his tense jaw. My eyes drop toward the steaming tub. Bubbles foam luxuriously. The scent of lavender invites me to sink beneath the surface. A symbol of relaxation the world over, and I'm imagining him dunking my head, holding me under until my soul leaves this God-awful place.

"Are you ready?"

I look at him again, still averting his gaze. My eyes drop to his waist. His entire body is stiff. I shudder at the thought before bracing myself and sinking into the hot water.

"Yes," I mumble. I let seconds pass, my body adjusting to the heat before I allow my injured hand to sink beneath the surface. The foam wraps around my body, comforting and shielding me from his view.

"I bought some feminine products for you." He opens a small, mirrored cabinet above the sink to reveal tampons and pads. I look away, mortified.

"No need to be embarrassed, darling. It is the most natural thing in the world. When will you be expecting it?"

I want to scream. I consider drowning myself rather than answer his intrusive questions. How dare he take something else from my control. "I just finished," I lie, looking away as I work out how long

I have before my next period arrives. Seven days. Seven full days to escape or die trying.

He kneels next to me, his white shirt sleeves rolled up. My head tilts away from him toward the rusty chrome taps at the middle of the bath. Water drips from the faucet, brimming on the edge before forming a drop and falling into the bath. I make these little drops of water my sole focus as his hand dips into the water.

"Lift your arm," I hear him say. My body responds, my mind on the *drip, drip, drip* of the water. Water splashes, he sighs contentedly. The scent of lavender continues to rise with the steam as he violates my body. The flimsy washcloth is no barrier against the feel of his hand, washing me like a helpless child.

"Lie back, while I do your hair," his voice heavy with lust. I sink back without argument, my eyes finding a water stain on the ceiling above as his fingers run, painfully slowly through my hair. Cold air hits my exposed breast. The weight of this invasion weighs heavy on my chest, almost enough to sink me. Silent tears fall, disappearing into the bathwater.

He stands abruptly. "You're all clean."

I've never felt filthier in my life. I don't think I'll ever feel clean again. He reaches for a towel then waits for me to stand up, his eyes averted as I take the towel from him. I feel that when I see Scott again, this thing, this animal, will have destroyed something within me. In order to return to him—to see his dimpled cheeks and smiling eyes—I'm allowing a monster to paw at my body. Agent Perez told me to stay alive at all costs. I can take the physical pain, but my heart and soul need to remain intact, if I'm to return to the world beyond these walls. *How dare he do this to me!* Rage bubbles within me, like a simmering volcano that suddenly erupts. My chest burns with it, it flows like hot magma through my veins, cooling beneath the surface and forming a solid barrier around my soul. Resolved to find my way out of this place, I towel myself dry before following him back to the bedroom.

"I'll wash your undergarments and have them back to you tomorrow." He smiles. I see the same dress I've worn since my arrival, laid out on the bed again, the black heels next to it.

"Do your makeup, and I'll be back soon. He moves to the door, switching on the light before turning back to me.

"I would like for you to bathe me too, maybe in a few days?" He hesitates inside the doorway, almost like a lost child waiting for affection. This is an opportunity for me to gain some trust, so I take it.

"That would be nice. My hands should be healed by then, that will make bathing easier." I smile. His eyes light up. *Maybe he'll think twice before breaking any fingers tonight!*

"I'll be back soon. Wear the red lipstick again. And tonight, wear more kohl."

I force a sweet smile. "Sure."

I turn away, facing the mirror. *You can do this, Faye!* The voice in my head is not my own, it's Savannah's husky southern drawl that reassures me.

After supper, he clears away the plates. I'm sitting at the table.

"Tomorrow, it will be your turn to clean the dishes." He walks around, gathering the used cutlery and cups, as if this whole scenario is normal.

"That's only fair. Thank you for cooking supper." I force a hard smile.

"I have a gift for you. Close your eyes." He comes around to stand behind me, his hand resting on the back of my chair. I do as I am told. I feel his arm brush mine as he places something on the table.

"Open it," he says excitedly, moving around to sit back in his seat. There's a small cardboard box tied with a red ribbon on the table. I struggle to undo the ribbon with my aching fingers. All the air leaves my lungs when I finally see the contents.

"I knew you'd be happy," he claps his hands together.

Tentatively, I lift the ornament, holding it up in front of me. Memories of that so precious night assail me. I can't allow myself to think of Scott in his presence. Tears threaten to break down my determination.

"You're not happy!" He jumps up. I clear the mist from my eyes, shaking my head, and offer him the widest, fakest smile I can muster.

"It's beautiful," I croak. "Thank you."

It's like walking a tightrope of his emotions, my responses dictating whether he stays steady or flips the switch on his disparate personalities.

"I knew you would like it. It makes me happy to see you appreciate my efforts. I would do anything for you." He reaches for my hand. "Come with me for your next surprise. Bring the ornament." I allow him to lead me toward the living room. In the far corner, lights twinkle on a Christmas tree.

"I brought it in from the barn. I thought you'd like to hang the ornament." He walks toward the tree. I nod enthusiastically. It's forced, but he doesn't seem to see past his own delusion.

"It's really pretty," I lie. The artificial tree's not only old and misshapen but also missing branches. And except for one string of twinkle lights, it's devoid of any cheer.

"Come, hang the ornament. Then we can start practice."

I move toward him. The shoes slip at my heels, the friction beginning to burn as blisters form. I ignore the pain and keep my face as cheerful as the tree. I place the ornament.

"You believe me, don't you?" He looks down at me, his eyes round with sincerity.

I can't remember what I'm supposed to believe. "What?" I ask, afraid to guess at his question.

He smiles, lifting me by the waist and swinging me around in a playful dance. "That I would do anything for you!" He laughs. "Let's practice our dance ..." He sets me down in the middle of the open floor.

"Find your position," he says, and lightly touches my cheek before he walks to the old record player.

The same song begins to play, no doubt on repeat for the night. He returns, opening his arms for me to step into his embrace.

"May I have this dance?" he asks.

I nod, taking his hand. He moves me into position. One shoe is already slipping from my foot.

"This is the closed position, Faye." He smiles before he begins the routine. I follow along as best I can. I look at this handsome man and wonder what could have happened in his life to make him this fucked up.

CHAPTER 18

DETECTIVE JOHN WALTERS

Gaining access into Scott Allen's apartment block wasn't easy.

"Luke! Scott!" I bang hard on the apartment door. I don't care if I wake the whole damn building at this stage.

A sleepy Scott answers. I look him over as he scrubs a hand over his unshaven face. He's still dressed in the clothes from two nights ago. It's clear that he hasn't stopped long enough to wash himself.

"Shit, what time is it?" Not yet fully awake, he hurries into the living room.

He kicks a sleeping Luke Anderson on his couch. "Luke, wake up."

I walk into the room. My eyes drift to the open laptops and papers strewn over the coffee table in the middle of the room. Luke groans, his mind playing catch-up as his sleepy eyes find me standing over him.

He jumps up. "What's wrong? Did you find her?"

The reason I'm here has nothing to do with Faye and everything to do with Luke.

"No, no news on Faye, yet." I swallow against the bitter taste those words leave in my mouth. "I've been trying to get through to *you* all night."

"Why?" he asks, walking into the small kitchen area. He takes down two mugs, then asks over his shoulder if I want one.

"Yeah." I nod, and he pulls one more from the cupboard. "I got a concerning phone call last night."

"Is that so?" He pours three cups of coffee, passing one each to me and Scott. I take a long sip, my eyes assessing Luke over the top of my cup. He's a tall man. Broad, strong and very rough around the edges. I ran a background check on him. His record is clean. No speeding tickets, no bar room brawls or violent incidents in his past. Despite his obvious strength, he has never used it in anger.

"Joe Cullen—you know, down at Joe's Guns and Ammo? —called to let me know that you've been approved to buy some firearms at his store. He thought I ought to know." My gaze flicks between them. Scott stays quiet.

"Yeah?" Luke shrugs, unapologetic.

"Luke, what is your plan here?" I sigh. "You can't go running around Wisconsin with a gun, looking for this guy. Having to check up on *you* is taking vital time away from my investigation. You need to trust *me* to do the police work."

"I appreciate the checking in, but really, that's not my intention. Though I don't plan on sitting around doing nothing. I can't. The gun is just for protection."

"Uh-huh."

"Are there any updates on the case?"

"Nothing major yet," I admit. "Savannah's being discharged today."

"Why the hell are they letting her out?" Luke barks, his burly arms crossing over his chest.

"She's discharging herself."

His eyes roll. "Why doesn't that surprise me!"

"Sounds like her, all right." Scott sighs.

Luke drops his mug into the sink. "I'd better go and get ready, Detective. We have a busy day ahead." He shoulders past me.

"Luke." I try one last time. "I can't stop you from buying a gun, but you're not thinking straight. Feeling guilty because you weren't there when she was taken will be *nothing*, compared to the guilt you'll feel if you charge in, guns blazing, to a situation that gets her killed."

"I'd never risk her life!" He storms away. I turn my weary eyes to Scott. "You need to call me if he gets out of control. Think of Faye's safety first." I walk over, setting my mug next to Luke's in the sink.

"He isn't as unstable as you think. But if I think you need to step in, trust me. I'll call you."

Leaving them, I head to the station.

I asked Jones to get a list of names from the bank, regarding the credit card receipts that Kitty Harmon provided us with. I want to go through them.

We're also running all the plates of drivers coming in and out of the gas station along Greenville Road leading into Appleton. This road would have given the killer access to Highway 41, north toward Green Bay. If we follow the profile, he lives or works in Green Bay. We're also cross-checking it with cars spotted at the vigil. The partial plate that

Luke got off the stalker's car is helping to narrow down that part of the search.

Perez sits at the head of the conference table along with two other agents, when I arrive. She smiles broadly when she sees the tray of coffees I hold. She makes the introductions.

Agent Ryan begins. "There are no other unsolved murders matching his MO or signatures, but we came across an assault case from 1998. The attack was on a female jogger in Crivitz's national park. The attacker attempted to break her legs with his bare hands. He failed, but did break both her arms before fleeing the scene and leaving her for dead. She regained consciousness a few hours later and called for help. Black ski mask and blue eyes were the only descriptors of the assailant. No arrests were made."

"Do we have the current whereabouts of the victim?" I ask.

"We're working on that. She left Wisconsin soon after the attack, moved to Washington DC. Then we lose her. We think she may have married and changed her name, so we're checking the marriage registrations for that time. Lynam is trying to trace any family members that might still be in the area around Crivitz."

I stand and move to the investigation wall, looking to the full map of Green Bay and surrounding areas. "If this is our perp, it means he was active as far back as '98." Tapping the map, I add a red pin to the location of the possible first attack. "OK. So we have Rose's house, place of work, and abduction site ..." I follow the red pins in each location from Rose's abduction, moving north toward Green Bay and Katherine's known locations, further up to Faye's abduction site and north again to Crivitz. "Crivitz is the furthest north. What does that tell us?" Stepping back, I look around the table.

Perez answers. "If she was his first victim, he would have sought her out in a location close to home. She may even have known him."

"If we run with that theory, then ..." I circle a ten-mile radius around each Oak Orchard Road and Crivitz.

"We know from the tire impressions at Faye's abduction, he drove toward Pensaukee. It stands to reason he went further north, toward Crivitz or beyond, so we start there." Stepping back, I examine the map with fresh eyes. The red circle encompasses endless country roads that branch off along that route, toward other small towns. It's a daunting task.

"There are hundreds of hunting lodges and cabins along this route that coincide with what you said in the profile ..." I look to Perez. "There are also farms and pockets of communities. Can we use that database of yours to cross-reference the list of names we're compiling from the bank receipts and the gas station against any property owners?" I wonder.

Agent Lynam chimes in. He has a strong New Jersey accent. "We could give it a try. I've compiled a list of a hundred men, aged between thirty and fifty, working in Green Bay in a field that involves bones. Including chiropractors, rheumatologists, anthropologists, dentists, physical therapists."

"Crosscheck it with anyone in that suspect pool who owns a property within this perimeter." I point to the wall. Perez continues along the same train of thought.

"Also remember, it's likely he comes from a single-parent family. He was most likely raised by his mother or grandmother. Factor this into your search. Include properties owned by women, widowed or single during the seventies and eighties and go from there."

"Great idea," I agree.

Jones pokes his head around the door. "Madison's crime lab is on the line."

His announcement has everyone sitting up. We've been waiting for the DNA test results from the clothing to come back. This is a big moment in the case.

"Transfer them in," I tell him, hitting the speaker button on the conference table phone.

"Detective John Walters."

A hopeful Jones sticks his head in again to listen. I beckon him in, directing him to close the door. He's worked hard on this case; he deserves to be here for this news.

"Detective, this is Amy from Madison Crime Lab. We processed the four items listed as urgent."

I lean closer to the speaker with bated breath to find out if his DNA was on any of the items, and if so, if it's in the nationwide criminal database.

"Go ahead when you're ready."

"OK. It's good news and bad news, I'm afraid. We tested the two articles of clothing sent to us, marked GB001 and GB002. We found traces of soil, wood, and hair particles, on both dresses. The DNA matched with Katherine Clifford on dress one. On dress two, it matched with Rose Bernstein. There was a third female DNA contributor found on both dresses. This DNA does not match anyone in the database."

"So, there's a possible third victim?" I look to Perez.

"Or our killer *is* a woman?" Lynam suggests.

"Or it's his mother's hair?" I add to the list of questions this news has brought.

"Sorry. Please continue, Amy." I return my attention to the call.

"No problem. Under UV light inspection, we spotted a stain. We determined that it wasn't a biological fluid like blood, semen, or saliva. Our forensic chemist tested it, and found it contained the chemical formula NH_3, or ammonia."

My brows furrow in confusion. "Isn't that found in most household cleaning products?"

"Yes, but at this concentration, it's more likely to be found in labs or in industrial cleaning products."

I continue to take notes, my mind already trying to tie that into all the other information we have. Perez asks some follow-up questions to clarify the information received before we thank Amy and end the call.

The energy in the room feels different, inspired even, as we process the crime lab results.

"What do we think of the ammonia?" Perez asks.

"Do you think he used it to try to remove DNA evidence?" I wonder.

"Hmm," she muses. "Ryan, can we look at what ammonia is used for in a laboratory setting? Let's start there and figure it out later." I nod, agreeing with her assessment.

"I'll start visiting some of the places that Katherine visited while in Wisconsin. It's a long shot, but someone might remember something."

LUKE

With Savannah next to me and Scott in the back seat, we make our way to Appleton.

"It feels a bit weird sitting in the back seat of my own car," Scott muses out loud. I asked him if I could drive, needing to be doing something.

My eyes slide to Savannah. The bruising looks worse now than it did a few days ago. The doctors told her she's lucky to be alive. One inch closer to her temple and the blow would have killed her. The stitches she got will leave a small scar, that will fade over time. The black and blue hues that mar her beautiful face will disappear. My knuckles pale against the steering wheel. My anger, fear, and concern all grip it with me, as I navigate my way toward Arnie Bernstein's home.

I glance back again at Scott. These two people, friends of Faye's, who have been on the periphery of my life for so long, but who mean the world to Faye, feel like my responsibility. At least until she's home. I've spent a few days with Scott, watched him fret and fear for Faye. I've listened to him crying over my little sister. The road ahead blurs. My eyes sting as breathing becomes difficult. I'm struggling to force air past the tightness of my chest. It takes all my concentration to pull over.

"Luke, are you OK?" Savannah's voice echoes around me. I wrench open the door, gasping for air as my feet sink into the snowy shoulder of the road.

"Luke, man. Breathe," Scott's hand thuds between my shoulders as I bend forward, gripping my knees. I've tried to keep my shit together, but the reality of how I failed Faye hits me like a sledgehammer to the chest.

"I.LEFT.HER." the words feel jagged as they tear out and release some of the weight on my chest.

"Luke. Look at me," Savannah's dusky tone fills me with a new wave of shame. The floodgates open, my tears are too heavy to hold back. They burst through my clenched lids as I stand up straight. Cupping my face, I try to hide, but the torrent takes over, slipping through my fingers as I try to rein it back in. Unable to anchor myself, I search for something to cling to. Savannah wraps her arms around my waist, holding me upright.

"We got you." Her words, her solid presence, and Scott's hand on my back help to steady me.

"Just breathe. You're OK." She continues to whisper, over and over. After a time, her soothing words take root, giving me something to hang onto.

"I'm sorry," I murmur.

"There's nothing to be sorry for." Scott slaps my back once more before stepping back, giving me space to compose myself. Savannah follows his lead, then asks if he'll give us a moment.

"I'll wait in the car." Scott's already pulling open the back door and sliding back into the car.

Savannah's blue eyes search mine. "You're not responsible for any of this: not for Faye, or me, or Scott, for that matter." She pins me with a serious stare. I nod, still wiping the wet mess from my face.

"My instincts told me to stay, and I left anyway." I allowed the pull of responsibility to outweigh my own feeling that Faye needed me, here in Wisconsin. I let the everyday pressures of life become more important than my own flesh and blood and the consequences have been tenfold. Faye is out there somewhere, still paying that deadly price.

"What are your instincts telling you now?"

Her question throws me. "I ... don't know."

"You do. Listen."

Since returning to Wisconsin, all I've wanted to do is find Faye. I haven't listened to anything *other* than the voice screaming *save her!*

"They're telling me to go pick up the guns and save my little sister."

"What guns?"

I tell her about my intended purchase and the detective's visit.

"Detective Walters is good at his job," she begins. "If anyone in that department can find Faye, it's him and that FBI agent. But *we*—" She makes a circle with her finger that includes both of us and Scott—"are her family. So, you need to trust *us* to help." She narrows her bruised eyes on me.

"You're already injured, I can't put you in more danger!" I protest. I won't ever forgive myself if she ends up hurt again.

"We need to stop at my apartment before heading on to Appleton. I need to show you something." She turns away, walking back to the car. "Come on, we're burning daylight," she calls over her shoulder.

At the apartment, Savannah runs inside. When she returns, she's carrying a wooden box. Sliding back into her seat she flips open the lid, revealing a handgun to us. My eyes widen.

"What the fuck? You have a gun?" My mouth falls open, but Scott laughs.

"You want a gun, don't you? This saves us going back to the city."

I turn to Scott. "Did you know she had a gun?"

Savannah rolls her eyes. "I grew up in Texas, Luke. Everyone there has a gun and knows how to use one." She lifts the small silver revolver out of the box, turning it over in her hand. "This here, is a Smith and Wesson 686. It has the most accurate shot of all the revolvers I've owned, plus the trigger is light. It's a classic." She opens the stainless-steel chamber and spins it, before loading in some brass-cased bullets from inside the box on her lap. I watch her, counting the bullets as they slide into the chamber. She holds up the last one, turning to face me.

"This is a.38 special. It's faster than a regular.38, and lethal." The feisty look in her eyes returns as she drops it in, then flicks her wrist so the entire chamber pops back into place. She handles it like a pro. I'm impressed, and a little turned on, if I'm honest.

"You know how to fire it?" Scott cuts in, sounding mighty impressed too.

"You're joking, right?"

He holds up his hands, grinning. "Don't shoot, cowboy!"

"OK, settle down both of you," I smile. The light, easy humor feels alien and wrong, but Savannah has somehow managed to distract us all for a moment.

"We'll find Faye, and we'll find him." She squeezes the handle of the gun before placing it back into the box and under her seat. I get it. The point wasn't to show me the gun. She wanted to show me that she can take care of herself. The fire in her eyes leaves me in no doubt.

CHAPTER 19

LUKE

Three boys throw snowballs at one another on the lawn two doors down from where Arnie Bernstein lives. Their laughter and shouts of excitement can still be heard through the closed living room window . His daughter, once a child like them, is dead. She's never coming home. All he has now are memories. Those memories are hung on every wall of this small room. Pictures of Rose on her graduation day, smiling into the camera. A wedding photo of Arnie and his deceased wife. Rose again: as a baby, a little girl, and a woman, fill the frames that hang on the walls and the surfaces of every table. He's a tall man, with tightly curled gray hair. Too young to lose everyone dear to him, too old to start over. I watch him move to the window, pulling the drapes closed and blocking the view of the boys' fun. They don't belong here and may never again.

"I was sorry to hear about your sister." Mr. Bernstein sits across from us. "I knew he would do this again." His eyes move to Savannah, before dropping to the floor. "When you agreed to help at the vigil,

I thought it would shine a light on whoever killed Rose. I never imagined it would drag you and Faye into the shadows with him."

"I'm not in the shadows. I'm here, with you ..." Savannah reaches forward, her small hand covering his as she continues. "None of us could have predicted how this would all play out. But right now, Faye needs us. Will you help?"

"I wasn't able to help Rose. How can I help Faye?" His voice breaks. Savannah's at his side in a moment. I watch her, both her hands holding his as she sits, allowing him to weep. There is no mending his shattered heart, there is no consoling him, all she can offer is kindness. I like seeing this soft side of Savannah. Scott and I glance at one another, knowing this could very well be us, if we don't stop this madman in time. We wait, allowing him his grief, feeling it as our own.

"I wish I could have known Rose. Everyone speaks so highly of her," Savannah says finally, when Mr. Bernstein seems to have exhausted his tears.

"She would curl up on that sofa." He points to where Scott and I are sitting. "Every night and she'd tell me about her day. All her interactions with her clients and animals. Oh, she loved animals. Especially the lame ones. She cared about every living thing." He shakes his head.

"Did she ever express fears about being followed?"

"No." He sighs. "I gave the police a list of the places she told me about." He stands up. Moving to the mantelpiece, he picks up a letter. "But this arrived this morning." He hands it to me. Opening it, I read it aloud.

Dear Ms. Bernstein,

Thank you for attending our recent academic information session. As a prospective postgraduate student at UW-Green Bay, we are happy to inform you that applications for next fall's Animal Science MSc. are open.

"She wanted to go to college?" I ask.

"She earned her degree in animal sciences last year. She attended the University of Wisconsin-Madison, and I know she hated being so far away from me. We had chatted about her going back to continue into veterinary medicine but then she got the job at the animal clinic and seemed really happy. She must have been making inquiries, gathering information before talking it through with me." She had her whole life ahead of her. She was making plans for a future she will never see, and tears fill his eyes once again.

We talk for over an hour. He shares the information he has managed to garner from the police. He visits the station regularly, hopeful there will be an update.

"I phoned Detective Walters before your visit. He's coming by tomorrow. I'll be telling him about the letter too," he admits as we all walk to the door. "If you find this man, what do you intend to do?"

"I'm going to kill him." I've never felt more certain of anything in my life.

"I hope you do." He nods in approval, then pats my back. "Go. Find your sister."

Turning away, I falter. My eyes meet his once more. "When all of this is over, would it be OK if I visited again?"

"I'd like that." He nods, closing the door.

When we're all back in our seats I start up the engine and pull away from the curb, heading toward UW-Green Bay.

Scott gets on his phone, looking for information. "Classes are closed for Christmas break. The gates to the campus re-open at nine a.m. tomorrow. The Animal Sciences department is closed ... but the building is open, until Friday. We could go by first thing tomorrow. Maybe we can get the name of whoever ran the information day Rose attended, see if anyone remembers her?" His frustration is felt by all of us.

"Let's just go now." I ignore the fact that we might not gain access to the building.

"It won't do any harm," Savannah agrees. I need to be doing something, even if it means circling an empty parking lot. We need to keep active and right now, I'm not sure what else we can do.

FAYE

My heart trembles, each quiver crashing against my rib cage, knocking the air from my lungs as he twirls me again. The living room blurs with speed, my feet burning as yesterday's blisters open.

"Shoulders back and slip step," he snaps sharply. I look at my feet, trying to recall what a slip step is. He blurts out directions that mean nothing to me.

"Head up," he growls, already moving me to my left. He moves too fast: 'I'm constantly playing catch up. "And turn!" he calls again, but the sudden jerk has the shoes falling off.

"HOW MANY TIMES?!"

It's impossible. There is no way that I can do what he expects. My hands swell and pulse, my aching fingers burning in his cruel grip. I keep my eyes on the coarse wooden floor. I don't reach for the shoes. I don't make any kind of sudden movement.

"I'm sorry," he croons. The softness in his tone sends a shiver of awareness up my spine. I can feel him glowering at me, his cold eyes waiting to connect with mine. We've been dancing for over an hour. I'm exhausted.

"Faye. Look at me."

Glancing to my right hand, still held captive in his, I slowly raise my eyes.

"I want to show you something." My stomach turns inside out. His erratic behavior is beginning to reveal some patterns. I recognize the evil lingering on the edge of his tone.

"Oh?" My lip quivers, my inner turmoil finally finding its way to the surface.

"Come with me." He steps back, allowing my left arm to fall from his shoulder. He pulls me along behind him. I instinctively dig my toes into the grooves of the wooden floor.

"No, please! I'll try again." I pull back. I have no idea where he wants to go, but I know it can't be good. My body responds instinctively, twisting and turning. My free hand is trying to peel his iron-clad grip from around my wrist.

"Please, no. I'll try again!" I scream, caught in a violent tug of war. My entire being fights to gain some ground.

"SHUT THE FUCK UP." His voice cuts through my pleading. The words are punctuated by the sharp strike of his balled fist, connecting with my cheek. The momentum I'd built pulling away works against me and the forceful blow sends me sailing through the air, landing with a heavy thud across the room. Until a few days ago, I've never been hurt so violently. An overwhelming need to be comforted rips through my chest. *I don't deserve this. How can he do this to me? Why me*? Self-pity and despair take their turns, gnawing away at my will as he paces. My mind screams to me: *get up, run, fight,* but my body remains a trembling heap on the floor.

"STOP CRYING!" His rage only provokes louder, wetter sobs from this mangled mess.

"Please! Let me go home!" I beg through gasps for air. My vision doubles as his legs pass by me again.

"Get up, Faye." I strain to hear his voice above my own gasps and sobs until his hot breath is at my ear. "GET UP," he growls out. The undercurrent of danger in his tone only serves to paralyze me further. He doesn't wait for me to comply. As if I'm a ragdoll, he lifts me by the fabric of my dress. Once I'm sitting, he wallops the same tender cheekbone again. Exploding white lights fade into darkness, and peace.

An icy breeze forces me awake. I'm outside. A sharp pain throbs across my face. One eye refuses to open as I struggle to take in my new surroundings. My arms and legs are bound to a hard surface; flat, except for a raised bit that's digging into my spine. I'm spinning. The cold air is like a thousand blades assaulting my bare arms and legs. *Focus, Faye!* I will myself to tune back in, to be present, to get myself out of this situation before he takes me out.

"Jeffrey?" I call out. I've lived in a state of constant trepidation for days. Mentally and emotionally spinning, he drifts, he wobbles, he spins off axis and breaks everything in his path. Now, I'm physically spinning. The tin roof overhead is my only point of reference. My breath puffs out in plumes of fear.

"I'm so disappointed, Faye. I thought you would be different," I feel his fingertips grazing my bare arm before I begin turning faster.

"In my previous relationships, I tried to avoid this. It was always a last resort. Tonight, watching you behave like a spoiled child, listening to you squeal, like a pig, forces me to behave just as brutishly."

"Jeffrey, I'm sorry. I will behave, I promise!"

He's standing over me as I turn. The spinning suddenly jerks to a stop. In spite of the freezing temperature, he is bare chested. A sheen of sweat coats his skin. He's frighteningly calm.

"Open your mouth," he demands. I can't tell if this is a test, or if complying will lead to my doom. I swallow hard against the uncertainty, then obey.

"Wider." A cruel smile spreads up his face. Tears sting my eyes, but I do as I'm bidden, my aching face stretching as he forces a rag into my mouth. A piece of duct tape seals it inside.

"Have you heard of the Catherine wheel?"

Nauseous, I shake my head and bite on the dry rag.

"It was also known as the breaking wheel. It was used during the Middle Ages, as a form of capital punishment." I listen as he begins to move, my head turning to watch as he circles me.

"An old wagon wheel, like the one you're lying on now, was brought out onto a public stage. And just like you, the punished were tied to the spokes of the wheel, spreadeagled before the public, who waited, salivating, knowing just what was to come." The pleasure in his voice freaks me out. Adrenaline rocks my body, pulling at the cable ties that bind me to, what I now know, is a wooden wheel. My screams, obstructed by the rag and duct tape are nothing more than muffled gurgles.

"Shushhhhh now." He pats my forehead, passing me again before disappearing into the darkness once more. The wheel, and my stomach, start to slowly turn as he speaks again. I shake my head against the sound. I don't want to know anymore. *JUST DO IT!* My mind screams into the abyss.

"Rose pushed and pushed, until I was forced to bring her here ..." I wish I could turn him off.

"I didn't want to hurt her. I don't want to hurt *you,* Faye."

I try to breathe, desperately inhaling air through my nose, my teeth biting down on the soggy rag.

"Don't make a sound, Faye." Laced in unadulterated pleasure, his whisper accompanies the feeling of warm breath on my hair as he stands over me again.

"I've decided to give you one last chance. But you have to know just how bad it can get for you. The executioners would usually break the legs first ..." He lifts another wagon wheel over his head. "I hope you appreciate how lenient I'm being here."

My eyes widen in horror. His hips thrust forward, his head thrown back, taut muscles exposed as he groans in pleasure. He slams the wheel down on my left arm. The pain drowns out all the aches of my previous injuries, pounding on my every nerve. His face contorts in ecstasy as he lifts the wheel above his head again, crashing it down on the same arm once more.

JEFFREY

"Jeffrey, this is the closed position. Now, follow my lead." The room swirls. I keep my back straight, my arms fluid, holding position throughout the dance.

"Jeffrey, you're slouching, again." Her curt tone hurts. I've been practicing hard every night, but she keeps getting angry with me. I keep trying, but she just gets mad.

My *mother made me stay up all night until I got this just right. "Do* you *want to have to stay up again, Jeffrey?" she grinds out. I shake my head no. I'm tired. The competition isn't for another three months. I know the steps. I'm doing everything she asks. We move around the room again, her hands gripping me with more force.*

"Jesus, Jeffrey. Fix yourself. Your posture is all wrong. Do I have to whip you again?" she yells.

I sniffle. "No, ma'am."

"From the top." We go again. The walls move around me as I keep focused, turning my head and arms as the routine demands. I pull back my shoulder blades until they meet, opening my chest. My feet slide gracefully from one step into another. I finish the routine. Sweat drips from my every pore.

"Not good enough. Again," she demands. I'm always so obedient. I'm a good boy. But the other boys at school call me a sissy because I dance. I don't want to be a sissy. It has me wound so tightly that for the first time, I snap.

"NO!" I yell, stepping out of her hold.

"You get back into position right now, Jeffrey." Her furious growl only spurs me on further. I take another step away.

"I already know the dance. I'm going to bed!" I jut out my chin in defiance and watch as her eyes fill with rage.

"No. Get back here. Now." She points her long finger to the floor in front of her. I turn on my heels, running up the stairs for my room.

"COME BACK HERE, YOU LITTLE BASTARD!" she screams. I don't look back as I race to the stairs. Her footsteps are gaining on me. I'm almost at the top when her hands grip my ankle ...

I sit up straight in my bed. My blanket slides to my waist, exposing my bare chest to the arctic night air. I collapsed into bed when we returned from the barn, exhausted. I rub the sleep now from my eyes, my shallow breathing making it difficult for me to pull myself from the nightmare. It's been so long since I've dreamed of Mother. I spent years training my body to be strong. Years spent focusing my mind and energy on being the dancer she wanted me to be. Faye has caused this. Her insolence is unearthing all the pain. I was merciful tonight. I overcame my impulse to break both her arms. Her silence at the end was all the confirmation that I needed. She will behave in future. My bare feet pad along the cold floor as I make my way to Mother's room. Unlocking the door, I open it, just a crack. Faye is still there, wrapped up warm under the heavy blanket. I tucked her in after giving her some sleeping pills. Hopefully she's getting the rest she needs for tomorrow's practice. Christmas is just around the corner. I want to spend it with Faye. I want to share those magical moments with someone who cares as much as I do.

She will help me get the dance right. Together, we can finish the steps. I know she is the one. Re-locking the door, I return to my bed. I have one more day at work, then the holidays will really begin then. She is my gift, and I am hers.

CHAPTER 20

DETECTIVE JOHN WALTERS

The FBI are still working on a list of property owners.

I shut my eyes and lean my head against the back of the chair in my office.

"I thought you might need this." A gentle knock and Della's voice brings my head back up. I smile at the outstretched coffee in her hand. "You know, you really should get rid of that plant. It's bad feng shui."

I follow her gaze to the plant corpse still on my window. "I call it my lucky dead plant," I joke, and she offers me a sleepy laugh. "It's late. What are you still doing here?" I prop my elbow on my desk and rest my own weary face into it. She sits across from me, shrugging.

"My mind won't allow me to sleep at the moment. I feel like I'm missing something. We need a little luck on our side." She groans, stretching.

I agree. I don't generally rely on luck. Hard work always yields results, and I feel we're gaining ground.

"Jones said that Mr. Bernstein called today. Did you speak with him?"

"Yes, he wants me to come by tomorrow. Said it's important but wouldn't tell me over the phone."

"I'll come with you if you don't mind? I could use a change of scenery."

"Agreed." I sigh wearily. "Let's get out of here. There's a bar next to that motel of yours, right?"

"I noticed that too. I'll grab my stuff." Standing, I pull on my coat. A cold breeze sweeps from down the hall when she opens my office door, gently blowing the paperwork in front of me. I grab the navy hardcover book sitting on the corner of my desk and use it as a paperweight. I consider the gold-embossed title. *Capital Punishment During Medieval Times.*

"Are you ready?" Della calls from the hall.

"Yeah, sorry. Let's go." I blink my sleepy eyes and follow her out, switching off the light and closing the door.

AGENT DELLA PEREZ

The days here in Wisconsin have been cold and long, the nights even more so. Sleepless nights spent trying to figure out the killer's next move, to get one step ahead of him, are beginning to take their toll. It's exhausting. Sitting here in the small bar with John, soft jazz music and low lighting ease some of the tension from my shoulders. The wine helps too.

John's drink rests on the dark wood.

"You like vodka?"

"I needed something to take the edge off." He shrugs, lifting the clear liquid to his full lips. I notice a small scar on his chin.

Without thinking, I point to it. "What happened here?"

He pulls back, as if I was going to touch him.

"Sorry." Heat creeps up my neck. "I don't know why I behave so inappropriately around you."

"No, it's fine." He pauses. "It's just an occupational hazard: when I see a hand coming for my jaw, I dip ..." Playfully, he dodges his head left to right, lifting his arms into a boxer's stance. "I got that scar while working in Madison. I was chasing a suspect, and he managed to clock me before I could get the cuffs on." He lifts his glass again, shrugging away the memory. I'm surprised, but happy that he shared the story with me.

"You mean he bested you?" I tease.

"He's currently serving life in Green Bay Correctional, so I guess that makes us even." A smug smile forms on his face. John and I have butted heads too often on this case. I allow myself to bask in this nice change of pace. The music changes. An instrumental version of "Jingle Bells" begins, the smooth timbre of the saxophone and soft piano fill the room. It fills me with nostalgia for home.

"Who will you spend Christmas with?" I wonder.

"You're full of questions tonight." He turns back to his drink, and I laugh. It bubbles up from my chest and erupts around us, louder than the mellow music.

"John, you're so suspicious!" I manage.

"I'm not suspicious ..."

I roll my eyes. "Yes. You are! I suppose you'll call that an occupational hazard too!"

"I might start calling *you* an occupational hazard soon," he grunts.

"So, you'll spend Christmas alone?" I push.

"I'll figure that out when the time comes. What about you?" He lifts his hand to the barman, ordering another round with a simple tilt of his chin.

"My family live in San Diego, but most likely I'll be in Milwaukee working." I throw my head back, the last few drops of chilled wine easing the lump in my throat. I haven't been home to visit with my family in over a year.

"San Diego's home?"

The barman slides my third glass of wine across the bar. My fingers twist its stem.

I nod. "Yes, it's where I grew up, but I was born in Tijuana."

"So basically, you have two homes. Lucky you."

"Home is where the heart is, John. And my heart is with my family."

"Home is also where fifty-four percent of murders occur." He shrugs.

His comment makes me laugh. "You're so cynical!" I giggle, taking a fresh sip of wine.

"My turn, John. You have to answer, question for question. Deal?" I narrow playful eyes on him, only to be met with his usual dubious frown.

"Hmph. Go ahead." He sighs.

"Where is your home?"

"Home is a few blocks from here. But I assume you mean where my family is. They're in Milwaukee." He looks pained.

"What brought you to Appleton?" I'm feeling brave, thanks to the wine.

He sighs again, heavily. "I worked in Madison for a few years. I was head of the homicide division, until I was in a high-speed car crash.

I suffered some broken ribs and long-term chest trauma. Needed rehabilitation. So, I decided a change of pace was needed."

"I'm sorry to hear that. Do you like it here?"

He shrugs.

"Would you rather be back in Madison?"

He ignores my question. "Your turn, Agent. Why the FBI?"

"I was living in California, studying psychology. I was always interested in the human mind, but I imagined myself in a cozy office, helping people cope with the challenges that life offers." I laugh.

"What changed?"

"I was in the second year of my degree, and we were looking at profiling human behavior and how that is used in the criminal justice system. I was fascinated. I excelled at my assignments and exams that semester. I went on to complete my master's, landed a job working with analyzing criminals and law enforcement personnel straight out of college. I loved it, and I learned a lot about police work."

"So, you were one of those shrinks they force us to see?" His lips twitch as he tries to hold back another smile, but his eyes betray him, revealing the warmth reflected in his soft tone.

"No! Many come of their own volition! I'd been doing it for two years when I heard about the FBI program. I had the educational requirements, made it through the testing and interview stages and passed basic training."

"Tell me this, Della ..." the gruff tone on my name sends a trickle of heat down my spine. I flush as his dark eyes find mine over the rim of our glasses. "Do you like being inside the minds of psychopaths?" He tips his head back, his Adam's apple bobbing as he swallows. My gaze drops to my wine. My suddenly parched throat needs relief and I too, take a large gulp.

"I like catching them," I finally answer.

"It's an art."

"Profiling, or catching killers?" I wonder, surprised he would describe it so.

"Both, I suppose." He smiles.

"You think we are artists, John?" I laugh.

"No, that doesn't sound right."

"Well, it is a skill, but you could say art."

"Yeah, but you describe our killer's work as art or that at least *he* feels that it is. So, to compare your work in the same way sounds odd. I think *skill* suits better." His eyes zero in on my face.

"I'm not sure. I think I was liking where that was leading. I think with my knowledge, I'd make a prolific—" I pause gingerly—"nuisance." I giggle.

"You are already!" He laughs. "But I agree: with your skill, I wouldn't want to be on your tail."

I peruse his body before locking eyes with him. Dark like roasted umber, they send my pulse racing. I want him. I want to know him. But it will never happen, his walls are too high.

"With your skills, John, I would willingly surrender."

Clearing his throat, he stands abruptly.

"I think we should head out; we have another long day ahead of us, and you look tired." His cool tone is like ice-water to the warmth I was experiencing only seconds ago. My shoulders stiffen.

"I'm good here. You head off." I turn from him.

"I'm not leaving you here, alone, at this hour!"

My hand moves to the gun on my hip. "I think I'll be OK. Unless you planned on walking me to my door?" I chance.

"No, I didn't," he admits. I appreciate his honesty. "Goodnight, Della."

"Goodnight, John." I try to keep the frustration from my voice, but this man is infuriating. I watch him leave. After waiting a few minutes, I pull on my own winter coat and walk the short distance to my motel room. The cold air helps to temper my mood.

LUKE

The smell of coconut always lingers in the air around Savannah. Her apartment is no different. Lying here, my tense body is unable to relax into the comfort of the oversized sofa beneath me. I toss and turn, each movement bringing a new waft of coconut. As soon as Scott's head hit the opposite couch, he was out for the count. He's emotionally worn out. Savannah is too, I can see it in the dark rings under her eyes.

Twisting again, I see the kitchen clock across the room. It's three a.m. Somewhere, my sister is alone and afraid. The ticking of the clock seems to get louder and louder, like time is running out. Sitting up, I rest my elbows on my knees. My hands grip fistfuls of hair in an attempt at calming my frazzled mind. *Sleep, I need to sleep.* If I can just get a few hours, I know I'll be able to think fast, act faster.

The wooden box, home to the.38 special, sits on the coffee table across from me. Savannah: true-crime obsessed and carries a gun. It surprised me, but it shouldn't have. I've fired guns before, gone on hunting trips when I was younger. The thrill of killing an animal evaded me. I've never really understood the fascination some people have with guns and killing. But right now, I'd take that gun and pump all six bullets into whoever has my sister. Without hesitation. I would go to prison for the rest of my life, if it meant Faye and Savannah were safe.

An audible gasp from Savannah's room has me up and at her door in seconds.

She's sitting up in bed, gripping her blanket to her chest.

"Are you OK?" I whisper into the moonlit room. Her eyes shift toward the door, her head shaking no. Her silence sends the hair on the back of my neck upright. My eyes start scanning her room.

"It's Luke." My hoarse voice is a deep whisper. Satisfied that the fear I see in her eyes is only a residue from a nightmare and not some new intrusion, I move closer to her bed.

"I—" she manages before her bottom lip quivers. Her wide eyes fill with tears and overflow. My heart aches to touch her. To comfort her.

"What if we don't find her?" She wails, as I drop onto her mattress, feeling it sag beneath my weight. My hand reaches for hers. She climbs onto my lap. Her auburn hair, messy from sleep tickles my nose.

"That's not an option, Savannah. I'll find her." There can't be anything soothing about my gruff tone. I would like to be a better man for her. Someone who is soft. Instead, she has a rough lumberjack with calloused hands and zero tenderness.

"I dreamed about his eyes." Distraught, she continues to cry. "He looked so *evil*, Luke. What if he's hurting her?"

"Come on, Savannah. We can't think that way. She's strong. She'll be trying to find a way back to us." I take her hand in mine, reassuring us both.

"I didn't see him; he came out of nowhere." Her body trembles as she tries to breathe through her weary sobs. I want to wipe her tears away, be worthy of her vulnerability. Instead, I tighten my embrace and hope she finds some comfort.

"Listen: tonight, you're going to cry this out as much as you need, then go to sleep. I'll be here. Tomorrow, you're going to wake up and we're going to get back out there and find Faye. OK?" I push her hair back from her face, feeling her nod against my chest before I lay her down on the bed. Her fingers still grip my t-shirt, pulling me toward her.

"Stay with me?" I feel her warm breath on my face, and I realize that I need her as much as she needs me.

"Of course, I will," I say, sliding in next to her.

"Goodnight, Savannah," I whisper. Resting my forehead against hers, my body relaxes for the first time in days. As she snuggles into my embrace, I finally sleep.

DETECTIVE JOHN WALTERS

Arnie Bernstein's grief is more apparent every time we meet. He's lost weight and the dark circles under his eyes suggest he may not be sleeping.

"How have you been?" I ask him, taking a seat across from him.

"The truth is, every day feels like hell. I get up, I suffer through it, and I remind myself of what Rose went through. There was no easy way out for her and there won't be for me." His frank response weighs heavily on me.

"Mr. Bernstein, I know I let Rose down. I'm sorry."

"Please, call me Arnie. And you haven't let her down unless you've given up on finding this monster." There's a kindness to his tone that I don't feel I deserve.

"I'll never stop looking for him. I can promise you that."

"Good." He hands me a letter. I open it up, reading as he continues. "This came yesterday. I thought you should know about it. Looks like she was planning on returning to college. She hadn't told me."

Agent Perez takes the letter from me, reading it over as I take notes in my notepad. I know that Katherine Clifford was in Wisconsin touring different college campuses. She was interested in math research. Faye's a radio DJ and Rose was working in an animal clinic. There doesn't seem to be a common link between all three, regarding their careers.

"He must be stopped! What about this poor girl, Faye? Her brother promised he'd find him." His hands tremble.

"Mr. Bernstein, we won't rest until we stop him. You now have the word of Detective Walters here, the FBI, and Luke Anderson. This will come to an end. And when it does, we will still be here, for anything you might need." Perez reassures him.

"Arnie, can I ask: in your chat with Luke yesterday, did you tell him about this letter?" I can't have Luke running around chasing leads before we even know about them.

He nods. "He could potentially be a nuisance to you, or he may be an obstacle for the killer. Either way, if his sister ends up like Rose, he won't lie awake night after night wishing he'd done more. I helped him, and some small part of me feels that I've helped Rose, somehow." This assertion brings more life to him than I've seen all morning.

"That makes sense," I admit. I could never understand the heartbreak that comes with losing a child, but I know the self-deprecation that comes from wishing you'd done more.

"I guess I'd better let you go follow up on that." He nods to the letter, still in Della's hand.

"Can we take it with us?"

"Of course. Savannah took a picture on her phone." He smiles mischievously.

"I'm sure she did." I smile back. He walks us to the door and stands, waving as we pull away.

"Do you mind?" Perez asks, rolling down her window. Cold air swirls in. Glancing toward her, I watch her inhale deeply, her eyes fluttering closed with each deep breath. "Are you OK, Agent Perez?" My brows crease in concern.

"Too much wine last night." She turns toward me, a rueful smile on her face. "Not really. The air was so thick with sadness and regret there, it's lodged itself here." Her hand comes to rest on her chest. My eyes drop to her slender fingers, before returning to the road ahead.

I sigh now, too. "That cloud of despair may never lift from around him."

"Rose was his reason for living. Her future was his. He hasn't just lost her, he has lost the possibility of grandchildren, the opportunity to walk her down the aisle, her love and support. I hope in time he finds a purpose."

When Rose went missing, Arnie was desperate to have her home. Today, I witnessed how that desperation is turning into an obsession with catching his daughter's murderer. He doesn't blame me; he blames Rose's killer. I need to remember that this isn't just me versus a killer. There are so many victims, so many people seeking out the truth, searching for answers and begging for justice.

"Talking to him always helps me to refocus," I admit.

"How so?" she asks.

"I want to catch this killer for them. Ego aside, I want to find him, I want to bring them justice." I shrug, my eyes staying firmly on the road ahead.

"Can I be honest, John?" I hate those words. They're always followed by some ugly truth that I never want to hear. I nod for her to continue.

"I think you're an amazing detective."

I wait for the *but*. Silence forces me to glance toward her. "Is that it?" I ask.

She laughs softly, her green eyes full of humor. "Yes, it's true."

"No 'but'?"

"Do you want there to be a 'but'?" She laughs again.

"No, *but* there usually is!" I laugh too at the silly moment.

"No. We all need a little positive reinforcement from time to time and you're a great cop."

We pull up to a red light. The engine hums beneath us as I try to figure out the catch. There's always a catch.

"Hmm." My doubt has her laughing again.

"You don't believe me?"

"I do. Thank you." I clear my throat.

"You're welcome."

There is no follow up. No *but*.

"We're almost here," I announce, changing the subject. "Will you see if this college is on the list of places Katherine visited?"

I reach over and pop my glove box, pointing out the list for her. She casually peruses the list as I head toward the University of Wisconsin Green Bay campus. Her demeanor is much the same as it was before. I find myself still stuck on her compliment. Certain that I don't deserve her kindness.

"Yes, it's here!" She looks toward the roof of the car, pondering. "You know, they would both have been working toward science degrees, which involves lab work."

"That could explain why we found ammonia on Rose's clothing," I agree.

"We should investigate who processes the college applications for the science departments. They would have access to all the potential students' personal details."

"I think we might be on to something here." My detective senses tingle as the dots begin to connect again.

CHAPTER 21

DETECTIVE JOHN WALTERS

I drive through the campus, following the same road that led me to Dr. Stanley's office. I pass by that red brick building on my right and pull into the lot for the animal sciences department on the left. We climb out of the car to find Luke, Scott and Savannah walking out of the animal sciences building.

"Jesus Christ." I shake my head in exasperation. Perez ducks her head, trying not to laugh. Three amateur sleuths running around Wisconsin with a gun are not only going to put themselves at risk, but the public too.

I approach, unimpressed.

"Luke Anderson, you are now interfering with my investigation." My steely gaze holds his.

"Looks like you're one step behind, Detective," he sneers.

"This isn't a game!" I bark.

"You think I'm treating this as a game? I'm on the street, looking for my fucking sister! Where were you? Behind your desk? I told you I'd stay out of your way. Now you stay out of mine." He pushes past me, his burly bicep catching my shoulder. I grab his arm. His unruly eyes cut to my hand, his mouth curling in anger.

"You got something you need to do?" He dares me.

"You get in my way again, and you'll be arrested. All of you." I look to the other two, who look just as defiant.

"That won't look great in the press. Or sound great on the radio, Detective." Savannah Phillips's husky southern tones sound in my ears. Dropping my hand, I turn to her.

"You think I care what the media says about me? I couldn't care less. What I care about is finding Faye; as quickly and as safely as possible. You might not see it, but this vigilante act will only do more harm than good."

"John, let's go." Perez intervenes.

"Is there anything else that I should know, before you leave?"

"No, the office is empty. There are only a few people around; no one remembers seeing Rose." Luke's jaw ticks with frustration. I nod, turning on my heel and leaving them as they return to their car.

"He needs to feel useful," Perez says softly.

"I know, but the last thing I need is more deaths on my conscience." I pull open the door and wait for her to go ahead. We walk through the building and find a member of the faculty, working away in one of the labs. Having knocked on the door, we enter.

The young female looks up from her microscope, smiling. "Can I help you?"

Perez and I introduce ourselves, showing our badges.

"We were hoping to speak with someone from the animal sciences department." The slim brunette places dark-rimmed glasses on her nose as she introduces herself.

"I'm Dr. Kelly Hughes. I'm an assistant to Professor Lee. He's gone home for the winter recess. Maybe I can help?" she shrugs.

"I'm sorry to disturb your work. We really need to speak with whoever oversees college applications and information sessions for the entire science faculty," I tell her.

"Is there a building that oversees that?" Perez wonders.

"Yes. When you first come onto campus, the large stone-faced building on the left is the office of admissions. Annie Bennett heads that whole department. She oversees the guided tours and information sessions too. She's the lady to speak with."

"Doctor, would you know of any reason ammonia might be used in your lab?"

"Most of our chemical cabinets will have ammonia. It's used quite a lot: in organic chemistry; as a base solution in analytical chemistry; and it does come into our studies here. But in general, we don't have cause to use it in a lab setting." she shrugs.

"Can you think of a reason any other lab might use it?"

"Well ... it would be used mainly in chemistry, or as a cleaning solution?" she offers.

"Thank you," Perez and I say together. When we reach the door, I turn back to see her hunched once more in front of her microscope.

"Merry Christmas, Dr. Hughes."

"You too, Detective."

I don't miss Della's curious stare.

"Do we have a thing for lab coats?" she teases.

"No, I was wondering how safe she is here alone," I answer, honestly.

"I'm sure she will be OK." She smiles.

"If ammonia is used mainly in a chemistry lab, we can check out the surrounding buildings. Look into the chemistry faculty too." I hold the door for her, glancing up at the security camera mounted on the corner of the building. I scan the other buildings around us. They all have similar cameras facing the sidewalk.

"We'll need to get the footage from these." I point toward the camera. "Hopefully we can pinpoint the date she was here, to save us trawling through hours of footage," I say as we climb into my car, heading toward the office of admissions.

Unfortunately, Annie Bennett has also finished for the winter recess, but the dean is still in his office. We're lucky enough to catch him just as he's getting ready to leave.

"Thank you for seeing us on such short notice, Dean Fiennes." I nod as Della and I take our seats across from his desk.

He waves it away. "Of course. What is this about, officers?" He tugs the hem of his reindeer sweater over his round stomach, before stroking his white beard. This time of year must make him the butt of many Santa jokes.

"We're investigating the murders of Rose Bernstein and Katherine Clifford," I begin.

He looks horrified. "Oh my. Well, how can I help? I don't believe they were students of ours?"

"No: prospective students. Both had attended information sessions or campus tours in the weeks before their disappearances." It's difficult to know how much information to give to a witness, but in this case, we need his help. The more he knows, the more inclined he'll be to help. I hope.

"Well, anything we can do to help, let me know."

"We wanted to get in touch with Annie Bennett. I understand she's the head of your office of admissions? We need to speak with her as soon as possible."

"Annie has gone home for the Christmas break, but I have her personal contact details. I'm sure she won't mind me passing them on, in this case." He turns to his computer screen, looking up briefly. "You understand, I'll need to call ahead and let her know to expect you."

"Of course. She's not in any kind of trouble," Perez interrupts. "We just need to ask a few questions."

He prints off a sheet of letter-sized paper, handing it to me.

"We also noticed that you have security cameras on the corner of your animal sciences building ..." I reach into my inside pocket and pull out the letter Arnie got yesterday. "Do you know what date this information session took place?" I pass it to him.

"Our information sessions run all year long, but I can look up this young lady's name. If we sent this letter, she must have signed up to have us contact her when registration opened. She should be in the system ..." He's typing away as he talks. "Ah, yes. She came in on October ninth. She attended the lunchtime session, between one and two p.m. I will contact Security and let them know to accommodate any requests you might have."

"We really appreciate how helpful you've been." Perez reaches over to shake his hand, as we stand to leave.

"The CCTV was installed to protect our students and faculty. I hope this is nothing more than a very sad coincidence, but nevertheless, it is my duty to protect our community."

I shake his hand before leaving and find myself wishing him a merry Christmas too.

JEFFREY

Shock had me rooted to the spot as I watched Detective Walters and Faye's brother in a heated discussion. Surrounded by the FBI agent, Savannah and *him!* They glared angrily at one another right outside my window. I was just about to finish for the Christmas break. A few seconds more, and I would have bumped right into them. News reports today confirmed that Katherine's case was connected to Rose's. *Detective Walters is finding another link!*

My instinct was to run, to get out of here before they located me. It took a few seconds to realize that I was safe. They were here to interview witnesses from the animal science building. There is nothing that they can gain from that line of inquiry. Yes, I watched her enter that building from this very window, but I never approached her. I waited in my car, to follow behind her when she left. When the detectives enter the building, I watch the others drive away before walking to my own car. The college is practically a ghost town. I'm one of the last to finish up for Christmas. Satisfied that I'm still safe, I pull out of my parking spot, my car creeping slowly along the icy road.

FAYE

The pain is gone. Sitting upright on the bed, I raise my arms out in front of me, rolling and twisting them with ease. I smile when I realize that I'm no longer tied to the bed. My bare feet dangle off the edge, the tips of my toes grazing the smooth wooden floor. Everything has changed. The floors are polished and clean, the wardrobe, the dressing table, all of it gleaming in the sunlight. Standing, I move to the window and look out at lush green fields and pine forest, fencing in the freshly painted red barn. It's summer in Wisconsin, bringing with it a wonderful heat. Sweat begins to prickle across the surface of my skin. My eyes track to my exposed arms, watching as the hot sun beams through the window, turning my pale skin blue. The soft rumble of tires on the gravel driveway holds me in place to see a black sedan come into view. *He's here!*

"Scott!" His name is a squeal of relief and pleasure. *He's here!* I rush to the door. There's no fear as I pull it open, laughing and calling out his name over and over, as I make my way down the stairs. My long hair is sticking to my neck. Sweat is oozing from every pore as my excitement builds with each step. I don't stop to admire the fully furnished living room, don't stop to listen as a different melody plays from the old record player in the corner. Instead, I push my tired feet to the door. My hand grips its handle. Freedom is within my grasp.

"Faye?" Scott's familiar voice calls to me from the other side. The door is jammed.

"Scott!" I call out again, pulling harder. My arms ache, the bristling pain weakening my ability to yank it open.

"Scott, push!" A cold chill ruffles my hair before dancing across my skin, leaving a trail of goosebumps in its wake. *HE's* here too. I look back over my shoulder. The room has returned to its decrepit state. His voice bellows from upstairs.

"FAYE," he growls. His footsteps, no longer light, fall heavy on the wooden floor as he nears.

"Scott! He's coming!!" My frantic pleas are joined by a swell of strength, and I pull open the door. Eager for Scott's embrace, the safety of his arms, I run headlong into the brick wall.

"Scott! ... Scott. ... Scott ..." Dazed, I close my eyes, continuing to call for him. A bone-chilling shiver rakes my body as Scott's voice fades further into the distance. Then I feel him, his weight next to me.

"Shusssssh. Faye, I'm here." His hands wipe at the sweat on my brow, in spite of my head twisting to resist his touch.

"Shusssssh," he continues, his fingers now at my wrists.

I peel open my sticky eyes and squint against a single bright spear of light lancing through the small gap in the heavy curtains. Its sharp intrusion divides the room in two but brings no warmth to the murky corners, leaving me shrouded in dimness and confusion.

"Scott?" I call out again, feeling the weight of my arms fall from the loosened binds. I'm so cold. My skin, pulled taut to accommodate the swelling, feels no relief.

"I'm going to forgive you, Faye. You have a fever." His words slice through my confusion, drawing my attention to his face. "You'll need to take these. I'm going to wrap your arm, it will help." He's already stuffing two pills into my mouth, lifting my head from the pillow as he presses a glass against my lips. Sipping, I swallow the pills. Nothing could be worse than this pain. I was dreaming. I thought I had escaped. The soul-crushing reality makes the pain of my arm pale in comparison. I close my eyes, hoping to never open them again.

"I saw that meddling brother of yours today."

My pulse quickens. Jeffrey's angry tone drags my eyes open and to where he stands in the doorway. He leans against the doorjamb, his hands tucked into the pockets of his black slacks, a white shirt neatly tucked in.

I woke up not long ago. The pain lingers beneath the surface, the constant threat of its return marked by every slight movement. Before his arrival, the room was pitch black. No moonlight could sneak through the now tightly closed curtains. I didn't need its light to know it was almost time for our nightly routine. He's going to make me dance again.

"Oh? Was he asking after me?" My heart pounds in my ears. The urge to plague him with questions is dizzying.

"Of course not; I didn't speak with him. He was hanging around my workplace with that *boyfriend* of yours." The words rip from his chest in a deep growl.

"He's not my boyfriend," I mumble. Hope swells beneath my ribcage. Warmth wraps itself around my tired heart, helping to slow the wild beats. I knew Luke would be looking for me. Knowing Scott is with him is like a balm to my battered soul.

"I KNOW THAT. DON'T YOU THINK I KNOW THAT?!" He moves quickly, bending over me, his hands on either side of my freshly bandaged arms as he yells. My lip quivers, tears pooling in my eyes as I nod in agreement. "He could never take care of you the way I can. Do you think he would risk the things that I've risked, to be with you?" His nose presses against mine, his expression ferocious.

"No!" I gasp.

"Good girl." His voice turns lustful. The quick shift in energy rips through my gut like a switchblade. *Not now,* I offer up a silent plea to the heavens. *Not ever*, I beg as his eyes sweep lower, to the rise and fall of my chest. My body seizes, his salacious perusal tensing every muscle. My arms tighten by my side, my legs go rigid, my lips clamp shut. Each quickened intake of air causes my nostrils to flare. His eyes snap back to mine, the hellish fires in his heated gaze extinguished by my icy-cold response.

"I'll be back in five minutes." Rejection returns him to rage as he lifts his weight from the bed. He doesn't look back. The heavy thud of the door lock unleashes a fresh wave of panic. Memories of last night's punishment flood my mind. His wild groans of pleasure, his arousal at my cracking bones. The desire in his eyes moments ago pales compared to the rapture he derived by strapping me to that wheel.

Surviving him means figuring out how to escape him before he brings me back to the barn. There is no other option. My arm aches, but with a renewed appreciation for my intact legs, I creep to the window. With one eye over my shoulder, I slip between the curtain folds. My shaking fingertips grip the wooden frame and lift. It doesn't budge. My arm pulses beneath the tight bandages that Jeffrey wrapped it in. I bite my lip against the pain, my swollen fingers grip along the rotting wood. On a deep inhale, I muster every ounce of strength and push upward. The base of the frame crumbles in my hands.

Oh my God! Tears of relief sting my eyes until the floorboards vibrate beneath my feet.

He's coming!

Mashing the broken pieces of wood back into place, I dash to the vanity table. The lock turns, the door thrusts open as he enters. With my heart in my throat, I spin around to face him.

"What are you doing in here?" His eyes flick from my clammy face to the vanity before narrowing on the gap in the curtains. He takes a step forward.

I fake a dizzy swoon. "Jeffrey, I feel a little hot. Could I have some water, please?"

His arm snakes around my waist, guiding me to the stool.

"Sit ..." He hushes me. "I'll wait here while you get ready. We will have water at supper."

He watches me slowly apply the makeup. He eyes each painful swipe of the dark kohl across my lower lids, then salivates when the tube of lipstick rattles between my broken fingers.

"That's enough." His patience gone, he stands. Taking my arm in his, he helps me down the stairs, and to the kitchen table.

"I thought tomorrow we could do up a grocery list for Christmas dinner!" He grins, filling my glass with water from a jug at the center of the table. I sip the tepid liquid, watching as he moves to prepare some food.

"Oh, sounds exciting." I try to smile. "Does that mean you have the day off?" I ask, keeping my tone light.

"I have three weeks off for the holidays." His shoulders tense, his stiff back to me as he waits for me to respond.

The water turns to bile in my belly, the sickening reality dawning. Three weeks. Together. "Lovely. Will we have turkey for Christmas?" *If he's here, how will Luke find him?*

"I'd like that." He relaxes, smiling again.

Our conversation over supper follows that same pattern. I pretend to be interested in his day, his life. Careful to avoid his suspicions, I avoid intrusive questions, but manage to figure out he works in a lab. If Luke was at his place of work, that information should be enough to lead police to him.

When it comes time to dance, I curl my toes, gripping the inside soles of the shoes. My bandaged arm screams in protest as he moves me with vigor around the room. I try to keep up and manage to succeed for most of the evening. He is pleased. His irritation, when the shoes finally do come away, is tame in comparison to yesterday's punishment. I push the fear of the barn and the breaking wheel to the back of my mind, determined to make it through the night with my legs still intact. I'm no good to him if I can't play out this sick routine. Completing the dance is his main objective, yet he makes it impossible for me to do it. My "mistakes" allow him to vent his rage on me. I'll never win this battle. I need to be smart. Tonight has proven that. I massaged his ego, and he didn't lash out as much during the dance.

By the end, my head is spinning. The lyrics of that song are repeating over and over in my mind. He walks me to my room.

"Tomorrow, I'll bathe you again." His hand cups my face, his fingers playing with my hair. I keep my composure; I know he's testing me. I stay perfectly still as he bends down. He's daring me to reject him, but I learned my lesson last time. His lips graze mine; I don't recoil. I close my eyes as he presses his lips again, more firmly. He doesn't use his tongue; I don't think I could continue with this pretense if he tried.

"Let's get you to bed," he whispers, his breath fanning my face. I'm surprised when he ties my wrists together, leaving them to rest on my stomach as I lie on my back. This is the first time he hasn't tied them to the bedposts. I've managed to win his trust. Indulging him in his madness has won me a small victory. I fall asleep consoling myself with the knowledge that tomorrow, I'm going to start putting my plan of escape into action.

JEFFREY

"COME BACK HERE, JEFFREY!" Her high-pitched scream startles me, as I race to the top of the stairs. Her high heels scrape against the wooden floors, clacking on the stairs as she chases behind me. My skinny legs tire with each step upward. Only one more step until I can lock myself in my room. But she's quicker. Her fingers grip my ankle and yank me back. I fall forward onto the landing. My nails try to dig into the polished floorboards but can't find purchase. I slide as she pulls me back toward her.

"NO!!" I twist and turn, fighting against her. My frantic pleas make it hard for me to breathe, harder to focus as my body is pulled over the edge and down two steps to where she stands on the stairs.

"YOU LITTLE BRAT! YOU'LL PAY FOR THAT," she screams.

It happens so suddenly, in a blur of panic and rebellion. One moment she's threatening to punish me, the next, my foot lifts, kicking her backward. My eyes feel glued to her body as she tumbles down the stairs. Her shoulder makes a popping sound as she hits the edge of one stair. Time is moving so slowly. The sound echoes around me as she continues her descent. Her neck cracks, the sound joined by a crunch as her jaw hits wood. My eyes are wide, taking it all in. Her legs crash through the spindles of the wooden railing. The broken pieces roll with her as the thigh bone pokes through the skin of her right leg. Her arms flop down at her sides when she lands on her back. I look down on her from atop the stairs. My panic subsides, replaced by a strange feeling in my groin. The way she's lying, she's looking up at the painting above her head. Slowly, I descend the stairs, watching her.

"Jeffrey ..." she gurgles, probably bleeding internally. Her eyes widen in horror as I stand over her, my head tilting from side to side, awed by the sight before me. Fascinated by the rise and fall of her chest as the rhythm slows. Her final breath is a whispered "help."

My eyes fly open. That's the second dream of Mother this week. A sense of calm replaces my usual panicked reaction. There's no pounding heart or ringing in my ears, no hyperventilating or confusion. Instead, the cloud of my warm breath mingling with the cold air holds my attention as my hand slides beneath the covers, skimming the surface of my slick torso down to my bulging crotch. Memories of Faye's kiss tonight have my eyes fluttering closed, my fingers gripping my arousal, each tug building momentum. Her soft lips, the fear in her eyes begging me to be gentle, burns deep, spreading like wildfire to my chest before erupting in a deep growl that disturbs the still night. I remember her on my wheel, her arms and legs spread, primed. The clear, sublime sound of the snap resurrecting itself in my memory propels my warm, wild release.

The months after my mother's death were a time of guilt and shame. Her attempt to enhance my dancing was thwarted by years in foster care. Precious practice time was wasted while I struggled to comprehend the mixed emotions the memory of her death brought on. The link between sadness and arousal silently fucked with my head. Then I was placed with a foster family who owned a dog. The skinny mongrel nipped daily at my heels. Breaking its leg stopped the biting and brought a similar thrill, not unlike what I had felt that night. The fear of being caught, combined with the power of holding its leg in my hand and feeling it snap, was electrifying. The mutt's vulnerability excited me as much as getting away with it. They never suspected me.

At sixteen, I joined a kickboxing club and managed to break an opponent's arm. The club banned me for excessive force. It brought unwanted attention. Social workers insisting I see a therapist for my 'anger issues.' I endured six months of therapy.

I had thought breaking his arm would quell the inner voice, the drive. Instead, I felt nothing. It was mother's face that appeared each night in my fantasies. To get ahead of these urges, I needed to relive that time with her.

At nineteen, I worked up the courage to attack a girl. After two years of watching women, imagining what it would feel like to break their bones, the desire turned into a compulsion. The park was the perfect hunting ground. Hidden behind the treeline, I watched as the blond jogged alone, taking the scenic route as she looped around the lake. I'd already decided that whoever chose that path was choosing me. It was destined.

At first, my fists felt muffled as adrenaline pumped through my body, so I beat harder, unaware of just how much power was behind each blow. Her moans exhilarated me. She lay there, like Mother, her eyes looking toward the lake. The sight sent all my blood flowing to my cock. It was masterful; until I tried to break her leg. I twisted it, stamped on it, bent it in every direction, until exhaustion took hold. The failure catapulted me into red rage, bolstered my strength as I grabbed her arms in fury. The first crack spurred me on until her eyes popped open, the pain pulling her from unconsciousness. Her screams propelled me into action. My fingers curled around her neck, wringing the air from her body until she succumbed again. Convinced I would be caught, I fled without checking her pulse.

A mistake I never made again!

For weeks after, I waited for the police to break down my door. They didn't come. They never suspected me.

Those dark needs disappeared for a time. I embraced college, explored relationships, and endured unsatisfying sex. Time passed in a haze of numbness.

Returning to the farmhouse after college reignited my passions. Back in Mother's world with the same record sitting on the turntable, I was her child again. A scared boy who wanted to please her: get the steps right, make her proud.

In that moment, it all became so clear. I could never bring her back, but I could make it up to her. I would finish out our routine. Perfectly. I would find a partner worthy of dancing in Mother's shoes.

At first, I brought street workers home. The first few times, they humored me and danced with me. Then, one called me crazy, causing a rage strong enough to blind me. When the red mist lifted, I found her dead on the living room floor. Her face was unrecognizable, and my fists were cut and swollen. It was messy, but I felt alive. Her corpse allowed me to explore my fascination with the femur. Through various experiments, I removed the muscle and tissues around the leg. I realized that though I was curious to see the broken bone, to see the result of my work, it added nothing to my enjoyment. It was hard to clean the bone and harder to wash away the blood. Ultimately, it sullied the experience. My pleasure was derived purely from the sound of that snapping bone. I examined bones every day at work. That was enough to satisfy my anatomical interests.

When I sat in on Dr. Stanley's lecture on medieval tortures, the images from his projector fascinated me. The brazen bull cooked people alive inside it. The rack pulled and stretched their limbs, but it was the breaking wheel that aroused my curiosity. That's when things truly changed for me. Learning more about the breaking wheel became an obsession. A new kind of fantasy. I knew there was an old wagon in the barn. I removed its wheels. It was easy after that. I added the iron and the handles to hold its weight.

I paid the butcher for bones and practiced, night after night, until I was strong enough to bring the wheel down in one fell swoop. Then I brought home a prostitute to practice on. Her thrashing caused the wheel to break her skin, but I knew that with less movement, I could avoid that in future. That taught me about how tight the binds needed to be.

Then, Katherine came into my life. I was lounging outside the office of admissions. Her bright smile stopped my heart, the appreciation in her gaze invited me into her world. When Annie called to her, the world stood still.

Katherine, the same name as Mother. And she resembled her too: blond, blue eyes and beautiful. There was no denying the spark between us. I needed to find her. I did, two weeks later, in Chicago.

She was the first to share this experience with me, but she fought me every day. Kicking, biting, and finally scratching at my face. When my work colleagues scrutinized my suspicious-looking injury, our connection dwindled.

Rose came three years later. I cared deeply for Rose, but she was weak, and unable to keep up with the rigors of practice.

Faye, now: she's really made all of this worthwhile. Her brother is a worry. I'm wondering if I should pay him a visit.

I'm tired, but I'm excited for tomorrow with Faye. I'm not going to let anything ruin it.

CHAPTER 22

SCOTT

I'm playing with the eggs on my plate.

"Scott, you need to eat," Savannah's bruised eyes swim with concern. It's day four and I miss Faye. I can't eat. Can't even think about it. I just want her to come home. I'm in a constant limbo between hope and hopelessness. I'm exhausted running the daily gamut of emotions. One moment I'm determined, certain we can find her. The next I'm angry, wanting to kill the man who did this. Then my emotions take over and I can hardly breathe with fear. Everything in between is just numbness.

"I will ..." I look across the table at them both. We're all huddled into the corner booth of a diner. Downturned mouths and worried eyes look back at me. "I promise."

The trip to the college yesterday yielded nothing. We're all feeling a little defeated.

"I wish I had an idea, something we could be doing. I feel useless!"

I look around the diner. Christmas decorations hang from the ceiling. The servers, all wearing Santa hats, are smiling. Families are doing their Saturday shopping in town, all caught up in the holiday cheer.

"Christmas is Faye's favorite time of year." Luke drags my eyes back to him.

"I hope she knows. I wish I could tell her how worried I am." My breath hitches, my eyes filling. My throat burns as I try to hold in the love I feel for Faye, but it's useless and the tears break free. In the middle of a busy diner during the Christmas rush, I cry like a baby. Pride is washed away by the onslaught of tears.

"Scotty." Savannah reaches across the table and squeezes my hand. Luke's large hand comes down over both of ours.

"Scott, man. Breathe." He repeats my words to him.

I nod. Reaching for some napkins, I dry my face and take a few calming breaths.

"I'm sorry. Let's refocus: what can we do next?"

Luke straightens. "What do we know?"

"We know that he killed two women," Savannah chimes in. "We know that Rose attended that information session, and we know that Katherine traveled to Wisconsin to tour different colleges."

I've avoided reading the newspapers so far, but Savannah has done a good job of keeping me up to speed.

Luke suddenly blinks, struck by a thought. "I've got it." He looks from me to Savannah. "Katherine came here. That was three years ago. If the killer was a student, they would have either finished their courses or be in their final year."

"OK, how does that help us?"

"Don't you see? If he met Katherine at the same campus as Rose, then he was there three years ago too, for Katherine. It rules out most students, but not *staff*."

Luke is right. This narrows down possible suspects for us to look at. The pendulum swings back to hope as I jump up from the booth.

"Savannah, can we use your laptop?"

"Yeah, but why?" She rushes behind us as we head back to the car.

Luke jumps into the back seat, not even taking the time to complain about the cramped conditions. "The college website might have pictures of their staff, maybe a photo gallery. We can start with the animal sciences department."

"Do you think you'd know his eyes if you saw them again?" I cut across, staring directly at Savannah.

"I could try. We can rule anyone out with dark eyes." She pulls on her belt. "What are you waiting for? Let's go!"

FAYE

My ankles are still tied to the bedposts; my hands, tied at the wrist, are resting on my tummy. Tears spring to my eyes. I'm not sure I can do another whole day of this. The fever is worse. My arm, swollen to twice its size, feels alien, as if it belonged to someone else and was sewn on. The infection has taken on a life of its own too. It pulses beneath my skin, flowing through my body and wreaking havoc with my immune system. I'm hot. I'm cold. I'm achy all over, or I feel nothing but numbness.

"Stop this pity party, right now!" I warn myself in a low growl, through gritted teeth. "You're getting out of here *today*. Stick to the plan." I repeat the words over and over in my head. I need medical attention: I don't have another twenty-four hours. One way or another, I'll be leaving this hell hole.

Things are clearer by the time he knocks on the door. He waltzes into the room and pulls open the curtains with both arms before turning to me.

"Rise and shine!" His wide smile, revealing straight white teeth, matches his upbeat mood. I should be relieved to see him so happy, but this is new, so I'm wary. He has never been so ... so giddy!

"I've a surprise, darling." He stands at the end of the bed, resting his hand on the bed post before releasing my right ankle. His fingers skim the welt left by the rope before moving to free my other ankle. Again, he glides his fingers across the red ligature marks, his glacier-blue eyes warming in pleasure. He'll never set me free; it brings him too much joy. He's convinced himself that these are acts of love, so he has free rein to hurt me.

"Oh, really? That sounds nice." I smile sweetly, not daring to sit up until he orders me to do so. I'm going to get through this afternoon and then I'm going home. If it means going out the window, so be it.

"I hope you'll appreciate my hard work."

The mattress sags sideways under his weight as he sits on the edge, leaning over to finally untie my hands.

"I hope this won't be forever." His eyes fall to the coarse rope in his hands. "Come on!" He tugs on my hand, too roughly for my aching arm, dragging me up off the bed. He walks me, barefoot, down the stairs and into the kitchen.

Laid out on the table are flour, eggs, sugar, butter and chocolate chips.

"I thought we could make some cookies!" He beams.

My eyes fall to my swollen arm, feeling ready to burst at the seams in its disease-ridden state. I stumble over my words, confused but wanting to appear upbeat. "Oh, OK ..." My lips curve unnaturally upward.

He stills next to me. "You don't want to?"

"No, no! Of course I do, but can you help with the heavy lifting?" I lift my arm, reminding him of my injuries.

"I'm at your full disposal." He bows low, then his lips press briefly against mine in a chaste kiss.

We spend the afternoon like this: in a world far removed from reality. I watch with tangled emotions, as the man who has kidnapped, confined, and hurt me, behaves like a little boy staring through the window of a candy store. He waits with wide eyes for me to reward him with approval every step of the way. My nerves are stretched like a tightrope, as I struggle with keeping up this facade, while balancing the emotional baggage of a lunatic.

"These are delicious!" He bites into the warm, gooey, cookie, then hands one to me. I take it, washing it back with some warm milk.

"Do you want to rest before supper?" he leans down, kissing me again, the contact turning the milk sour in my stomach. I nod, breaking my lips free from his.

"Yes, please."

"I'll need to bathe you before supper, but yes, go first, and rest." His fingers sweep the loose strands of my knotted hair behind my ears in his parody of affection. The sour milk churns, my stomach begging to evict its contents all over his grotesque touch.

DETECTIVE JOHN WALTERS

It's early afternoon on the Saturday before Christmas when Annie Bennett finally returns my call.

I hit the speaker button on the call so all the agents in the room can listen in.

"Thank you for getting back to us, Mrs. Bennett," I begin.

"Oh, that's no problem, at all! Dean Fiennes mentioned you might call, but I forgot my phone this morning. It's always hectic this time of year. I have family visiting from Ireland tomorrow!" She rambles. We all smile, allowing her a moment to share.

"I wondered if you might be able to help us with some queries we have, regarding the campus tours and information sessions?" I begin.

"Well, if I can't answer them, no one can." She chuckles.

"We're trying to figure out if there's one person who takes care of the paperwork regarding prospective students?"

"Oh no. We have so many courses available, and thousands of applications, so different staff members deal with one or two departments each," she explains.

"Mrs. Bennett, my name is Agent Della Perez. I'm with the FBI. Could you tell us who oversees the science department for that task?"

"Oh! That department is quite big. That would be Alex Bardell."

Agent Ryan is already typing the name into the database.

"Can you tell us a little about Alex?" I push.

"Oh sure. He's a great guy, and hard working too! He's a little quiet, but he's very friendly and polite."

Ryan turns his laptop around. We all look at the photo of the middle-aged, balding man with brown eyes.

"It's not him," Perez whispers. I nod and continue.

“Is there anyone from the science department who is heavily involved in the information sessions or tour guides from that department?”

“No, I attend a lot of the information sessions myself. The tours happen daily, we try to be as non-invasive as possible during lecture times.”

“We’re investigating the death of Rose Bernstein. She attended an information session there in October,” I finally reveal to her.

“Oh, yes. I remember Rose: a lovely girl. I was so sad to read about it in the newspaper.” We all look at each other, shocked.

“You spoke directly to Rose?” I confirm.

“Well, yes. I ran that session. She held back, to talk at the end. She wanted to continue with her veterinary training if I remember correctly. She asked for information on financial aid and grants. I spoke at length with her, about all her options. She seemed happy with the information when she left.”

“Was she alone?” Perez asks.

“Yes. I believe she worked close by, at an animal clinic. She said she was on her lunch hour.”

“Can I ask why you didn’t come forward before now?”

“I—I didn’t think it was important. Should I have?” Her voice breaks and Perez cuts in.

“No, Mrs. Bennett. You’re being very helpful now.” Perez throws me a warning glare. My harsh tone was unintended.

“Tell us, again.” Perez keeps her tone light. “You didn’t see anyone hanging around her, nobody asked about her, after she left?”

“No.” She sounds certain.

"Mrs. Bennett, another young woman may have attended one of your campus tours, three years ago ..." Perez begins.

"Is that the other girl in the papers?" Annie interrupts.

"Yes," I confirm.

"I thought I recognized her face, you know? But my husband said I was imagining it." She harrumphs.

"Her name was Katherine Clifford. Is there any way to confirm her attendance?"

The room is silent for a moment. We listen to some shuffling down the line and the sound of typing.

"I brought my work laptop home with me. Let me see what I can find."

"Katherine Clifford, right?" she asks, typing away.

"That's it," Perez confirms.

"Yes. I don't have much. She visited all right. It was one of our last tours that semester. We generally conclude classes by the end of April. That's all I have, I'm afraid," she sighs.

"That's OK," Perez answers. A thought occurs to me.

"Mrs. Bennett, you mentioned that you complete your classes at that time. When does the college close down for summer?" I flip through my notepad looking at the dates of Katherine, Faye, and Rose's abductions.

"Oh, the college never closes down. But most of the teaching faculty finish up in mid-May. Our admissions office is fully operational all year round."

"Do the teaching faculty have an October break?"

"Yes, at the end of October."

My pulse races. "Can you send us a list of all the teaching faculty members who have been employed by the college for over three years?"

"I'll need to confirm with the dean, but I'm sure I could." Her voice shakes.

"Annie, it's nothing to worry about. You're being very helpful," Perez reassures her again.

"Mrs. Bennett, if I can ask one more favor: could you start with all the science departments first?"

"Of course. Let me call the dean, and I'll call you right back," she promises, before hanging up.

Standing, I roll out my shoulders and prowl around the room. I think better on my feet.

"Guys, you need to look at this," Agent Lynam calls to the room. He's been going over the security camera footage from the college for the past hour.

Perez and I move behind her leaning to see the screen.

"At 12:45 p.m., we see Rose's car enter the campus," he pulls up another screen, pointing to Rose's car as it comes into view.

"This is her pulling into a parking space behind the animal sciences building, and then," Lynam continues, opening another screen, "less than sixty seconds later, she enters the animal sciences office." Again, he zooms in on Rose. All of our eyes are glued to the screens as he fast forwards the recording. "No one follows in behind her. Forty-seven minutes later, she leaves. Nobody walks out behind her, and she gets into her car and drives off," he finishes.

"Shit." Another dead end, I sigh to myself. He looks over his shoulder at me, shooting me a warning glare.

"Hold on." He clicks into another screen. "Right here. In the corner of this shot, we can see a black sedan pull out after she passes." He gives us a wider view of the road exiting the campus. Sure enough, when Rose turns right out of the campus, the other car follows behind.

"Where did he come from?" I lean in, squinting at the blurred license plate. "Go back to the first clip, of her driving by the animal sciences building." My eyes scan the parked cars that line the road and fill the lot where she pulls in.

"Pause it here." I lean in closer to the still image on the screen and can just make out the trunk of the same car that follows Rose off campus.

"He didn't go after her on foot. He saw her get out of her car and walk in," Ryan says exactly what I'm thinking.

"What buildings are across from the animal sciences department?" I ask. He's already pulling up a Google Maps street view.

"There are three main buildings in close proximity. The school of psychology, social science, and philosophy; the forensic science department; and the chemical science building."

There's a knock on the conference room door. It's Jones.

"Sorry to interrupt, but Luke Anderson, Scott Allen and Savannah Phillips are all demanding to see you both." His eyes are on Perez and me. "They say they have a lead on the killer." Color creeps up his neck as all eyes focus on him.

Blood is pumping hard around my body. *We are so close!* I swallow back my frustration at the interruption and try to keep an open mind. I nod toward Jones. "We'll be out in two," I say, before turning back to the team.

"Ryan, get on Annie Bennett and get that list. Use it to check with the DMV against any faculty members that drive a black sedan and own a second vehicle. Look over the profile. If they don't fit, put them at the bottom of the list of suspects." I nod around the table, everyone nodding back. The air around us is crackling with tension and a renewed sense of fire. Perez exits the room with me.

"They're in your office," Jones announces.

"You left them in my office?!" I growl, hurrying through the door.

LUKE

Detective Walters's office is as unwelcoming as he is. Impatience, coupled with a morbid need to know whatever the police do, has me moving behind the desk and reaching for a large book sitting atop a stack of files.

"Luke, don't!" Savannah whispers as I pick it up. I read the title, noting the page earmarked before my eyes drop to the manilla folder beneath it. I look up at Scott who nods for me to read it. Savannah looks nervous but positions herself beside the door.

"Hurry," she hisses.

I open the folder and see Rose Bernstein's name. I scan the first few lines quickly; my heart picks up its pace as I read the heading.

Cause of Death: Multiple broken bones, leading to serious infection and death.

The words jump from the page, punching me in the gut, each new sentence another blow. I should put it down. I can't. I won't. I need to do whatever I can to find Faye. I hear Savannah hiss my name in warning, but my eyes can't leave the page. He broke her fingers, her arms, her legs and beat her. She was mutilated over the course of three weeks.

"What the hell are you all doing here?" I look up, still holding the report in my hand as Walters storms toward me.

"Is this what my sister is going through?" I spit. Faye has been with this psycho for four full days now. Already, visions of her torture are plaguing my mind.

"Is he breaking her bones, for fun?" I yell.

"Luke!" Savannah steps forward, her eyes glistening with unshed tears, asking me to calm down. I glance between her face and Scott's. His eyes are wide with fear. I force myself to push down the anger, but it's replaced by terror.

"Oh Jesus, we need to find her. Right now," I move around the desk. Agent Perez is standing in the doorway. She offers me a sympathetic nod but doesn't move out of my way. I stand next to Scott and Savannah. Savannah takes my hand and squeezes it gently. I take a deep breath.

"You told me if I found anything to bring it to you." I take the paper I have in my back pocket out and hand it to him.

"What's this?" he asks, unfolding the page.

"It's a list of suspects."

Scott moves forward, between me and Savannah. "We went through all the available faculty members on the university's website. Savannah was able to rule out practically all of them, but two of those names had no picture up, just a bio, and the other two had blue eyes," he explains.

"What departments are these from?" Walters looks up from the page. His eyes dart straight to Agent Perez, who levers herself off the doorway and moves to meet him, taking the page.

"What makes you think he's a faculty member?" Both cops have that guarded expression. My heart picks up the pace. We're on to something, and they know it.

"We figured it out. If Katherine Clifford was kidnapped three years ago, and Rose only two months ago, most students would have graduated within those three years, but the staff stay." My words are rushed as I explain all this to him.

His eyes come up from the list again, this time landing on the book in my hand. If he has registered anything I just said, it's not obvious.

"Jesus Christ," he says softly. He moves quickly, taking the book from my hand and rushing back to the conference room. We rush after him and the agent lady. They're in the room with the door closed too quickly to see what's going on. He knows who has my sister. I reach for the door handle, but the deputy from before puts a hand on my arm, and stands in front of the door.

"You'll need to wait out here."

"You'll need to step out of my way." I tower over him. To my grudging respect, he doesn't back down. I don't really want to get arrested, but no one is going to stand between me and finding my sister.

CHAPTER 23

DETECTIVE JOHN WALTERS

Beneath my shock, I'm impressed. I listen as Luke explains how they came to the four names on this list and read through them.

Prof. Kalvin Nell

Prof. Paul Simons

Prof. Daniel Stanley

Dr. Jeffrey Carson

Mentally, I cross a line through Dr. Stanley. I already know that he doesn't fit the profile, I've met him. I furrow my brows at the fourth name. *Carson?* I repeat it over in my head until it finally dawns on me: Dr. Stanley's assistant was called Dr. Carson. I'm digesting this information while Luke continues to talk. My eyes stray to his hands. A flashback of Dr. Carson suggesting to me how the killer could break the bones of his victims is like a taser to my brain. The electricity fills the gaps in my mind, bringing the picture into full view. And his eyes, an icy blue. Just as our witnesses have described. Perez must see me connecting the dots. Her eyes turn serious just as I reach forward, snatching the book from Luke's hand and rushing toward the conference room. I hear the shuffling of feet behind me and the clamoring of people trying to get into the room.

"Stop what you're doing!" I burst through the doors. "Ryan, I need you to get me everything you can find on a Dr. Jeffrey Carson. He is employed at the forensic sciences building in UW-GB.

I turn to Perez, ignoring the scuffles beyond the conference room door. I know Luke Anderson is trying to burst in. I'll deal with him in a second.

"What have you got?" she asks.

"His job is in the forensic anthropology department. He interrupted my meeting with Dr. Stanley, a few weeks back. He's midthirties, tall and well built. When I asked about a possible weapon, he suggested this ..." I open the page earmarked on *The Breaking Wheel*.

Perez takes the book from me. When I first looked at the image of a man tied to a large wagon wheel, I dismissed the theory as far-fetched.

"Tell me I'm crazy to think that the killer would hand me the murder weapon on a plate?" Running my fingers through my hair, I grip a tuft, hoping to make quick sense of the events unfolding around us. *I couldn't have gotten it this wrong.*

"Ryan, have you got anything on this guy yet?"

"Almost."

Perez looks at me again and then at the room. "OK, everyone, listen up. This guy matches the profile. He is tall and strong. He works in a field dedicated to the study of bones. He works in the building across from where both of our victims visited. He inserted himself into the investigation. Get me everything you can on him." She returns her gaze to me. "This is our guy."

"OK, here we go," Ryan calls out, silencing the room. "Jeffrey Timothy Carson. Born November '82, to Katherine Milton and Jeffrey Carson Sr. Grew up on Carson's corn farm, Crivitz, Wisconsin." I move to the maps on our wall. Crivitz is where the first victim was attacked. "His father died in a farming accident in '91. His mother also died, accidentally, in the home in '93." He looks up from his screen, the color draining from his face. "Says here she fell down the stairs. Suffered multiple broken bones and died of her injuries. Carson Jr. bounced from one foster home to another until he was eighteen, when he inherited the family farm and his mother's life insurance policy. He started a degree in archaeology and social anthropology at UW-Madison in the fall of 2002. His master's specialized in forensic anthropology, which he completed in 2006, before transferring to UW-Green Bay, where he wrote his doctoral dissertation on skeletal trauma."

"Where was he in the summer of '02, when we saw our first attack at the Thompson national park in Crivitz?" I ask, grabbing a marker to make a timeline on our whiteboard.

"In November 1999, his request to leave foster care was approved. He spent three years at the Green Bay young adult housing complex—"

"OK. Do we know when he left that complex?" I watch him type away furiously.

"It looks like he was there until his move to Madison in August of 2002. His file is closed, so I can't see any information regarding his behavior."

"OK, so we know he was in the Green Bay area in the summer of 2002, which is an hour away from Crivitz, where he grew up. So he knows the area. He leaves, goes to college, and during this time we have no similar assaults. So, he comes back to Green Bay, when?"

"He started working with Dr. Stanley in the fall of 2006 as his field assistant while teaching at the university and working on his doctorate, which he completed in 2012."

I turn to Perez. "He was dormant from 2002 until 2017? That's fifteen years. Why would he start killing suddenly?"

"It's not unusual for a killer to become dormant, especially if they find other outlets for their emotions. He was caught up in the study of bones, learning everything he could about them. He completed his doctorate on skeletal trauma! Ryan, do we have any missing persons in Green Bay, between 2012 and 2017?" she asks, before turning back to me. "I think he might have started to refine his methods in that time. The deaths of Rose and Katherine were well-planned and strategic. He didn't just wake up in 2017 and begin to live out this fantasy."

"There were eight missing people during that time. Three are street workers of different ages and race, none matching our victim profile ..." Ryan's head bobs as he reads out the information before him. "The others are elderly or delinquent teenagers. None of these match, I'm sorry."

"That doesn't necessarily mean they're not connected. He may have developed his victim's profile over those years, practicing on street workers, figuring out what makes him tick. He got away with kills: no one knocked on his door, so he started to take risks. Katherine, Rose and Faye are all blond women, aged between twenty-four and twenty-eight. He was attracted to their wholesomeness ... Ryan, what do we know about his mother?"

"Katherine Milton Carson, born 1945, in North River, near Chicago. She was a dancer with the International Dance Academy from 1957 until 1976. She competed all over the world. She was good," he muses. "In 1976, she left the academy and moved to Green Bay to start her own dance school. That closed down in 1979. She worked odd jobs until she married Jeffrey's father in April of 1981, and moved to Crivitz. She lived there until her death in 1993."

"Do we have an address for Jeffrey Carson now?" I look around the room.

"Working on it." Agent Lynam stands up from his laptop at the other end of the table. I look at him to continue. "Ammonia is used in anthropology. It helps to lift tissue from the bone." he tells me.

"I have something too." Agent Ryan pipes up again. "A brown Chevrolet Caprice station wagon is registered in his name, as is a black 2017 Buick Regal."

The room is buzzing. Everyone's typing away, throwing information to me and Perez, who continue to connect the dots. All roads are leading to Jeffrey Carson.

"OK, people. Jeffrey Carson Jr. is our main suspect. We need a recent photo of him."

"I'm looking. He has no social media accounts, and there's nothing on the university's website. I'm printing his college student card now—" Ryan says as the printer rumbles to life in the corner.

"That'll do." I grab my coat from the back of my chair and make my way to Ryan. I look down at the old college student card and despite the ten years since it was taken, I recognize the man as the same one I met in Dr. Stanley's office.

"Perez and I will head to Kitty Harmon's to get a positive ID. Everyone else, get me everything you can on this guy: all known locations. I want to know where he is right now. Lynam, once I get the ID from Kitty, we should have enough for a warrant to search his properties. You go with deputies Jones and Clarke and prepare it with the DA." I'm already moving out of the conference room.

"What the fuck is going on in there?" Luke Anderson jumps up from a bench as soon as I open the door. I'd almost forgotten about him. I don't stop moving, instead passing by him, to retrieve the bulletproof vest from my office.

"Luke, I need you to wait here. I'm tracking down an important lead." I ignore him as I fasten the Velcro over my white shirt, before pulling on my heavy winter coat. Perez is next to me, securing her own vest and her standard-issue, navy FBI jacket, her badge already hanging from a silver chain around her neck.

"Bullshit! You know who it is. I'm not staying here." He follows behind us. I turn on him. We don't have time for this crap.

"Listen. I *will* have you arrested! This is a police investigation; you need to wait here until we get back. I need to focus on getting your sister home right now. *You* need to stay put." I leave no room for doubt: he will not be tagging along.

I'm surprised by his curt nod, but I don't stand around to discuss it with him. I'm already jogging to my car with Perez.

We use flashing lights all the way to Kitty's house. It's six p.m., and already dark. The snow has been coming down heavily all day.

"Ryan says the Carson corn farm is still owned by Jeffrey Carson, but he has a property here in the city too." Perez is reading messages that are coming in, in rapid succession on her phone.

"Tell them to get warrants for both addresses. He's more than likely holding her at the farm, but we need to be sure." She nods in agreement, before texting the instructions back to Ryan. With sirens blaring, I speed toward Kitty's home. We pull up to the curb within minutes, both jumping from the car before slogging through the thick snow. I pound heavily on her door before moving to the edge of the porch and rapping on the window. Breathless and impatient, I move back to the door-pounding again.

Moments later a flushed Kitty opens the door. Her eyes blink as fear turns to relief.

"Officers?" she pants, clutching her throat.

"Kitty, I'm sorry for showing up unannounced, but I want to show you a photo to see if you recognize the person in it."

"Kitty, if you *don't* recognize the person, then please say so," Perez cuts across.

"Come in. Let me get my glasses." She moves to the hallway. I hear snow crunching with approaching footsteps.

"Is she here? Is this where my sister is?" I turn to see Luke Anderson rushing up the drive, a gun in his hand. Automatically, our training comes into play. Both Perez and I step to block the door, moving toward Luke. With raised guns, we issue our warnings.

"Put down the gun, Luke!" Perez shouts.

"Is my sister in there?" He stops, his eyes looking beyond us to the empty doorway.

"NO! Luke, drop the gun."

"DROP. THE. GUN." Perez yells again. His confused eyes skitter over our heads to see Kitty appear in the doorway.

I call to Kitty to get back in the house. Luke puts down the firearm.

"ON. YOUR. KNEES." Perez continues to call out. He follows her instructions, dropping to his denim-clad knees into the thick snow.

"Hands behind your back," I order, kicking the small revolver out of his reach. He does as he's told, and Perez cuffs him.

"I'll put him in the back of the car." She rolls her eyes, looking as frustrated as I feel.

"I just wanted to get my sister back." His anger has subsided into a desperate plea. I get it, but he's hindering our investigation.

"Where are the others?" I hear Perez ask him, as she puts him in the back seat, her hand on the top of his head to keep him from hitting the door frame.

I knock gently on Kitty's door and explain to her who we just arrested. Her eyes fill with sympathy. I apologize again for the intrusion, and she waves it away.

"Come in. Finish what you came for," she steps aside to let me enter. "The lighting is better in here."

She pops on a large, blue-framed pair of spectacles and looks closely.

"He's a few years younger in this photo, but this is the man who bought the ornament from me." She confirms.

"Thank you, Kitty." I'm already rushing out the door.

"Of course, Detective. Good luck with finding his sister!" she calls after me. "Go easy on him."

"I will," I promise, before hurrying back to my car.

"We've got him." I say as I jump back into the passenger seat. I'm already phoning Deputy Jones.

"Jones. Get me that warrant and take Clarke and Ryan to the apartment in the city. Tell Lynam to meet us at the farm. Phone the local sheriff's office in Crivitz, and tell them I'll need backup, and to have an ambulance and fire crew on standby."

"What about this vigilante?" Perez thumbs into the back seat. I sigh heavily.

"What the fuck were you thinking?" I bark.

"I was thinking that my sister was in that house." He has the decency to look embarrassed.

"You could have gotten yourself *shot*, running at two officers with a gun!" Perez's dusky tone does nothing to mask her fury. "*Idiota!*" she grumbles.

"I'm all she has. So, call me an idiot, but I'm willing to risk my life to save hers."

"Where are Scott and Savannah?" Perez asks.

"Probably following us."

I check my rear-view mirror. If they were following us, they're not now.

"You're staying in the car. Do you hear me? Cuffs on," I growl.

I pick up speed. We have an hour's drive ahead of us. The local sheriff can take Luke into custody, for his own safety, when we get there

FAYE

The daylight hours slip away into early evening. The sound of the squeaky bathroom taps and rushing water force my eyes open. It's time. I've spent the last two hours going over my plan in my mind. Like me, it's weak, but it's all I've got. I can't keep up this act much longer.

The door swings open.

"Bath time, darling," he smiles, and I force my lips wide, silently snarling through my smile as he unties my ankles. I glance at the door. The keys are dangling, still in the lock. He unzips my dress, kissing the back of my neck. Tears sting my eyes as I fight my body's urge to recoil. It's been four days; I haven't got another one in me.

The dress pools at my feet. My underwear is still on when he leads me to the bathroom. Standing in front of me, he unwraps the bandages on my arm. I look away briefly before shifting my eyes back to my swollen, purple arm lying heavily against my bare breasts. Even his eyes widen in horror at my mutilated body.

"I'll get some ibuprofen for you."

"Thank you," I manage. He grips my hips, helping me sit into the bath.

Kneeling next to me on the tiled floor, he begins by pouring hot water on my head, and shampooing my hair. Silent tears mingle with the bath water that streams down my face. His fingers massage my scalp, his breathing heavy as his hands creep closer to my neck before sliding across my shoulders. I tremble under his touch. His hands still.

"Is everything all right?" he asks, his gruff tone adding to the knot twisting in my stomach.

"Yes," I curl forward, lifting my legs to my chest, my trembling chin resting on my knees as his fingers continue their journey down my back. I tightly squeeze shut my eyes, my weighted arms holding my body still, as he traces the full length of my spine, dipping beneath the water and slowly circling my coccyx.

"Why are you upset?" he asks, moving around and tugging at my chin, forcing me to look at him. His stare is cold enough to freeze the water.

"The shampoo got in my eyes," I lie.

"I'm sorry, darling. Why didn't you say?" He turns on the tap. "Here, rinse them out," he whispers gently. Doing as I'm told, I cup my palms together and inch toward the running water. My arm screams in pain as I lift the frigid water toward my face. The sting of the icy fresh water offers a moment's relief from the agony.

He turns my cheek to face him again, "All better?" he smiles, his eyes never leaving mine. I nod in agreement.

"Good. Let's get you dry."

He brings in the small stool for me to sit on next to the vanity. After rewrapping my arm in the bandages and helping me back into the same dirty dress, he begins to comb my hair, humming that same dreaded tune. The room is dark, the only light streaming in from the hallway, through the open bedroom door.

"You've got the silkiest hair," he whispers, bundling it up in his hands and leaning down to bury his face in its scent. *His* scent. I imagine wrapping my locks around his neck and choking him with them. Standing, he drops the comb. He locks eyes with me in the mirror.

"I've made us spaghetti and meatballs for supper, and tonight we'll finish the dance. I know you're almost there." He nods, his hands resting on my shoulders. "I knew you were special, Faye. The others disappointed me, but not you," he squeezes.

"Others?" I ask, unable to resist.

"Oh, don't be jealous of Rose and Katherine. They tried, but they came nowhere near to finishing the dance." His fingers clamp tightly on my shoulders again.

"I'll go get ready and collect you in ten minutes," he finishes. He switches on the light and locks the door behind him. I have a moment's doubt about acting, until his last words register in full. *They came nowhere near finishing the dance.* And neither will I. *It's now or never,* I remind myself. I will my mind, my body and my nerve to hold strong.

Rising from the stool, I creep to the window. My bare feet tiptoe over the creaky floorboards, my heart leaping from my chest at the slightest sound. My ears are trained on the door, listening as he moves around his bedroom. I've counted: there are eight footsteps from his door to mine. This old house has done me one good deed during my stay. Once I put this plan into motion, it will take him only a few seconds to get in here. When he does, I'll either get extremely lucky or I'll die. Glancing out the window, I map out the quickest route toward the treeline. I'm hopeful that the trees and dark sky will help me to hide. My eyes drop to the thick blanket of fresh snow on the ground below. My footprints will be easy for him to track. I look to my bare feet, my head drooping. The odds are against me, but I'd rather die cold and alone than on his breaking wheel. Resolved to go through with it, adrenaline floods my body. Heat spreads like wildfire, burning away my fears and leaving my doubts in ashes. Gritting my teeth, I grab the wooden stool and throw it through the window. I watch as the stool, and much of the glass, clatter to the ground below. A jagged piece of glass glints at me from the rotting frame and without a second thought, I pull it free. I stick it in the pocket of my dress before getting into place, behind the bedroom door. I'm just in time for the lock to turn. Steeling my breath, I freeze as his voice, booming out my name, enters the room before he does. He runs straight to the window. My feet feel as heavy as cinder blocks and my heart is ringing in my ears, but I edge around the door and pull it shut behind me. He charges toward me, but I turn the key with ease.

"COME BACK HERE, FAYE!!" he screams wildly, his thumping fists rattling the door as I jump back. I can't believe it worked. I stand there, dazzled by my success until he roars again. Taking the keys, I run down the stairs. My feet are moving faster than my mind will allow me to catch up. I'm at the cellar door in seconds, fumbling with the keys as I start trying to unlock it. A louder bang overhead has me looking up to the ceiling. His shouting of my name over and over is replaced by his footsteps pounding on the landing. *He's out*! One key turns, opening the door. I lock it behind me again. I rush down the wooden stairs, stepping in some broken glass. I don't pause to register the pain to my abused feet. My eyes scan the dark space for an exit. There's pounding on the cellar door. *He's kicking it in!* It busts open just as I find the outside cellar door. Climbing the three steps and using my back, I push upward. I'm thrilled as the two wooden doors part. I leap into the night.

I'm running fast, but the frozen ground acts like tiny shards of glass cutting into my already shredded feet. I'm leaving bloody footprints. The pain reminds me that I am alive, I am escaping as I head toward the treeline. Then, without warning, I'm tackled from behind. His hard body crashes into me and we both tumble into the snow.

"YOU BITCH!" he yells as I struggle to free myself. His hand wraps around my ankle as he pulls me back. We roll around in the snow, my poor arm useless against his onslaught of violence. I try to kick him off and away from me. He slaps me hard across the face, as I continue to wriggle against him. Remembering the glass in my pocket, I reach for it. My arm is in agony, but with all my strength I plunge the glass through his white shirt. My confidence is bolstered as I feel it pierce his skin. The sight of his blood empowers me. *I can do this*, I think. Then his balled fist comes across my cheek. The force of the first blow dazzles me. The second one knocks me out.

JEFFREY

My feet are bare, and the searing cold of the snow has me chasing after her with vigor. I don't think. I lunge for her, dragging us both to the ground. She's like a feral cat squirming beneath me. I almost laugh at her pathetic attempts to claw at me until I feel the sharp stab against my chest. *She fucking sliced me.* The white snow is spattered red with my blood and with it, my wrath is released on her face. I beat her once, twice, three times, until she lies still beneath me.

As I stand, my pained groan turns into a guttural roar. I look down at her, clenching my fists again. The intensity of my outrage has me gripping my hair in my hands. I look up to the starry night sky and bark at the moon again. I thought she was the one. *How dare she treat me this way, after all I have done for her? She's left me with no choice!* She's sprawled at my feet, blood in the snow at her head and feet. Decided, I smile. Soon she will be strapped to my wheel. I need this.

Carrying her to the barn leaves me breathless. Panting heavily, I drop her onto the wheel. Standing back, I see the crimson on her dress.

My blood.

Rage, like shards of pointed glass, stabs at my core. A loud roar rips free as I tie the ropes around her ankles with ferocity. *She* won't *escape again*.

Checking her bindings one last time, I storm toward the house. Stepping over the damaged door, the smell of tomato sauce and garlic greets me. The pleasant aroma infuriates me further. She spoiled dinner, ruined our night.

Rolling out my neck, the light cracking helps me to gather my thoughts. I'm surrounded by Faye's destruction, the sting of her rejection far worse than pain of my wound.

She fooled me; convinced me that she wanted to share this with me. I'll tend to my injury and dress for a different kind of evening. Tonight, the wheel will turn, but for Faye, it won't be in her favor

CHAPTER 24

DETECTIVE JOHN WALTERS

We're met by three patrol cars, an ambulance and a fire truck, two miles away from the farm. Fifteen minutes ago, the team in Green Bay entered his apartment. It was empty, but they found newspaper articles from the murders stacked on his living room table. A forensics team is moving in now, to scour the place for any evidence that the girls might have been there.

Perez and I leave Luke in the backseat when we climb out onto the cold country road. Six officers move toward us, gathering at the front of my car.

One of the officers steps forward to take my hand. "I'm Officer Duggan." I shake it, then he offers it to Perez.

"Do you know the farm?" I ask him. He unfolds a map onto the hood of the car, and we huddle around.

"This is the farm, here. You can see it's surrounded by forest. The only way in or out, by car, is along this lane." His fingers move around the map, pointing out the laneway entrance before continuing.

"The place has been vacant for years. As far as I know, there's is no way into the house. The downstairs windows and doors were sealed up with cement blocks, years ago." His eyes lift from the map to meet mine.

"Shit. He must be getting in and out somehow."

"Is there a cellar or basement? A lot of old farmhouses have outside cellar doors," Perez offers.

"I reckon you're right, although I can't say it hasn't been sealed off."

"John, we can't risk going in hard." Perez eyes me.

"What do you suggest?" I ask her.

"We go in quietly: use the treeline to shield us, until we can get a read on an entrance into the house."

"We'll be going into the house blind," I remind her.

"We have no choice; time is running out."

Turning from her, I address Officer Duggan again.

"OK, tell me all you know about that farm's layout, as quickly as you can."

"It's about two miles down this road. You'll see the sign "Carson Corn Farm." Take a right at the sign. There is a tree-lined drive, approximately two hundred yards, then you'll see the red barn on your left-hand side with the main house directly ahead. Wooded areas all around the property. Two miles beyond the house there's a lake."

I pull my gun from the holster on my hip, checking it's loaded with the safety off. Perez is doing the same as we listen.

"Is there anything that might hinder our efforts?" I need to figure out how we'll get onto his land undetected.

"Well, beyond the lake, there are only rocky hills and bush all the way to Lake Superior. So, even if he flees, he won't get far on foot, especially in this weather."

My eyes fall to the map as I begin to call out instructions. "We'll drive to the sign and go in on foot from there. I don't want him to hear the cars approaching. You and one of your men enter from the left along the tree line. Cut across the old cornfield, flanking the house from the left. You two, take the treeline to the right and flank the house on the opposite side. Perez and I will go up the drive and secure the barn first. Keep off the radios unless you establish an entry point or his whereabouts." I look up from the map at all the officers. "That goes for everyone. We don't want to spook him. That could cause him to harm the victim." There is too much at stake here.

I point to the remaining officers. "Once we're on the property, I want you to drive your patrol car to block his exit. Headlights off and as quietly as possible. Once we secure the barn, I'll radio for you to follow up the drive. The plan is to find an entry point into the house. But no one enters without my word. Is that understood?" They all nod. "Perez, anything else?" I look to her.

"This guy is dangerous; we have no idea what we are going into, so keep your eyes peeled. He won't be expecting us, so we have that advantage, but he is smart. Keep your head low. Remember: bringing Faye Anderson home alive is the priority here, so don't get trigger-happy. Flashing lights off, and let's go."

I confer quickly with the ambulance and fire crews. I want them to stay as far back as possible until we radio for them. Once that's sorted, Perez and I climb into my car, following behind the patrol cars.

"You need to uncuff me!" Luke begs.

"I can't have you putting her at risk, Luke. You need to stay in the car."

"Look, if I promise to wait in the car, will you uncuff me?"

"No, I'm sorry." I refuse to put him at risk. He can spend the rest of his life hating me for it but at least he'll have those days.

Pulling her mane of curly hair into a ponytail, Perez turns to Luke. "Luke, we are so close to ending this. You need to trust us."

"I just want her home." His eyes shift out the window, his voice breaking on the last word. I find him in my rear-view mirror, a silent tear trickling down his face. The weight of his love for her reinforces my own determination to succeed.

"You will be bringing her home, but I'll be bringing her through that gate. I can't risk you coming onto the property. Faye will react to seeing you. She may put herself into further danger, in order to get to you. You have to think with your head now and allow me to do my job."

We pull up behind the patrol cars. His eyes find mine in the mirror. With one firm nod he agrees. "Go get my sister."

"I'm not leaving without her," I promise.

"I've never trusted her to anyone. Don't fail her."

Luke's faith in me was hard-earned, but I've no intention of failing anyone tonight. With a sharp nod, my boots drop into the slush on the old country road. Inspecting the property before me, I instinctively feel we're right where we need to be. It's time to end this: for Faye, for Katherine, and for Rose.

FAYE

The light throbbing quickens to a burning sensation beneath my skin. My eyes peel open to find myself strapped to his wheel. I gave it everything, fought with all my strength, but it wasn't enough. I'm helpless. Hopeless. Tired.

My urge to sleep is abruptly washed away as icy water rains down on me. I gasp. My eyelids are too swollen to fully see through. I catch a glimpse of him. I feel his fingers next to mine as they grip the rim of the wheel, spinning it violently. My head flops sideways. Dazed and disoriented, I vomit, the motion too much for me to take.

"Please, stop!" I whimper. I can't take anymore; I want it all to stop. The wheel, the pain, the hope, all of it needs to end. I just want to stop. My entire body is in agony, every inch of skin is on fire, burning through to my aching muscles before melting like lava onto my broken bones. I close my eyes and try to find peace. My mother's face is smiling, surrounded by lush grass and wide blue skies. I reach for her outstretched hand. I'm home, at the farm where I grew up. My heart fills with joy as we run through the fields. I can see my dad, my grandmother and grandfather, all waiting for me. I run faster. The pain is gone. I'm free.

"Faye, Luke needs you." I hear her voice. It's in the wind, inside my mind, but she is no longer next to me. Gray clouds roll above me.

"Mum! please don't leave me," I beg. Watching our old house fall into disrepair, the ground beneath growing darker, its shadows moving toward me. I turn, trying to outrun it. It's no use. My ankles are gripped as I'm sucked back to reality.

"YOU'LL PAY FOR THIS, YOU LITTLE BRAT!" he roars. His ear-piercing scream causes the room to shake. My eyes open painfully. He's standing over me, with another wheel above my head. He won't let me escape his punishment. Not here, and not in my mind.

DETECTIVE JOHN WALTERS

Weapons in hand, our guns low, Perez and I hasten up either side of the drive. We stick to the edge of our path along the tree line. Trudging through three inches of untouched snow, we round a bend, pausing as the barn comes into view. My hand comes up and Perez stills with me. The air is still, our heavy breathing disturbing the silence of the night. I point to the house beyond the barn, my eyes assessing the situation.

"The upstairs window is smashed," I whisper across to her. My words dissipate into white vapor across the drive. She looks in that direction. I'm about to suggest that she take the barn alone when a blood-curdling scream shatters the eerie calm.

"YOU'LL PAY FOR THIS, YOU LITTLE BRAT!" The violence in his tone spurs us into action.

Without a second thought, we rush to the barn, both reaching the wide wooden door within seconds. It's ajar. We position ourselves on either side. Perez uses her foot to push it farther open. I nod once, and she slides her body through the small gap, entering ahead of me. We pause inside, our eyes adjusting to the dark. Beyond the machinery that obstructs our view, a dim light beckons us. We hear a moan of pain, another angry scream. I point to one side of the machinery. Perez nods, moving to the other side. Our eyes meet one last time, her green eyes bright in the darkness, a silent nod to stay safe. I swing right, and move between the machinery, using it to shield me until I can get close enough to see what I'm facing. My gun is raised, my eyes scanning the rafters of the barn, securing my location as much as I can with the poor visibility. I remain in the shadows; my eyes find the light source first. Swinging over a workbench, a bare bulb casts dancing shadows on the walls and illuminates his creation. I try to make quick sense of what I am seeing. Faye lies strapped to an old wooden wagon wheel that spins at the height of his waist. He holds another large wagon wheel at his chest. I don't wait for Perez to come into view, but step out as he moves around her, taunting her as she writhes in pain. The only weapon I see is the wheel in his hand. He moves it above his head.

"POLICE! FREEZE!" I yell, my feet shuffling as I edge around the barn, closer to him and nearing his workbench. I see his back stiffen, the muscles taut with rage at the sound of my voice. Slowly, his head turns toward me. His cold stare meets mine across the barn.

"Step back and put down the wheel," I warn. His biceps are beginning to shake under its weight.

"Help me, please!" Faye cries out.

"It's OK, Faye." Perez's reassuring tone fills the barn, pulling Jeffrey's attention in her direction. I glance toward her, taking note of her location as she steps out and flanks him on his left side.

"Carson, step back, and put the wheel down," I call out. He begins to circle the wheel, rotating it with him, holding Faye hostage beneath him.

"Stop moving!" I snap.

"Don't shoot, or I'll drop it on her face." He snarls, continuing to inch around until he faces us both. Clever. "I'm going to set the wheel down." He glances back and forth between us. My eyes narrow in suspicion, and I yell for him to step back.

"Step away from Faye and slowly lower it," Perez warns him. When he begins to move back, we both take a small step closer. His hands come down slowly, lowering the wheel.

When his face and upper torso are shielded, he backs up quickly.

"Don't move! Put the wheel down!" I roar. With one quick movement, he throws the large wheel forward, away from himself. Shots ring out as both Perez, and I fire at him. The wheel lands with a clatter, next to Faye. I'm already chasing after him.

"CALL THE PARAMEDICS!" I call over my shoulder to Perez. Faye's in a bad shape.

LUKE

Twisting sideways, I manage to open the back door and slide out of Walters's car. Despite being handcuffed, I make my way up the country road toward where the patrol car is blocking the entrance to the property.

"Hey you! Get back to the car." I stop moving when an officer steps out from in front of the car. He glowers at me from beneath the rim of his wide-brimmed hat.

"Now, let's not make a ruckus," I bluff. I intend to let them do their job, but I'm not sitting in that car another second. A second officer is starting to march toward me when gunfire erupts through the quiet night.

"Don't. Move." They both turn away and run up the drive. I hesitate, momentarily conflicted by my natural inclination to run in there and help, and the fear that maybe I'll make things worse. When more sounds of violence echo down the drive, my feet move before my rational mind can catch up. Hunched forward, I rush down the drive, slipping twice on the icy ground before tearing myself up by the knees and rushing toward the mayhem. I can't see any cops and there's silence when I reach the end of the drive. I pull my shoulders back, my chest heaving as I try to catch my breath. I see two officers, one entering the barn and the other circling around back.

More officers emerge from behind the house. Another two come out of the bush on my left as I rush into the barn.

"He's on foot, heading northeast, through the woods. I'm in pursuit." Detective Walters's voice crackles over one of the officers' radios.

"Get the ambulance crew here, now!" I recognize the voice of Agent Perez. I push my way to the front of the barn to find Perez leaning over Faye, who's lying on a … table? I freeze. Unable to look away, I take in my little sister. She's so still. All of my worst fears are realized.

"*Madre de Dios!* What is he doing here?" She sees me but addresses two officers. "You: go and move the patrol car so the ambulance and fire crews can get in. You: he's on foot. Go help Walters. Luke, get over here and help me."

"Luke?" Faye's weak voice cuts through the chaos. *She's alive!* Relief washes over me, allowing me to move toward her. She's tied down to a wheel, her beautiful face swollen, black and blue.

"Oh, Faye, what has he done to you?" I crouch next to her. "I'm here, little sister. I'm here. You're safe," I repeat, over and over. Perez moves behind me, unlocking the cuffs. I watch as she grabs a box cutter from the workbench and begins to cut the cable ties that hold Faye down. I stroke Faye's hair. She's crying, the tears barely squeezing out through her swollen eyelids.

"Take this." I look up to find Perez handing me a gun. "Anyone comes through this barn that isn't police, ambulance or fire crew, shoot them." She's up and leaving me here to protect Faye. My urge to chase after the man who did this is nothing compared to the need to reassure her.

"Where are you going?" Perez is a good agent.

"I need to help John and the team find him. Have you got this?" Her eyes tick to Faye.

"Yeah. Go." That fucker won't get near her, ever again.

"Luke, I'm sorry!" Faye's voice pulls my attention to her. She's badly hurt, but she's alive. She'll get through this. I know she will.

"Faye, don't talk. I love you. Savannah and Scott are waiting for you to come home, OK? You need to stay strong." I kiss her forehead, wiping the tears from her swollen eyes. Emotion courses through my veins. I want to kill him, maim him, but more than anything, I want to take away her pain.

"Luke, don't let them see me like this." Her heart-wrenching sob brings tears to my own eyes. I can feel my heart break with my words.

"OK, it's OK," I whisper. "Just hang in there. Help is coming." I tell her, over and over. I want to lift her off the wheel but I'm too afraid that I'll hurt her further. Seconds feel like hours until the paramedics arrive. I step back as they work with quick efficiency to get her on a stretcher. One officer stands guard with me. His radio comes to life just as they begin carrying Faye out.

"Shots fired. Officer down!"

CHAPTER 25

DETECTIVE JOHN WALTERS

He escaped through a broken wall panel at the back of the barn. Following behind, I lose sight of him as he disappears into the forest. The thick layer of snow slows me as I track his footsteps into the night.

"He's heading northeast on foot through the woods. I'm in pursuit," I call out over the radio. My ability to talk is hampered by my labored breathing. My chest burns, but I plunge forward, following his prints. As I move into the woods, the snow on the ground thins, making it easier for me to run, but making it harder to track him. I trudge on, slowing my pace, my eyes focusing on the disturbed ground at my feet.

"What's your location?" Perez's voice sounds over my radio. I cringe at the noise and quickly turn it off, stepping back behind a tree for cover. I look out into the woods that he knows so much better than I. There's no movement. Bolstered by the knowledge that he has no weapon, I move out from behind the tree, and continue deeper into the gloom.

I don't hear him coming. One second, I'm rounding a large pine; the next, a fist makes contact with my cheekbone, a heavy body slamming me against the tree. My gun skitters across the forest floor. Startled, I shake my head against the white lights that burst in my vision, in time to see his fist coming at me again. Dodging low and to the side, I watch as his full weight goes into his missed punch, allowing me an opportunity to get out in front. He hits the tree as my fist connects with his ribs, my knee coming up to his stomach. I expect him to fall. Instead, he whirls around, catching me in the side of the head. I push him back, creating some space between us, and heave in some fresh air. He bounds forward, coming in low. My fist clips his jaw before he wraps both arms around my chest in a bear hug. My elbow comes down hard on his back, and he slams me into another tree. We scuffle, my back scratching against the rough bark. We're throwing punch for punch. He's strong. Focusing on his strikes, I wait for him to throw his left fist in again and shift to my left. Caught off guard, he loses balance, just as my elbow catches him in the jaw. His head jerks to the side, his body twisting in the air before he lands on his stomach at my feet. In an instant, he's rolled onto his back, a vicious snarl on his face as he points my own gun at me. The shot rings out before a hard pressure explodes against my chest. My shoulder burns, my leg next, as I'm thrown back into a patch of undisturbed snow.

"FBI, freeze!" The ferocity in her voice, deepens Perez's Spanish tongue with a growl that thunders through the gunfire.

My vision blurs. "Della—" I reach my hand up, toward her voice.

AGENT DELLA PEREZ

My heart races as I gain speed, my eyes dipping to the snow-covered ground. John's footprints lead me. My legs feel heavy with the cold and fear as I enter the forest. My eyes struggle to adjust to the lack of moonlight beyond the treeline. The snow glow in the clearing gives the illusion of going from day to night. I squeeze the handle of my gun and push on, with burning lungs and tired limbs. I hear the grunts before I recognize them as the sounds of a scuffle, the urgency propelling me forward. I come upon them just as John knocks Jeffrey Carson to the ground. Without warning, he rolls onto his back, revealing a gun in his hand. Time stands still. I watch John's eyes widen with recognition of his peril before three shots ring out. My throat dries, sending all of its moisture to my eyes, as John's body falls backward, landing on the cold winter ground.

Raising my gun with one hand I point it at Carson.

"FBI, freeze!" I scream, my free hand trembling as I call for backup.

"Shots fired, officer down!" I call out, as Carson jumps up, already turning the gun in my direction.

"Drop the gun," I warn.

His arm lifts higher, the gun at the ready. I make the decision to shoot. Cupping my right hand with my left, I aim and fire. The gun kicks up as the bullet leaves, its power reverberating through my body. I fire again and watch as the gun flies from Carson's hand. His body spins around before falling next to John. With only a few feet between us, I move cautiously. My foot finds the gun and I kick it out of his reach.

"This is Agent Della Perez. I'm approximately half a mile northeast into the forest directly behind the barn. I have an officer down. Suspect is down. I need backup and medics here." The radio crackles in my ear, the signal unable to hide my shaking voice.

Frazzled, I try to focus on my training. I've never shot a suspect before. All the training in the world could not have prepared me for the physical aftermath. My body shivers with shock as I run through the protocol. I've secured the weapon. Keeping my gun trained on him, I turn him over onto his back. Blood seeps from his shoulder and abdomen. His eyes are still, he is motionless. Satisfied he's down, I move to John's side. Hunching down, I keep my body facing Carson as I check for John's pulse. The light thumping beneath my fingers sends warm relief through my veins.

"John. Can you hear me?" I sniffle. Holstering my gun, I run my hands along his vest. A bullet hole in the center would have pierced his heart had it not been for the vest. Pulling at the Velcro, I lift it up and find his shirt soaked in blood. He's been hit in the shoulder. My eyes scan the rest of his body and find blood seeping through one of his pantlegs.

"John ...?" I gently tap his cheek, staining it with his blood before pushing down hard on his shoulder injury, to stem the flow of blood. His eyes pop open, wincing.

"Della! Behind you!" he croaks. I twist my head just in time to see Carson standing above me. His fist whacks me across the face. Pain explodes in my jaw as I fall backward next to John.

As I'm reaching for my gun, he swipes it out of my hand. My eyes widen in horror as it disappears into the snow next to John. Icy blue eyes bore into mine, an evil glint of pleasure flashing as I scuttle back, turning to get up. He grabs my ankle and pulls me back down onto my stomach. I turn around to face him.

"Let. Her. Go." John's painful growl draws our attention to the tree. Standing now and leaning one shoulder against it, his body sagging forward, John points the gun at Carson. He drops my foot and lunges for John. The popping sound of a shot echoes around me as Carson's head snaps back. His body seems suspended in the air for a moment, before falling next to me on the ground. His blue eyes are still open, smoke curling from the bullet hole between them as he lies, lifeless, next to me.

John sways, then drops to his knees.

"John!" My voice is hoarse as I rush to his side. I grab him around the waist, trying to haul him back up.

"Come on! Put your arm around me." His weight flops to the ground. I'm too weak to pick him up. My fingers are blood-stained when I pull out my radio again.

"Officer down! Backup needed, hurry!" I keep my voice sharp, my instructions clear as I turn John over onto his back.

"This is going to hurt, but I need to slow the bleeding," I warn him. I plug the bullet hole in his shoulder with my fingers. I expect him to scream out in pain. Instead, he lifts his hand, still holding the gun.

"Take the gun." His words are barely a whisper, then his eyes roll back.

"John, wake up!" I cry out. "HELP!!" I scream into the quiet forest. Seconds later, the sounds of sticks and leaves crunching surround me. Agents Lynam and Ryan rush from the darkness, followed closely behind by four police officers.

"We need to get him out of here!"

Lynam crouches next to Carson and checks for a pulse. "He's dead," he confirms before he and Ryan move to my side.

"Bring in the medics," Ryan calls out over the radio before looking to me. "They're close by." he nods reassuringly. His eyes scan my face. "You're injured, Perez," he says, his focus on my cheekbone. He touches John's neck to check for a pulse. He's trying to distract me. The change of subject does a good job of it. The wallop Jeffrey gave me is beginning to demand my attention, the sting getting sharper as the adrenaline leaves my body.

"OK, ma'am, we have it from here." Two male paramedics arrive on the scene. They're both carrying large medical bags and sharing the weight of a stretcher.

"His pulse is faint. Do what you can here, but we'll need to get him out of here soon," Ryan says. Moving to my side, he helps me up from the ground.

"He'll be OK. Let's get you cleaned up." He's gentle with me. His strength is the only kindness I need right now. Looking down at my hands, covered in John's blood, I nod.

Lynam hurries over to us, radio in hand. "A helicopter is on route. It'll take Faye and John to Wisconsin Memorial."

"OK, great." Somehow, I manage to form a plan of action. "Ryan and I will follow John and the paramedics out of here. You should stay behind and secure the crime scene until forensics arrive. Once John is in the air, we'll secure the house and barn."

John and Faye are airlifted in the same chopper. An officer just left, heading to the hospital with Luke in a patrol car. Flashing lights illuminate the farm in blue and red, patrol cars and black SUVs littering the entrance to the lane. I'm resting for a moment, watching from the wooden porch steps. Lynam sits down next to me.

"Put this on your face." He bumps my shoulder, handing me an ice pack. Half smiling, I nudge him back and press the cool gel pack against my throbbing face.

"That's gonna be one hell of a shiner," he says.

"Will Faye make it?" I ask, forgetting about my own injuries. I've been avoiding the question since the chopper lifted off the ground.

"They both will," he nods. We turn at the sound of a deep male voice calling from behind us.

"Agent Perez?" Officer Duggan's at the side of the house. "Agent ... Lynam, is it?" Lynam nods. Addressing us both, Duggan beckons.

"You might want to come look at this."

Groaning, I pull my aching body up. "What is it?"

"We've gained access to the house. I wasn't sure if you wanted to go in first?" he asks, passing me a pair of latex gloves. Taking them from him, I hand over my icepack.

"Let's go."

We follow as he leads us both to a low cellar door. Lynam and I reach down, each pulling up one of the wooden doors from the ground. Lynam takes out his flashlight and gun, motioning me to follow behind him. Together, we descend into the cellar, two officers following behind me. We all move carefully through the dark space, before finding the wooden stairs up into the house. Carson is dead. The likelihood of an accomplice is minimal, but we won't take risks.

I allow all three men to enter ahead of me. Once I hear them yell out "clear!" I climb the stairs into the living room.

"Kitchen, clear," Lynam calls out. I glance around, dazed. With each step forward, I feel as if I'm stepping back in time. Outdated furniture is pushed against the walls. A large portion of the floor space is worn and scuffed. Moving to the freestanding record player in the corner, I drop the needle into the groove of the record in place. Sounds from the Everly Brothers' "All I have to Do is Dream" echo around the room.

"Upstairs is clear."

Startled, I jump around to find Lynam holstering his gun as he re-enters the living room.

"You OK?" His eyes search mine.

"Yeah ..." I shake my head, turning a half-circle to look around the room again. "It looks like he was dancing with them." I point to the scuffed floor. Moving behind me, he lifts the needle off the record player, so the song stops.

"I don't see any other records." His brows furrow in confusion.

"He might have played the same song on repeat." I shrug, moving to the bare Christmas tree. I note the single ornament, similar to those Kitty Harmon showed John and me.

"This is just all so sad." I sigh. Human behavior still manages to surprise me. Carson was once an innocent child who probably brought home paper Christmas tree ornaments from school to his mother. How much trauma did he endure before growing into a man who tied women to a wheel to break their bones?

"It's like he was stuck in a time warp," Lynam muses, hunching down next to the sofa at the other end of the room. Moving toward him, I agree.

"Same song on repeat, maybe even the same dance steps, over and over. Then you look at the fact that he built a *wheel*, which turns in the same spot, never going anywhere. He didn't want to break these cycles." I crouch next to him and see the missing button from Rose's dress. John had it noted in his files when I first arrived. Seeing this piece of the puzzle brings another layer of closure. It's over. We have the killer, and Faye is alive. Standing up, I clear the thickness from my throat before speaking.

"Let's do a quick sweep of the house, before forensics gets here," I croak. I don't wait for him to follow, instead moving quickly about the farmhouse. Upstairs, I find the room he kept the women in. Stepping over the door, now broken in pieces on the floor, I note the metal lock still attached to the door frame. *Faye must have escaped.* The broken window confirms my suspicions that an attempt at escape was made. Moving toward the back bedroom, again, I'm careful not to touch anything. Instead, I'm just absorbing as much information as I can.

There is a dark energy here. The innocence of a child's room, frozen in time. He kept it all just the same: he slept in a child's bed, under bed linen printed with toy cars. He woke up looking at superhero wallpaper, his small dancing shoes and dirty sneakers still lining the wall next to his dresser. Photos of a young Jeffrey Carson holding trophies crowd the shelf over it. Dusty trophies and ribbons cover every surface.

"Forensics are here," Ryan's head pops in at the door.

Rolling back on my heels, I nod. "Can you ask everyone to clear out?"

Following behind Ryan, I stop midway down the stairs, my eyes catching the large painting hanging at the bottom for the first time.

It hangs above the spot where the report says his mother died. The reason he left his victims by bridges and waterfalls becomes clear. It was all about her death. He was reliving his childhood memories. Her broken bones, where she died, how she looked. They must have danced together; he must have watched her die. My feet plod heavily down the last few treads, the heaviness of it all spreading from my chest to my limbs. The forensics photographer is already at work as I leave.

"Make sure you get this," I say, pointing to the button. With a curt nod, he moves straight to that corner and begins snapping photos. Ryan and Lynam are all sitting in the black SUV, waiting for me when I get outside.

"You should get that looked at," Ryan nods at my cheek. My fingers gingerly feel my swollen cheekbone.

"I will," I sigh, too weary to deny the pain of my injury. "Can you drop me at the hospital? I'll check in on John and Faye and see a doctor there."

CHAPTER 26

LUKE

A mass of auburn hair is splayed across my lap. Savannah's drooling through my jeans as she sleeps. Her lithe body stretches over three waiting room chairs as we wait for news on Faye. Her injuries are extensive, but the fever was their biggest concern when she first arrived. My brave sister has a broken arm and fingers, her face is black and blue, and her blood is pumping a dangerous infection around her body. But, for the first time since this all began, I know she'll be OK. She's stronger than I ever knew. Scott sits silently across from me. He jumps up when a female doctor, still in blue scrubs and a surgical mask, walks in.

"How is she?" He frets, wiping nervous hands on his jeans. I gently nudge Savannah awake. She jumps up too, at the sight of the doctor.

"Is there news?" She rubs her sleepy eyes, looking up at me. The doctor steps forward, addressing me first.

"The ulna bone on Faye's left arm was shattered. It's badly swollen and infected." She pauses, shifting her gaze to Scott, then Savannah before finding me again. "We will need to get the infection under control and the swelling down before we can operate. We will eventually insert metal plates and pins to help keep the pieces in alignment as the bones knit back together. She has a long road to recovery, but it looks as if she was saved just in time." We all fire questions at the doctor, who graciously allays all our concerns. She agrees that we can see Faye, before heading back on her rounds.

"Luke, do you mind if—?" Scott turns to me. I don't have to think about it, already nodding before he finishes the question.

"Thank you." His eyes water and we watch him rush straight to Faye's side.

"Sorry about your jeans." Savannah's rueful voice brings my attention to her downcast eyes looking at the wet patch on my thigh.

"These are my favorite jeans," I tease.

"Those!?" She recoils in disbelief; her affront tickles me. A deep rumble of amusement fills my chest, and I allow the sound to fill the small waiting room. Relief mingles with my joy as laughter spills out of me.

"Yeah, these. They're my favorite." I smile, wiping the tears from the corners of my eyes.

"You've got terrible taste in clothing." She mocks me, pushing at my shoulder. Grabbing her small hand in mine, I pull her close.

"Yeah, well you didn't mind resting that mane of hair on these terrible jeans, a few minutes ago." A slow smile curves up my face. Her eyes widen as our noses graze.

Without thinking, I tug her even closer to me, closing the gap between our lips. Testing her response, I move my lips gently over hers before leaning back, my eyes assessing her expression, waiting for her to slap me or join in.

"We shouldn't," she whispers.

Waiting, I keep my eyes trained on her, my breathing even as I allow her to process what I'm asking of her. Faye's her best friend, and they've both been through so much. I want Savannah, but not if it means causing her more heartache. The tension is thick between us when she finally speaks.

"I need to think ..." She shakes her head, pulling away and taking her warmth with her.

"OK." I smile, feeling confident. My eyes follow her as she walks on shaky legs to the door. She pauses, her hand on the handle.

"I'm going to grab a coffee. Do you want one?" she mumbles.

"If that's all you're offering..." I pause, a slow smile creeping up my face. "I'll settle for that, for now."

Laughing, she flees the room without responding. Savannah feels exactly the same way I do. She just needs to accept it. Relaxing back into the cold metal chair, I try to get comfortable. I'll be playing the waiting game in more ways than one.

FAYE

Beep, beep, beep.

The sound rouses me from my sleep. I blink slowly. The skin is tight along my cheekbone, the discomfort helping me to recall my last few minutes of consciousness. *I tried to escape. He beat me. I woke up on the wheel ... did I escape?* My heart begins to race, the *BEEP, BEEP, BEEP,* becoming louder as my left eye opens wide enough for me to see through. I can't move my arms. I try to cry out, but my mouth and nose are covered. I start to panic.

"Faye?" Scott's voice is so clear. Closing my eyes again, I realize that my legs are free. *Am I dead?*

"Faye, it's me, Scott. You're OK, you're at the hospital." His soothing voice is so close.

"She just woke up," I hear him say.

"Faye, my name is Charlotte. I'm a nurse at Wisconsin General hospital." Her gentle tone is followed by a harsh, bright light in my eyes. I squirm against it. "The doctor will be along shortly to explain everything, but you're safe—"

"I can't move!" The words grate on my parched throat as they leave my mouth, muffled by the oxygen mask covering my nose and mouth. She lifts the mask, resting it gently beneath my chin.

"We had to put your arm into an open splint. It has to be elevated to reduce the swelling and to help the healing process. I know it's uncomfortable, honey."

"Scott?" I call out. *He was here. Where is he?*

"I'm here." His words drift closer, as he rounds the bed.

"Scott, is it really you?"

"It's me." The warmth of his smell envelops me as he leans forward, his lips softly kissing my forehead.

I hear a door open and beyond, I hear the faint sound of music. That song is playing.

"It's Jeffrey! ... He's coming, Scott ... HELP ME! Scott!" I plead. I close my eyes tight, the beeping of the monitor speeds up.

"Faye, you're OK!"

"Scott, I'm on the wheel."

"No, Faye, you're ... you're in a bed."

"The room is spinning, Scott ... I'm spinning ... I'm on the wheel again!" I wail.

The nurse steps in, telling him to wait outside.

"Oh Scott! Don't leave me."

"I'm NOT leaving her!" Scott's determined growl is the last thing I hear. I fall into sleep.

It's been two days since my rescue. Luke, Savannah and Scott have been by my side in relays. Right now, Scott is here. Luke and Savannah have stepped out for coffee. It took some time, but the reality is finally setting in. I'm alive and Jeffrey is dead. I can't deny I was thrilled to hear the news. And while I'm still haunted, I know he can't physically harm me anymore. I'm surrounded by the people who love me. My recovery and my focus have to be on that.

"Scott, I'm sorry about yesterday." I turn my head to face him. He's sitting in a chair next to my bed.

He sits forward. "Please don't apologize. You don't have to."

"But I want to try to explain my outburst ..." I swallow against the lump wedging itself in my throat. "And I find it hard to tell you."

"Whatever it is, Faye, tell me when you're ready."

"When the nurse came in to give me a bed bath ..."

"I stupidly offered to help. It should be me apologizing." He looks down at his hands.

"I wasn't expecting to have that reaction, but it put me right back there, with *him!* You see ..." I inhale deeply, trying to hold back the emotion. "It was part of his sick ritual."

Scott rubs my hair and gently catches my tears with his fingers.

"I wish I could take you in my arms right now and comfort you. Hold you as tight as I could, so that you could feel safety like you've never felt before. That's what I want to give you, Faye." His voice trembles.

"I want that Scott. It might take some time ..."

"There is plenty of time. I'm going nowhere, Faye. I love you. It's selfish to tell you now, but I can't wait another second." His nose grazes mine.

"I love you too, Scott. I love you so much."

DETECTIVE JOHN WALTERS

"Aren't you a sight for sore eyes?" Jones's voice interrupts my reading.

Dropping the newspaper in my hand, I groan, audibly, at the sight of him. Leaning lazily in the doorjamb of my hospital room, he's suited and booted in his uniform. Despite myself, I mirror his smile. He is the first visitor to my bedside.

"Shouldn't you be out writing up parking tickets?"

"Just sent a tow truck to impound a hunk of junk out on an abandoned farm in Crivitz," the mischievous gleam in his eyes glistens further as he pushes off the doorjamb with his shoulder. Stepping closer, he brings his hands out from behind his back.

"I got you these."

My eyes widen at the bunch of flowers in his hand before a barking laugh erupts from my chest. He joins in, and we're both howling at the absurdity of his gesture. My shoulder screams with pain as my body rocks from laughter.

"Stop, stop," I beg, my eyes tearing up.

"I figured I should bring you a get-well-soon gift."

"While I appreciate the gesture—" One of the many nurses who has taken care of me walks in. "Perfect timing. Gemma, Deputy Jones was just telling me he got a bunch of flowers for the nurse's station," I lie. She moves to the end of my bed, reading my chart before looking over the rim of her glasses toward Jones, who is now holding them out in her direction.

"Why don't you take them out to Mary, she'll happily accept them." Her lips twitch, holding back her own smile, as Jones looks over his shoulder to see a pretty brunette behind the nurse's station.

"Don't mind if I do!"

Gemma mutters to me, her eyes full of humor. "Mary's allergic to lilies." She winks at me before heading back out.

I return to the newspaper article I was reading, holding it at arm's length until the words come into focus. *I'm getting old,* I sigh to myself. *It might be time for reading glasses.* Finding a comfortable reading distance, I view the face of Jeffrey Carson, taking up much of the front page. The media is going crazy for the serial killer obsessed by the sound of breaking bones.

"What do you think of the article?" Jones is back.

"I think it was too soon to be revealing these details to the media. We didn't have time to speak with Katherine's family, or Arnie

Bernstein. How's he taking it all?" I'm disappointed that Agent Perez interviewed for the piece.

"You know what the FBI are like, they want all the glory." He rolls his eyes. "Agent Perez wasn't happy about it, but her superiors told her to get ahead of the media frenzy." He shrugs.

"She deserves the credit. Her profile was bang on. I'm concerned about Arnie and the victims."

"Mr. Bernstein came by the hospital to see you, yesterday. Della—I mean Agent Perez—told him you were still recovering from surgery, and to try again later this week. He's thrilled we caught the guy."

"Perez was here?" I'm too casual, and the broad smile widening on Jones's big head confirms it's not fooling him.

"She was." He wiggles his brows. I nod, pressing my lips firmly together. I refuse to ask him for more information. My heart monitor begins to ping faster, the beeping belying my show of indifference. I thought Perez had flown home without so much as a goodbye. I scowl at the machine, and deliberately slow my breathing until the beeping subsides.

"I spoke with the captain ..." Jones recalls my attention. I'm happy enough to change the subject. He's shifting from one foot to the other. I wait as he crosses and uncrosses his arms. "Turns out, once I finish my degree next year, I'll be eligible to shadow a seasoned detective. Such as yourself ..." He clears his throat.

"Are you asking a sick man, only one day out of surgery, if you can have a promotion?" I ask drily. I dig deep for the most stoic expression I can find.

"Well, it's not a promotion. As such. I'd just be more involved when you're out in the field, learning from the best homicide detective we have," he stutters.

"Oh, I'm the best, am I?" I smile now, giving the kid a break.

"One of the best, is what I meant to say."

"I'll agree if you answer one question."

"Go ahead." Pulling his shoulders back, he steels his glare, ready to answer whatever I ask.

"You'll be qualified for any unit. Why homicide?"

I wait as he considers his answer.

"Honestly, working homicide is the elite in police investigation. I've worked patrol for years. I've got a good record. I know I joke around, like to flirt with the ladies, but I'm a fine police officer and a hard worker. Last year, I solved a burglary within minutes of getting on the scene because I've got a keen eye and my interviewing skills aren't too bad. They're not good enough yet, but that's where you come in." He nods solemnly.

"Do you want to be the best, or do you want status among your peers?" I clarify.

"This case confirmed for me that homicide is where I belong. I liked working for you; you're tough, but you get the job done and I'm not afraid of hard work."

"OK. Focus on passing your course. Keep your head down and the hard work up in the office. When you get that piece of paper, I'll show you the ropes." I can hardly believe the words coming out of my own mouth: I prefer to work alone. But Jones has shown great initiative, and we all need a dig out from time to time.

"You won't regret it!" He claps his large hands together gleefully.

"I hope I won't, especially when they stop pumping all these meds into me."

"OK, I'd better get back to the station. Do you need anything?" He's already heading for the door. I chuckle at his excitement. He is, really, like a kid at Christmas.

"I'm good." I shake my head, laughing.

"Oh—" He turns back abruptly. "Agent Perez left something for you, on your desk." He wiggles his damned bushy eyebrows at me again before almost skipping out the door.

I spend the next twenty-four hours wondering what the hell it could be.

CHAPTER 27

DETECTIVE JOHN WALTERS

My mom drove in from Milwaukee to bring me home for Christmas. She refused to bring me to the station to collect paperwork. I was "officially on leave," and she was going to make sure I rested. Unfortunately, having to use a wheelchair to get around until my shoulder heals enough to use crutches meant I was relying on her to push me everywhere. She loved every moment of it too. The prodigal son was home, and he wasn't going anywhere without her say so. After two weeks of being constantly fed, doted on and scolded because of my dangerous career by both my parents, my brothers and sister, I was itching to get back to work. I wondered a lot about what Agent Perez left on my desk. Half of me hoped it was something personal, the other half dreaded that it might be.

My plan today is to do a follow up interview with Faye Anderson. She's still in hospital, but all reports indicate she will regain full use of her arm. I have a mountain of paperwork to catch up on, but Jones has volunteered to help type up my reports until I'm fully recovered. Having a shadow detective might not be too bad, after all.

It's still dark outside when I get to the station. The overhead lights blink momentarily before the fluorescent bulbs engage, brightening up my dark office. My gaze is already on the middle of my desk surface. The heavy thud of my heart irks me. Pulling at the collar of my shirt, I shrug against the discomfort of finding a small box sitting there, waiting for me. Leaning into the single crutch, I hobble over. The gunshot to my thigh was a flesh wound but it hurts like hell. I drop into my leather chair and stare at the box and attached envelope that simply reads, "John."

My name, not "Detective Walters." Tapping the edge of my desk first, I walk my fingers over. Gripping the letter between my thumb and index finger, I turn it over in my hand like a piece of evidence, before ripping open the white envelope.

> *John,*
> *Thank you for saving my life in the woods. You are a fine detective. It was a pleasure to work with you (most of the time!). I thought it was time for a new plant in your office. The cactus requires less TLC so don't let this one die!*
> *Merry Christmas, Detective Walters.*
> *Della.*

Reaching into the black box, I take out the small cactus plant. She was right, it is still very much alive, despite having spent two weeks in a dark box, without water. Standing, I move to the windowsill, setting it down. I lift the dead weeping fig and throw it in the trash can next to my desk.

Picking up my phone, I pull up Della's phone number. My thumb hovers over the call button, before I decide to fire off a text message instead.

A cactus?...

Do you like it?

I'm not sure if I should be offended? Are you saying I'm prickly?

Maybe a little, but the spines on a cactus are meant to protect the plant, not to harm others!

Her words, while fun and meant in jest, are true. I've absorbed enough heartbreak and disappointment in love to last me a lifetime. Half of me can't, the other half doesn't want to even try to make room for love again. With that in mind, I decide that professional is the only way forward.

Thank you, Agent Perez, I appreciate the thought.

You're welcome, John.

I don't reply. I'm not sure trying to be friends is a good idea. For now, I lean back into my chair, acknowledging to myself that if anyone could make me take that leap again, it might just be Della.

LUKE

Upright in her hospital bed, Faye winces as she turns to welcome me.

"Ugh. I keep doing that." She rolls her eyes at herself as she carefully rests her shoulder back against the pillow. Her face, while still stained yellow from bruising, is healing. Light is beginning to return to her eyes. Each day that passes brings a little piece of my sister back.

"Just stop. Don't move." I narrow my eyes at her. Coming around her bedside, I fluff the pillow behind her back. "There. Where's Scott?" I wonder, noticing for the first time that he isn't in his usual spot by her side.

"Today's their first day back. He and Savannah are working tonight." Faye has a beautiful smile. When it's natural, it can light up a room. When it's forced, like now, you know she's trying to be brave.

"That's right. And you'll be back too, in no time." I don't offer her sympathy, just hard facts. She needs to heal her body first and then her mind.

"I know. I woke up today feeling like I need to get back to *normal*. Seize the day and re-start my life." She shrugs, wincing again. The pain is another reminder that she's not there yet.

"Has Dr. Price been around today?" The hospital arranged for the psychologist to visit with Faye a few mornings each week.

"She was here earlier. She's lovely, it's definitely helping." Her smile warms.

"Good. I was looking into therapists close to home. I was thinking it would be a good idea to continue with treatment for a while, once you're released." I keep my tone light. The last thing I want to do is tell her how to heal, but I want to help. Most of the time, I feel useless. The flush of her face tells me I might have stepped over the line.

"You don't have to; it was just a thought!" I hurry to add, waving my hand in the air to push that idea to the side.

"No, I will continue. But ..." She chews on her bottom lip.

"What is it?"

"Scott and I have been talking, and ..."

My eyes narrow, I've no idea where this is going.

"I'm moving in with him. When they release me."

Her words and fears linger in the air between us. If I could erase the events that brought us here, help her feel safe and secure, I would. But I have worried if coming home might impact her recovery.

"I understand. You know, the cabin doesn't even feel like home. I'm not sure it ever will again."

"Scott's worried you'd be afraid on your own." She laughs. Clearly Scott has been teasing me when I'm not around. If it made Faye smile, I could not care less.

"He's a good guy; he'll keep you safe." I'm learning to trust others when it comes to our little family unit.

"He is. I know it won't be easy, Luke. Getting over all of this, won't be easy. But with Scott, I know I'll come through it stronger." Hearing her speak, listening to the wisdom of her words and the conviction in her tone brings tears to my own eyes.

"I wanted to protect you. I feel like I failed you." My voice breaks.

"You were with me, every step, Luke. In my heart and mind. When the police found me, you found me too. Knowing my big brother was searching for me helped me get through each day. Don't ever say you failed me. You saved me. You all did. Oh, I wish I could hug you!" She growls out the last part in frustration.

My big hand envelopes hers, squeezing it gently. I nod through my tears.

"Enough blubbering, from both of us. Tell me: what's going on with you and Savannah? She can't meet my eyes any time I mention your name!" Her abrupt change of subject makes me laugh.

"She's been avoiding me since I kissed her." I wait for Faye to react.

"OK, so why is she being weird?"

I laugh again.

"She's Ms. Independent. Plus, I think she's afraid you'll object. I'm not giving her any more time to convince herself that she's better off without me. I'm planning on talking with her after the show."

"Go for it, Luke. You're each as fiery and stubborn as the other. I think she's perfect for you," Faye offers me one of her full smiles. She means it, and that means everything to me.

Scott met me at reception thirty minutes before Savannah's show ended. I waited outside the studio door, listening to her wrap it up. Her voice, deep and husky fills the airwaves, flowing into the homes of people all over Wisconsin, and around me in the hallway of the station.

“She’s off the air.” Scott pokes his head out the door of the adjoining room.

Their colleague Don follows as they both head down the hallway. “She’s all yours!” He winks.

Without waiting, I walk into the studio, locking the door behind me. Standing with her back to me, I watch her pack up her bag for the night.

“One second, Scott.” She turns, and her eyes pop when she sees me. Her hair tumbles around her shoulders. Her lips part. I smile remembering how good they felt against mine.

“What are you doing here?”

I smile wider, stepping slowly toward her.

“I’m taking you home.” I shrug, ignoring her shocked expression. She keeps her eyes on me. I move closer, into her space, wanting to grab her, kiss her. I still myself, waiting.

“What are you talking about? Where’s Scott?” She breaks our eye contact for the first time, trying to look around my shoulders toward the door.

“He’s gone to sleep at the hospital with Faye.”

Slowly and with great restraint, I reach around her, picking up her bag from the chair.

“What are you doing? I’ve got that.” She steps back, reaching for the handle. I tug it, pulling her closer. Our bodies collide.

“No more waiting, Savannah. You need to decide if you’re going to take a chance on me or not.” The words sound smooth and controlled, revealing nothing of the turmoil in my guts.

"But, we can't ..." She shakes her head, stepping back again and looking away. I hold tight to the handle of her bag; she doesn't let go either.

"We can."

"No, Luke: Faye is my friend, you're—" Her nose scrunches as she struggles to find the words to describe me. I laugh. Maybe I'm way off base with this, but I push on.

I don't hide the fire in my eyes. "I'm the guy you're dying to ..."

"Ugh!" She pushes against my chest. "Move out of my way. You're such a pig! This is exactly why I refuse to go there with you ..."

I reach for her, but she pulls back. Her southern drawl thickens as the outrage fills her gut. "After everything we've all been through, you want me to risk my friendship with Faye, for sex?! No thank you. I'd rather suck on a dead dog's nose!"

Dropping the handle of her bag, I grip the collar of her shirt, pulling her lips to mine. My kiss is rough and angry. Her bag lands at my feet. Her hands slide under my flannel overshirt, fisting my t-shirt as she meets me, blow for blow, our tongues plunging, mouths sucking, demanding more with each lick.

"You didn't let me finish," I say, pulling back. I'm enjoying the glint of arousal that has replaced the anger in her eyes. "I'm the guy you're dying to fall in love with!" I smile.

"Oh, dream on! You are so conceited! You could strut sitting down, do you know that? I believe you're the one who showed up at my workplace—" I crash my lips against hers, silencing her again. She laughs against my kiss. Lifting her from the floor, I growl when her legs wrap around my waist, squeezing the air from my lungs as she grinds against me.

"Fuck me, we should go." She fists my hair in her hands, her arms enveloping my face as she looks down into my eyes. She is stunning, and more woman than I deserve.

"Savannah ..." Restraining myself, I look in her eyes. "You scare me." I swallow.

"I'm a Texan, Luke. You should be afraid." Her eyes twinkle.

"Oh, I know you could beat the crap out of me, but it's my heart that I'm worried about."

"Don't you worry, sugar. I've got my gun back; I'll keep you safe." She grins again before pulling on my hair and forcing my face to tilt upward. She sobers, one hand dropping to my chest, where my heart thuds beneath it.

"Are we doing this?" The vulnerability I hear, has me squeezing her tight.

"We are."

"OK. I've got you, if you've got me?" Her eyes water.

"I've got you."

EPILOGUE

FAYE

"Good evening, Green Bay! And thank you for tuning into the Late Show with myself, Faye Anderson, and my disgustingly happy co-host, Savannah Phillips." I look across at Savannah, who beams beneath her headphones.

"That's right, folks. I've got my best friend and partner in crime back with me for the first time in more than a year, and I couldn't be happier!" she gloats.

"I'm glad to be back," I admit, my eyes finding Scott in the control room.

"We've all missed you." Her voice fills with emotion.

"No tears tonight! Let's get this show on the road!"

It has taken me longeAr than a year, and the road to recovery is not over yet. I've got a long way to go, but being here, doing what I love, is going to help me heal.

"On that note, Faye: you wanted to open the show discussing the amazing services available to victims of violence?" She looks to me.

"I did. It's something close to my heart and I wanted to take time out to acknowledge all the support services available, here in Green Bay."

"I know you said no tears, but I'm not sure I'll make it through this segment without a few." Savannah's already sniffling at her mic. I grin at her.

"I brought extra tissues." I laugh. "First up: we have a group of wonderful women running the Safe Haven Center, for victims of violence. Anyone who has experienced trauma, through physical or emotional abuse, can get in touch with these ladies ..." I dive straight in. Within minutes, it's as if I never left. The studio is my own safe haven.

The rest of the show goes smoothly. I'm on a high when we wrap up. With every day that passes, I feel more like myself again.

"How does it feel to be back?" Savannah asks, as we pack our bags.

"Like, I never left."

"Yeah. It was kinda great just being 'us' again." She blushes. Since they got together, she and Luke have been inseparable. As a group, we've dined together plenty of times at our apartment. I'm not ready to get fully back out in public settings, yet. Tonight was a huge step forward for me.

"Will Luke be staying with you tonight?"

"Yeah. He was fishing with Arnie today. I can't wait to see him later."

Luke has formed a strong bond with Mr. Bernstein. It brings me comfort, knowing Arnie isn't alone. I know better than anyone what Katherine, Rose and the other women went through. The police investigation confirmed the names of the streetworkers Jeffrey killed.

Mary Louise Gable and Cheryl Clark deserved so much more of our attention. Savannah and I have decided to highlight cases that the general public know very little about when we restart the true crime segment.

"When does Luke leave for Washington?"

"Next week. He'll be away for four weeks, so we're going to see each other as much as possible before that." She beams.

"He told me we got an offer on the cabin." My throat constricts, and I have to force the words out. It's been tough saying goodbye to our family cabin, but to this day, I've been unable to return. Selfishly, I left Luke and Savannah to deal with the sale. Savannah was kind enough to pack my belongings, with Scott and Luke working together to bring them from the cabin to the apartment for me.

"If you're not ready—" she begins, but I cut her off.

"No. I'll never be able to live there again, and it's time. You and Luke can buy a place with his half from the sale, and Scott and I are looking at buying something bigger too." The cabin is our past. All the good and the bad that belong there. I want to push forward and make new plans.

"OK." She nods. Walking around the desk, she hugs me. I wrap my arms around her back and squeeze tightly. I'm so grateful to be able to hug again. My arm is covered in scars from my surgeries, but I can move it, and use it, and I'm alive. It'll never be as strong as it was before, but these little moments remind me to be grateful. Things could have turned out so differently.

"Let's get out of here." Scott, his hair flopping, bounds through the door. His hand is outstretched, waiting for me to grab hold. And I do.

I link my fingers in his, look up into his dimpled smile, intending to hold onto him forever.

THE END

DON'T...

Leave me this way!
Join my newsletter today at christinewinstonauthor.com and download a FREE bonus epilogue!

You can also keep the suspense alive with book two of the *Killer Signatures Series.*

See book details below!

The Girls Who Got Away

She survived one serial killer; can she defy all odds and survive another?

Detective John Walters resumes his role as homicide detective in Appleton, Wisconsin, a town that has finally found peace after his explosive showdown with the bone-breaker killer. However, the arrival of a new and sophisticated murderer propels an old survivor into a fresh and deadly threat.

When Deputy Jones enlists John's help to investigate the targeted cyber-hacking of his childhood friend, someone who survived a serial killer two decades ago, he can't refuse. She's dedicated herself to rebuilding her life, vigilant and proactive in her home security and self-defense against the demons of her childhood. As John probes further, what initially appeared to be a distant online attack conceals a disturbing up-close and personal connection to her past.

In a parallel pursuit, FBI Agent Della Perez, well-acquainted with the sinister minds of serial killers, tracks a new menace. A killer who roams the country, targeting survivors of past murderers. His twisted trail leads her back to Appleton, and Detective John Walters. Working together again, they face a chilling question: Can they stop a madman who seeks to strike terror into the hearts of those who've already escaped the unthinkable?

The Girls Who Got Away releases February 1st 2024

Acknowledgments

I began writing this book back in 2017. It fell to the wayside when I stepped away from writing for a few years. But it was this story, these characters, this idea that compelled me to write again. It has been a long and rough road, but with the help of so many people, I got there.

With that in mind, I'd first like to thank my parents, Biddy and John, who encouraged me to not only self-publish this book but to do it the right way. My sister Janet, who has read this book almost as many times as I have, your critique is always spot on.

To my beautiful daughter Isabelle, I love you to the moon and back. Everything I do is for you; I hope you'll be as proud of me as I am of you every day. You are my world, thank you for being so understanding of the late nights and the running around. You're my little *neglecterino*!

Thank you to all my family and friends who encouraged me to keep going.

Thank you to Tiffany Tyler, the first developmental editor I've ever worked with. Your feedback and patience were invaluable.

To Nicole McCurdy at Emerald Edits who took on this book for a second round of developmental edits. I'm in awe at your ability to write the most beautiful words of encouragement. They lifted my mood and spurred me to keep going with this story.

To Jill at Bright Owl Edits, you did an outstanding line and copy edit on this book. Your attention to detail and hard work helped to transform this book. Thank you.

To Deirdre Winston, thank you for all the long nights, all the tweaks and all the great ideas that truly elevated this book and these characters. It was a grueling task, but the rogue tears and revolving arms made it worth it! LOL

To Orla Doyle, thank you for proofreading this book. As always, your work is impeccable. Thank you for the wonderful feedback too, it is always welcomed and valued.

To Helen, my Beta reader. I can't thank you enough for your online support and for taking on *The Girls That Break*. I loved your passion and your honesty, and it was a joy to read through your feedback. It was a huge help in the final few hours of editing.

To Alison, my book cover designer, who created a cover that I absolutely love. Thank you for allowing me to explore different creative ideas and for all your patience and alterations.

To all the wonderful readers around the world who accepted an ARC of *The Girls That Break!* and took a chance on an unknown author from Ireland. I am truly grateful to all of you.

And last, to all my readers. Writing a book is a wonderful achievement, but there is no better feeling than knowing you guys are buying, reading, and enjoying my books. I can't tell you how uplifting it has been, every time someone reached out to tell me they can't wait to read my next book. On the tough days it spurred me to keep going, to produce the best story I could for you. I hope I've created something you can love. Thank you all from the bottom of my heart.

Chris xx

Made in United States
North Haven, CT
08 September 2024